THE LAST EXODUS

THE LAST EXODUS

THE EARTHBORN TRILOGY BOOK 1

PAUL TASSI

TALOS

Talos Press

Talos books may be purchased in bulk at special discounts for sales promotion, corporate gifts, fund-raising, or educational purposes. Special editions can also be created to specifications. For details, contact the Special Sales Department, Skyhorse Publishing, 307 West 36th Street, 11th Floor, New York, NY 10018 or info@skyhorsepublishing.com.

Talos® and Talos Press® are registered trademarks of Skyhorse Publishing, Inc.®, a Delaware corporation.

Visit our website at www.talospress.com.

10 9 8 7 6 5 4 3 2

Library of Congress Cataloging-in-Publication Data

Tassi, Paul.
The last exodus / Paul Tassi.
pages cm. — (The earthborn trilogy ; book 1)
Summary: "Earth lies in ruins in the aftermath of an extraterrestrial invasion. The few survivors must work together to escape the planet. But if they don't find common ground, all will die, stranded on a ruined Earth"—Provided by publisher.
ISBN 978-1-940456-37-9 (paperback) — ISBN 978-1-940456-48-5 (ebook)
1. Extraterrestrial beings—Fiction. 2. Space warfare—Fiction. I. Title.
PS3620.A86L38 2015
813'.6—dc23
2015014969

Cover design by Paul Tassi, Victoria Maderna, and Fredrico Piatti
Cover planet photograph: NASA Earth Observatory image by Robert Simmon

Printed in the United States of America

For Doug, the pioneer
For Mike, the motivator
For Nat, the mentor
For Michelle, the believer
For Mom, the editor

1

The war was over. And everyone lost.

Lucas walked down what used to be an interstate in northern California. It was January, he thought, and a sweltering eighty-eight degrees. The landscape was barely recognizable, and when he finally made his way to the ocean, he found himself overlooking three miles of beach where a few feet used to be. Every time he returned to the shoreline he found the murky water harder and harder to see in the distance. It was probably only a matter of weeks before it was gone from view altogether.

The ice caps had melted, but no floods came with the oceans mostly evaporated. Judging by his surroundings, he guessed Antarctica might be the most comfortable place on Earth right now. A while ago he heard that if anyone ventured south of San Francisco, their skin would start to fricassee like steak on a grill. Bet the cannibals would love that.

He wouldn't survive the summer, he knew that. But all that was left was walking. *Only a few more miles to Portland*, he kept telling himself. *Only a few more miles to home.*

It hadn't rained in weeks, and the last time it did, if he had been caught outdoors he would have been permanently scarred. The downpour was so acidic it killed off all the remaining plant life that hadn't already been burned to a crisp in battle or the ensuing endless wildfires. It was unclear whether it had been them or mankind itself, but something had killed the sky, and the sun was now masked by a haze of red clouds that stretched all the way down to the horizon. Every crash of thunder hinted at another deadly storm, but true rain never came as the clouds seemed to know their work was done. The planet was dying, and would be a husk soon enough.

If he could ignore the weather, the worst part was the hunger. The constant, pervading, consuming hunger. Wildlife was nonexistent. The animals had been killed in the war or the storms or had been hunted to scarcity by survivors. The only reason they stayed alive for so long was that there were barely any survivors to hunt them. Lucas found sustenance by eating cockroaches, the one creature everyone predicted would survive the end of days. But now even they were scarce, as they realized they were a rare commodity in the current conditions and had burrowed underground, to return once the Earth and the rest of its former inhabitants had turned to dust.

Why hadn't he eaten man? He certainly had the opportunity. His high-end rifle gave him more than a fighting chance in most encounters, and he'd created plenty of dead bodies he could sample from. But he knew the end result. When a desperate soul started eating human flesh, it ceased to be human itself, and at that point why bother living at all?

Outside of cannibals, he occasionally came across one of *them*. Staggering around, wondering where all his brethren had gone and how they had the audacity to leave him behind. Power armor cracked and disintegrating, guns dangling, useless, having lost their charge long ago. They might have tried to fashion some sort of makeshift weapon out of scrap metal, or attempted to fire a human gun with their misshapen hands, but out of their element they were rather easy prey, as most of their spirits were broken as well. He saw them eating the dead in their desperate hunger, so he didn't see a problem eating them. The last one he took down fueled his journey for an entire month. He didn't feel a bit of remorse.

Their arrival often crossed his mind during the endless hours he trudged north. It had happened the way few predicted. The first ship showed up and the world went crazy. It just hung there like a painting in the sky, silent and motionless, observing the world's reaction. People flooded to New York to see it, and Manhattan came to a standstill, overstuffed with everyone clamoring to get a view. They eventually had to shut the bridges and tunnels down, and people had to be content with watching it from the shore or on television.

Many worshipped it, naturally. Why wouldn't they? Many had suspected this day would come—but not for millennia or eons, certainly not in their lifetime. It was like a dream.

The military was more cautious. They began pushing people out of the city and set up shop in Central Park. They launched jets and helicopters to try and communicate. In retrospect, it was something that shouldn't have been provoked. It would have been wiser to let it sit there in its mystery and simply hope it would choose to share its intentions.

But after a week of no response, the metal behemoth just sitting there without making a sound, the government sent a crew to investigate. It landed on top of the colossus and began sending live reports back down to the ground. Not much to see; it was metal, seemingly impenetrable. It wasn't until they broke out the plasma torches and started cutting that anything happened. The feed went black. All communications went dark. There was a video on the Internet purported to be the last three seconds of the feed. Amidst bursts of static a door could be seen opening, and in an instant a swooping figure grabbed whichever head the camera was attached to.

The military scrambled. Not just America's fighting forces, but the world's. Already on high alert, they now deemed the thing hostile and were preparing to react accordingly.

But that's what it wanted. It was testing the planet, seeing what kind of firepower it had, judging its behavior. By now the rest of its kind had gotten the message that life had been found. And then they showed up, guns blazing.

The war was less one-sided than many would figure. They had no impenetrable shields, no molecule-evaporating ray guns. They were tough to kill, but killable. The problem was there were just too many. The firefight raged for months, with no clear sign of what the end goal was other than destruction. Someone said they saw them scooping up civilians. Another saw one with a massive hose dropped into the ocean. Still more said they had ships with giant laser drills touching down and blasting their way into the ground.

At first it seemed like Earth was winning. Though humanity's forces suffered heavy losses, the alien ships seemed to be going down with enough firepower. But for every one that was killed, two would show up from the stars in its place, and the ships grew bigger as the invaders realized they needed more reinforcements than anticipated.

As the ships became more massive, Earth started throwing nukes. It worked, most of the time, but they started playing hardball as well, launching detonating devices that would wipe entire cities off the map.

That's when the lights went off and the sky caught on fire. Most electronics were fried from the blasts, and any reports of action in the field were all hearsay with no Internet or television or even radio transmissions in most places. The sky had always been full of smoke and fire since the war began, but something had changed, and whether it was from mankind's nukes or their own doomsday tech, no one knew.

And then as quickly as it started, it was over. There were no more bombs to be launched, and no more ships to launch them at. As the survivors picked themselves up from the ashes of their cities and towns, some saw a few lingering ships flying into the clouds, presumably to report back that whatever mission they'd come for, they'd failed. Or succeeded. It really was anyone's guess.

But there was no celebration when they left. The Earth itself was mortally wounded from the conflict, and everyone knew it. What few of its inhabitants were still alive began scrambling for the scraps. How many years ago was that now? It was hard to keep track when each day was a constant, bleary nightmare. A journey across the continent shouldn't take this long, even on foot. But with no maps, no landmarks, no sun and no stars, it was easy to go in circles. As the years passed, there were far fewer survivors left, and far fewer scraps to fight over.

Originally there had been a group, a wretched collection of the lost that had been attracted to him by the rare sense of purpose he seemed to possess. But with not enough food to feed one most of the time, how was he supposed to provide for five, or six, or ten, or even two? Those kinds of things never ended well.

He had watched two sisters claw each other's eyes out over a bottle of spring water. He witnessed a college student swan dive off a freeway overpass rather than drag himself one more step in the heat. He still had the scar on his elbow from when Carl, the mechanic from Coral Springs, tried to bludgeon him while he slept and make off with his weapons and the remaining food. Fortunately he raised his arm in time to stop the crowbar, and his knife quickly countered, almost on instinct. Carl looked apologetic in his last breaths. The group soldiered on, but eventually disintegrated along with everything else.

The truth was, if you were still alive now, you'd killed plenty of people to stay that way. At first, human instinct had been to band together to try and overcome the devastation. But once hope died, the descent into madness was swift, and only a fool would trust anyone they met.

Some made it perfectly clear to stay away. Lucas once came across a man wearing what had to have been a child's skull around his neck. He was almost naked, wearing only scraps, and he screamed and flailed about when he saw Lucas, like some sort of primal defense mechanism when a creature encounters something he knows outmatches him. A makeshift spear made out of a broken pipe and a military bayonet was no threat to him, but the man himself was a vision of terror, a personification of what the world had become. Who did this cursed soul used to be? A dentist? A teacher? A janitor?

Lucas let him scramble away into the remains of a nearby forest, too transfixed by what he had witnessed to even fire a shot and rid the world of the monster. But the Earth was full of only monsters now, a lesson he had to learn quickly.

He had run into his first honeypot about four months after the sky's death, back when emotions like empathy and compassion still existed. His pack was full of water and preserved food he'd collected, and he only felt the need to carry one weapon. A novice mistake.

Roaming through a city street in a suburb outside of Atlanta, he heard a cry for help: a woman's voice, faint, but clear. It echoed down through the abandoned subdivision, occupied by shells of homes, upper middle class mini-mansions ravaged by early looters, which was an improvement over other population centers that had been leveled completely by bombs and fire.

As he turned the corner he saw her. She was trapped under a collapsed section of a house. He presumed she was scavenging for food like he so often did, and the damaged home had made her pay for it.

"Oh thank god," she gasped. "I've been here for almost a day now. I didn't think anyone would come through."

Her legs were trapped under a thick piece of wood, and when Lucas looked into her eyes, he was taken aback. The woman was strikingly gorgeous, a true rarity in the midst of a scarred world. In a previous life, she would have stopped men in their tracks on the street, and judging from their current circumstance, it appeared she still had that power. Her wide, light green eyes overflowed with tears and pleaded with him for aid.

He immediately did the human thing and went to go find something to lift the debris off of her.

"Thank you so much," she moaned.

He found a metal pole that was once attached to a street sign. He dragged it over and thrust it under the wood plank across her thighs. The wood appeared heavy, but when he applied force to the pole, it shot upward so fast that Lucas fell backward onto his heavy pack. Canned tomatoes and peaches spilled out everywhere.

Before he could even comprehend what was happening, he saw the woman rise above him, a military-issue Glock in her hand.

"You still don't get it do you?" she snarled. "There are no more heroes."

She pulled the trigger.

Lucas rubbed his shoulder, which still ached after all this time. Fishing the bullet out by hand had been excruciating enough, but it was the subsequent infection that almost killed him.

She left him with nothing, and he had had to claw his way back to where he was today. But the lesson she had taught him was more valuable than anything she'd stolen.

He'd encountered a few other honeypots since then, beautiful young women feigning distress in auto accidents or cannibal assaults. They always looked well nourished, which was an obvious red flag in the current era. Their strength came from the supplies of a dozen survivors they'd tricked with their sorrowful eyes and purposefully torn clothing. Lucas now left them lamenting in the dirt, no matter how pitiful their cries as he approached or vulgar their obscenities as he passed. Trust was something that no longer existed in the world, and he had more than a few scars to prove it.

He trudged down the road, the sun's invisible presence above the clouds causing his vision to blur from the eternal heat. Rows and rows of abandoned cars on the freeway were all painted a singular color by dust. The heat was unbearable, and he had to rest. His weapon was a necessary burden, but he suffered carrying it through sweltering temperatures. Setting the barrel down on the pavement, he ran his thumb over the inscription crudely etched into the stock, NATALIE. A long-dead lover, but not his own. It started as a simple nickname for the appropriated weapon, but over time, it had become more than that. Natalie was his protector, savior, and friend, however mad that made him seem. But sanity barely seemed worth holding onto in those days.

He caught a reflection of himself in one of the car's side view mirrors. Wiping the dirt away completely, he was stunned to realize he barely recognized the man before him. Gaunt from hunger, his cheeks were hollow and his gray eyes had sunk into their sockets. His sandy brown hair was crudely cut short and his face roughly shaven. He had to make do with his knife, as too much hair meant even more unbearable heat. His cotton T-shirt had lost its sleeves months ago and was torn and stained from a litany of past events. Digitally camouflaged cargo pants held much of his remaining ammo, and his combat boots were forever caked in dried blood. He broke the car mirror with his knife in disgust and trudged further down the corridor of cars.

Automobiles had a very short lifespan in the aftermath of the war. What gas hadn't been used to fuel military operations had been vaporized by airstrikes. Even if the cars could run, most roads were too damaged for them to travel more than a few miles unimpeded. Lucas had tried out an all-terrain dirt bike for a few days, but quickly found the whine of the engine radiated for miles in this silent world and attracted too much attention from humans and creatures alike. Every so often he might stumble upon a bicycle, which would cut time off his journey until his tires were shredded by a rogue nail, a piece of glass, or the roots of a human tooth.

It had to be only a few more miles. That's what he'd been telling himself each day he trudged further north. Though there were rumors of havens in this part of the country, in his heart he knew they were dead. They had to be. After he made sure, he would be at peace with leaving this wretched world like so many others. What was the point of remaining behind? To witness the exact moment when the planet breathed its last?

He had been a religious man before they arrived. Their appearance broke his faith like it did so many others, but not to the point where it drove him to participate in the mass suicides that happened around the world. Priests, rabbis, clerics, and their congregations had all been driven mad by physical proof that everything they had devoted their lives to was a lie. Some had ended it all when the first ship came; others waited until the rest arrived. But regardless of their apostasy, their purposeful deaths avoided at least one hell, the one currently in existence everywhere around him.

Lucas didn't think about God much anymore. If He did exist, what could He be doing right now? Washing His hands of the world He created, now a broken toy needing to be replaced by another? It was better to imagine He wasn't there at all, as Lucas didn't need to waste his energy with hate. Survival was the more pressing concern.

He was down to his last water bottle and was not looking forward to attempting another dry spell. His record was two and a half days without a drop, and he knew any more than that was certain death. Thankfully he had learned to ration efficiently and trained himself to think a mere sip was ecstasy that would last him the better part of the day.

Fortune had favored him one day when he heard a shot ring out. He had scrambled for cover, but realized it had come from further up the road. He approached cautiously, creeping up behind dead cars. A man lay in the middle of the freeway ahead of him, his hulking shotgun lying useless beside him, blood pooling underneath his body. His pack had burst open and four giant bottles of Absopure slowly rolled down the incline toward him. And to think, they used to mock the very concept of bottled water. It was the only safe way to consume it these days.

Lucas scoured the horizon for the person responsible, seeing nothing. Surely they would come to collect their prize, and when they did, Lucas would collect them.

Then, further down the road, Lucas saw movement on the ledge of a billboard. It was an advertisement for some TV action-drama in its first season, its run cut short by the apocalypse. The figure scurried down the side and hustled toward the spot where the man lay. Lucas remained crouched behind a car some ways down the road, mapping out a possible approach scenario. He could let the sniper take the water and run, avoiding a potentially dangerous skirmish, but it had been too long since he'd had anything to drink, and he could feel every ounce of his body burning, lusting after the water that lay there. One bottle continued to roll slowly in his direction.

The sniper was nearly at the body now, approaching cautiously in case the traveler somehow survived the .50 caliber slug that had caved in his chest cavity. The man was scrawny and tattooed. Lucas wondered if he had perhaps been a gang member before the war, but as he moved closer, his torn Black Flag shirt and gauged ears implied a more musical background. His sniper rifle was military grade, presumably picked up from one of the millions of fallen soldiers scattered across the countryside. It was surely a pain to lug around, so it was no wonder he spent his time camped out in the shade of a billboard, looking through the scope.

Satisfied with his prey's demise, he grabbed one of the water bottles and took a quick drink. Like Lucas, he was a professional survivor at this late stage in the game and knew how to savor what little moisture still existed in the world. The urge to inhale the whole thing was a hard one to resist, but veterans of the apocalypse knew better than that.

The sniper quickly scooped up the rest of the nearby bottles, and shuffled through the man's pockets. He picked up a few shotgun shells and tossed them away. No need to carry another heavy weapon around in the heat. His gaze then shifted to the water bottle that had rolled a few yards away toward Lucas.

Underneath the car, there was a bit of a respite. The shade kept Lucas's body cool, and he'd slept in similar places on many an occasion, the way a lizard might. Shelter was often hard to come by due to most structures having been flattened by blast shockwaves. He saw the bottle and the man's feet approach it. He was wearing combat boots, again looted from a soldier, and they were worn and sticky with blood.

There would be no warning shot, no ultimatum of "if you leave now I'll let you live." Those days were long past. Lucas looked through Natalie's scope and fired one round. The echo practically deafened him underneath the car. The sniper hit the ground, clutching his shattered shin, the rest of him now visible to Lucas in his makeshift bunker. Another round went directly through his forehead, effectively ending the pain in his leg. The Earth's population was one soul closer to zero.

Lucas finished the last drop and put the final empty container back in his sack. Who knew, maybe one day the rain might stop being the devil's fiery piss. But he doubted it. He felt he was probably close enough to Portland where that would be the last drink he ever needed. The last intact sign he had seen said eighty miles. But how many days ago was that? How many weeks? He had lost track, but it had to be soon, even if his pace had slowed to a crawl.

He was inland now, having left the coast to make his way toward the city. The dry beaches sometimes provided supplies hidden away in wrecked yachts or beached aircraft carriers, but mostly they'd all been picked clean. Now back on the main freeway heading northeast, it was the usual expanse of an endless automotive graveyard surrounded by the burned sticks that once made up a vast pine forest.

Trudging forward, Lucas felt that old familiar wrenching pain of hunger gnawing away at his insides. Ideally he'd stumble upon another creature and, after a short fight, could have a feast on his hands, but such ideas were only a fantasy at this point. The creatures were worse at adapting to the new landscape than the humans most times, so there were barely any still roaming about.

Ahead, he saw the collapsed remnants of a freeway overpass sign. He scanned the ground until he saw what he was looking for, a faded green sign that read DOWNTOWN PORTLAND EXIT TWO MILES with a diagonal arrow. *At last,* he thought, and he turned the corner. The road became steeper.

As he rounded the bend, what he saw perplexed him. The road ended. In its place was a giant pile of earth covering the street and the cars on it. A landslide? *No. Then it's . . . No, it couldn't be.* But of course it was.

Lucas mustered his last bit of strength and started sprinting up the rocky cliff, loose dirt giving way under his feet. He understood what the makeshift mountain was, and was dreading the view from the top. But he had to see it. He had to.

Above him the red sky roared with thunder and lightning jumped from cloud to cloud. The mound became steeper and he was forced to drop to his knees and climb up with his hands. Rising higher and higher, he didn't look behind him to see the remnants of the freeway below. His muscles burned and he was almost blind from stinging sweat, but he ignored all of it. All that mattered was reaching the top.

At last, he arrived. What he saw was a familiar sight, but it shattered him all the same. He was standing on the brink of an enormous crater, looking down at the ruins of a metropolis now blown to dust and resting in the middle of a desert.

The city was gone. All of it. The devastation was from one of their bombs, because otherwise his skin would have started boiling days ago, cooking in radiation. The landscape was almost entirely bare for miles until it was bookended by the opposite crater wall. In a city of skyscrapers, nothing stood above a few stories, and what did was a mere mask, a wall or two standing as a memorial to the building once rooted there.

They were gone, like everything was gone. His fool's errand to cross the entire country to return to them had been a worthless pursuit. He ran his hand through the dirt and ash at the top of the crater. *They're no more than this now*, he thought as he let the particles slide through his fingers. He would have cried if his body had any liquid to spare. Instead his vision blurred, then blackened, and his body went limp. He cascaded down the side of crater, rolling across the smooth surface of dust until he came to a stop at the bottom. Darkness consumed him fully.

2

He woke minutes or hours later, he couldn't be sure which. The thunder had stopped and a hot breeze blew through the sandy wasteland around him. Pulling himself upright, he found his head throbbing and his arm in a good amount of pain. Searching himself, he found no blood. Sitting with his arms folded around his knees, he stared out into the shifting sands. Nothing remained. Behind him the crater wall rose up two hundred feet. Even if he had the energy, the climb would be impossible. But where would he go? Where could anyone go with the world in such a state? He stood up and looked around. Scraps of twisted metal poked out of the black earth, but all were maimed to such a degree it was impossible to imagine what they had once been.

His journey was over. Reaching into his boot, he pulled out the picture of his wife and son. It was the one thing on him he hadn't taken from a corpse. The photo was torn and faded, but he could just make out their smiles. It was time to join them at last.

He took Natalie off his shoulder and quickly checked the magazine. This would be her final mission: to reunite him with his family. He always knew this would be her purpose in the end. Positioning the barrel under his chin, he put his thumbs on the trigger and raised his eyes to the sky.

Above him, he saw a patch of clouds that had somehow turned blue among the angry red.

He stopped. He looked down. He hadn't pulled the trigger yet. This wasn't some portal to the afterlife above him; the clouds were actually blue. The sand swirled around him as he looked at the mysterious apparition above. Was it something just above the clouds, or something shining up? Focusing more intently he saw trails of light reflecting off the sand. They narrowed to a focal point he couldn't see.

He dropped Natalie from his chin and slung the rifle back over his shoulder. Marching through shin-high shifting ash and sand, he followed the path of the light. It flickered briefly, then went out. The landscape was lifeless again, the clouds red. He paused, then continued forward and the light flashed back on for a second or two before it was extinguished once more.

As he progressed further, the winds died down. The sand and soot stopped swirling, and he could now see more than a few feet in front of him. But there was nothing around but charred rubble. The clouds lit up again as the light reappeared and he saw exactly where it was coming from.

Along the side of the crater wall, a few feet up from the ground, there was a hole. The light shone brilliantly from it, then went out again. Lucas could hear some sounds that resembled electrical fizzling. Looking around, he walked toward the opening. The light remained off, but he could now hear mechanical whirring coming from within. He approached the hole and peered over the top with Natalie leading the charge. He hadn't seen anything with power in months. *What the hell could this be?* With nothing to lose, he climbed in the hole, Natalie at the ready for any snake that might be lurking there.

The light turned on again and engulfed him with its radiance. He had to shield his eyes from the blinding whiteness of it, and his retinas felt like they were on fire. When the light dimmed again, he could see nothing but red blotches. As his vision slowly returned, he looked to his left and saw an offshoot tunnel. The fizzling and whirling spooled up again, and he jumped inside. The light shot past him unimpeded out into the sky. *Can't go that way,* he thought, *at least not without my Ray Bans.* He laughed. It was the first time he had done so in recent memory. This strange new mystery had reinvigorated him. Lucas forgot how hungry he was, how much his muscles ached, and even about his family, now a part of the dirt that surrounded him. The light had transfixed him.

He started down the alternate tunnel, and after a few moments in blackness, saw a blue glow. It paled in comparison to what had just blinded him, but it at least allowed him to see through the darkness. At the end of the tunnel, he approached an open, metal doorway and immediately knew what he had discovered.

The room he entered was a cathedral of machinery, and not any of this world. In front of him loomed two giant objects with a familiar blue glow at one end. They pointed at an upward angle into the sand. The glow amplified. The objects were producing the brilliant light.

Of course, he should have recognized that light. The engines of the creatures' crafts had soared past him many times, but always at supersonic speeds. He'd encountered many a crashed ship in his trek across the wasteland, but none that were operational. What normally was unrecognizable when dashed into a million pieces on the side of a cliff was here fully formed, and, apparently, fully functional.

Outside of the two rear engines there were panels lining the walls of the room. The interfaces were holographic, and Lucas ran his hand through the closest one. He half expected a missile to fire or a self-destruct sequence to initiate, but the ship didn't seem to recognize his presence and kept whirring along, spurting out occasional flashes of light from the engines.

Lucas approached stairs that led to the upper deck. He could see a door leading to what looked like an engine room, where a red light was flashing overhead. With the craft apparently working, there had to be someone, or something, inside it. Was there really a crew of creatures still alive to resurrect the behemoth? Lucas clutched Natalie feverishly. Sure, the pair of them had taken down straggling creatures before, but they were starving, delirious, and lacking equipment most times. But here? On their home turf with their armor and weapon systems possibly as operational as this ship? He wasn't taking any chances. In a craft this size, there could be dozens. But how had they survived for so long?

His eyes and barrel constantly darted to every creak and beep coming from inside the room. Then he heard a sound he recognized instantly. Gunfire. The popping noise was unmistakably an automatic weapon of some sort, judging by the frequency. Sticking his head back out into the dark tunnel, he thought he could hear voices as well. Creeping back through the blue glow of the passageway, he saw the bright flash of the engine light in the main pathway up ahead. He turned his back to it, and hoped his silhouette wouldn't give him away.

As he approached the lip, he dropped to his stomach and peered out into the crater. The scenario he saw unfolding in front of him was something he hadn't witnessed in a long while. A trio of people, together, not tearing each other apart, but working as a unit against a common enemy. An enemy that was the eight-foot-tall creature slowly backing up toward the hole where Lucas lay prone.

The creature's head turned back and forth frantically, and he ducked as another volley of shots was fired over his head.

"What's wrong frogman? Where are all your buddies?" a man wearing goggles holding the light machine gun called out to him.

Another stood to the right, clutching a shotgun.

"Once you tell us what you got stored in that glowing cave of yours, you're gonna make a real nice dinner."

The third figure was hidden from view by the backside of the creature. But a woman's voice spoke.

"He can't understand you, idiots. Just shoot him and we'll figure it out ourselves. I'm starving anyway, and I'd really rather eat him than you."

"Aw, we're just having a little fun aren't we?" Goggles said. "He's not going anywhere."

And indeed he wasn't. Despite his working ship, the creature had no power armor or guns. Instead he was clutching a glowing cylinder, which didn't appear to be a weapon, or else he would be using it.

Thoughts raced through Lucas's mind. Presumably if the trio murdered this creature and found him inside the hole, they wouldn't exactly welcome him into their merry gang. From the looks of the two he could see, they had the crazed tremors of cannibals. He still couldn't make out the woman.

Lucas made a judgment call. Hell, did consequences really matter anymore? As Goggles raised his rifle to finish his game with the creature, Lucas raised his. He fired one slug that passed directly through his eyeball, and by the time he hit the ground, Lucas was trained on the shotgunner. As the man whipped to the right to see what had happened to his partner, Lucas fired a spray that ripped up through his tattered outfit and sent him tumbling to the earth. His shotgun veered upwards and fired a blast into the sky.

At that point the creature stumbled and fell on his back, looking side to side, unaware of what was going on. In front of him, Lucas saw the woman with a raised .45 Magnum. It was pointed at the creature, but she quickly shifted its focus to Lucas when she saw him in the hole behind the downed alien. Lucas fired, and so did she. Her shot buzzed by Lucas's ear, but his found a soft target in her flesh. She screamed and lurched backward, her gun flying from her grip.

Lucas exited the hole and made his way toward her. The other two lay motionless, with mortal wounds, but he could hear her gasping in agony ahead of him. He passed by the creature, who looked up at him and instinctively scrambled backward, away from the additional human threat.

Lucas reached the woman and kicked her Magnum further away. He had hit her in the arm, a pretty far distance from her head, which was where he'd been aiming. She was clad in torn pants and a black tank top. A checkered cloth was wrapped around her nose and mouth, as was true of her two cohorts. It was probably to avoid the whirling sands in this area, but it made them look like Old West outlaws. He raised his rifle to finish her off and saw the woman's wide eyes staring at him, anticipating her final moments. Her brilliant, green eyes. Wait. Had he . . . ?

His thought was interrupted by a sharp crack across his back. The creature was on his feet and had struck him from behind. Lucas rolled over and raised Natalie but the gun was swatted from his hands and cartwheeled across the sand. The creature swung at him with a three-clawed hand, and Lucas rolled left and right to avoid it, though one swipe grazed his face. He brought his knee up into what he thought would be a solar plexus, and the creature reacted accordingly, crying out in pain. Lucas then got a foothold on his chest and pushed the beast over the top of him, and he landed with a muffled thud beside the woman, who was now on her feet and staggering over to her Magnum. Lucas veered over to tackle her before she got there while the creature lay on his back moaning. He swung his fist and struck her, knocking her out cold, but as he raised it again, it was grabbed by the creature's claw. He was pulled up and off of her, and flew into the sand as the creature loomed over him. He kicked the creature in the stomach and went to his boot for his pistol. The creature lay sprawled on the ground, then slowly sat upright and held his arm up in a submissive manner. His left arm didn't have a claw. In fact, it had nothing but a stump where a claw should have been, the wound long healed over. Lucas saw the sign of defeat, and hesitated.

"Is this your ship?" he yelled over the roar of the wind.

The creature just looked at him and made no sound.

"Is this your ship?" Lucas repeated. He leaned in closer, brandishing his gun. The creature made a guttural sound and nodded.

"Can you understand me?" Lucas asked in a cracking voice. He had never thought to try and talk to these things before; he was usually too busy barbecuing them.

"Are there more of you inside?" he asked.

The creature made another noise and shook his head slowly from side to side. He patted his chest with his good claw.

Lucas slowly circled around the creature, his gun still trained on him. He reached down and picked up Natalie sticking upright out of the sand.

"Can you fly it?"

The creature pointed to the glowing cylinder he had dropped a few feet away. Lucas wasn't sure exactly what it was, but he had an idea.

"So you found the keys . . . Alright, inside. Get up."

The creature staggered to his feet, and Lucas slowly backed up to where the woman lay. He pointed his gun at her head.

The alien started emitting a cacophony of sounds and thrust his arms out toward him. Lucas immediately jumped back and trained his sight on the creature again.

"Whoa, whoa! What are you doing? Get back!"

The alien raised his arms and slowly circled toward the woman. He pointed at her, then at the ship.

"You want to take her inside?" Lucas lowered his weapon. "Why?"

The creature had no response but bent over and scooped up the woman, a light burden for the tall creature. He slung her over his shoulder and walked toward the hole. Lucas grabbed her pack left lying on the ground and followed him toward the opening, which was still intermittently flickering with bursts of light.

Inside, the ship still sputtered and whirred. The creature sauntered over to a panel at the base of the two engines, inserted the cylinder into a slot, and tapped a few virtual keys. Immediately the engines ceased their groaning, converting to a dull hum, and the light shone a constant cerulean blue and more brightly than ever. Lucas felt the floor beneath him shake.

But then it all stopped. The creature swirled his hand around in one of the arrays, and the entire room powered down completely. He turned and trudged up the stairs, practically walking downhill as the entire ship was buried in the earth at a sharp angle. Lucas found his footing and followed him, Natalie always at the ready in case the creature attempted another assault, but he seemed to be paying him no mind.

They walked through the doorway of the engine room and down a long hallway lit by a pale green glow that seemed to pervade the ship. There was a massive door at the end of the hall, but the creature diverted to the left where there was a smaller one. Lucas followed him cautiously, expecting an ambush at any time. But there was none. Instead he turned to find a small empty chamber, one with no windows and a solitary light embedded in the ceiling. The back wall was full of metal cuffs, and the floor was caked with dried black blood.

The creature set the woman down on the floor. He walked back a few steps and played with some controls. A white wall of light flickered to life across the middle of the room. It stayed there for a few seconds until it disappeared, and the creature made a sound of dismay. He walked back inside and grabbed the woman by the hand. Lifting up her limp wrist, he inserted it into one of the wall cuffs, which automatically snapped around it, her body dangling lifelessly underneath. The creature turned, grunted, and motioned toward the door. Lucas slowly circled around him, his gun still raised and his hands shaking from a combination of anxiety and exhaustion. Breathing a sigh, the creature walked slowly out the door with a slight limp, presumably acquired during their last altercation. As he moved toward the door, Lucas looked behind him and saw a mummified hand lying on the floor next to the unconscious woman. One bigger than his head with three claws.

He followed the creature out the door, which slid shut smoothly behind him. They walked to the end of the hallway where a tiny circular room waited. It turned out to be a lift, and Lucas soon found the ride up a few levels was painfully long. How could a ship so advanced have an elevator that moved so slowly?

Ahead, two giant doors opened with a hiss, and the pair entered what must have been the command center of the ship. A giant circular table was in the middle, and flickering above it was a hologram of Earth. Red dots appeared all over its surface. Surrounding the central hub were panels with holographic interfaces similar to those in the engine room. Some were glowing a constant blue; others were flashing an angry red. Lucas saw that the far side of the room was completely open, made of a transparent material that resembled glass, but was assuredly far more durable. Instead of an expected view of stars and galaxies, it was black with dirt and ash. In front of the viewing area sat what appeared to be some sort of seat, albeit with a massive amount of technical and holographic add-ons whose purposes were unknown.

The creature walked over to this area and made a few hand motions. The ship roared to life, and it almost knocked Lucas over, in combination with the tilted floor. Another claw swipe and the ship powered down again. A grunt of approval.

For the first time, the creature turned to look directly at Lucas. He was large, but Lucas had seen bigger. He looked kind of pathetic in a way, his naked form far less impressive than the ones Lucas had come across all suited up in armor. He was breathing heavily, and Lucas wondered if he had knocked the wind out of him earlier. Bruises were already beginning to form where he'd struck him.

These things had two arms, two legs, two eyes, and a long-snouted mouth filled with razor sharp teeth. Their pupils were entirely black with a singular ring of color running through them; this one's were gold, but Lucas had seen a full spectrum in his travels. Their legs were bent backwards like a bird's, but their arms and hands seemed to function as one might expect, with three clawed fingers and toes. They were all shades of varying gray, and had darker patches of natural armor plating across much of their chest, abdomen, and back. They had no tails, nor wings, nor tentacles, nor anything one might expect from a Lovecraft novel, but they were certainly built to give mankind nightmares nonetheless.

Lucas called out from across the holotable.

"How do I know I can trust you?"

The creature put his arms out and looked down, as if to say he had nothing on him that was dangerous.

"Yeah, well that doesn't really matter does it?"

Lucas pointed to the scratch over his eye made by one of the creature's claws minutes earlier.

It grunted and pointed in the direction of the prison area, then down at the floor.

"Yeah, yeah, you want her here, I know. But why?"

That was an answer that couldn't be communicated with gestures.

"You can understand me, but you don't have a way I can understand you?"

The creature motioned to his right. Lucas turned and saw a cracked screen with a cluster of controls flashing red beneath it.

"That thing?"

The creature nodded. Sparks erupted from the controls every few seconds; clearly whatever the unit was, it would take some time to repair, if it could be salvaged at all.

"Where's the rest of the crew?"

The creature grunted, and flung his claw toward the darkness in the viewscreen behind him.

"I'm going to guess that means they're not coming back."

It shook its head and walked toward the holotable. Lucas readied Natalie again. The creature gave an annoyed grunt and put his arms out again presumably to signal he had no ill intentions.

He pointed at Lucas, then at the hologram of Earth floating in the middle of the table.

"Yes, I know, you destroyed my planet."

A few flicks with his good claw into the console's holocontrols summoned a three-dimensional scene that flickered to life in the center, replacing the globe.

3

The holographic recording was a first-person view, shot from the perspective of a creature—this one, Lucas presumed. Amidst a flurry of overlaid symbols he recognized from the controls around him, two clawed hands tinkered with a piece of machinery. One was then inserted into some sort of glove device and started searing a metal object in front of him with a hot orange glow. He was surrounded by complex machinery, and on the opposite wall there were tanks filled with fluid. *Did something just move in there?*

A loud bark came from his left side. The creature turned and in front of him was a figure that towered above him, decked out in full power armor. A soldier. He grunted at him and the smaller creature grunted back. The soldier grunted louder and threw a weapon at him. The creature caught it in his claws, and looked at it like it was a foreign object. He gestured toward his lab. *A scientist.*

A holographic data pad was presented to the scientist. An array of unintelligible symbols scrolled across while the soldier was saying something in the background. Pointing toward the device on the table, the scientist barked in protest, but the larger creature grabbed him and started dragging him out the door. The screen cut to blackness.

It booted up again almost immediately, this time in the heat of a firefight. Around the scientist was a squad of other creatures, all wearing full power armor. They marched down a city street, firing indiscriminately, but the creature's viewcam showed him not using his weapon at all, rather ducking any time a blast rang out nearby.

The scene around him was chaotic. Fighter jets strafed alien ships, and tanks and Humvees were exploding on the ground. Bodies lined the streets. From the burning skyscrapers, Lucas thought it looked like Portland. Amidst all the carnage, Lucas was fixated on only one thing: the sun. *I'd forgotten what it looked like.* The feed cut out again.

It reappeared indoors, the creature squad was now inside what appeared to be an abandoned school. Outside, muffled explosions and gunfire could be heard, and the occasional jet or alien aerial fighter would scream by overhead, shaking the walls. The hallways were dark, and the team had dwindled in number to four, including the commanding officer who had approached the scientist initially. He was covered in mud and a mixture of black and red blood. A real cocktail of war.

The camera twitched frantically from left to right, mimicking the panicked mental state of the scientist forced out onto the battlefield. The school was a mess and had clearly been evacuated in a hurry. Locker doors were hanging open, ungraded tests and assignments littered the ground. Only a few lights still worked, and even in holographic form, the mood was undeniably tense.

Suddenly, a wave frequency began to fluctuate on the scientist's display. A heartbeat. The lead creature raised his hand and made a fist with his claws. The heartbeat increased in frequency. The group slowly crept forward again down the hallway, and the singular heartbeat was soon joined by a chorus of others, causing the lines on the grid to go off the charts. The commander motioned to a door that was shut, which was conspicuous as all others down the hallway had been flung open. He removed something from his suit that immediately dissolved the hinges of the door. Shouldering his weapon, he grabbed the sides and flung the wooden door backward as the two other soldiers jumped in front of him with weapons drawn and fully charged. Screams rang out from inside the room. The two creatures pushed back the mess of tangled desks and chairs in front of the door and wrestled their way inside along with the scientist, given a firm push by his commanding officer. There in front of him was a small group of children, all flocked around a young woman who looked to be their teacher.

All of them were shrinking against the opposite wall, trying to crawl further backward away from the creatures, but with nowhere to go. There was pure terror in their eyes, and almost all of them were crying and screaming. They couldn't have been older than eleven or twelve, middle school students, he imagined, and the teacher herself didn't appear to be more than few years out of college. The lead creature went over to the blinds and ripped them off the wall with one swift swipe of his claw. Sunlight poured in and destruction could be seen and heard outside.

He turned to the scientist and barked something, then gestured toward the huddled, shaking group of students. The scientist looked at them, then back at his commander and made some low, guttural sounds. The other two soldiers in the group each vocalized a thought and stepped up, weapons raised at the humans, who shrieked and tried to sink further into the wall. The leader snarled at them, and they immediately stood down. He turned and grabbed the scientist's gun, and pointed it toward the cowering students. The scientist looked at them, tears streaming down their cheeks, now mute out of fear. It was deathly silent, except for the occasional muffled explosive thud outside. The scientist paused, lifted his rifle, and then swung it toward his commanding officer.

It caught him by surprise, but the officer reacted quickly. He grabbed the gun and flung it upward, causing it to fire and blast a hole in the ceiling, which drew a cry from the children. He ripped it away from the scientist, and then jammed the butt of it into his stomach. The camera keeled over toward the ground and then peered up again just in time to see the gun come crashing down. Everything went black for a few seconds, but then the image resurfaced. It was unfocused and blurry, but showed a sideways view, as the scientist's head was resting on the ground, looking at the students and teacher on the far wall.

The room erupted in a blaze of light and sound, then the screaming stopped. The heart rate monitor went flat. Everything went black.

Lucas looked up at the scientist. He motioned for Lucas to direct his gaze back toward the hologram.

The scientist was now being dragged through the hallway in the ship he and Lucas had just walked through moments earlier. He was thrown through a doorway and two creatures set upon him, tearing off his armor piece by piece. When they were finished, they pulled him over to the wall, emitting noises that sounded vaguely like sneers. They put his arms in two restraints on the wall, then backed out of the cell. The white wall flickered to life and stayed that way. The camera panned up toward one of his imprisoned claws, and back down toward the door. Cut to black.

The hologram flickered to life again, this time the scene was in a state of panic. Droning sirens echoed through the brig, red lights flashed every few seconds. The scientist looked from side to side, but could see nothing relevant through the translucent force field, just the closed door. He heard footsteps and frantic cries outside, when suddenly, the room started spinning.

Everything shook and the sirens intensified. The impact of the ship's crash made the image cut out again.

The scientist awoke with the force field now deactivated. The sirens were silent and the only light was from flashing emergency strobes. Everything else appeared to be offline. He looked to his right, where he saw one of his claws had broken out of the cuff, which had burst open. Glancing to the left, he saw the other claw was still trapped. Blackness again.

He woke once more, the emergency lighting was no longer flashing, and instead produced a constant, ambient glow. Holding his right arm out in front of him, it was deathly skinny, as were his legs and torso when he looked down. His gaze shifted upward toward his trapped claw. He pulled at the cuff, which, unlike its counterpart, had apparently suffered no damage and wasn't budging.

Breathing heavily, and then drawing shorter and shorter breaths, he reached up and plunged his claw into his own wrist. Lucas probably would have winced had he not been bathing in gore these past few months and was all but immune to its appearance.

The scene quickly escalated as the creature found his dulled claw wasn't enough for the task at hand. He hoisted himself upward, and sunk his teeth into his own flesh. He pulled back and a big patch of skin and muscle tissue was missing. Alerts went off on the heads up display, but the scientist went back for more. This time there was a loud crack, his mouth wrestled with his wrist, and finally he ripped it away. He quickly backed up and his claw hung there in the cuff, like some sort of bizarre light fixture.

He stumbled out of the door and into the main command center. It was empty and baked in a dull red ambiance with no control panels lit up or functioning. He approached the central hub and pounded on it. Eventually, an image flickered to life, a globe with a pulsating red dot where Portland used to be.

The hologram shifted from the scientist looking at the globe to the globe itself. Lucas looked up at the creature across the table.

"You're a traitor."

The creature shook his head. He rewound the video to the part that showed his squad taking aim at the children. He pointed toward them and grunted angrily.

"They're the traitors? I hate to say it, but they seemed to be the majority opinion."

He rewound the video further to when he was tinkering in his lab.

"You're just a scientist, you didn't want this. I get it. I didn't think you things had a moral compass."

The creature remained silent. This was now officially the longest conversation Lucas had been a part of in months. And no one was dead yet. Amazing.

"So you've spent all this time repairing the ship? How did you manage that?"

He swirled his claw and the globe zoomed into the surrounding area around post-crater Portland. There were certain points flagged with symbols. The display was magnified further and the wreckage of a ship came into view. It panned out, then back in on another point, where a different ship lay in ruins.

"You salvaged the pieces from other crashed ships nearby. Damn. That's a dangerous move in this current climate. I imagine you ran into a few folks who weren't happy to see you."

The scientist motioned toward a set of power armor hanging on a wall nearby. An energy rifle lay next to it on a console. Both items looked battle scarred and broken down.

"Yeah, I would imagine it would have helped when those were operational."

The creature chortled.

"Where have you gotten food, water, while the ship's been down? I know even you things need them."

He pointed at Lucas, then raised his claw to his mouth, clenched it, and bit down.

"Well, I guess we can call that even then."

The mere thought of meat made Lucas's mouth water.

The creature held up one claw and pointed to the display screen. It showed a video of a bay door opening, and a giant, flexible pipe was lowered down into a body of water and made a low humming noise.

"And?"

The screen flickered and changed to a security camera–like shot of a giant cargo bay. Huge clear drums of water were stacked in rows, backlit by blue lights.

Lucas's jaw dropped.

"Take me there, now."

In the lift, Lucas was lusting after what he'd seen on the monitor. He didn't think stores of water so vast even existed any more, and as little as he thought of the creatures, this one in his underground desert castle had turned out to be incredibly resourceful. But his finger never left Natalie's trigger. He might have saved his life, but the nuances of alien honor codes still escaped him, and to him there seemed to be no reason he couldn't turn on him at any moment. And why had the scientist spared the woman? She was clearly intent on murdering him, and with his knowledge of English he likely heard her threats. Why was he so determined to keep her alive?

The doors finally opened, and the sight that awaited him was simply majestic. The bay was cavernous, and lining the path in front of him were rows upon rows of tanks, glowing blue and filled to the brim. They were about twice as tall as he was, and as wide as grain silos.

"This . . ." he stammered. "This is all water?"

His guide nodded.

"And it's . . . safe?"

The scientist turned to the right where a smaller container sat, about the size of an oversized refrigerator. Tubes connected it to the closest two tanks on either side. Opening a compartment, the creature took out a metal cylinder, and brought it up to his mouth. Water spilled out the corners of his face as he drank.

Lucas's mouth was open in amazement. As soon as the creature brought it down, he grabbed it from his hands. He threw the container back and downed the remainder. It wasn't just water, it was *cold* water, something he hadn't tasted in the better part of a year. He couldn't detect any traces of salt, meaning if the hose he saw had been in the ocean, it had been expertly filtered.

He threw the container down to the floor where it bounced with a loud clang that echoed throughout the storage bay. He immediately unhooked another container from the compartment and guzzled it all down. Finally, no more need for restraint. With how much was there, it could last indefinitely. Tossing the second empty container aside, he grabbed a third.

The creature put his claw on his arm. Instinctively, Lucas snapped it away and raised his gun at the scientist, who retreated. Immediately, Lucas turned his attention back to the water container, and raised it to his lips again. The liquid was the best medicine that still existed on Earth. Almost instantly he could feel some of his lost strength returning.

But then he felt something else. He choked halfway through the container. His stomach began rumbling and intense nausea filled him. Dropping the cylinder, he vomited up everything he had just drunk, which splashed down to the metal grated floor looking as clear as it had when it went in.

Panting, he brought himself upright again. *Of course*, he thought. After endless bouts with starvation and dehydration, his stomach had shrunk, and too much of a good thing wouldn't fit in the now-tiny capsule. He would still have to pace himself after all.

The creature stared at him blankly for a minute, took another cylinder from the tank, and started walking back to the elevator. Lucas peered outward toward the tail end of the bay, wondering what else he might find down there. But he turned and followed the scientist, as he felt it was still in his best interest not to take his eye off him.

After another interminably long ride on the lift, they were back in the command center. The alien set the water cylinder on the holotable and played with a few more controls, causing unidentified whirs throughout the room. He walked over to the damaged console he had motioned to before. To the side lay a crate with what appeared to be tools sitting on top of it. The scientist opened some drawers within it and pulled out a strange device that looked like a cross between a power drill and blow torch. He tore a panel away and peered inside of it. Sparks greeted him, and he made a dismayed grunt.

Turning to look at Lucas, he pointed toward the water cylinder next to him. He then motioned toward the hallway door, where the woman sat unconscious and bound a few levels down.

"No. You take it to her."

The creature pointed to himself, and then to the damaged console. He then motioned to his mouth, then to Lucas, then to the sides of his head, where ears would be if he had any.

"Oh, that's the thing that lets you talk to me?"

A nod.

"How do I know you won't just lock me in there and electrify the floor or something?"

The alien simply shook his head, turned around, and activated the odd-looking power tool. The smell of smoldering metal filled the room.

Lucas shifted Natalie uncomfortably in his arms. He wouldn't stop being suspicious, but between this creature's alleged betrayal of his own kind and his gift of endless water, he figured there probably was no immediate threat. For the first time in about an hour, he slung the rifle back over his shoulder and his tired arms breathed a sigh of relief. He grabbed the water and made his way toward the door that led to the main hallway and the lift.

When he reached the bottom level, he walked a short way down and peeked into a few other doors, which also looked like formerly functional jail cells. All of them opened immediately in front of him to show some fizzling controls and empty rooms. A few of them were bloodstained, but no more missing limbs were present. When the ship was fully operational, he imagined there would have been more security in place than a series of motion-sensing doors that opened automatically like at a local supermarket. The scientist must have deactivated all that to move about the ship more freely as he rebuilt it. There was no point in stopping every two minutes for another password entry or DNA scan when you were the only one around.

He turned and entered the last room before the engine bay and saw the woman still slumped over unconscious, one hand raised above her head locked in the cuff. For an advanced race capable of jet setting across the galaxy from god knows where, it was a rather primitive means of imprisonment, but he remembered the force field that should have been operational. That was a little more Star Trek, he supposed.

Drawing closer to her, with a cloth no longer masking her face he could see that the woman was maybe seven or eight years younger than him. Twenty-five, twenty-six perhaps? She wasn't even stirring, which, after a quick, albeit solid, punch to the face, seemed a bit suspicious. In the wasteland she had surely endured worse on many occasions.

Lucas set the water cylinder down and reequipped Natalie. The woman's long legs lay stretched out in front of her, and Lucas kicked one of her dusty boots, but she made no response. He got down on his knees and thought of a new means to test her commitment, if this was indeed a charade. He unholstered his buck knife, another of his longtime allies, though one without a name, and brought it to her shin where the boot stopped and her torn pants began. He found a tan bit of flesh exposed by a rip and balanced the point of his knife on top of it. He'd kept it sharp on stones and metal wreckage, and he spun it around until it quickly drew blood from the point where it rested. Again, not even a flinch. He supposed she really was still gone.

He shouldered his rifle and leaned in closer, raising his hand in an attempt to check her pupil's dilation so he could see just how under she was. But as his hand was an inch away from its target, her head lifted slightly and her bright green eyes opened.

"Shi—"

He didn't even have time to finish the expletive as she brought up her free hand, which hadn't reached the other cuff, originally meant to house eight-foot-tall creatures. By instinct alone, he managed to stop it before it collided with his face, and looking right, he saw there was a sharp point of metal protruding from a cloth strip wrapped around her wrist. It hung motionless a few centimeters from his eye for a moment before he thrust her arm back into the wall. He leapt backwards as she swung at him again, and as he did so, bumped into the water, which spilled all over the floor and ran down the angled surface away from the woman. Her attention was immediately diverted by what she saw leaking out onto the ground and she lost all interest in assaulting Lucas. She made an effort to dive over to the floor to lick up some of the water that was pouring forth, but she couldn't quite reach it. It was an almost pathetic sight, but Lucas could empathize. He'd done far worse things for a drop of water over the last few months.

He quickly picked up the cylinder, which was rolling away down the incline, spilling most of its contents as it went. Still seated, he shook it, and it seemed to still be about a quarter of the way full.

Realizing she couldn't reach the water on the floor, she looked at the cylinder, quiet splashes indicating its remaining volume. She lunged for it, but it was out of her reach, and Lucas pulled it back even further.

"Give me . . . that," she said in a cracked voice drenched in venom.

"Yeah, you definitely just made your case for being released on good behavior. How about we start by you throwing me that blade?"

The woman looked angry, but grabbed the protruding spike with her thumb and forefinger, pulling it out of the wrapping that contained it. She lobbed it in Lucas's direction where it clanked on the metal floor.

"What else you have on you?"

She glowered.

"Fine, play this game." He brought the water to his lips, and the desire in her eyes was palpable.

She reached into her boot and took out a switchblade, tossing it toward where Lucas sat.

"Keep going. If you've survived this long, I know you're as well prepared as I've been."

She reached behind her back and came back with a grenade, pin mercifully still in place. Lucas's eyebrows instinctively flew up.

"Wow, and in what scenario is that your weapon of choice?"

"Not this one, but you'd be surprised." She put the grenade on the floor where it rolled down to the opposite end of the cell.

"That's it. I've been running a little low on artillery these days. Now give me that."

Lucas handed her the cylinder. She took it down in one gulp.

"Trust me, you don't want more than that."

She wiped her mouth with her free hand.

"Cold? Where the hell did you get that? And more importantly, where are we?"

She looked around the room and saw the working lights and strange symbols attached to the door controls and surrounding consoles.

"No, it can't be," she said with a look of horror slowly creeping across her face.

"One of theirs? Yeah."

Her mouth remained open and she panned around the room.

"But it's . . . working?"

"More or less. I think there's still a piece or two missing, but it's being sorted out."

"Wait, that thing. You didn't kill it? It's running this place?"

"Correct on both counts." Lucas twirled his knife around in his hand. After examining the woman's face for the past few minutes, he had determined it had to be her. A little more gaunt, a little closer to psychosis, but it was her.

"So how did . . ."

"Let me ask *you* a question, green eyes. How did you get all the way up here from Georgia?"

The woman looked taken aback.

"How did you know I was in Georgia?"

Lucas furrowed his brow.

"You don't remember? We've met before, and when we did, you shot me and left me for dead in the heat."

She cocked her head.

"You're going to have to be more specific; that doesn't exactly narrow it down."

"A suburb outside of Atlanta, you were trapped, I saved you. You shot me and took my entire pack of supplies, everything I had."

The memory found her.

"Ohhh, I remember you. The hero," she sneered. "You looked so concerned when you got there. And I remember that pack was one of my biggest hauls. You were quite well stocked. That was very . . . gentlemanly of you."

Lucas rubbed his eyes. He was exhausted. He had to participate in actual conversations today, and now someone was actually talking back to him. It had been a while since social interaction that didn't end up with someone dead in a matter of minutes. But hey, the day wasn't over yet.

"Didn't make that mistake again. You weren't the last person to come up with that scam, but I see it's taken you far."

She looked off to the side, her mind drifting elsewhere. "Not far enough."

"Why are you in Portland?"

"I was making my way to Alaska. I heard the heat was still at bearable levels there and it even still got a little bit cold at night. Also, rumor had it not all the water had boiled yet."

"And what about the idiot twins out there?"

"Jonas and Miller? They may have been insane, but they had what it took to survive out here, I'll tell you that."

"You don't see humans working together too much out there anymore."

"When we met, they were very intent on having me for dinner, until I convinced them I could use my . . . skills to get them more food and water than they were accustomed to."

"Skills that involved tricking passersby into coming to your aid, only to end up with a hole in their head?"

She rolled her eyes.

"I shot you in the shoulder. And no, that hasn't worked in months. I have however, had a flawless ambush record since those days. Well, almost flawless."

She grabbed her arm that had been grazed by Lucas's bullet earlier. Blood still trickled out of the wound.

"You'll live."

"I'm sure you're thrilled. Speaking of, why exactly am I still alive?"

Lucas stared at his knife, still flittering through his fingers. He had been wondering the same thing.

"I don't know, my friend seems intent on keeping you breathing for some reason. He's quite adamant about it." He pointed to the scratch over his eye.

"How long have you two been working on this little science project? And do you have any bread to go along with that wine?" She motioned toward the cylinder.

"I just got here today. And I haven't sorted out that second issue yet."

"And you haven't eaten him? What the hell are you waiting for? Those things are like a seven-course meal. Go take that fancy rifle of yours, do it now, and we can split him between us."

"Believe me, the idea crossed my mind. But look around you. Look at all this!" He motioned to the humming controls and radiant lights. "Who knows what else he can do with it."

"Yeah." She paused. "It is something."

"Apparently he's a scientist, and he got in a bit of trouble by betraying his own race before they all left without him." He pointed to the decaying hand on the floor.

The woman's eyes widened. "That thing was his? And wait, you can talk to it?"

"It understands me somehow, but I haven't been able to process what he's been grunting yet. He does seem to have mastered basic human body language though, so his nodding and pointing helps. Right now he's working on a part of the ship that I think is supposed to act as some sort of translator."

"I need to eat," she said. "It's been days."

"I can drag in your two friends from outside if you'd like a snack."

The woman scoffed.

"I never went down that road. I saw how much it messes with your mind, and you need to be sharp, not just nourished, to survive out here. Those two would be the prime examples of the dangers of man-eating. Though that was something I did know something about in a former life. Metaphorically of course."

Lucas's eyes narrowed, "What's your name?"

The door behind them opened, and the scientist was standing there holding a small device with his good claw.

"Holy shit!" the woman exclaimed, and instinctively started scrambling backward, but she was already against the wall.

Lucas stood up.

"Believe me, you don't have anything to worry about. He's the only reason you're not laying out there in the dust with your pals."

The scientist walked into the cell with the handheld device. He held it up to the woman. A bright light scanned over the surface of her face and it let out a high-pitched whine.

"What the hell is he doing?" she asked, turning her head so it was flush with the wall.

"I have no idea. But I would recommend sitting still."

The creature grunted in agreement. He flipped over the piece of machinery and held it up to her wounded arm. Gel shot out of it like a caulk gun, covering her wound. It hissed and started smoking, and the woman looked shocked. But in a few seconds it was over. The wound had regrown skin and the bleeding had completely ceased.

Lucas was stunned.

"You come here with that kind of technology and you choose to share your antimatter bombs instead?"

The creature said nothing. Lucas continued.

"Can I get some of that? You did some damage to me earlier." He brought a finger to the scratch over his eye.

The creature bent down to look the wound over and then shook his head. He held up two claws and put them close together to make what appeared to be a "little" symbol and scoffed.

The woman spoke from the floor, "I think that's alien for 'it's just a scratch.'"

The scientist walked through the door and motioned for Lucas to follow. He did so, but first went through the cell, scooping up the spike, the switchblade, and the grenade the woman had unloaded. As the two exited through the doorway, she called out after them.

"What, I have to stay here? You said he liked me!"

Lucas answered without turning.

"I said he wanted you alive. And you *have* tried to kill both of us in the last hour."

The door slammed shut behind them.

Back on the bridge, the creature returned to work on the console, which was still spitting out sparks every few seconds, as were many other stations around the room. Lucas wondered if the ship was in fact operational, as it looked like, well, like it had been through an intergalactic war.

He slumped down to the floor next to the woman's pack he had brought in from the desert. If he was lucky, he'd find some rogue scraps of food. She hadn't looked all that decrepit, so clearly she was eating something. He dumped out the contents of the bag and a host of objects fell out with a clamor that made the creature stop and look at him. He shook it and another grenade fell out and started rolling down the tilted floor.

"Shit, shit, shit, shit!" Lucas exclaimed as he lunged for it. *How many of these things did she have?* Thankfully the pin was still in place.

The biggest noisemaker was the cacophony from about thirty .45 shells hitting the floor. He took her Magnum from the back of his pants and opened it; five shots remained. He replaced a single bullet and kept digging. He turned up a hatchet with dried blood on it, a few books of matches, and a copy of *Paradise Lost* with the edges singed. He flipped through the pages until he found a bookmark near the end. A photo, creased and partially burned, but he could make out the woman wrapped in the arms of a man. It was readily apparent that before the war she had been stunning. The photo showed her in full makeup with her dark hair voluminous and curled at the ends. The image was the most breathtaking thing Lucas had seen since the million gallons of water sitting below him. The man behind her was young, with blue eyes and a wide smile. She grasped his wrist with her hand, and he could make out a large diamond ring on her finger. A fiancé? Husband? Even the she-devil, snarling with rage and loaded with weapons, had lost someone. Everyone had.

Lucas put the picture back and turned his attention to what appeared to be a silk dress folded around something. Not much occasion for such clothes these days, but he supposed it must have been in her honeypot wardrobe back when that was still a viable tactic. He picked it up and immediately felt something hard inside. Recognizing the shape, Lucas could hardly contain his excitement as he whipped the dress open. Cans flung out of it and clanged on the floor. Lucas scrambled to keep all of them from rolling away, but two escaped his grip and were sent tumbling down the slanted floor. The creature was on his back, fiddling with a new tool on the underside of the console. One came to rest on his hip, which caused him to look down in surprise. He flung out his arm to catch the other one rolling his way. Lucas looked over at him as he grabbed the other can and rose up from the floor.

He looked at Lucas, then back at the canned tuna fish in his hand. Tearing the top off hungrily, he threw it back like a shot into his open mouth. Looking supremely satisfied, he turned back to Lucas and flung the remaining can at him. Lucas caught it and opened it quickly. He scooped out the fish with his fingers, and licked the insides when he couldn't scrape any more out of it. Looking down at the other cans he saw pears, peaches, olives, salmon, and more tuna. There were about a dozen cans in all, more than he'd seen in one place for months. As much as he despised the woman, he was now exceptionally thankful for her resourcefulness.

A can of tuna in forty-five seconds was not good enough rationing, and his stomach immediately began to regret his sudden indulgence. But he kept himself in check, and managed not to coat the floor with his recently consumed meal, unlike he'd done with the water. He folded the cans back up into the dress and began scooping the floor's items into the pack.

All around him multicolored lights glowed softly. There was no telling what time it was in the buried craft, but Lucas's body told him night had come hours ago. In a world where he routinely faced death and desolation, the day had gone above and beyond in every way, and so he drifted into unconsciousness, on the floor of an alien spacecraft.

4

Lucas stirred back into consciousness when he was lightly kicked by a clawed foot.

"Awake," a mechanical, grizzled voice said.

He jolted up and instinctively reached for Natalie, slung around his back. Pointing it up at the creature who loomed above him, he did a mental double take.

"Did you just say something?"

The creature now had a sort of collar around his neck. It was metal with a bit that wrapped up and around his throat. A small blue hologram protruded slightly from the front of it.

"Yes."

Lucas jumped to his feet, dropping the gun to his side.

"You did it. You fixed your translator."

"I was able to repair the console to a degree where it allowed me to program my . . ."

The voice became a garbled mess of sounds.

"Your what?"

"You humans do not have a word for it. It takes certain psionic brainwaves and translates them into audible speech, though sometimes it cannot translate something for which your language does not have an equivalent term."

The creature was indeed talking without moving his mouth and was only grunting occasionally. His new voice was metallic and deep, but not without inflection or even emotion. It was a welcome change from growling and pointing, and suddenly the creature was feeling less like a creature, and more like . . . a man? It was as if a gorilla suddenly opened his mouth and was telling you about his day.

"Well this makes things easier. But how have you been able to understand me this whole time?"

"I am able to process your language mentally, but my biology does not allow me to speak it, just as you could never vocalize my native tongue. I studied all the languages of your 'Earth' intensely in preparation for our mission here. It allowed us to learn of your culture before we arrived, and it was key for intercepting transmissions between your leaders. It would also have been useful for interrogation of prisoners, but that was never an authorized command, only extermination. Speaking the language was never a necessity, but this was a device I had been working on in my spare time, and I am glad to see it is functioning properly. Is my grasp of your language understandable?"

Lucas slowly nodded his head, which was internally spinning. This might be the first face to face conversation that had ever taken place between a creature and a human. There were so many questions, his brain felt like it was about to implode in on itself. He spat out the first one that came to mind.

"Why did you come here?"

The alien looked out the black viewscreen.

"Why we always come. To conquer. To pillage. To strip your planet bare to fuel our war."

"Your war? The war against Earth?"

The alien paused.

"I did not say our war was with you."

Lucas opened his mouth to further investigate, but was stopped short.

"I know you have many questions, and there will be time for answers, but we have a more pressing matter to attend to. We need to retrieve the [garbled] from the [garbled]."

"I didn't catch most of that. What are you talking about?"

"First, we need the female."

He turned to walk out the main door toward the prison wing.

"Wait, what am I supposed to call you?"

The creature turned.

"I am known as [garbled], but for simplicity's sake, you may refer to me as 'Alpha.' And what are you called?"

"Lucas."

Alpha nodded in acknowledgment.

"Come, there is much to do."

"Whoa wait, that thing can talk now?"

The woman was awake and stunned at the new development.

"I could always speak, now you can simply understand me."

Lucas kept Natalie trained on her. She seemed in better spirits now that the hole in her arm had been sealed. Her wrist was red from the cuff, but he imagined she was still quite some time away from chewing her own hand off. Alpha approached her slowly.

"Hey, back up, what are you doing?" Lucas exclaimed as he twitched nervously. "You're not letting her go are you? She's incredibly dangerous. Yesterday I was where you're standing right now and she almost took my eye out."

Alpha glanced back.

"You removed her weapons did you not?"

"Yeah but . . ."

"There is no time to waste; she is essential to what we must do."

The woman stopped squirming as Alpha examined her arm.

"Wait, what?"

"She is in fair health. However, she needs nourishment."

He stood up and went over to the console outside the broken forcefield. The cuff slid off of her and her arm dropped limply to her side. She rubbed her wrist and slowly got to her feet. Lucas took a step back and pointed Natalie at her chest.

"Relax, I'm done fighting. Just get me some damn food. I know you found it in my bag. I killed eight people to amass that stash and I'll be damned if I'm going to let you two eat it all."

She pointed at Alpha.

"I know what tuna fish smells like, asshole."

Alpha was nonplussed.

"Come."

The trio exited the room, Lucas letting the lady go first, not out of respect, but so she wouldn't yank the revolver out of his belt and blow his brains all over the extraterrestrial hallway. She obliged and they turned toward the lift to the bridge.

As the door opened she saw her pack leaning against the holotable. She raced over and ripped it open. Lucas had a sudden thought and sprinted over to catch her. But by the time he got there, it wasn't an axe or a grenade she pulled out, but the can of peaches. He stopped abruptly.

"What's your problem?" she asked as she opened the can and threw a slice in her mouth. Lucas bent down and picked up the rest of the pack. He opened it, fished around, and pulled out the axe and grenades. He slid the former into his belt and the latter into his pockets.

"Keep 'em. But I want my gun back."

Lucas laughed.

"Yeah, okay."

Alpha was playing with some controls on the holotable. They were zooming around the globe, focusing in on various points that were all flashing red. Finally it came to rest on a green dot that wasn't pulsating at all. It looked to be in . . .

"So what the hell is going on?" the woman cut in. He was really going to have to learn her name at some point.

Alpha looked up from the table and slowly walked around to their side.

"Your planet is dying. That much should be obvious to you by now. Scans indicate that there are still inhabitable regions to the north and far south of our present location, but within six months time, those will be desolate as well. Your atmosphere is corroding, your planet's temperature is rising and it will be unable to sustain any life at all within a year's time."

Lucas leaned up against the table.

"Yeah, that's what I figured."

The woman was uncharacteristically silent. Lucas pressed.

"So what are you proposing?"

"With the acquisition of the [garbled]—With the acquisition of this functional energy source, the ship is now mostly operational. Some systems remained damaged, but the engines and life support are online. As is water filtration, which I fixed long ago, and inter-ship communications, which I brought online last night when I programmed this [garbled]. This translator."

Alpha turned back to the holotable, which zoomed out from Earth to the solar system, and then further out to a star cluster.

"With current functionality, we only have enough power to get to these neighboring star systems, none of which are inhabited, and few possess planets that could even theoretically sustain life. This is a [garbled] class ship, and it's lacking the [garbled] capabilities of a [garbled] class."

"Your translator appears to be on the fritz there," the woman chimed in.

"These words do not exist here. This ship is a smaller vessel not suited for long-range travel. A larger ship has these capabilities, but all of that class have been destroyed in our civilizations' battle. Also, those ships have crews of thousands and would be impossible to fly without a hugely coordinated effort. From what I have seen, such a thing no longer exists."

He swiped the hologram which turned into a three-dimensional model of the ship.

"This is a lower class of craft, but still requires a basic crew to function. Normally there would be at least twenty onboard operating the ship at all times, with a hundred soldiers for transport. My calculations put the absolute minimum number of bodies needed to operate the ship in its current state at three. I thought this a lost cause, as I have seen what the world has turned both my and your people into, and was planning on attempting to make the trip alone, with bypassed automated systems attempting to handle the load. I would have certainly failed."

Different parts of the holographic ship lit up and were marked with symbols Lucas couldn't decipher.

"I believe the two of you could perform the necessary functions to mobilize the ship and acquire the remaining part needed for long-range travel. That is why I kept her alive, and that is why I did not kill you when you slept."

Lucas was stunned.

"You want us to fly this ship?"

The woman was equally skeptical.

"And to where? 'Long-range travel'? What does that mean? Where are you trying to go?"

Alpha swirled the hologram around so it zoomed back in on the green dot.

"Our ultimate destination I will discuss later. We do not have time at the moment. The [garbled] we need is halfway around the world, and is quickly becoming incapacitated."

Lucas was confused.

"The what? I can't understand what you're talking about. What is this thing?"

"It is a core for the larger vessels that allows them to travel long distances. Across star clusters, across the galaxy. It is not meant to be fitted to a vessel as small as this one, but I believe I can modify the ship so it will be able to house and use the core safely. That is part of what I have been working on in solitude all this time. All

I need now is the core itself. I was unable to acquire one until I found a power source that would allow the ship to fly locally. I have now located the last remaining active core on Earth, but it will not remain operational for much longer, as it is degrading at an exponential rate. This is the need for urgency."

"So where is it?" Lucas asked.

Alpha summoned the rotating globe once more and it zoomed to a point in Scandinavia.

"The device is located in a [garbled] class ship that was partially destroyed in the region you once knew as 'Norway.' Readings indicate that the area in which it is located, while devoid of water, still has habitable temperatures, and the vessel has at least 28 percent of its systems online, including the [garbled]. Including the object we require."

The woman interjected.

"You want us to fly this thing to Norway? How exactly is that going to work? We're buried in a mountain, and also, I can't speak for him, but I've no idea what any symbol in this room says, nor how to use them to make this thing move."

Lucas said nothing, but was thinking the same thing. He glanced around the room bristling with foreign devices and couldn't begin to process how he would be able to meaningfully contribute to such a mission.

"It is difficult, but possible," Alpha insisted. "We have [garbled]. We have thirty-four hours to reach the device before it degrades to the point of uselessness. In that time you will learn what you need to comprehend about this vessel to get our party there."

Lucas was incredulous. "You're telling me we can learn to operate this thing in a day and a half?"

"You will need to do so in twenty-nine hours to allow time for travel to the destination."

The woman laughed.

"You mean to tell me you can't zip this thing over there in five minutes? It still takes hours to get somewhere halfway around the planet? Does this thing run on biodiesel?"

Alpha's mechanical tone shifted into something resembling annoyance.

"Our journey must be made at a far lower speed than usual and at a far lower altitude in order to avoid detection."

"Detection by what?" Lucas asked.

Alpha hesitated, but continued.

"My brethren have left scout Sentinels behind in the outer atmosphere. They monitor the state of the corroding planet, scan for missed resources and would undoubtedly be alerted to our presence if we decided to fly at high speed across the world, as there are no other functional [garbled] ships left on Earth."

"Why wouldn't they help you?"

Alpha shifted his gaze outward and looked slightly . . . forlorn.

"My betrayal is not only known to the former crew of this ship. It is a permanent mark upon my being, and as I have been branded a traitor to my people, any communication I make is flagged as such, as is any vessel I may be operating, which will be viewed as an outlaw craft. Compounding this is the fact that if you two were detected onboard, the Sentinels would immediately obliterate the ship on sight."

Alpha waved and the hologram broke into a series of diagrams and symbols. He turned to the pair of them.

"We must not delay any further. Will you join me on this endeavor? It may be the only hope for your preservation, and for the survival of your entire species."

Lucas mulled over the question. His mind turned to his long journey through hell. He thought of the horrors that lurked outside the walls and a barren world where vats of water, cans of tuna fish, and casual conversation ceased to exist.

He considered his other option, death. It was a choice he had been about to embrace before this new mystery invigorated him. Though he had no knowledge of the endgame of this creature's plan, there was something about it that awoke a spark within him. A curiosity, a purpose. One could argue death was a similarly interesting mystery, but it was one he could always solve later.

"Alright," Lucas said.

Alpha nodded, and turned to the woman. "And you?"

Lucas imagined she was having similar thoughts to his own. She leaned back on the console with her hands in her pockets. Looking up at the ceiling, she blew out a large breath.

"Sure, why not?"

With the skeleton crew assembled, Alpha's next objective was to divide up the responsibilities of the team. His assignments were surprisingly simplistic.

"You will fly," he said, motioning to Lucas. "And you will shoot," pointing his stump at the woman.

"And what will you do?" she asked.

"I will ensure we do not explode," he said as he brought up a hologram of the engine room. "Though we have power, this vessel's engines are still extremely unstable and require constant monitoring and correction."

Lucas hadn't flown so much as an RC helicopter before, but something told him that even if he was a master F-18 pilot, that wouldn't help him much presently. The alien CIC was a puzzle wrapped in an enigma, and he didn't even know where to start.

"What exactly am I going to be shooting at?" the woman inquired.

"If we manage to secure the core, we will need to . . . outmaneuver the Sentinels. Without manually operated offensive capabilities, we will surely fail. You will man the [garbled], as the [garbled] has been damaged beyond repair."

"Come again?"

"You will man the light guns, as this ship's main cannon is no longer operational. Even the smaller, active weapons may only work for a brief time, as all spare power must be diverted to the engines."

Alpha zoomed in on northern Norway once more, where a bunch of red dots surrounded the big green one.

"Additionally, scans show a number of life-forms near the entrance of the downed vessel we must enter. Whether human or [garbled], I do not know. It is reasonable to assume they will be hostile however, and as such, suppressing fire will undoubtedly be required."

Lucas thought he saw a glimmer of excitement in the woman's eyes.

"Take this," Alpha said, handing the woman a small chip laced with tiny holograms.

"Go through that door and take the [garbled]. Take the lift down three levels. Exit and you will discover the light cannon nest. Release that device from your hand while seated, and your training will begin."

The woman didn't waste any time, blowing past Lucas, bumping his once-wounded shoulder as she did. Some water and peaches and a new objective had flooded life back into her. Lucas felt the same way, to an extent. Alpha turned to him and presented a similar chip.

"You will remain here, as your station is the commander's chair." He motioned to the large seat full of electronics and holograms.

"And this chip is going to teach me how to fly this ship?"

"Ideally, yes. I've translated the programs for each of you into your own language. Some information may be lost, but we require only basic skill for our present flight. This is a program we give to our [garbled]. To our children at a young age."

"I guess the war starts early, huh?"

"There is not one among us who is not trained in some aspect of combat. It has been our way for millennia."

"But you're a scientist."

"Inventing weapons of destruction for my superiors, rarely able to focus on my own creations." He tapped his translator with his claw. "And as you saw, even I was made an unwilling soldier. As are many of us . . ."

Alpha's gaze trailed off before he snapped back into focus.

"But you must begin. Be seated and I will retreat to finalize preparation of our engines so that we may extract ourselves from this crater wall."

Alpha turned and exited out the main doors, leaving Lucas all alone in the great mess of technology that was the central command. He walked up to the massive chair, unslung his rifle, and laid it against its side. He sat down, leaned back, and released the chip. It hovered in the air for a moment, then shot into a slot near his left arm. All of a sudden, a host of cables with flickering nodes on the end shot out and attached themselves to his arms, legs, torso, and head. The black viewscreen in front of him flickered to life.

5

The training program was an elaborate video game–type exercise that made use of the huge viewscreen, projecting a photorealistic holographic setting where blackness used to be. Lucas's virtual ship appeared to be on a landing pad amidst a vast and rocky wasteland where unfamiliar moons hung in the sky.

Holograms wrapped themselves around each of his arms, and in broken English, the translated commands in his field of vision showed him how various gestures controlled different parts of the ship.

The cables connected to parts of his body allowed him to experience the simulation in a way that mirrored realism. When he clenched his fist to start the engines, he felt them thunder through his bones as they came to life, though no such thing was happening in Alpha's engine bay. He felt the sensation of motion in the pit of his stomach the first time he ascended in the virtual craft, and a sharp sting of pain when he promptly crashed it into a nearby mountainside.

Something about the program soon seemed to be crawling its way inside his brain. He felt himself processing information far more quickly than normal, and the longer he stayed plugged in, the more the controls began to feel second nature. He wondered if the cables attached to his scalp were creating this effect, and imagined what else he might learn with such a device. It was a complex series of actions just to make the ship move in three-dimensional space, but his ever increasing knowledge of the intricacies of the controls caused him to crash less and less as time went on and he progressed through various training stages of increasing difficulty. Pain avoidance was certainly a motivator as well, since each failure brought a marked increase in the amount of hurt received. Did Alpha say this was a program for children?

Lucas was jolted out of an eighth-level mission by a complete shutdown of the system. He thought it was a power failure, but turned and saw Alpha standing next to him. He held out his claw and the chip released itself from the console and floated into his hand. He tapped it, and a hologram shot out with a bunch of alien symbols of various colors.

"Hmmm," Alpha mused. "It seems you have passed [garbled]."

Lucas was pleased.

Alpha clarified. "It seems you have passed the equivalent of fourth grade. And barely at that. But it will suit our purposes."

Lucas scowled.

"Don't I need to keep going? I was almost through with the eighth set."

"It has been fifteen hours."

Fifteen hours? It had seemed like barely one, if that. Now he understood why his son had been able to play his video games for massive stretches of time without so much as a blink. His son. He had avoided such thoughts for more than a day now, but again, there was no time to grieve as Alpha barked an order.

"Fetch the female and return here. Both of you must rest or you will be useless during the upcoming campaign. Your biological readings indicate neither of you have slept in almost thirty hours.

Lucas wondered what device was able to take such readings, but as he got out of the chair his legs buckled and he knew those statistics were accurate.

Alpha motioned to the doors the woman had walked through. He picked up Natalie and, with the gun once again secure on his back, walked through them and down a long corridor with a lift at the end.

Bracing for another long ride, Lucas noticed that the symbols on the elevator marking the levels of the ship were now in English. Alpha must have programmed elements of the ship for translation now that two thirds of his crew needed access to its decks. The five levels read COMMAND, BARRACKS, LABORATORY, ARMORY, and, finally, ENGINE. He swiped his hand across ARMORY, the ship's controls now registering his presence, and the slow descent began.

The doors opened and he could see flashes of light almost immediately from a hallway down and to the right. As he made his way to the divide, he first looked left, and with a swipe through the door controls, peered into a vast room full of racks and storage cubes, all apparently bare. He imagined the original crew had cleared out whatever weapons remained when they evacuated the ship, but the area would warrant further exploration when time was not of the essence.

Heading right, the hallway wound around and he found himself entering a spherical room with a chair similar to his own but smaller in the center. The woman was seated, strapped in with the same sort of cables that had bound him, shooting at virtual spacecraft on a great curved screen. Her eyes darted back and forth, not noticing his presence as he stood next to the chair. He could hardly make out what type of ships were being shot at before they began exploding. It seemed her training might be going a bit better than his.

He encroached further into her gaze, but still, no recognition. Finally, he waved his hand over the console and the chip shot out and the screen went black. The cables retracted and she looked around, suddenly confused as he had been.

"What the . . . ?" She finally saw him. "Why did you stop me?"

"Alpha say it's time to go."

"Alpha? Is that his name?"

Lucas was taken aback, but quickly realized that he had only shared that identifier with him.

"Sort of. Call it a nickname."

She tried to wave her hands over the console, but it remained black.

"I just started this."

"It's been fifteen hours."

She looked incredulous.

"Yeah, I know. These things mess with your mind a bit."

She swiveled around the chair with a gesture.

"You know this is insane right?"

"What is?"

"This entire thing."

Lucas leaned back against the black viewscreen, rubbing his eyes with his palms.

"Of course I know that, but what about the last few years hasn't been?"

He slunk down to sit on the curved floor of the spherical room and continued.

"But I'm tired of walking. I'm tired of starving. I'm tired of this dusty, ashen, barren world. If he can take us somewhere away from here, don't you at least think we should stick around to see where that is?"

"I don't like leaving my fate in the hands of a . . . thing whose friends destroyed my life and the planet I lived on. At least out there I was in control of my own destiny."

Lucas scoffed.

"You really believe you were in control?"

"Of course, you don't?"

"What about that unstable freeway overpass that could have crumbled when you stepped on it? What about that one burning rainstorm that could have caught you when you were just far enough away from cover? What about that lone wanderer whose shot you couldn't have heard until it was inside your brain? You weren't in control out there; that was just a delusion. You think that being alive right now makes you some kind of superhuman, but really all it makes you is lucky."

She looked past him, brow furrowed. "I earned the right to be alive. You should know that better than anyone," she said, pointing to his shoulder.

Lucas threw his hand up dismissively.

"And what if I knew better by then? What if when I came along I just blew your head off without a second glance?"

"And what if tomorrow was a bright sunshiny day with a high of seventy-one?" the woman said fiercely. "There's no point in that kind of thinking. I'm alive for a reason, and now this, this could be my reason. I know what I've done to be where I am today. Don't tell me it's luck that I can butcher five grown men waiting in ambush without suffering so much as a scratch. Don't tell me it's luck that I can charm two psychopaths to do my bidding like a pair of loyal dogs for months. Don't tell me that I'm one of the last people alive on this planet because of pure chance. Maybe you stumbled into this ship after months in the desert on a whim and prayer, but I doubt it. You crawled your way here over the bodies of millions like I did, which means you're made of some of the same stuff."

She turned and shot him a piercing glare.

"Why are *you* doing this if you just think we're mere flies that are simply fortunate enough not to have been swatted yet?"

Lucas tilted his head upward, keeping her gaze. After a lengthy pause, he spoke.

"There's something to be said about discovering the unknown. To have a task greater than just surviving the next day or hour. I thought Portland was the end, but maybe it wasn't. Clearly he has a plan, and I don't think it involves going back to his homeworld and being executed for treason. There's something he wants to show us."

Suddenly, a familiar metal voice rang out.

"All crew report to command immediately."

Alpha was growing anxious.

The woman got up from her chair to leave and Lucas rose from the floor.

"I think it's about time you told me your name," Lucas said.

The woman paused on her way out of the room, her back to him.

"Asha."

"Lucas."

"Let's go."

Upon their return to the command center, Alpha quickly checked Asha's marks on her chip, which he deemed satisfactory. Lucas couldn't tell what they were, but he definitely saw far more green and less red than when his program had displayed a similar screen.

Alpha then escorted them to the barracks level, which was a room full of rows and rows of translucent pods. Many were cracked or remained dark when Alpha powered up the room, but there were a few dozen still functioning. Lucas remembered Alpha saying this was a transport, and at one time there were over two hundred soldiers plus the crew who manned the ship. Presumably at one point, they all slept here. Well, they were about to *sleep*, right?

"In a sense," Alpha explained. "Your higher brain functioning will be shut down for a period in which your body will recharge. Normally it would be fed supplementary nutrients during this time, but this ship's supply has long been depleted."

"So how is this not sleep?" asked Lucas.

"It is inefficient to wait for the individual to fall asleep on their own schedule. Rather, unconsciousness is induced with the aid of the [garbled]. It produces a state you might refer to as 'sleep,' but in truth it is far deeper than that."

He flipped a holoswitch and a metal halo-like device descended from the roof of one of the open pods.

"I don't like this." Asha said flatly.

Alpha had no time for what she liked.

"You will be unable to perform the complex functions required for the upcoming task without the aid of the [garbled]."

"I've been blowing up alien ships for the last fifteen hours just fine."

"You have undoubtedly noticed an increase of information flow to your cortex, and a distortion of time. These processes take a toll on the body, and readings indicate this is especially the case for you as humans are unaccustomed to such levels of stimulation."

It was hard to disagree with this point, as Lucas had felt dizzy and borderline nauseous ever since his simulation had ended. His muscles ached and a wave of fatigue had come over him that went deep into his core. Asha had to be feeling the same way, and the dark circles under her eyes gave her away.

"There's nothing to lose at this point, right?" Lucas said as he stepped into the machine.

"Your cooperation is appreciated," Alpha said as he closed the pod's door.

Lucas felt the gelatinous backing of the pod conform to the shape of his body; it was surprisingly comfortable. He looked up and saw the halo descending toward him. Alpha and Asha peered through the glass, and they were the last thing he saw before blackness.

But blackness was not what remained.

He awoke in the same hotel bed he had been in that morning. The same call from his wife jarred him awake, and once again he rubbed his eyes and squinted out the window into the bright Miami sunshine. It was the same moment, and one that was burned into his mind for all eternity.

He answered groggily.

"Hey . . . what's up?"

"Oh thank god. Are you watching this?" his wife said hurriedly on the other line.

He winced his eyes shut, and found that he had the hangover he expected. It was a familiar side-effect of his cross-country trips for work. The light was too much too bear, and the volume on his receiver seemed deafening. He pulled it away from his ear.

"Watching what?"

"It's three hours later there. Are you just waking up?"

"No," he lied, and they both knew that. But her voice was frantic, not angry.

"I've been calling for hours, but this is the first time I've been able to get through. All the lines are jammed. Turn on the news."

He fumbled around for the remote, which was buried deep in the bedcovers. He flipped on the TV, wondering what channel the news would be on in this unfamiliar city. But it didn't matter, it was on all of them.

It took him ten seconds to fully process what he was seeing. A giant object loomed in the sky above New York City, the caption UFO Appears over Manhattan beneath it as five correspondents all tried to talk over each other at once. It took Lucas a solid minute to even speak a word.

"Honey? Honey, are you there?"

Lucas found his voice at last.

"I'm coming home, right now. Stay there."

"Okay, talk to Nathan, he's been—"

The phone cut out, a dropped signal as the entire cellular network was assuredly in a state of meltdown. Redials were met with an endless busy signal.

Lucas let the phone slide from his grasp as he watched the TV with a fixed gaze. He didn't even notice when the door to the bathroom opened and she strolled out onto the carpet in her underwear. He jumped when she spoke.

"What is that?" she asked, as she saw the newscast on the flatscreen.

He turned to her.

"I need to go, now."

Suddenly the woman decayed into ash as the walls of the room expanded outward and drifted away into a starry sky that now enveloped his view. He flew toward it.

6

He woke with the halo slowly rising off his head. His vision was blurred, but within a moment he recalled that he was in the pod. A dream? No, a memory. A crystal clear, perfectly rendered memory. He could even still smell the beach for a few lingering seconds, taste the vodka on his breath, and then it was gone. Why had he just relived the most astonishing, terrifying, and ultimately tragic moment in his former life? He'd thought about it often, but never actually had to fully experience it again. His drinking had finally caused him to make a mistake he never thought was possible, a line he vowed he'd never cross. And on that night, on that day, of all days. Since that moment, there hadn't been an ounce of alcohol in his veins, and he spent the years since trying to fulfill his promise to come home. On the way, he often viewed his hellish march as penance for his sins. True, the journey had made him a mass murderer in an effort to stay alive and find them, but he preferred the content of his character now to the wreck of self-loathing, deceit, and addiction he once was. The apocalypse made many men worse, but few better.

The pod's door slid up and open, and he stepped down into the corridor. He was shaken from his vision, but physically was feeling noticeably better. How long had he been in there?

Across from him, the door to another pod opened to reveal Asha. It seemed Alpha had talked her into a nap after all. She looked disoriented as the halo rose up from her head, but she soon regained her bearings as she stepped out. Lucas saw she looked noticeably disturbed as well.

"Did you see anything?" he pressed, but she cut him off quickly.

"No. I was out like a light."

But he knew she must have been plagued by a similar phenomenon as he. Alpha's voice ended any chance of further questioning.

"Crew to command."

Asha walked quickly out into the hallway, avoiding Lucas's gaze.

When they reached the CIC, Alpha asked them about their slumber.

"Are you feeling more rested?" he inquired, though his only real concern was likely for the integrity of the mission.

Lucas shifted.

"Yeah, but there were . . ."

Asha cut in.

"What the hell is that thing?"

Alpha looked confused. Well, as confused as a creature can look.

"What did you experience?"

"Memories, and not good ones," Lucas offered.

"Strange," Alpha said. "The [garbled] is programmed for almost complete neural shutdown during rest. There must have been an unforeseen complication with your . . . biology. I will have to investigate further at a later date."

"Please do," Asha said, as she stood with her arms crossed, clenching her fingers to her skin, which was rife with goosebumps. She looked uncharacteristically unnerved, which made Lucas curious about what she had seen.

Alpha continued, tapping a mechanical cuff on his bad arm, which Lucas was surprised to see now had a robotic hand attached with six spindly fingers sprouting out of it. A small hologram shone out of his wrist.

"In any case, your biological signatures indicate the last five hours spent at rest have increased your neural functioning by

60 percent. I've finished the last of the preliminary engine work during that period and we must now depart."

Lucas began to sweat, something he hadn't done in a long while due to the complete lack of water in his system. But now with moisture back in his skin, the old indicator of nerves had returned. Hologram training was one thing, but could he actually fly this ship halfway around the world?

"Report to stations," Alpha said with unusual command presence. "We will have visual and audio contact with each other at all times."

Then, as if he sensed Lucas's tension, he caught his eye and continued.

"Your training will be sufficient."

Not exactly an inspired motivational speech, but Lucas felt comforted Alpha trusted him to some small degree. He nodded and walked toward the central captain's chair as Alpha and Asha disappeared down their respective hallways.

This time when he sat down, only the cables that attached to his head reappeared. He assumed the rest were for the simulation only. Holograms sprouted up all over his field of vision and around each of his arms. Overwhelmed for a moment, he reached into his mind for the information he knew was there. He found it almost instantly, and began running through the preflight checklist he had learned as his first lesson in training. Unlike his virtual ship however, this one was still damaged, and from the translated read-outs he saw it was functioning at only 73 percent capacity. How that would affect his ability to operate it, he had no idea.

Two floating windows appeared in his field of vision. One was a fixed shot of Alpha in the engine bay; the other showed Asha sitting in the turret down below. Alpha looked into the camera. Or was it a camera?

"Visual contact confirmed. Confirm audio."

"Um, audio confirmed," Lucas spat out hastily.

"Confirmed," said Asha.

"Lucas," Alpha said, which was the first time he'd uttered his name aloud. "This takeoff will differ from your simulation."

Fantastic, Lucas thought.

"What do I do?"

"Divert all available power to the underside engines. We will need every bit of it to free ourselves from the crater wall."

"Alright," Lucas said. His mind raced and he managed to remember the location of the engine control grid he had been playing with earlier. He brought up a floating blueprint of the ship and tapped each of the bottom engines. Bringing his hands together, all available power was thrust into them. He clenched his fist.

The ship roared to life and the lights in the entire CIC went dark. There was only a hint of light on the faces of Alpha and Asha in the monitors now. It seemed he really did mean all available power.

"And now rise," Alpha said coolly through the screen.

Lucas turned his fist upward and slowly raised it. The ship shook violently, far more than it ever had in the simulation, and Lucas would have been thrown from his chair had he not been strapped in. He saw Alpha buckle in the monitor. It kept shaking for five, then ten seconds, then Lucas finally felt a sense of elevation. They were moving. Alpha scrambled to secure the engines as alarms were going off all over the bay. Asha clenched her hands wrapped in the gun controls, unaware of what they might find once they surfaced.

A few seconds later, ash started streaming down the black viewscreen, which began to get increasingly lighter. Then, in an instant, they burst through the top of the crater wall with a massive groan that Lucas was worried had torn the ship apart, but as they rose, everything felt as it had when he successfully took off in the simulation.

"We are free," Alpha said on the comm. "Keep elevation under [garbled] and speed under [garbled] at all times."

"Please repeat," Lucas said, stunned he had been able to successfully surface the craft.

"Elevation under 3,254 feet and speed under 1,238 miles per hour," corrected Alpha, as his translator converted to the appropriate units.

The lights in the ship came back on, and Lucas looked out the viewscreen, which now had a full view of the surrounding area. The crater that once was Portland was vast, and as he looked west, even at elevation he couldn't see any ocean, only an endless beach littered with the skeletons of innumerable ships, planes, and presumably, people. The crater, conversely, had almost nothing in it, just a few husks of the bottom floors of skyscrapers that Lucas had seen from the ground. Somewhere down there had been his wife and son, before god knows what wiped them from the Earth.

The craft dipped slightly and it made Lucas's stomach churn. As the ship stabilized, Lucas realized that his heart was thundering in his chest, and fatigue, hunger, all of it, had faded away. He was fully aware he was at the helm of an alien spacecraft. It felt like a dream, but then again so had the entire last few years. His awe was interrupted by Alpha, who was waving various screens about on the monitor.

"Here are the coordinates of our destination. Enter them into the console."

A longitude and latitude appeared in front of Lucas, and he wiped it over into a spinning globe. It zoomed in on the green point and the ship lurched forward, pinning Lucas back in his seat for a moment. He had to quickly dial the speed down to match Alpha's specifications, and soon, despite traveling at 1,200 miles an hour, Lucas felt like he was sitting comfortably in an airplane. An impossible, interstellar airplane.

He put the ship on autopilot with elevation and speed locked, and a countdown timer appeared to his left. Three hours and thirteen minutes until they reached . . . what was this place called?

"Kvaløya" it seemed, and it was far enough north that it was equivalent with parts of upper Russia, Canada, and Greenland. Lucas sifted through the menus to try and find out the temperature there, but gave up as not enough of those commands had been translated into English. He was also a bit unnerved by all the glowing red dots surrounding the green one on the map. He wondered if this thing could detect remaining life anywhere on Earth if they were reading signatures from that far away.

"Are we there yet?" said Asha sarcastically on the comm.

"Three hours," Lucas said.

"Stay alert," Alpha added.

Lucas wiped away most of his controls with a flick of his hand and turned his attention to the vista through his viewscreen. They were speeding over what was left of the United States, which was, in effect, nothing. Forests of charred trees had given way to fields of ash. Every so often they'd fly by a tattered town, ravaged by looting, but there were dozens of giant craters that marked where larger cities had once been. They were low enough to still be under the endless suffocating cloud cover, so there was no chance to see the sun. Lucas thought about raising the ship just to take a peek, but knew Alpha would probably lock him up in the brig rather than risk detection by the Sentinels. And rightly so. He peered into the clouds and wondered how far out they were, and how wide-reaching their equipment was. He supposed they were a problem for another time.

It was only a few minutes later when they reached the Rockies. They were mostly free of major devastation from the war due to a lack of tactical significance, but they were missing the signature snow cover that normally adorned their peaks. Snow. The concept was almost humorous now.

Soon they were in southern Canada, following the curve of the Earth to their final destination. The country had normally been spared in times of conflict throughout history, but when the creatures realized the United States had hidden nuclear silos scattered throughout their northern neighbor, Canada suffered the full wrath of the onslaught. Additionally, wildfires, acid rain, and widespread panic cared naught about borders, and so the lands looked as ravaged as any Lucas had seen further south. Eventually they flew over what appeared to be a small metropolis, less ruined than most he'd seen. The display hadn't bothered to translate the names of such minor cities into English. Tapping through the holocontrols, he still couldn't figure out how to scan for nearby life, but he supposed it didn't matter; if anyone was holed up there, the rising temperatures would cook them in a month or two.

He thought about what it might take to try and save other survivors before they left the planet for good, should they not all die in this upcoming endeavor. But as the types of people left alive at this point were like him or Asha or worse, he couldn't imagine filling a ship with such personalities. Violence would undoubtedly erupt as there still was barely any food, and even the last heralds of the human race would likely ensure their own destruction. No, it was better with only two, he thought, though he wasn't entirely convinced one wouldn't kill the other in due time.

Lucas wondered about their final destination. A place to start over? Such a thought was likely overly optimistic, as wherever Alpha had come from brought a promise of endless war and bloodshed. A sentence Alpha had spoken previously came back to him.

"I did not say our war was with you."

Though the ship was on autopilot, Lucas kept his hands wrapped in the controls and stared intently out the viewscreen for the next two hours. When he finally managed to see the Atlantic Ocean, which began about two hundred miles east of where it was supposed to, it was a murky reddish brown, and didn't look like it could sustain anything remotely resembling life. As they reached Iceland on the virtual globe, Alpha spoke through the monitor.

"Slow to 239 miles per hour."

Lucas was jolted out of his thoughts and dialed the speed down to Alpha's suggested level, wondering why they were decelerating if time was so precious. Alpha answered his question.

"We must now investigate the crash site so that we may formulate an entry path."

"Meaning finding out what exactly those red dots are, and how we're going to kill them?" Asha chimed in.

"That seems likely," Alpha agreed. "Lucas, release a [garbled]. Release a probe."

Lucas scanned through the navigation system. The cables attached to his temples allowed him to find the launch program immediately, despite only using it once briefly during a fifth-level training simulation. A virtual image of the probe appeared before him. It was a small mechanical sphere with tiny jets on all sides of it. He'd seen more than a few of these whizzing around the city during the height of the brief war, never knowing their purpose. Pulling up the coordinates, he flung them into the virtual probe, then hit the holographic "Go" button, which he assumed was a rough translation that probably should have read "Launch."

But go it did, and from the viewscreen, he saw it shoot out of the underside of the ship and off into the horizon. The readout hovering in front of him indicated the probe was traveling at a blistering 4,313 miles per hour.

"When the [garbled] approaches the destination, I will control it from here," Alpha said as he pulled up a holographic screen on the wrist of his six-fingered metal hand. It showed a landscape moving incredibly quickly, and Lucas assumed it was the view from the probe. Alpha made a motion with his claw and that theory was confirmed as the display suddenly engulfed his entire viewscreen and, from the looks of it, Asha's as well.

The probe blew past what remained of Iceland and soared over the dark ocean at an incredibly low altitude that wasn't displaying on the readout. A few minutes later it hit the shores of northern Norway and slowed dramatically to a few hundred miles an hour.

The probe's positional locater moved slowly toward the green dot on the globe and increased its elevation. Alpha had now taken manual control and was steering it through several mountain passes, which, much like the Rockies, were desolate and bare rather than covered with their usual blanket of snow. He weaved in and out of them, often veering dangerously close to the slopes, but always correcting at the last moment. The probe then turned and went straight up the side of a large mountain and shot out over the top of its peak. Then they saw it.

He had only seen them far up in the sky, with the last one he spotted jetting away into the upper atmosphere when he was somewhere in Mississippi. But here a mothership had fallen to Earth and had cut what used to be a charming little fishing village in half. A small town was spread out before them, encased in the valley with the massive downed craft slumbering behind it. Sporadically, blue lights would flicker in the upper regions of the ship, while the floors below remained black. There was smoldering debris littered throughout the town and visible damage all over the hull. Lucas wondered what might have brought it down for good. Not a nuke, as there would be a lot less of it left and they wouldn't be able to land if that was the case. A coordinated, massive fighter strike perhaps? It would have taken a whole fleet of planes shooting in all the right places to take something like this out. Did Norway even have an air force?

The probe dipped down the backside of the mountain it had just climbed, and as it drew closer to the village, Lucas realized that the smoke coming from the ground was actually . . . campfires?

"What the hell is this?" Asha said slowly on the comm.

Alpha stopped the probe completely, and after a few twirls the video feed zoomed in ten times, fifty, then two hundred.

The village was alive. Lucas couldn't contain his astonishment as his jaw hung loose. As the probe zoomed closer, he could see people walking on the ground. Some toted weapons, others lumber or rocks. A few had slabs of meat. There were dozens, maybe a hundred. The life detection system had not prepared them for this. They had found an actual society, a miracle in the current state of the world. But as the view drew closer, Lucas began to wonder what sort of society they had found.

The probe panned down to the bay and showed a long convex wall made up of all sorts of wood and twisted metal. It was hard to see exactly what it was composed of, but further magnification implied felled trees, stone, and scrap metal. Makeshift guard towers lined the top of it, and men with long rifles overlooked the empty bay full of shattered docks and the carcasses of dozens of former fishing vessels.

The camera panned further up to inspect the village itself. Though the ship's crash had leveled many buildings, a large number still stood, their solid stone craftsmanship holding resolute. There was an ornate church, a clock tower attached to a building that was likely some kind of city hall, and rows of tightly packed houses. It was unclear how much of the village had been swallowed by the ship. Lucas imagined that years ago, this would have been a picturesque destination, flanked by snow-capped mountains and crystal clear water. But as the probe turned its eye toward the town square, it became clear this wasn't paradise, nor was it some hidden utopia in a dying world.

In the cobblestone square stood Y-shaped pieces of metal and wood shoved into the ground. Strapped to each of them was a nude man, each in a different stage of emaciation. Some appeared dead or unconscious, but a few stirred. Lucas counted eighteen of them, with ten or so more empty Y-crosses scattered around near them. Nearby, a human body roasted on a spit. They were cannibals, but from the looks of the town, organized ones.

Two of the men walked over to a prisoner tied up on a stake and one of them promptly slit his throat with a knife. They cut him down and dragged his convulsing body to the other fire, which had no meal roasting on it yet. But it seemed it was about to.

The cannibals' exact level of brutality was not of primary concern, and so Alpha panned the probe up the sloped ground to where the alien craft met the Earth. One section of the ship seemed of particular interest to Alpha. In front of it stood a large mansion—almost a castle.

As they watched, the doors of the building opened and a hulking bear of a man walked out. Or was it a creature? The probe zoomed in further, and it looked like the giant was wearing stitched together pieces of alien power armor, and he was toting a matching massive energy weapon. How he managed to assemble such a suit to fit a human and still have it function after all this time, Lucas had no idea, and judging from how long Alpha lingered on him, he was intrigued as well.

Men began running through the streets down toward the bay, and Alpha shifted the probe's view to follow them. There was nothing to see at first, but after zooming out, it was clear what all the commotion was about. A party of about fifteen cannibals was returning to camp with six other humans in tow. Two were smaller, scraggly men of unknown age, the others were four women who looked badly battered.

The men near the wall swung open a part of it that doubled as a gate. As they did so, Lucas saw two pikes protruding from either side, one skewering a human skeleton while a creature's bones rested on the other. *So this is what "society" looks like in this world now?* Even with all he'd seen, the existence of a place like this made Lucas feel nauseous.

The captives were shoved inside the gate. They were lead through town as other men jeered at them from the sides of the road. The men were immediately dragged over to vacant Y-stakes in the town square. Two cannibals lifted each of them up and, after raising their arms, shoved something sharp through each of their wrists, pinning them to the wood

Guess they ran out of rope, Lucas thought as the men screamed in agony while blood ran down their forearms.

Meanwhile, the four women were stripped of their remaining rags and thrust into the nearby church. Lucas caught a glimpse of other figures inside before the door was slammed shut and a wooden slat was threaded through it to ensure they stayed put.

He could see Asha seething on her monitor.

Alpha flipped a switch and the view from the probe went thermal, or something like it. Inside the hut they could see about two dozen huddled glowing figures, with some appearing to have their arms chained to the walls and others lying prone on the floor. A harem of sorts? The thought was sickening, but as only men wandered around outside, it seemed the likely answer.

Lucas thought that through for a moment, instinctively attempting to formulate a rescue plan for the captives in the church and on the stakes. But it was entirely possible, if not probable, that these prisoners were every bit as dangerous as their captors. They had to be to have survived this long, and they were merely stripped of their weapons and clothing, overpowered by superior, more organized foes. And this many men, all working together? Such a thing was unheard of since the early days of roving bands of rogue police and marine patrols, but those hadn't existed in the US for months. He wondered how long this miniature fortress had stood here at the base of the wrecked colossus. Asha had some thoughts of her own about the village, which she relayed through the monitor.

"I bet they came here in search of creatures to eat, because they must have been pouring out of that thing at one point, and I'm sure many stuck around. But when they ran out of meat they started eating their weak, and eventually sent out raiding parties to bring back more."

"Why haven't they turned on each other by now?" Lucas asked.

"Their system works, so why mess with it? They have food, shelter . . . women," she said, gritting her teeth. "There's no reason to kill each other."

It made sense, but trust was something Lucas thought had vanished from the world completely. Though looking at his two new compatriots in the monitors, he supposed that under certain conditions, that wasn't exactly true. Was it possible to eat your fellow man and not go insane?

Alpha spoke through the monitor. "There is no time to waste; we must obliterate that installation and make our way to the ship's core."

"I like the sound of that," Asha said.

Lucas looked up at the monitor and watched flames engulf the recently executed man, now mounted on a spit. He liked the sound of that as well.

The aerial assault plan was drawn up quickly. Lucas would strafe the ship over the town while Asha rained down fire and brimstone from her cannons until everything was rubble. If the main gun was online, they could have obliterated the entire village from three miles out, but Alpha insisted it was beyond repair, and even if it wasn't, it could irreparably damage the weakened ship that made up the north wall of the encampment.

Lucas asked if they could just hover above the fray while Asha unloaded, but Alpha said that in the ship's unstable state, concentrated small arms fire could damage vital systems. The assumed leader's appropriated alien weapon could actually tear a hole in weaker parts of the craft if it was fully charged. They would have to do a few fly-bys and hope that Asha would be able to eliminate enough ground targets so their subsequent entry would be easier. Lucas couldn't imagine storming the gates on foot. Despite what the tatters of the uniform he wore might indicate, he was in no way prepared for that kind of combat. A few bandits or cannibals was one thing, but a city full of them? Impossible.

The probe returned and Lucas dialed the ship up to cruising speed once more, making landfall a few minutes later. The village at Kvaløya was only a hundred or so miles ahead, and Lucas took manual control of the craft for the first time since launch hours earlier. Lowering his altitude, he weaved through mountain valleys the way Alpha had steered the probe, but the ship felt like it was made of lead. Sure, it was no fighter jet, but it felt far more cumbersome than the equivalent virtual model in training. Lucas couldn't tell if that was a flaw in the simulation, or if the damage done to the vessel had altered the way it was supposed to fly.

"Prepare for contact," Alpha said through the monitor.

Asha clenched her fists tightly, each wrapped in holocontrols. "Ready."

"Ready," Lucas said as he brought up a screen of Asha's turret view so it floated in his field of vision. He'd have to concentrate on flying, but needed to make sure her shots were lined up as well. This had been the stage in the training program he was flying through when Alpha interrupted him. Hopefully he'd learned enough.

Mikkel sunk his teeth into a hunk of human thigh, which had recently finished cooking on the fire. It tasted even worse than the last one, which was likely because the wanderers they dragged in were increasingly nothing more than skin and bones.

He began to hear a low whine, which steadily increased, and then he watched as the empty shell casings started to dance on the table near the fire. He turned to look behind him and saw a sight he hadn't witnessed in a long time. Grabbing his rifle, he cupped his hand to his mouth and shouted with a deep, booming voice that would have shook the snow off the mountains if there was still any left.

"*Alarm! Frem med våpen!*"

He turned, raised his gun, and was instantly blown into a dozen pieces.

There was fire in Asha's eyes as she tore through the village with her first volley. Her monitor indicated five confirmed kills, though she'd only seen two of them explode on her viewscreen. Her shots ripped up the street and blew large holes in nearby stone buildings. The incendiary shots set ablaze anything remotely flammable, and she watched with delight as a man stumbled out of a house fully engulfed in flames. As Lucas steered the ship past the camp, she swiveled around and kept firing, her canister shells igniting a few more rooftops before she was out of range. Asha's heart pounded and sweat poured from her brow. A small smile crossed her lips.

"Circling around," Lucas said on the monitor.

The ship was far too bulky to do anything resembling a vertical turnaround, so Lucas banked hard right until the craft, moaning and creaking as it went, made a full loop and had the village in its sights once again.

This time around the cannibals had armed themselves, and Lucas heard gunfire pelt the hull of the ship. Readouts said that no actual damage was being done, but he was still waiting for the glass of the viewscreen in front of him to shatter from a bullet. *Though it's probably not glass, is it?*

Asha fired back with another volley from her cannons as Lucas roared by. This time her blasts tore through the center of town, incinerating a dozen more hostiles and several of the prisoners tied to stakes. The ones she missed scattered like roaches in every direction.

Suddenly, an alarm sounded.

"What the hell is going on?" Asha shouted into the monitor as they flew past the town and into the mountains once more.

Alpha frantically went back and forth from control to control in the engine bay.

"The guns are overheating the ship's weak core. We will soon have enough power to fly or fire, but not both."

"So what does that mean?" Asha yelled over the sound of the alarm.

"This next pass will be your last," Alpha said as his metal hand flittered through readouts.

"Make it count!" Lucas said as he veered the ship around once more. He slowed down his approach to give Asha more time to fire, should she not get the opportunity again.

Once more she lit up the town, ignoring the blaring of the alarm in her ears. She watched the shells eat through the clock tower where two men were blown out of the top before the rest of the structure crumbled. On the ground, scores of cannibals sprinted for the gate. Focusing her fire on them, she tore across the ashen sand, catching eight of them in the open before her fire blew a hole in the forward wall near where the gate stood. It was hard to make out if any of them had successfully fled, and if they had, they were too far under the ship to target. Asha quickly focused her gaze back to the village, when a rocket-propelled grenade whizzed by her turret and struck the underside of the ship. Attempting to return fire, she was greeted by a flashing red error message in loosely translated English. No Fire, it said, and judging by her unresponsive controls and the smoke pouring out of the gun barrels, she knew what it meant.

Lucas felt the engines sputter a bit, and the craft dipped suddenly as it left the smoldering town in its rearview.

"Alpha?" he yelled worriedly.

"Systems are overheating and we suffered a direct hit to the [garbled] from that explosive device. Weapons are offline, engines at 43 percent." There was a hint of panic in his voice.

"What do we do?" Lucas asked over the blaring of the alarm.

"We must land, immediately."

Lucas brought up a topographic map of the area and scanned through it. The region was quite mountainous, and the computer indicated the best place to land in the area would be . . . the bay.

It hadn't seen water for years, and the sands were vast enough to accommodate the relatively large craft. At least the walk to the mothership would be short. The life detection readout, flickering on and off, revealed there were still plenty of people alive down there, though he couldn't tell which were cannibals and which were prisoners. Their bombing run of sorts had softened them up, but there was still more work to be done.

Lucas wheeled the ship around, and when he glanced down at the monitors, he saw that while Alpha was still playing with the flickering controls in the engine room, Asha was no longer in her turret.

He turned back to the viewscreen, and approached the bay, which fed into the walled entrance to the village. There was no sign of movement on the ground, only smoke rising from flaming buildings and crisp bodies. Had they forgone fleeing to start hiding? Where had they gone?

Lucas easily recalled the landing sequence procedures from training, thanks in part, he assumed, to his external neural enhancements, and performed the operation like it was second nature. The ship touched down softly in the sand, though it moaned one last nerve-racking time before Lucas shut the engines down on Alpha's command. In the viewscreen ahead, he could see the town's wall up at the top of the sandy shore and smoke rising in front of the massive wrecked ship that loomed behind it. Above it, the same angry red clouds were present that Lucas had found all across America. Transfixed by the scene of extraterrestrial devastation, he didn't even notice Asha, until he heard the bolt click.

Shit.

He instinctively reached for Natalie, propped up against the ship's command chair, but the weapon was already gone. Asha was standing behind him, pointing his own gun at his head with a stern look on her face. Looking down, he saw she was barefoot, and he had to applaud her for doing a damn fine job sneaking through the CIC unnoticed. However, he was disappointed in himself, as he would have never made such a mistake in the wild even a few days ago. He slowly turned the chair to face her.

"Hello," he said flatly.

"Give it," she replied, motioning toward him with the raised rifle.

"Give what?" he asked, bemused.

"It's saved my life more times than I can count, and if we're going out there I need it, along with my other supplies."

He noticed that she had already picked up her pack, which had been sitting forgotten at the base of the central console. Lucas was still perplexed.

"You want . . . what exactly?"

Asha looked exasperated.

"The revolver, idiot."

Though it had once been creating quite the annoying sharp pain in his lower back, Lucas had forgotten about the gun he confiscated from her when they first met. Well, second met.

"Oh you mean this?" he said as he took the revolver out of his belt and quickly pointed it at her with the hammer already drawn. She raised Natalie and took one step forward.

"That's the one."

"And why would I let you have both guns, just like that?" he asked, trying to remain calm and playful.

Asha raised an eyebrow. "Because you still have one in your boot, and you can have this thing back once I get mine."

"You'd just give me my gun back? Trade a fully automatic machine gun for a six shot revolver?"

"The way I see it, there are only about six of them left out there anyway, and that's all the shots I need. And let's just say it has . . . sentimental value."

Natalie had sentimental value as well, but Lucas would be damned if he was going to say that out loud. He had to resist referring to it by name during their conversation out of force of habit. It had been the only one who had listened to him during his long trek these last few hard months.

"So how do you want to do this then?" he asked, letting his grip loosen on the Magnum just a bit.

"Exchange on three?" she said, as she drew closer to him.

"Alright."

They both began counting.

"One . . ."

As they spoke, Alpha marched straight into the room from the lift corridor. Walking right up to them, he promptly snatched Natalie from Asha and the revolver from Lucas before either knew what was happening. He walked over to the holotable and threw each gun on it. They were both so stunned they couldn't speak.

"The time for dissent has past," he said plainly. "We must take inventory of all our weaponry for our approach to the ship."

After Asha and Lucas recovered from the shock of the sudden end to their standoff, the table soon became piled with weapons and ammunition. Natalie had about four spare clips left, while the revolver had thirty odd shells, despite Asha's insistence she wouldn't need them. Lucas put his boot pistol on the table, which only had the clip that was in it, and his buck knife. Asha had her two grenades and a hatchet, but no other firearms. Alpha had spent the last few minutes attempting to activate his old power armor and gun with his spindly mechanical fingers, his other hand clutching another sort of alien power tool like the one Lucas had seen earlier. Finally a few lights came on in the suit, with fewer lit on the gun.

"Will that thing work?" asked Lucas.

"The [garbled] is only at 18 percent power, but it will function well enough for our purposes. The material alone will make me largely bullet resistant."

"Great, and what are we supposed to do?" lamented Asha.

"Do what you have done previously," Alpha said as he strapped the armor over his chest. "Survive."

After suiting up, passing around a can of tuna fish and downing a few ounces of water, they exited the ship through a port Lucas hadn't seen before as it had been about a hundred feet underground when he first boarded the ship. After they left, Lucas turned back and saw the vessel he was flying for the first time in its entirety. He'd seen many swooping overhead during the war, but none this close, and he felt a strange kinship to the ship despite only having flown it for a few hours. Some of the plating was heavily damaged, but the jet-black surface was unscathed near the top, and the arcing lines and flickering blue lights made it look impressive, even if it was a mere transport.

Out in the open, he found the air felt different here. It was still stuffy, but not suffocating, and it was certainly hot, but not hellish, as Lucas remembered they were north of the Arctic Circle in the middle of winter. Even if it was milder, a familiar problem presented itself. The whole area used to be filled with bays, inlets, and islands, but now it had transformed into a desert like the rest of the world. If Alpha was correct, it would be uninhabitable within a month or two. Judging by how fast he'd seen temperatures rise recently, Lucas believed it.

His clothes were soaked in sweat, partially because of the heat, but mostly due to the task at hand. Looking up at the camp's wall, Lucas wondered what condition the survivors were in, and how many would pose a threat. It was the first time he could remember feeling actual fear in months. He thought he'd just grown numb to it, but the pit of his stomach told him otherwise, and he had to steady his hands as they clutched Natalie with white knuckles.

He looked to his left, and saw Asha holding her Magnum in both hands with no signs of tremors. Her hatchet was threaded through her belt loop, and she trudged through the sands in her ripped black pants and knee-high combat boots. Two grenades jangled on her belt like keys.

On his right, Alpha looked far more impressive than he ever had, now that he was fully encased in power armor. It may have been cracked and half functional, but the plating still made him look imposing, and he carried himself with far more confidence than the slouching scientist Lucas had seen in the holoscreen recording earlier. He supposed Alpha had seen and done a lot since then. They all had.

Alpha's good hand clutched the long, standard-issue alien energy rifle that Lucas had seen a thousand times when the creatures swarmed the streets. His mechanical, six-fingered claw (which, he explained, was not weaponized, and only for complex technical procedures) was wrapped tightly around the ship's glowing core, which he said was necessary to stop the mothership's larger core from deteriorating further once they reached it.

As they made their way through scores of wrecked fishing boats and approached the wall, the smell of the air became acrid. Whether it was rotting flesh, burning flesh, or some combination of the two, Lucas couldn't be sure, but it was enough to make his eyes water.

Periodically as they moved up the slope, Asha and Lucas slowly turned around to make sure they weren't being flanked from the rear. Life indicators in the ship didn't say there were any stragglers outside the camp, but then again, the system wasn't functioning correctly much of the time. Alpha's powered down armor didn't have its heartbeat sensor online either. It was one of many functions that fell by the wayside after extreme use. They were going in blind.

The wall was a twisted bramble patch of wood, metal, and stone, stacked high enough that it would be exceedingly difficult to climb without being shot by a sentry. But now the makeshift guard platforms that lined the inside had collapsed or were vacant. The gate looked like the most reinforced link of the entire chain, though on the ground now lay the bones of its two heralds. The human and creature skeletons formerly occupying pikes were shaken loose thanks to a blast from Asha that had decimated an entire section of the wall next to the gate.

The crater was still smoking as they carefully stepped through it, weapons at the ready. Smoke clouded their vision, but dissipated as they progressed, and they saw the town laid out before them. On the ground were the bits of Norwegian cannibals that had been caught in Asha's line of fire. Further up, there was a man slowly crawling away from them through the sand, missing the lower halves of his legs with wide burn marks across his back. Judging by the length of the trail, he'd gotten pretty far from where he'd originally been hit. He didn't appear to have a weapon, but . . . *thunk*.

Lucas jolted as an axe appeared in the back of the man's head. Asha crept a little further up to him and removed the hatchet with a crunch, wiping it on the man's rags before sliding it back through her belt loop. Alpha and Lucas hurried up to follow her, and the three fell back into formation. Silence was still of the utmost importance, as they didn't want to start a gunfight if they didn't have to.

As they reached the street, it became clear the once bustling cannibal carnival was now a ghost town. There was no phalanx marching out to meet them, as perhaps they imagined that with a functional, deadly creature ship also came functional, deadly creatures. These men hadn't survived this long without running away from a fight or two they couldn't win. But where were they?

The stone buildings hinted at what shops used to reside within. Though only scraps of Norwegian words remained, a bicycle wheel here, a torn up winter jacket there indicated what the stores used to sell. The glass in all the windows had long since shattered, probably during the firefight that took down the ship, or the crash itself. The trio scanned each vacant window carefully until Lucas finally saw what he was looking for.

Without a moment's hesitation, he raised Natalie and fired two slugs at the man in the third-story window. The shots echoed down the empty street as the pair of bullets passed through his throat and skull. Lucas heard him collapse in a heap alongside the sniper rifle he had been clutching moments earlier. Alpha and Asha had their gaze jolted upward after the shots, but when two cannibals rounded the corner to see what had happened, they shifted focus. They each raised a weapon and Asha fired her revolver. The right man's chest caved in and he flew backward as blood arced out of the wound. At the same moment, Alpha let loose a blast from his energy rifle that took off most of the other man's head who then crumbled into a heap and his remaining singed brains spilled out onto the pavement. No further adversaries showed themselves as the sound of the two blasts bounced off the walls and down the street.

Bodies littered the road as they marched toward the center of town, stepping over the two fresh ones barring their way. Their clothes were streaked with blood, but the camouflage they wore was unmistakable. *Soldiers*, Lucas thought. *It was always the soldiers.*

Asha had made quick work of many of them from the sky, and there were few corpses that hadn't lost a limb or two. Unrecognizable, charred chunks indicated there were even more dead than they could see. But still, it wasn't enough. Where had the rest gone?

As they reached the main square, the ground was scarred with crisscrossing burn marks from each of the ship's passes. Many of the surrounding buildings were on fire or had already burned down. The field of stakes further ahead in the square was mostly uprooted and splintered, and Lucas couldn't see any bodies hanging from the ones that remained.

Further ahead stood the ornate church the captured women had been shoved into. It was fully engulfed in flames, seemingly ignited by a nearby building unless Asha had specifically targeted it. Lucas raised his weapon as he saw movement at the doorway. Someone was struggling with the heavy plank that barred it. He was about to fire, but as they drew closer, he saw that it was in fact an older woman wrestling with the blockade.

"What the . . ." Asha said breathlessly.

The woman had to keep shielding her eyes from the flames above and was coughing due to the smoke pouring out from the cracks. She finally managed to lift the plank from the handles, and as she wrenched the doors open, more smoke and flames shot out, knocking her to the ground. She yelled something in Norwegian, but there was no reply from within. All those inside were either dead of smoke inhalation or the flames themselves. She fell backwards to the ground and began to weep.

Lucas walked toward her, gun still raised, but his grip loosened slightly. As he moved forward, she raised her head from her hands and saw him. Her eyes widened in horror and she scrambled to her knees with her arms outstretched above her head. She was wearing a torn apron with a worn dress underneath and was covered in soot from head to toe with visible burns on her forearms and hands. From the wrinkles caked on her face, she appeared to be almost seventy, a true rarity in the current state of the world. She was moaning something in Norwegian as tears continued to stream down her face.

"*Hjelp! Vær så snill, barna! Barna!*"

"What's she saying?" Asha asked as she slowly approached.

"I have no idea," Lucas said. "Alpha?"

"We have no time for this. End her or leave her, but we must press on," he answered curtly.

Lucas turned to leave, but the woman sprang to her feet and grabbed his arm. Asha quickly raised the revolver to her head, but was stopped by a look from Lucas. She began tugging on his arm and pointing to another part of town to the east.

"*Kom hit, kom hit!*" she said pleadingly. Lucas tore his arm away and shook his head.

"*Barna! Barna!*" she cried.

"I don't understand. We have to leave." He noticed for the first time the broken shackles on her wrists. "You're free now, go!"

The woman looked panicked and then sprinted off in the direction she had been pointing. Lucas briefly thought about shooting her, as this place was now a ruin and she likely had nowhere else to go, but he ultimately decided it wasn't his place. Asha lowered her gun as she apparently came to a similar realization.

"What was she saying, Alpha?"

"I do not know this language," he said quickly. "We must continue; time is of the essence."

Lucas stared in the direction she went, but slowly turned and kept walking toward the downed ship.

They moved into a more residential part of town and immediately became far more wary; they could hear cries echoing from building to building. Some out of sight cannibals appeared to be injured, wailing from their houses or nearby streets. Others were shouting with more authority. The sounds bounced around too much to pinpoint where they were coming from. The voices sounded distant, but it was hard to be sure, and Lucas clutched Natalie tightly. Searching the rooftops for any sign of movement, none of them were focused on the ground below. Not until Asha's boot hit the tripwire.

Buried in the rubble that lined the street, none of them had seen the net that hoisted them into the air. Lucas and Asha were caught so off guard they lost their grip on their weapons, which clattered on the stone street below. Alpha would have likely dropped his as well were it not attached to his suit. Inside the net it was a wild tangle of limbs, rocks, and wood. They thrashed violently out of instinct, but Lucas quickly cleared his head.

"Cut!" he yelled, as he squirmed to reach the knife strapped to his chest. He heard holographic menus opening and closing and when he looked over saw that Alpha had already activated a humming saw on one of his metal fingers and was slicing into what appeared to be a military cargo net that was mercifully not laced with spikes or electrified. Lucas had seen such traps before. Squirming uncomfortably, Asha desperately tried to reach her hatchet, but was twisted in such a way that grabbing it was impossible. Lucas cut through one link with his knife, then two, then three. Alpha was having considerably more success with his automated tool. From her upside down vantage point, Asha saw men enclosing on their position.

Alpha's slices met Lucas's and the three of them were sent tumbling to the ground below. Ignoring the pain of the fifteen-foot drop, Lucas and Asha scrambled for their weapons as Alpha raised his, but they were already both in the hands of a bald, one-eyed cannibal standing in front of them. With a wide grin, he had Natalie propped on his shoulder and he pointed Asha's Magnum at them. Lucas instinctively went for his boot pistol, but stopped when the blackness in the corners of his vision subsided, and he could see that they were surrounded by cannibals on all sides, each brandishing a weapon pointed directly at their heads. Lucas began to raise his hands but his muscles tensed as 10,000 volts of electricity ran through his body, thanks to a cattle prod between his shoulder blades. As he fell limply to the ground, he saw Alpha and Asha set upon in the same fashion, and the searing pain gave way to darkness.

7

There were no dreams this time, as Lucas's unconsciousness lasted only minutes, not hours. When he came to, he felt his arms hoisted above him. When he looked up, he was glad that the cannibals had found some rope and he wasn't crucified on the stake where he hung. At least, not yet.

To his right he saw Asha, still unconscious and miraculously with all her clothes still intact. She had a throng of admiring cannibals at her feet, as they surely hadn't seen a woman like her in years. One reached out to touch her torn pants, but his hand was swatted away by the one-eyed cannibal who barked something in Norwegian.

On his other side was Alpha, taking up quite a bit more room on his stake with his feet almost touching the ground. He'd been stripped of his power armor and weapon, and there were bruises on his body, likely from multiple impacts by the stun baton. Though he was conscious, he looked worse than either of them and his breathing was heavily labored. He'd even been stripped of his translator, as any foreign technology was probably assumed to be dangerous.

Before them lay what was left of the village folk, a ragged assortment of cannibals all armed to the teeth. Most had long hair and beards, though a few were inexplicably clean shaven or had only light stubble. The majority were tall and blond, as was to be expected given the region, and many were wearing the remains of military uniforms. A few appeared to have scraps of riot gear on, which would explain the electric batons. There were a couple of bulletproof vests scattered amongst the crowd with the word POLITET on them. It was no stretch to imagine what that meant. The military and police had been best equipped and trained to survive a warzone like the one Earth had become, and as such he had run into them often in his travels. His own digitally camouflaged cargo pants served as a similar warning to any others he came across. A dozen or so other men were in dirty plainclothes, but then Lucas saw the man they had watched on the monitor earlier.

The colossus was even bigger in person and had to be about seven feet tall, though the power armor made him look eight—a giant in a town of monsters. It was clear from a primal perspective why the rest rallied around him. When he spoke, his voice boomed through the town square.

"*Spør dem hvem de er!*"

The man with one eye and both their weapons walked away from Asha, who was now conscious and looking annoyed, and stopped in front of Lucas.

"English?" he asked in a surprisingly high-pitched voice with little trace of an accent.

He looked over the tatters of Lucas's uniform.

"Yes, English," he concluded. "He wants to know who you are."

Lucas said nothing and glowered at the man.

"No? No name? No rank?" the man asked with a smile that was eerily out of place in their current predicament. He turned and said something to the chief who did not look nearly as amused.

"How did you fly that ship? Where did you come from? Why are you here?"

Lucas answered the barrage of questions with further silence. The one-eyed man smiled.

"Okay!"

Without a moment's hesitation, he whipped a familiar-looking buck knife out of the back of his belt and jammed it into Lucas's thigh as he lay bound on the stake. He was silent no more, his scream reverberating through the crumbling buildings around them.

"Better? You will talk now?"

The man removed the knife quickly from Lucas's leg and blood spurted out of the wound. Lucas cringed and bit his lip so hard that it too bled, but still said nothing.

The chief grunted and said something in Norwegian, motioning to Alpha.

"Why are you traveling with this . . . thing?" the smiling interrogator asked.

"Why are all of you so damn ugly?" Lucas spat out.

The one-eyed man laughed. "He speaks!" he said, turning to the crowd of thirty-odd men behind him, some of whom gave a low chuckle. He walked over to Asha, knife still in hand.

"And what about you? Do you speak? Do you think we are ugly?" he asked her with the same sickly grin.

Asha stared daggers at him and attempted to spit, but her mouth was too dry.

In the back, a few men were going through Alpha's power armor, attempting to activate it. Only a dim, flickering red light was lit on the gun. A few yards away, two other men were turning the glowing core over, trying to understand its purpose. A shorter man with a large scar across his lip was wearing Alpha's translator like a crown.

Back in front of them, the one-eyed man's smile faded.

"You attack our town, which we've worked so hard to build. You destroy our food, kill our men, and burn our women, and now you have nothing to say?"

The look on his face turned downright menacing.

"You will have something to say."

He paused.

"Cut her down."

"No!" Lucas shouted as two men sliced through the ropes binding Asha's arms. As they came free, the first cannibal got a broken nose and the second claw marks across the cheek. When her right foot came loose, she knocked the front teeth out of the next closest man. But more cannibals converged on her and pulled her down from the stake.

Whatever their problems had been back on the ship, Lucas was now in a frenzy, shaking his stake back and forth violently trying to free himself to reach her. As his head jerked back and forth, he caught Alpha's gaze to his right. He growled something, but without the translator, it was indecipherable. He turned his head to the side and closed his eyes. Lucas couldn't heed his warning.

The right half of the assembled crowd erupted in a blue fireball. The force of the blast sent a shockwave that not only flattened everyone still standing, but knocked over all three stakes, which splintered at their bases. Lucas hit the ground with a thud. His vision was spotted and white from the light of the explosion and the impact of the ground. Looking up, the red sky was brilliant and blinding, and a shadowy figure soon came into view. As his vision came back into focus, he saw it was Asha with his knife, still dripping with his own blood. As soon as she cut his arms free, she flung Natalie at him, which he caught out of reflex, despite his diminished motor skills. She was yelling something at him, but he couldn't make it out and only heard a low, dull tone in his ears. As he got to his knees, he saw the one-eyed man on the ground to his left, his throat slit and blood pooling in the cracks of the cobblestone.

Asha continued yelling and her voice slowly began to overpower the ringing in his ears.

"FIRE! FIRE!'"

She grabbed him by the collar and pulled him to his feet, where he faced the crowd. Though many were clearly dead due to the initial blast, some were beginning to rise with their hands over their eyes and ears. Nearly all were disarmed, and Lucas finally realized a unique moment was at hand. He and Asha began unloading into the smoke. Natalie's thirty-five-round clip emptied into the living and dead alike, and those trying to regain their footing immediately came crashing down again, now riddled with bullets. At this close of a range, Asha was making short work of the cannibals with her Magnum, and its .45 caliber slugs made six heads explode before she ran out ammo. Her throng of attackers must have shielded her from the blast, as she seemed in much better fighting form than anyone, Lucas included.

After their initial barrage, the smoke began to clear, and no one was attempting to get up anymore, save one. The chief. Protected by his power armor, he had only been winded by the explosion. He got to his feet and let out a roar that needed no translation. Attempting to fire his power weapon, he found it non-functional, and in a rage sprinted toward Lucas. A few clicks told Lucas that he too was out of ammo. He prepared to swing his rifle like a baseball bat, but the chief was on top of him before he could bring it around. As the pair of them hit the ground, he felt his bottom two ribs snap and an explosion of pain surged through his body. Natalie cascaded down the stone street out of his reach. The chief lifted a fist the size of Lucas's head and prepared to merge his face with the ground. Asha had dropped her own empty gun and she flung herself at the chief, grabbed his arm, which was almost as thick as her waist, and pried him off of Lucas using every bit of her strength. He tossed her aside, but as he did so, Lucas saw his knife stuck in the man's shoulder blade. He didn't even seem to notice.

Lucas winced from the pain and scrambled to find a weapon. Nearest to him was a sawed-off shotgun with a severed arm still clutching it. Lucas stripped the limb away and raised it at the chief who had now turned his attention to Asha. The blast caught him in the chest, but the armor, even in a unpowered state, was enough to deflect the buckshot. As he staggered back a few paces, Asha sat up and raised a police-issue pistol she'd found on the ground.

The man put his hand up and cried out in pain when she shot two rounds through it. She continued pulling the trigger, but the gun jammed and she threw it away in disgust as she rose to her feet. Lucas ran up to the behemoth, now clutching his pierced hand in agony, and with a well-placed shoulder lunge knocked him off balance onto the remains of his dead comrades with a crunch. Lucas stood over him with the sawed-off shotgun in hand.

The chief caught his breath and slowly lost his wrathful demeanor. Growing calm, he looked at Lucas and spoke softly.

"*Jeg var en skolelærer . . .*"

Lucas pulled the trigger and the man's face exploded into a mist.

Asha walked over to the headless corpse.

"What did he say?"

From behind them, a deep mechanical voice spoke.

"He said he was a schoolteacher."

Alpha had freed himself from his downed stake and was re-securing his translator to his neck, which miraculously was still intact. As was the glowing core he was holding at the end of his re-affixed metal claw.

"We were fighting that thing and you were getting dressed?" Asha said incredulously.

"You looked to be in control of the situation," Alpha said matter of factly.

"I thought you didn't speak the language," said Lucas.

Alpha fiddled with the controls on his mech arm and stayed silent. As he turned, Lucas could see that he had burns up the right half of his body.

"Are you . . . ?"

"I have suffered no permanent damage. [garbled] are much more resistant to heat than you humans. We also heal faster."

"What the hell just happened?" Lucas asked, as Asha scooped up her Magnum and pulled her hatchet from the one-eyed man's belt.

"As soon as we were in the net, I activated a countdown on my suit's core."

"You did what?" Asha said as she turned her head his way.

"Capture was imminent, and I knew it was our best chance of survival."

"What if you were still wearing it?"

"They would not let us keep our weapons, and would certainly strip me of the suit. I had hoped it would be placed close enough to cause sufficient chaos, but far enough where the blast would not consume us all. My calculations were . . . almost accurate." He winced as he touched a burn on his chest with his claw. Predicting their next question, he answered it.

"The suit was built with such functionality in the event of enemy capture. Though usually the occupant would incinerate along with it."

He pointed to Lucas's thigh.

"You must tend to that until we get back to the ship."

Lucas had forgotten about his injury during the adrenaline-soaked gunfight, but saw that he was still bleeding profusely. And that wasn't even counting whatever had happened to his ribs. As he searched his body for more pain, he discovered his right arm ached from crashing out of the net.

"Here you go," Asha said as she threw him a scrap of non-bloody fabric torn from a dead cannibal's outfit. Outside of a few bruises, she looked none the worse for wear, despite what the unhinged mob had almost done to her. Though, despite her cool attitude, her hands were visibly shaking for the first time. Lucas tied the cloth around his leg firmly and Alpha seemed satisfied about his ability to continue.

Asha finished picking up her confiscated gear and slung a non-melted tactical assault rifle over her shoulder, throwing a few clips into her pack. Bending over one of the hole-filled corpses, she pulled off his bulletproof vest and secured it to herself. Lucas thought it might be wise to do the same, and digging through the gore, found another intact vest for himself. Picking up a few shells from the ground, he decided to add the giant-slaying sawed-off to his arsenal, and then walked over to pull his buck knife out of the chief's shoulder. There was a veritable cornucopia of weaponry to choose from, but Alpha stopped them from scavenging further.

"This . . . detour has taken far too long, we must continue to the ship."

He strode onward, back to his old armorless form, only adorned with his translator and metal claw.

The trip back through the residential area was largely uneventful, though they kept careful watch on the ground for any more lingering snares. They couldn't be sure the entire population of the town had now been killed by the air assault and their recent ground skirmish, but they heard no more echoing voices from the rooftops as they had before. Eventually, they did come across one more wounded cannibal who had propped himself up on a bench on the side of the road. His clothes were drenched in blood, and it was impossible to tell what uniform he might have once worn, if any. He didn't even look up as they approached, and simply kept breathing with a painful whine as his eyes were fixed straight ahead. The extent of his injuries was unclear, but no longer mattered after Lucas put a slug through his temple from ten yards out. Leaving him was a needless risk.

They moved through the stone houses until they eventually reached another clearing, one quite different from the gory town square they'd just left. Before them loomed the massive mothership, and in front of it, a few hundred yards away, was a mansion that could easily be classified as a small castle. It was the building they had seen the chief emerge from in the bird's-eye view of the probe, but it, like him, was far more impressive up close.

Like practically everything in the city, it was also made out of stone, but looked quite a bit older than the other buildings. There were circular towers with slits in them for archers, and Lucas imagined this might have been a small fortress in a medieval age. In modern times it was likely owned by the mayor or some rich fishing baron until it had been appropriated by the cannibal chief. The stonework was crumbling in places, but looked impressively intact for a building that had been cut in half by a downed alien spacecraft.

They approached the mansion, moving through a long courtyard as they did so. The once manicured grass had now turned brown and crispy, and shrubs that had been symmetrically planted with precision were mere sticks. A giant stone fountain stood in the middle of the yard, and three angels held a bowl aloft, though it and the surrounding base were long empty of any water. One was missing a head and another a wing, but it was in quite good condition given the town's current residents, and the entire area looked free of damage from Asha's hellfire barrage. Presumably she was saving the section for a later pass that never came.

The three of them kept their eyes trained on the windows of the mansion, all of which were broken, but no yellow eyes or glinting sniper scopes appeared in them. No roommates for the chief it seemed.

As they reached the door, Alpha brought up a hologram from his claw that showed the layout of the mothership. It spread wide over their field of vision, and after a few swirls of his claw, it pointed out that the nearby entry bays were either a hundred feet in the air, fifty underground or on the other side of the mansion. Lucas and Asha began to pry open the ornately carved oak doors, which let out a prolonged creak as they parted.

The interior was dim and likely hadn't seen electricity in years, but light seeped in through the broken windows and several holes in the ceiling. A grand staircase unfurled before them, and Lucas was surprised to see the expensive-looking furnishings in the foyer were intact and arranged properly. Peering into a nearby sitting room, he saw a similarly organized setting, as did Asha when she walked into the living room to her right.

"Stay together," Alpha said quietly. They moved under the stairs and crept down a long hallway. It was lined with pictures that were perfectly hung but often cracked. Many were portraits of stately looking men with curled mustaches and women with billowing dresses. At the end of the hallway, they came to the kitchen, which was pristine with every cabinet door shut and every appliance properly aligned on the counters. But on the main preparation table lay a butchered human with most of his torso carved out and dried blood smeared everywhere around him. It was a jarring contrast to the rest of the highly organized and immaculate household.

They pushed deeper into the house and walked through a pair of double doors. Before them was a vast library, and against the shattered window sat a desk where many books lay stacked, a few open. In the center was a hefty tome full of handwritten words and an old-fashioned, ink-stained quill lay next to it. The barbarian chief, a tidy homemaker and an author. Who would have thought? Lucas remembered his dying words translated by Alpha about his former profession. He scooped up the book and tucked it into his pack.

Alpha and Asha were transfixed on a different part of the room. They were staring at the opposite wall, which was black and smooth. Alpha was running his claw across it.

"Is that . . . ?" Lucas asked.

"The ship, yes," Alpha replied. "We must find the port."

They exited through a door on the right, and found themselves in a guest bedroom, complete with sheets that were perfectly tucked into the mattress without a wrinkle in sight. Again, the far wall was the same metal material, but there was still no opening.

The next room was brightly lit, and looking up Lucas saw that a ceiling simply didn't exist. Though the walls were expertly wallpapered with a green and gold pattern, there was no furniture in the entire room. On the back wall, at last, there was a closed oval shaped port. As Lucas approached, a circular holographic interface appeared before him. He waved his hand through it, but it immediately turned from blue to red and disappeared. Lucas looked closer at the black door and wall and saw there was writing on it. A few silver pens lay strewn on the floor, and as he stepped back and the light caught the reflective ink, Lucas saw that the scribbling encompassed nearly half of the entire wall.

Alpha brushed Lucas aside and the interface returned. He made a complex series of motions as the symbols darted about on the controls.

"To think that a human could decode the key to our ship. Humorous."

Lucas saw different aliens glyphs written among the Norwegian on the wall. Was this how the chief spent his free time? Trying to break into this ship? Looking at the floor and edges of the wall, he saw black blast marks that appeared to indicate a more brute force method of entry had been attempted earlier. *I guess that's where the ceiling went.*

Alpha had far better luck, and the controls had already turned green by the time Lucas walked back over to him. The door disappeared into the blackness and he stepped inside. The glowing core served as a beacon of light in the dark, and Lucas felt a tap on his shoulder. Asha handed him a small flashlight that she said she procured off a spec-ops–type weapon in the town square's corpse pile. She had one for herself and affixed it to her Magnum as Lucas clipped his to his own barrel.

"These lower levels have no power due to the impact," Alpha said as he plugged one of his metal fingers into a socket on the wall. A virtual image of the ship appeared in front of them.

"Readings indicate that the bridge and a few surrounding floors are still functional, though all primary systems are offline, including life support. The core continues to deteriorate in the engine bay. We must make haste."

Their journey through the bowels of the ship was hurried and confusing. Lucas and Asha chased Alpha as he raced down a seemingly endless number of dark hallways. Their light revealed bits of architecture that looked familiar from their own ship. Alpha had closed the schematic and presumably knew the layout by heart. It was hard to keep up with his long strides, particularly in the dark, and Lucas soon tripped and fell with a clatter. As he got to his feet, he shone his light at where he'd fallen and his heart skipped a beat when he found the culprit. A fully mummified creature skeleton lay on the ground. Still clad in power armor, its bones poked out of the material and its lifeless fingers wrapped around an equally lifeless energy rifle.

Alpha saw what had happened and read Lucas's mind.

"There are no life-forms onboard. Watch your step."

Either the creatures had died in the crash, or they'd left their downed craft to be picked up by another. He wondered if there had even been any left when the cannibals came to town.

Eventually, they moved out of winding hallways and into a room that contained pods like the ones they'd been instructed to sleep in back onboard their own vessel. Lucas shined his light into them as they passed, but most of the glass was opaque. He looked over to Asha, who was directing her light upward instead. Even with minimal illumination, it was clear the room they were standing in was massive, far more so than their own barracks. There were thousands upon thousands of the pods lining the walls and arranged in columns like some oversized wasp nest. Lucas knew the ship was big, but he hadn't realized it had housed this many creatures. And was this even the biggest craft in their fleet? He turned to ask Alpha, but he had left the pair of them behind in their awe and was just a faint blue glow up ahead. They picked up the pace to keep up with him and eventually left the empty hive behind, sidestepping another set of dusty creature bones as they went.

There were more hallways ahead, and Alpha's assurance that there were no living beings onboard did not make the surroundings any less foreboding. More mummified creatures lay on the ground, and sporadically there was a splash of long-dried black blood on the walls. The surviving creatures must have been ordered out of the ship in a hurry to leave so many of their fallen behind.

Alpha's pace was quickening, and it was getting physically painful to keep up, particularly with the recent knife through Lucas's quadricep and his now free-floating bottom ribs. Even Asha appeared to be getting winded, but despite his own injures, Alpha was sprinting ahead with long-legged strides.

Gas streamed out of a broken section of the wall, but as Alpha plowed through it without hesitation, Lucas assumed he could as well. Moving through the mist, he thought it smelled a bit like sulfur, but mixed with . . . oranges? That couldn't be right. Whatever the compound was, it hadn't melted his skin, so he trudged onward as blood seeped through his makeshift bandage with each step. Asha swatted away a swath of cables that hung down like vines from the torn apart ceiling.

The blue glow they were chasing, emitted from Alpha's core, began to grow brighter, and it was getting lighter in color as well. As they rounded the next corner, they saw it was no longer his core producing the light.

The room before them was circular and massive, a far cry from the dank hallways they'd been running through. A few lights flickered around the room, but in the dead center rested a point of brilliant white light surrounded by thick columns of machinery. Every so often it would falter in sync with the others and go out, leaving the room in utter darkness, but would soon kick back on. It reminded Lucas of his first encounter with the sputtering blue light in the red sky back in Portland.

Alpha wasted no time and leapt down an entire staircase to reach the center of the room where the white core rested. He jammed his own core into a slot in one of the pillars. A holographic interface appeared and he began furiously swirling his organic and metal claws over the display. Eventually, the core stopped flickering and shone more brightly than ever before, illuminating the surrounding room like sunlight. Soon, it was almost impossible to look at the core directly, and Lucas was already seeing spots. Asha held her hand over her eyes.

"Never thought I'd need sunglasses again," she said. It really was the closest thing to the sun either of them had seen in years.

Alpha pressed a few more virtual buttons and a cylinder slid up and over the core, decreasing its brightness dramatically. Grabbing a piece of the metal that lined up the top, he detached it completely from the unit. It was larger than the blue core, but only just so. It measured about three feet tall and eighteen inches in diameter, but Alpha hoisted it off its pedestal with ease. Either it was lighter than it looked, or his bionic claw was dramatically increasing his strength. With his other hand, he pulled the blue core back out of the device and the room was lit with a dim combination of white and azure light. He hadn't spoken in some time, and finally appeared to be out of breath himself.

"So, we saved it?" Lucas asked, motioning to the white core with his rifle-mounted flashlight.

Alpha nodded.

"The core was at 0.8 percent capacity when we reached it. It would have been unsalvageable in a short while. That was the reason for our haste."

"And what exactly is this again?" Asha asked.

"The scientific complexities of the device would escape you. Suffice to say it is . . . what is the colloquialism? It is 'our ticket out of here.'"

"And you're saying it can make our ship travel into space?" said Lucas as he raised his eyebrow.

"We have that functionality currently. What it will allow us to do is leave this star system entirely and return to [garbled] by means of attempting a [garbled] [garbled]."

Alpha was visibly annoyed by his own translation limitations.

"I cannot convey the exact nature of what we are about to attempt, but we will leave this planet, and you will never return. That is, in the event I am in fact able to equip our vessel with this [garbled] core, and we do not end up as stardust once we activate it."

"How reassuring," Asha said.

Their trip back through the bowels of the ship was more relaxed, and Lucas's thigh was incredibly grateful. He was still wheezing thanks to his ribs, but the slower pace made everything less painful. Their way back was even more brightly lit from Alpha's supplementary white light source, though it was nice that it was no longer burning their retinas, as the polarized cylinder kept it a reasonable brightness.

They backtracked through the ship, the mansion, and town until they once again came upon the grisly pile of bodies in the square. Blood trails on the ground indicated a few of the cannibals weren't quite dead when the group left and had limped or crawled away. One of the trails ended with a lifeless man about thirty yards away, but a few continued down adjoining streets. Lucas scanned windows, but they were likely not in fighting shape, and hunting them down wouldn't be worth the risk. To their left, the once burning church was now a smoldering ruin.

Asha had stepped into the body pile and was picking through equipment and weapons. Alpha stopped and turned around.

"There will be time for that later. We must get the core back to the ship while avoiding further ambush."

"Juuuust one for the road," Asha said as she picked up a compact submachine gun and slung it over her shoulder. Lucas scooped up a few lingering shotgun shells resting in a pool of blood and continued onward.

Nothing jumped out from the shadows on the way back through the destroyed shops, and their nerves had finally settled by the time they reached the mouth of the bay. Their ship loomed ahead of them, past the sea of wrecked boats in various stages of decay. Their craft was indeed quite large and would dwarf any man-made airplane, but it was miniscule compared to the mothership they'd just left. Though he didn't understand the specifics of the device they now possessed, Lucas wondered if fitting the new core to their ship would be like putting a Ferrari engine in a Fiat. It might be a hell of an upgrade, but it could probably blow the entire thing up as well.

As they drew closer to the craft, an unfamiliar shape lay against the disturbed earth where the landing gear had touched down. It appeared to be a body, and after a quick signal from Lucas to the rest of the party, he and Asha raised their weapons as the unarmed Alpha fell back behind them. The form was lifeless, however, and as they approached Lucas could see who it was.

The old woman who had been pleading with them earlier at the church was now lying against the ship's landing prong, and she appeared to be even more badly burned than she was previously.

"Guess she wanted a ride out of here," Asha said as she instinctively bent down to search the body for loot. But she immediately jumped back with a look of complete terror on her face, an expression Lucas had never seen her wear. He approached the body and saw what had shocked her so.

An infant lay in the woman's burnt arms. A live infant.

Behind him, Alpha spoke.

"*Barna, barna*," he said slowly. "The children, the children."

8

The three of them stood on the bridge of the ship staring at the child, which had been placed on the holotable. Its breath was shallow and it was skinny, obviously malnourished. Its left arm and shoulder were covered in burns that Alpha had treated with his pocket-sized healing device, which had also sewn up Lucas's leg wound with a hissing gelatinous substance. A few dirty plastic bottles of milk lay strewn around it, taken from the dead woman's pack. It was Asha who finally spoke.

"Goddamn . . ."

It was a mix of revulsion and reverence. Lucas kept silent, but he agreed with the sentiment. He hadn't seen a child in years, except for his own in the picture in his boot. To be standing before one now was stranger than being on an alien starship. Finally, he spoke.

"I knew they were setting up some sort of society down there, but I never imagined they'd take it this far. Did they really think they could start over?"

"More like they didn't know how to perform an abortion after knocking up one of their chained rape slaves," Asha said with disgust. Lucas speculated that perhaps she *had* targeted that church on purpose. An act of mercy, in her eyes.

Alpha was scanning the child with a small device, and read through the information that sprung up in front of him.

"He is stable."

They hadn't bothered to check if it was a boy or girl yet, and this was the first they'd heard of its gender. He had opened his blue eyes only briefly until he succumbed to whatever Alpha had given him, and currently lay asleep with wisps of singed blond hair on his head, his face smudged with dirt and smoke. He couldn't have been more than six months old. Eight maybe? It had been a long while since Lucas's own son had been that age, and he was never good with those sort of estimations.

Asha asked the impolite question on everyone's mind.

"What do we do with him?"

Lucas had killed many things over the past few years, human, animal, and creature, but there was something gnawing at him about this child. Could they leave it here? Throw it back into town to die of exposure or become some surviving cannibal's mid-morning snack? The thought was gut-wrenching.

"He has food," Lucas said helpfully, motioning to the bottles on the table.

"That will last a few days at the most. Have you never babysat before? Jesus."

Lucas didn't reveal his past experience raising a child. Though to be fair, he hadn't been around all that often.

Alpha spoke after turning the thought over in his mind.

"We have barely enough food to feed ourselves, much less a child. Such a specimen, however, would be fascinating to study as I know little about the early development of your localized species."

"It's not a science project," Lucas said, a bit annoyed.

Alpha ignored him and continued, "Furthermore, it is a preferable companion to the remaining bloodthirsty citizens of your planet. You do not wish to further preserve what little is left of your kind?"

Lucas was flustered.

"Of course I do, but Asha's right, how do we feed it?"

Alpha paused, then checked a readout on his wrist hologram. It showed a spinning image of the mothership.

"There may be a way."

Alpha outlined a plan that involved returning to the ship they'd just left. Apparently, when he plugged into its "mainframe" (his translator was garbled until it finally settled on that word), he saw that, among the upper levels of the ship that were online, an entire room full of rations was still being kept fresh. It wasn't "food" in the traditional human sense, but rather "nutrients" was as best as Alpha could put it. The substance was made up of proteins and other essential vitamins that would sustain the life of his species. Usually they were fed to them in a gaseous form during their nightly rest inside the pods. This ship's supply was dry, but the manifest revealed the mothership had a large supply under lock and key. Alpha didn't know how the nutrients would react with human biology, but explained it was the only hope for all of them, the child included. He mused that the child could in fact survive and potentially even thrive on the gaseous diet. None of them raised the point of what they would do with the child besides feed it, but that was a concern for another time. The general consensus was, however, not to throw him out into the desert. Even with all the stone hearts in the room, forged out of years of misery, they couldn't inflict such a horror on something so helpless.

"If this thing cries all the time, it's going out an airlock," had been Asha's final word on the subject, even though Lucas suspected she hadn't meant it. In truth, the child hadn't cried once since they'd brought it onboard. Lucas wondered what sort of traumas he'd endured in the village, and how long they'd stay with him as he grew. That was, provided he survive for any length of time under the watch of two mass murderers and a traitorous extraterrestrial.

The plan was for Lucas and Asha to be dropped onto the roof of the mothership by Alpha, as trekking up through the bottom was impossible with those floors mostly destroyed. There would be no way down to the engine bay or any of the adjoining areas, which Alpha explained was why they hadn't gone in that way in the first place.

Alpha took the captain's chair and raised the ship as Lucas and Asha made their way to the storage bay from which they would depart. The child was secured inside a scrap metal cylinder lined with whatever fabric they could spare, which included Asha's old dress and the cloth in which the dead woman had wrapped him. Everything else had been too drenched in blood to be sanitary. The cylinder was secured to the floor with Alpha's fusion tool, and he claimed he would create better accommodations for the child once he had finished installing the new core. He said that would be a time consuming process, as every calculation had to be perfect, or else they would be "torn asunder on the molecular level." He was developing quite a flair for the dramatic.

The storage bay was empty, save for a few metal crates that had been pried open and looted. As they soared over the village and approached the top of the mothership, Alpha spoke through the comm, his voice booming through the barren metal chamber.

"When the floor opens, step into the light."

At that moment, the floor did indeed open, and about forty feet down was the top of the ship. A column of blue light shone around the opening.

"You first," Asha said, forever cautious.

Lucas was hesitant, as an unimpeded fall would surely kill him, or at the very least snap his legs like twigs. But he was beginning to take Alpha's word as gospel. It was strange to be able to trust someone again. He jumped.

After a split second of terrifying freefall in which his stomach rose into his lungs, his descent slowed dramatically as the beam of light caught him. He'd never experienced true weightlessness, and wondered if this was always what it was like. He was perfectly comfortable, and barely had time to register the fact he was floating until his feet touched down on the ground.

Satisfied Lucas had not ended up as a stain on the ship's hull, Asha made her own leap of faith. Lucas stepped out of the light and watched her combat boots heading down the column. As her face came into view, she too seemed amazed by the process. She looked almost angelic as she descended, silhouetted against the blue light with the red crackling sky behind her. An angel of death perhaps, but ethereal nonetheless. She landed gracefully on the top of the ship.

Above them, Alpha took the transport and steered it back toward the bay, its engines shining a bright blue as it retreated. Lucas took out a small cylindrical disc Alpha had given him and a holographic countdown timer appeared. He'd be back in a little over three hours.

As the ship moved into the distance, they looked out over the town. It was an angle they hadn't seen from the air, and the smoke was finally starting to clear from the burned buildings. Nearly all the remaining fires had died out. Lucas thought to try and look down on the mansion, but resisted getting too near the edge. The winds were gusting strongly a thousand feet up, and it was hard to keep his balance. Asha was staying low and having an easier time of it.

A hologram in his hand pointed the way to an entry port on top of the ship. He tried yelling at Asha, but the wind was too loud for her to hear. She put her hand to her ear and shook her head mouthing "what?" He pointed up ahead of him and started walking that direction, taking each step with care. Asha understood where he was going and followed. When he arrived at the portal, he stuck the disc in the center like Alpha had instructed him. According to him, the device was multi-use. It would display maps and other data, but more importantly, Alpha had designed the device as an improvised hacking tool, a key that would open any door on the ship.

It did its job quickly, and the controls turned green as the door slid open. Lucas peered inside with his rifle-mounted light, and saw the floor a short ways down. He sat on the edge of the door and lowered himself down slowly. There was no reason to further agitate his healing leg, and his ribs still made every breath hurt even though Alpha assured him they were on the mend.

Lucas landed as softly as he could manage. Light filtered in through the hole above him. Though these levels once had power, they were fully offline now that Alpha had removed the central core. Reaching into his pack, Lucas pulled out the blue core that powered their own ship. Alpha said even a sliver of the more powerful white core's energy would be more than enough to power their own craft, and the blue one would be necessary to "turn the lights back on." It was amusing to watch him get the hang of common English phrases.

Asha dropped down behind Lucas, landing on a tangle of cables spilling out of the wall and almost falling on her face. It was a somewhat less majestic descent than the one she'd made from the ship. Lucas held the core up like a lantern while consulting a three-dimensional map on the disc in his other hand. Despite Alpha's proclamation that the ship was free of life, Asha had her Magnum drawn anyway, with the small flashlight fixed to its barrel.

They crept through a winding corridor for a bit, Lucas keeping his eyes trained on the dot moving through the three-dimensional blueprint sprouting out of the device in his hand. The path soon dead ended at a massive door, a much larger version of the ones they had in their own ship. A small holographic interface appeared at Lucas's eye level, and he held the disc inside of it. It took a few more minutes to sift through the symbols, but in the end, the door slid upwards with a groan. It clearly hadn't been opened in ages.

According to the map, this was the bridge. A long corridor stretched out before them, and with their dim lighting, Lucas couldn't even see where it ended. Consoles lined the walls, but no lights flickered. He and Asha moved slowly toward the end of the room, her gun still trained on whatever ghosts may have been lurking in the tomb. The light revealed a number of skeletal creatures lining the ground, some with power armor, others without. One's skull was fully lodged inside a shattered workstation. A fine film of dust coated everything, and particles danced in the air around them, disturbed by the unsealing of the door. As they approached the center of the room, Lucas saw a much larger version of the holotable they had in their own ship. It was what he was looking for, and on Alpha's instructions, he searched its base for an opening. He found it around the back side of the console and slid the blue core inside.

The bridge came alive in an instant. Screens and control clusters surged to life all around them, and at the front of the room, the main command center was now online. It was a wide, curved interface that looked to be manned by four or five officers at least. Above it was a massive viewscreen that was a jumble of alien information, though pieces of the screen were glitching and a few remained completely dark.

The holotable now displayed a galaxy that Lucas recognized as the unmistakable spiral of the Milky Way. Of immediate interest was a series of annotations that marked it. Points were tagged along many of the arms on the right side. Though it was impossible to read the symbols, it was what they were describing that caught Lucas's eye. Each point of interest showed a planet. They weren't any Lucas had ever seen, and most were largely white, brown, and green with small pockets of blue that had to be water. One of the furthest out dots was Earth, which had more blue than all the other bodies, save one large sphere that had oceans even more vast than their own. Nearby the large planet was a distinctive red rock streaked with only minimal amounts of blue and green.

"What is that?" Asha asked as she walked over, finally lowering her gun.

"I think it's our roadmap out of here."

He waved his fingers through one of the planets. What were all these places? *Where* were they? He tried to play with the foreign controls, but received no response or further information.

Consulting the pocket map once again, they left the room through an adjacent door and headed down a ways toward their next objective. The nutrients were a few sections away, but it was now much easier to travel with the area powered up. The corridors they walked through were damaged, but hardly to the degree the lower floors had been, crushed under a million tons of steel or . . . whatever the hell the thing was made of. He'd have to ask Alpha about that at some point.

The broken English on the map readout informed them they were now approaching the Nutrient Surplus Area Room, ahead of them on their left. A long door was embedded in the wall, and Lucas had to search for some time to find the controls. Asha was already poking around the next corner, but returned to him when the door slid up into the ceiling.

The room was a mess, with storage cubes scattered around everywhere, a few having burst open with tiny clear vials coating the floor. Lucas consulted his readout, which Alpha had programmed with a visual depiction of the nutrients, and saw that they were in fact the small cylinders littered all around them. An open crate, about three feet by three feet, revealed rows upon rows of the stacked containers. There had to be thousands in each crate.

Asha looked at the holographic unit and realized they had found their prize as she picked one up off the floor. She held it between her thumb and forefinger and inspected it with care. The inside was cloudy, and the compound constantly swirled around like a white-ish fog.

"How many of these do we need?"

Lucas checked the readout.

"Not sure, it says here 'six units.'" Alpha was not yet fully versed in human systems of weights and measures.

"Six crates?" Asha asked. She bent down and tried to pick it up. It lifted a few inches off the floor, impressive for a woman of her size, but came crashing back down, a centimeter away from crushing her fingers.

"This might take a while."

It wasn't until they'd lugged the fourth box back to the entrance that they discovered a device at the far end of the room meant for loading and unloading. It had a singular ball at the bottom, which seemed unlikely to support any weight, but when a cube was placed on top of it, the device balanced it easily. Some sort of internal gyroscope perhaps. Once loaded, the entire contraption could then be moved by the mere push of a finger. Lucas's aching back, ribs, and leg made him wish they'd found it sooner.

The discovery of the device led them to bring back ten crates in all (better safe than sorry), as the rest were scattered around the floor, where many vials lay loose or broken. They stacked them in the area where they'd entered the ship, and after the last crate was loaded, Lucas checked his readout. Twenty minutes until Alpha returned. He pushed the device and the ball rolled seamlessly down the hallway. He turned to close the storage room door behind him, but realized he didn't know how. He waved the disc around in its general direction, but there was no response.

"Screw it."

When he got to the bridge, he turned left to make the trip back to the loading area, but stopped when he saw Asha staring up at the viewscreen. She'd been waiting there after unloading her last crate, but now had found something far more interesting than nutrient packs.

An enormous face loomed across the entire length of the viewscreen. It was a creature, and one unlike any Lucas had ever seen. It was dark, almost black, as opposed to the usual gray. Its eyes glinted with rings of bright blue. Pieces of well-polished armor could be seen around its neck, shoulders, and head, though the rest of it was out of frame. It was grunting and snarling, speaking in a language neither of them could understand. Lucas froze as the cube slowly drifted away from him. A few yards ahead, Asha stood enraptured by the imposing creature.

It continued speaking, its voice growing increasingly louder. Eventually in frustration, it waved its hand in front of him and the viewscreen cut to black. The pair of them stood in silence for a minute until Lucas spoke.

"What did you do?"

Asha turned around and put her hands up, her Magnum was in one of them.

"Nothing, I swear, I came back through here and he was just there, growling something. I tried to yell at it, but I don't know if it saw or heard me."

She holstered her gun. If he had seen her, she probably didn't exactly look like a friendly ambassador of Earth, adorned in weapons, shouting unintelligibly.

"Are there more of these things still on this planet?" she asked.

"None worth a damn that I've seen," said Lucas. "Any I've come across have been on the verge of death, and I'd never seen a working ship until well, ours. That thing didn't look like it was marooned here."

"Well it knows we're here, or at least that someone is here."

Alpha needed to know about this.

As the last crate was moved into the exit bay, Lucas had an idea. There were still about ten minutes left on the clock, and he beckoned

Asha to follow him back to the bridge. This time, there was no creature on the viewscreen to greet them.

"Help me with this," Lucas said as he bent over one of the dead creatures. He began to pry loose its power armor with his knife.

"What the hell are you doing?" Asha said incredulously, as she stood above him with her arms crossed.

"Alpha lost his armor and gun," he said, slicing through a strap around the creature's ribcage. He peeled the chestplate back and threw it on the ground next to him. He set to work on the shoulder brace next.

"And if we ever have to fight these things head on," he pointed at the viewscreen, "we're going to need a hell of a lot more than this." He tapped his POLITET bulletproof vest.

Asha was still skeptical.

"How are we going to wear one of these? They're enormous."

"Didn't you see the chief?"

"He was enormous."

"Well, I bet Alpha could work some magic and come up with something. If you haven't noticed, he's sort of handy with this kind of thing."

Sliding the long rifle out from where it was lodged under the console, he threw it onto the armor pile. Asha paused, then began hacking into a nearby body with her hatchet.

Lucas sat on one of the cubes and checked his timer. Eight zeros were blinking on the readout. Alpha was late. Asha sat across from him, her arms resting on two piles of alien power armor. They'd excavated three in total, along with the attached weapons.

"What are we doing with this kid?" she asked, bringing up a question he'd all but forgotten about. His mind was consumed with the dark creature and the galaxy map.

Lucas slowly tilted his head back and rested it on the wall.

"I don't know."

"This is no place for a child. And lord knows the three of us have no business near one. Do you have any idea how to raise a kid?"

Lucas thought back to missed school plays and baseball games, and the subsequent angry phone calls.

"No, I don't," he said. "But you want to leave it here? Just throw him away?"

Asha stared up into the hole above.

"The world used to do that long before everything went to shit."

There was something in her tone that intrigued Lucas. Was this going to be some actual, personal information? But she fell silent. After a minute, Lucas pressed.

"What do you mean?"

"None of your business, asshole."

"You brought it up. And you'd think in our current situation, it wouldn't be the worst thing to know something about each other."

"Oh yeah? And what do I know about you?"

They were interrupted by a familiar roar of engines from overheard.

"It's about damn time," said Asha, as she hopped to her feet. Conversation over.

The ship came to rest above them and the blue column of light shot out and came streaming through the hole. Immediately, one of the cubes began to lift up into the air. Lucas realized that unloading would be a breeze, and began to herd the rest of the cubes into the light. They trickled up and out of the ship and into the sky above. Next came the piles of power armor, and as they ascended they hung limply in the air like they were being worn by wraiths. The guns trailed under them a short distance below. Asha didn't wait for a "ladies first" as she stepped into the light and began to soar away. Lucas followed her up, and took one more look at the village as he rose above it. He landed gently in the storage bay, and immediately yelled into the air. He still wasn't sure exactly how comms worked in this ship.

"Alpha, don't leave yet. There's something you need to see."

After being told what they'd experienced on the bridge, Alpha turned ashen—even more so than usual—and immediately headed down into the ship to view the transmission for himself. Lucas and Asha stayed on the bridge while the ship hovered in autopilot. Alpha had warned them not to touch anything while he was gone, and Lucas thought that might be for the best as he didn't want to be swirling through a random console menu and accidentally dump all of their water.

On the floor, the child was awake and squirming uncomfortably, but still not crying. Asha scooped up one of the bottles from the holotable and placed it in the baby's tiny hands. He began sucking at it profusely. He was so thin Lucas swore he could almost see the liquid trickling down into his stomach. Asha watched him solemnly for a while, then spoke.

"My mother was a whore in Mumbai."

Lucas jerked his gaze toward her, caught off guard by the unexpectedly frank revelation. Asha continued, ignoring his surprise.

"She was forced into it by her father, who took every cent she earned and fed her with scraps. When he died, she was stuck in the life as there were other men who took his place and wouldn't let her out."

Lucas was stunned she was sharing something so personal. He kept silent to avoid saying anything to cause her to seal up again. Her eyes were fixed on the child as she continued.

"A white American businessman who had recently moved to the city got her pregnant. It was an unspeakable shame, and by the time she knew it for sure, her dishonor was doubled by the fact that the child was a girl. Her friends pleaded with her to abort, the men who owned her threatened to kill her if she didn't. She didn't listen. She fled to Murud, a nearby village. When she had me, the women there told her to throw me in the jungle and leave me there. One even tried to steal me in the night and do it for her. I was a bad omen, a cursed child."

She absentmindedly spun around the cylinder in her Magnum as she spoke, never making eye contact with Lucas.

"She refused. Instead, she went back to Mumbai and tracked down the businessman. She found out who he was. Someone prominent. A captain of industry. He was shocked and horrified to learn of my existence. At first he refused all contact with her, but after she threatened to tell his family and his company the truth, he offered her fifty thousand dollars to never see him again. She demanded a hundred. She got it."

Flinging the loaded cylinder back into the gun with a snap, she paced around the baby's makeshift bed as he continued to inhale the contents of the bottle.

"She used the money to escape to America, to buy a home for us, to send me to the best private schools. She worked as a maid and saved every penny she could for my future. She was at my first runway show with tears in her eyes. She framed my first contract and hung it on the wall. She died before I landed my first TV pilot, but I know she would have been on set with a plate of tandoori chicken for the cast and crew."

She finally turned her eyes toward Lucas.

"Ten million girls in India were aborted or executed over the past twenty years. My mother said no."

She looked at the child.

"I have to say no too."

Lucas was amazed by this entirely new side of her. But it was short lived.

"So you better not let this goddamn kid die or I'll slit your throat and feed you to Alpha."

Lucas paused.

"I won't."

He turned to face her.

"I had a boy once," he finally admitted. "I wasn't the father I should have been. The least I can do is to try and take care of the last son of Earth as best I can."

If the child wasn't the youngest person on the globe, he had to be close. And if all went according to plan, soon he would in fact be the planet's last infant.

Lucas walked over to the child and, for the first time, picked him up. He was shocked at how light he was, and it felt like he almost weighed less than his usual companion, Natalie. The child dropped his empty bottle, which rolled across the floor. He stared into Lucas's eyes curiously, but neither smiled nor screamed.

Glancing up at Asha, Lucas realized that her story explained a great many things about her. Her iron will, her constant resourcefulness, and her eternal will to survive. It even explained her exotic looks and how she was able to convincingly pretend to be a wounded damsel in distress on the road. She'd been an actual actress.

Some people were born survivors. Lucas wasn't. He was made one. He had no such backstory to give him that sort of steel constitution. Strength was something he'd found only after the world ended.

He looked at the child. What sort of strength would he have, should he survive? The offspring of a cannibal rapist and his slave in a crumbling hell? At least he didn't have to spend all that much time there.

"What should we call him?" Lucas asked, suddenly realizing another question they hadn't addressed. "We can't just go around calling him 'the kid.' And it's not like he came with a collar with a name on it."

"We probably couldn't even pronounce it if he had," Asha replied. She hesitated.

"We're not parents, you realize that?"

"Of course not, but 'guardians' is probably more of an appropriate term now than it ever was."

After thinking for a moment, she spoke.

"What about Noah?" she said.

"The one who survived the flood?"

"That's what I was thinking."

"You're religious?" Lucas said, surprised.

"Not anymore."

"Me neither, but it's hard to deny that it fits."

He held the child out in front of him.

"Noah, huh. Well there you go."

Noah had no opinion about his new name, and stared over Lucas's shoulder to the lights of the holotable while chewing on his hand. His burns looked less angry, but were still noticeable. Lucas set him back down in the cylinder. They really were going to have to figure out a better place for him to sleep.

"Is that what this is? Our ark?" he said as he looked up at the ceiling and all around the bridge with his arms spread wide.

"Now the ship needs a name?" Asha asked with a sneer.

"Didn't you ever name your car?"

She shook her head.

"I guess it's a guy thing. Your gun then?"

"No, why, what's yours named?"

He glanced at Natalie's barrel over his shoulder.

"Never mind."

The Ark. But one with only two species of animals onboard.

9

Asha busied herself cleaning her newly acquired gun and Lucas played around with the holotable controls. They didn't even hear Alpha enter the room; Lucas merely spotted him out of the corner of his eye. His gray form was stiff and rigid.

"You saw it?" Lucas asked hurriedly.

"What did it say?" said Asha, standing up from the ground, which was littered with submachine gun parts.

"The message . . ." There was a twinge of something resembling emotion in Alpha's voice. "The message was for me."

Alpha threw a flat disc like the one he'd given Lucas on the holotable. An interface appeared and he waved it over in the direction of the viewscreen to transfer the image to it. It was the dark creature. The video began to play. It was the same series of aggressive grunts and growls they'd seen on the mothership's bridge.

"It's for you?" Lucas asked. "How is that possible?"

"As I said previously, any ship I operate is tagged with my unique biological signature. When we activated the ship, they were able to locate me and deduce I was alive with a working craft. They contacted the [garbled] ship when you boarded it as they tracked the transport's signature to this location. This is a short-range transport vessel and does not have a long-range communicator, so they looped that message through the [garbled] ship in hopes that I would see it when I came here. They know what I am planning."

"And they were trying to contact you, specifically? Why?" asked Asha.

Alpha paused.

"I have not been entirely forthcoming about my position in the [garbled] combat force."

The video continued to play, the menacing creature taking up most of their field of vision behind Alpha.

"I am a scientist, tasked with mainly military projects to aid the cause of my race. My father was also a scientist, and possessed the greatest inborn intelligence quotient of anyone across our entire system. I was sent here as punishment for a time when he disobeyed a direct order from him." He motioned to the creature on the screen.

"Who is he?"

"High commander of the fleet. I will not even attempt to tell you his actual name. Refer to him as . . ."

He stopped to try and think of an identifier.

"To use your own simplistic alphabet once again . . . 'Omicron.'"

Lucas didn't bother to correct him that the alphabet he kept citing wasn't even one Lucas knew. But perhaps he knew that. Lucas couldn't even picture what a Greek omicron looked like.

"He is an extremely important military figure, and he decided sending my father's youngest son into battle was the best way to keep him in line with the cause."

Alpha looked toward the commander's face on the viewscreen. The volume was low so the grunts and growls were muffled.

"The message says that my father is dead, my brothers and their families along with him. How, I do not know. He says it was a [garbled] strike that killed them, but I am . . . unsure."

Lucas didn't know whether to say he was sorry, but the words escaped him. Asha was silent as well.

Alpha continued, though his voice was much lower than usual. Grief? Pain? It was hard to tell. He paused the video, and the commander stared intensely at all three of them.

"The sum of the knowledge my father had was vast, and he taught us everything he knew about genetics, electronics, physics, [garbled], and [garbled]. Our clan was highly revered for our scientific contribution to the war effort."

"Why did they send you here in the first place if you were so valuable?" Lucas asked.

"As I said, a lesson to my clan. But I was never supposed to be in actual combat. I rode on a transport ship and was merely tasked with scientific research of your planet. My commanding officers were killed and I was assigned new overseers who were not well enough informed of my station. I was forced into battle and subsequently imprisoned. The situation would have been resolved had the war not ended abruptly."

Lucas thought back to the hologram video when he'd first boarded the ship, how Alpha had pleaded not to be sent into combat.

"Omicron states in this transmission that they are coming to collect me, and my reported treason during the Earth campaign is forgiven. He says I must continue to serve the [garbled] the way my clan has for generations."

"But you don't believe him . . ."

"How or why my clan was killed, I do not know. Either they were exterminated accidentally as they say, and they want me to spend the next few centuries slaving away to rebuild the scraps of my father's military work, or they were killed purposefully and I am being hunted down."

"Why would your family have been killed by your own people?" asked Asha.

"I do not know. My father frequently sparred with his superiors over the applications of his work, which was used to cause much harm and suffering. But it must have been something of incredible significance or danger for my entire clan to be slaughtered."

Lucas finally found the words he felt were required.

"I'm sorry."

Alpha's expression didn't change.

"It matters not. Escape is now more important than ever. I wish to be neither a slave nor a corpse, and I must begin work on the [garbled] core immediately or they will intercept us in a matter of days. I presume it does not even need to be said that as humans you would be summarily executed on the spot if we are caught. Even the child."

He motioned toward Noah who had fallen asleep.

"I figured as much," said Lucas.

Alpha fled to the engine bay to continue installing the core. Lucas had attempted to ask him where exactly they were planning to escape to, if his own kind wanted him dead, but Alpha deflected the question, claiming he had no time for further explanation. The long-range core needed to be installed as soon as possible to avoid the demise of the entire group. He instructed them to return to the village to scavenge for supplies, as the journey ahead of them, should they escape, might require certain items they didn't yet possess.

They attempted to leave the ship but were caught by a wave of fatigue. They hadn't stopped to rest since the cannibal assault and the race to the core, and their bodies were shutting down. Lucas, taking a seat for only a moment, fell fast asleep in his captain's chair. Asha curled up in the rear of the room, using her pack as a pillow, a half assembled submachine gun on the ground next to her. Noah, conversely, was awake, but still mercifully refrained from screaming.

They woke some hours later, and on the monitor Lucas saw Alpha hard at work in the engine bay. They let him know of their departure, and he claimed that he would watch Noah after they left via a holoscreen in the bay. They doubted how much attention he would actually devote to the child, if any, but with unknown amounts of cannibals still lurking in the town, they figured he was safer on the Ark (the name had caught on) than strapped to one of their backs as they prowled through the streets.

There was an assortment of items they were hunting for. Obviously food would be the most welcome find, but they didn't expect to find any of the non-human flesh variety. Additionally, Alpha said if they wanted anything resembling "quarters" they'd have to furnish it themselves. He postulated that long-term "hyper sleep" in the pods might drive them insane or kill them, as even short-term stints seemed to already have adverse effects. Their trip into the unknown was going to take an indeterminate amount of time, depending on the functionality of the new core, but they would want to prepare for a long haul. Furniture, bedding, things of that nature would be useful. They were also keeping an eye out for anything that might benefit Noah, though Lucas imagined the cannibals weren't big on stuffed animals and diaper changes.

Exiting the ship, they walked past the shallow grave where they'd hurriedly buried the woman whose final act was to save the child. It was an admirable deed in a world beyond redemption, and she deserved better than to rot in the heat. They moved through the fishing boat graveyard and crept back through the splintered wall, guns always at the ready. It was daybreak; they'd slept through most of the night. But much like the first time they entered, the village was deathly quiet.

They already knew where their first stop would be. Quickly moving through the shops, Lucas and Asha reached the town square. It was time to increase their arsenal, should they end up running into Omicron and the rest of Alpha's pursuers. Sure, they might just be blown out of the sky immediately, but there was always a chance they'd have a more personal skirmish.

They managed to locate a relatively large wooden cart with metal wheels. It was empty, but the blood caked on the bottom implied that it had been used to transport more than a few bodies across town. It took each of them grabbing one of the outstretched poles to move it, and it wasn't easy to drag over the uneven cobblestone street. Placing it near the grisly pile of corpses, they began to sift through the mess for intact weapons.

Asha picked up a blood-soaked assault rifle and locked it into firing position. She discharged a bullet into one of the fallen men in front of her, and the noise echoed around the square. Lucas jumped out of instinct and swung around to find the perpetrator.

"What the hell are you doing?" he yelled.

"We need to see if these actually work. Some of them might have parts that were melted by the blast."

"Don't you think we're giving away our position a bit?"

"To who?" She flung her arms out and spun around. "There's no one left here."

"We know a few of them got away."

"Yeah, with serious injuries and no medical treatment."

Lucas supposed anyone in the surrounding buildings could see them anyway if they were looking, as the square was visible from practically all of sections of town. They just had to hope there were no more snipers lurking behind the dark windows. He picked up a long shotgun and fired it into a nearby body. Satisfied, he threw it on the cart.

Soon they had it loaded up with a dozen or so guns of various size and caliber, along with reams of ammunition loosely scattered around that they'd have to sort through and match up later. Asha loaded up her pack with grenades of all shapes and colors, and Lucas managed to extricate a few of the electric stun batons buried in the gore. A rocket-propelled grenade launcher was not test fired, but added to the pile regardless. They excavated a number of bladed weapons that could prove useful: a machete, several hunting knives, and what looked like a medieval short sword. The final addition was the chief's energy rifle, which lay a short distance away from his headless body. It hadn't worked when he fired it at Lucas, but could possibly still be salvageable. They hauled the entire load back to the ship and brought it into the armory, which had been stripped bare long ago. The new weapons joined the three sets of power armor they'd taken from the mothership.

They dragged the cart back through the sand, which was an exhausting processes, and the bumpy cobblestones almost seemed like a break afterward. Their next destination was even further away, but they knew it was their best option. Rather than go house to crumbling house in the main residential block, they headed to the mansion, where they knew many pieces of ornate furniture and supplies were for the taking.

After rolling through the barren courtyard under the watch of the three stone angels, they released the cart in front of the door and caught their breath. Lucas's back ached, and Asha was vigorously rubbing each of her thighs to get feeling back into them. And this was when the cart was empty. They were thankful this wasn't back in the States, where the temperature was sure to be at least twenty degrees higher.

Lucas approached the door but stopped when he drew near. It was ajar, and he specifically remembered closing it when they left a day ago. Further inspection revealed half of a bloody handprint on the oak. Pointing it out to Asha, the two advanced into the mansion with weapons drawn.

Blood droplets led them to the large staircase in the main foyer, and red smears on the gold hand railings let them know they were going the right direction. Each step was made with caution, and they kept absolutely silent. When they reached the top, a blood mark on the wall told them to turn left, dried droplets stained the varnished floor. It creaked underneath Lucas's toes and he cringed, stopping to avoid further noise. They probably should have employed Asha's earlier tactic used to sneak up on him and walked across the floor barefoot. But it was too late now.

Ahead, there was a large set of double doors with one slightly open. More blood indicated they'd found their prey's hiding place. Lucas slowly pushed the door inward with his foot and peered around the corner into the room, Natalie's barrel leading the way. They'd apparently found the master bedroom, as a giant four-post king size lay in front of them. The covers were strewn everywhere and the silk sheets were stained with a large amount of blood. Someone had clearly rested there.

The someone flung himself out from behind the door and swung at Lucas with a large bronze axe. Lucas raised Natalie just in time and the blade crunched into the middle of the rifle as he was almost bowled over from being caught off balance. They wrestled for a moment with the two stuck weapons, but behind him, Asha quickly fired a revolver shot into the man's kneecap, which disintegrated instantaneously at such close range. He dropped to the floor and howled in agony, his lower leg held on only by a few sinews of muscle fiber. Lucas tossed Natalie to the floor, with axe still embedded, and drew the knife from his belt. He dropped to one knee and plunged it under the man's jaw. Blood erupted from his mouth and spilled over an old scar on his lip. He twitched, then when Lucas withdrew the knife, collapsed back and lay motionless as blood pooled out of his throat and leg onto a very nice oriental carpet. His original injury appeared to be a gutshot, as the stained bandage wrapped around his midsection indicated.

Lucas fell to the floor and lay on his back, his heart pounding furiously. Above him, he could see the red sky through cracks in the ceiling. An open first aid kit lay next to him, and he could see several others under the bed. The chief had apparently been in charge of dividing up the important supplies, and this man tried to find some for himself. On the wall to Lucas's right was a round shield with an axe jutting out of its left side. The axe meant to go on the right was now firmly lodged in Natalie near his feet. He immediately sat up and grabbed his wounded companion.

"Damnit, Natalie," he said out loud as he cradled the gun in his arms. He pulled the axe out of it and threw it across the room where it took a chunk out of a dresser and clattered to the floor. The blow from the weapon had cut deep into the center of the gun, and the entire barrel was now bent up at an awkward angle. He ran his fingers across the torn metal. It didn't seem like this was an injury that could be healed.

Asha holstered her own weapon.

"Natalie, huh?" but her tone wasn't mocking. After all, she'd expressed her own attachment to her revolver on the ship earlier, practically willing to put a round in Lucas's head to have it back.

Lucas looked down at his broken friend. It was silly to be so attached to an inanimate object, but they'd had a long journey together.

"What, was it like your first weapon out of basic or something?" Asha asked.

Lucas pulled himself to his feet and lumbered over to a nearby leather chair. He sat down and put Natalie on a small ottoman in front of him.

"I was never in the service. I'm not a soldier."

Asha appeared confused as she looked down at his ripped camouflage pants, dog tags, and combat boots. Raising her eyebrow, she pressed him.

"Go on . . ."

"I'll tell you how I met Natalie," he said, as he rested his head on his hand in the chair.

It was back in the days when humanity still thought it best to stick together for the common purpose of travel and survival. Yes, they'd suffered losses. A few members of the group had turned on each other, there were several suicides, and Carl the mechanic had tried to murder Lucas in his sleep not too long ago, but outside of that, the community was still relatively strong and full of many folks willing to have each other's backs.

Lucas had been appointed de facto leader for reasons he couldn't quite understand. The eleven of them left spanned many ages and cultures. Bryce, the youngest, was fifteen, and could kill a rabbit at a hundred yards, though there weren't many left to shoot. Lois was the oldest, probably sixty, though she'd never tell. They'd been through a lot so far, and survived much that others hadn't. Many started out soft but were being tanned into tough leather, Lucas perhaps more than any of them.

They still had some food and water, as they'd been on a lucky streak raiding gas stations and grocery stores lately. But the heat was starting to get unbearable, and Lucas knew they should change their direction to go more north than west, though that would make his trek to Portland even longer. Most of the group had family along the coast, which was why they were sticking together. They'd lost six so far, and Lucas was hoping the wheat had now been separated from the chaff, and there'd be no more turning on one another.

Lucas wasn't exactly sure where they were. They hadn't seen a road sign in some time, and the last time they came to a bridge that had been blown out, they'd had to take a detour around that took almost a full day. It was hard to get any bearings when at any moment there might be no more road to follow. Every automobile they'd come across for a hundred miles had been dead, the batteries wiped clean by some sort of EMP blast. Whether it was mankind's or the creatures', they couldn't be sure. Even if they were still functional, there were so many chunks cleaved out of the road it was impossible to drive for more than a mile at a time without having to abandon a vehicle. He'd attempted it back in Florida. His stolen Range Rover got about three miles up the coast before its tire exploded on a piece of shrapnel from a downed F-22.

The war had been over for about a month, and Lucas had seen the last giant creature ship ascending into the clouds about three weeks earlier. He'd had no contact with his wife since the hotel room, as the phones and Internet were the first things to stop working. The official word from the military had been it was a widespread malfunction of the networks, but Lucas suspected the creatures had purposefully decimated known means of communication to cause widespread panic. And it worked.

After taking down their camp from the previous night, the group had set out without incident in the morning down a stretch of interstate that was surprisingly untouched. There were the usual cracks and potholes, but no huge swaths torn out of it and only minimal amounts of abandoned vehicles to navigate through.

They walked for about two hours, drinking tiny amounts of rationed water as they went. It felt at least a few degrees hotter than the day before, and Lucas knew they had to get out of the south as quickly as they could. He didn't understand what had happened to the sky, the sun and moon replaced by constant red cloud cover, but it was heating up the area like a pressure cooker. He wondered if it was a localized effect, or if this could possibly be the case worldwide. Even if the crazies had been expelled from the group at this point, the rest were starting to murmur about the changing weather and increasingly hostile conditions.

In the distance ahead of them was a shimmering mirage. Figures approached over the rise of the horizon, and Lucas squinted to try and make them out. They were mere abstractions, but as they drew closer, a larger shape appeared behind them. A vehicle. They hadn't seen one mobile in a week. The group began to talk amongst themselves, and Lucas kept his hand on the trigger of his long-barrel Remington shotgun—pilfered from the back window of a pickup truck. They were too short to be creatures, were they . . . soldiers?

As they came into focus, Lucas saw that was indeed the case. At long last! There were about twelve of them along with the vehicle, and Lucas saw it was an armored transport with a .50 caliber turret mounted on the back, manned by another soldier. There were sighs of relief within the group. Who knew what they had? They needed food, supplies, but more pressingly, information. Was the war truly over? What was going to happen now? Questions flooded through Lucas's mind.

As the two groups came within a midrange distance of each other, the transport stopped, and the troops with it. The passenger door opened and a man stepped out. He looked to be about Lucas's age and his bars indicated he was a major? A captain? He wasn't quite sure about the exact rankings of military brass, but the man certainly looked like he was in charge of this brigade. His face was surprisingly clean shaven for the current conditions, and he walked methodically toward them.

Lucas shouldered his shotgun and told the group he'd ask all their questions for them. He approached the Captain and the other soldiers turned to look at him. Their faces were all smeared in black, presumably to reflect the heat, but they had a gaunt, desperate look to them that unsettled Lucas. His eyes met the Captain's. He had an intense gaze, but smiled warmly.

"Good to see you, citizen, we haven't come across a group of this size in days. Glad to see you're weathering the storm."

Lucas broke into a smile himself, relieved at the man's pleasant demeanor.

"Yeah, the same. I haven't seen a soldier in weeks, much less a whole squad. Where are you guys coming from?"

"Laughlin Air Force Base," he said. "But it's gone now. Those damn things wiped almost every one of our southern installations off the map. I've heard similar things out of the east. Nothing from the north."

"What's happened to the government?" Lucas asked.

"DC is a crater, but reports are that the secretary of education was sworn in as president, and cleanup is beginning worldwide.

We were sent out here to try and find survivors and tell them to go to designated population reestablishment zones."

"But I need to get to Portland. Most of us have family along the West Coast."

"Oh, the coast wasn't hit nearly as bad as around here. They're probably already in zones themselves."

The Captain looked over at the group, who were nervously awaiting Lucas to come back with information.

"How are y'all for supplies? We have some we could spare," the Captain offered, his Texan accent a bit more pronounced. Lucas lit up.

"We have some food and water, but not much. Anything you could spare would be appreciated," he said.

"Absolutely, the zone is only about forty clicks just outside of Baton Rouge. It should be enough to get you there."

He put his hand firmly on Lucas's shoulder.

"Take some rations from the transport. We should have enough for the lot of you."

"Thank you, really."

The Captain guided him through the soldiers toward the rear of the vehicle. The .50 caliber gunner eyed him cautiously as he passed. Lucas imagined a vehicle of this size could hold quite a bit of cargo and was curious as to what he would find.

What he found was a sharp crack to the back of his head and his vision exploded into stars. The Captain had slammed his rifle butt into Lucas's skull from behind and he reeled to the ground. After ripping the shotgun from Lucas's back and landing another blow across his forehead, the Captain turned to his men.

"Take them," he said.

The infantry began marching toward the group with the Captain walking slowly behind. Out of his spotted vision, Lucas could see the horrific scene unfold, and he was powerless to stop it. Everyone looked surprised to see the soldiers advancing, and no one even had time to scream before the troops unloaded their weapons into them. Lucas tried to cry out, but his voice had vanished. After the initial blasts, the popping of gunfire started to die out. From his vantage point on the ground, Lucas saw them beginning to pick through the bodies of his companions.

Struggling against pressing unconsciousness, Lucas forced himself to his feet, his vision still blurred and head throbbing. He crouched behind the vehicle, out of the sight of the Captain and his troops, and began to hyperventilate.

Shit. Shit. Shit.

Patting up and down his body, he only found his knife. The Captain had stripped him of his primary weapon, the Remington, which was now slung across the man's back. He was shouting orders to the other infantrymen. Two more shots rang out as a soldier finished off someone who wasn't quite dead.

Lucas looked up to the gunner on top of the vehicle and made an adrenaline-fueled decision that would have seemed insane five minutes ago. He scrambled up the back of the transport, almost losing his grip because of how much his head was swimming. When he reached the top, he drew his knife and without stopping to think, launched himself at the gunner. The soldier was taken by surprise and couldn't react before Lucas pulled his chin to the left and plunged his blade into the right side of his neck. The man gasped and sputtered as blood filled his esophagus, and Lucas pulled him up and out of the turret station and sent him cascading over the side to the ground. Lucas took control of the .50 caliber, and caught the eye of the Captain.

"Oh . . . *shit.*"

The Captain dove to the ground as Lucas opened fire on the soldiers looting his comrades' bodies. The heavy gun tore through them like paper, limbs were ripped away from torsos, chests and heads erupted as no amount of body armor made a bit of difference with a gun of this size. Lucas steered the barrel down toward where the Captain was crawling toward the vehicle, but the angle was too severe and the turret wouldn't point that low. The Captain reached the front of the transport and pulled himself up. He fired a stream of rounds from his rifle, which caused Lucas to duck inside the vehicle to avoid losing his head. Inside, he found himself staring at the driver, who had a stunned look on his face as he found his gunner had been replaced by an enemy who had just butchered his squad in front of him. He drew his weapon but Lucas grabbed the gun and shoved the man's hand into the side of the seat.

The pistol fired, and the round ricocheted throughout the armored vehicle, hitting nothing, but making Lucas's ears ring loudly. He kicked the soldier in the face, and his broken nose caused him to lose his grip on the gun. Lucas pulled it away, quickly fired it, and the man's brains were plastered across the inside of the windshield. Behind the mess, Lucas could see the Captain staring at him with a look that went past hatred, all the way to insanity.

Pushing off the rear of the driver seat, Lucas slid to the back of the transport, where he scrambled to find a handle for the rear door. It was a latch that swung upward and, on its forceful release, Lucas tumbled out onto the asphalt. His gun slipped from his grasp and clattered onto the pavement. He reached for it, but it was immediately kicked away by a combat boot. The Captain rounded the rear of the truck and pointed an impressive-looking assault rifle at Lucas. Just as he pulled the trigger, Lucas sprang at him from the ground, catching him in the midsection. The shots went over Lucas's back and he felt a hot singe as one grazed him. The pair of them hit the ground and began wrestling on the asphalt. Lucas's muscles strained as he clasped the rifle and had to use all his might to keep the barrel from pointing at his face. The Captain's back arched in pain as he was ground into the shotgun still slung behind him, and Lucas used the brief distraction to smash an elbow into the man's eye. The Captain lost his iron grip on the assault rifle for a split second, and Lucas seized the opportunity to wrench it around so it pressed on the man's throat. Both of them were in a significant amount of pain and surging with adrenaline. The back and forth with the rifle seemed to last hours, though in reality it was only a few seconds. Lucas looked into the Captain's icy blue eyes and saw his furious stare begin to soften. His grip weakened and the rifle dug further into his throat. Lucas mustered up all his remaining strength into one giant surge and thrust the gun downward until he heard a sickening crack. The man's eyes went vacant.

Lucas rolled off of him and gasped for air. The clouds above were swirling, and they seemed to be even darker than usual. He looked over at the lifeless Captain and breathed a huge sigh. His hands were bleeding from where they'd dug into the metal rifle, and there was blood streaming down his face from his initial head injuries, also caused by the gun.

He picked himself up slowly and drew the Captain's rifle as he walked past the dead transport driver and toward the pile of bodies further up the road. When he reached them, no one was stirring. None in his group and no soldiers. The hot winds whipped through the empty landscape around him. He was alone.

He decided to take the Captain's uniform, as his own clothes were streaked with blood. Also, he figured that it would make him all the more imposing as he continued his journey down the road. Soldiers weren't to be trusted anymore; they were to be feared. And Lucas realized he needed to be feared. This was not the same world any more.

He looked at the dog tags that read "J. Stanton, USMC" and he put them around his neck. The boots were close to his size, but when he put his foot in one, something felt odd. He reached inside and pulled out a photo. It was of a beautiful young woman with platinum hair and green eyes. She was biting her lip softly, and her blouse was unbuttoned to show just enough cleavage to allure without being overtly crass. A former flame? No, a ring both on her hand and the Captain's said otherwise.

Was he just trying to get home too? Is this what you had to become to survive?

Lucas looked at the mass of bodies around him. He turned the worn photo over.

John,
Make it back to me, I'll be waiting.
All my love,
Natalie

Lucas placed the picture gently on Captain John Stanton's lifeless chest and folded his hands over the top of it. He hoisted the assault rifle upward for inspection. It was in pristine condition with a magnified scope, dual clipped magazines, and a host of other attachments that Lucas couldn't identify. He buckled his new belt, which was loaded with clips, and turned west, looking down the scope. Pulling back, he held the gun out in front of him. NATALIE was crudely etched into the rear stock, either as an identifier, or a reminder.

If Natalie had helped John survive this long, perhaps she could help him as well.

10

Asha sat quietly after Lucas's story ended. His voice was dry from talking for such a prolonged period and he reached into his pack for some water to ease his cracked throat. The blood had finally stopped spilling out of the cannibal and had seeped into the rug and floorboards around him. Natalie lay dead in front of him, her journey finally at an end. She had protected him to her last breath.

Finally, Asha spoke.

"Soldiers were the worst of them."

She was sitting cross-legged on the corner of the bed, not minding the dried blood staining the sheets inches away from her.

"I remember early on, a brigade told me to come with them to safety. Within an hour, they were rummaging through my bag and trying to rip my clothes off."

"How'd you get away?" Lucas asked.

"Nothing quite so Rambo as your story, though I did pull a pin on one of their vest grenades and got the hell out of there."

Lucas was hardly surprised to hear she'd experienced something similar. After the war, the shell-shocked, battle-hardened soldiers took advantage of their positions of trust and power, and Lucas had many more run-ins with them after his first encounter. It had helped he was dressed as one of their own.

"Population reestablishment zones, the secretary of education as president. You know that's all bullshit right?" Asha asked.

"Of course, though I kept hearing some variation of that lie among survivors. Sometimes it was to trick, sometimes it was to give hope. Either way, it was cruel."

Whatever had happened to the government during the war and shortly after was never made explicitly clear, but in a few years it became obvious to those who remained that a dying planet had no need for leadership as it marched toward its end. Lucas was sure there had been some squabbling among the remaining politicians and military brass in the immediate aftermath of the creatures' departure, but once every day became a fight for food and water, the regression into animal nature was swift. Wolves might have pack leaders, but they don't have executive, judicial, or legislative branches. That was as much leadership as there would ever be again. The headless chief a few miles away in town was a monument to the kinds of rulers that still existed. And even they would all be gone soon.

"Well that's a shame about poor Natalie there, but at least she died doing what she loved," said Asha.

"I suppose," said Lucas, but it hurt that his trusted companion was lying mangled in front of him. He got up from the chair and slung the gun over his back once more.

"You're keeping it?" asked Asha.

"I'm not convinced she's shot her last clip yet."

The huge gash into her middle said otherwise. Lucas knew it, but didn't care.

Asha had a sudden realization.

"So if you're not a soldier, what did you do then . . . before the war?"

"Nothing that mattered."

After clearing out the mansion's latest resident, the move-out process could begin. They'd have to find a balance between items they needed and what they could actually physically carry back to the ship in the cart. Lucas found the chair he'd been sitting in while telling his story to be quite comfortable, so he hauled it down the stairs. There were a few flecks of cannibal blood that had reached it, but he figured he would be able to rub those out.

Rather than take entire beds from the numerous guest rooms they discovered in the house, they just took the mattresses and piled sheets and blankets on top of them. They added a pair of small end tables, an oak desk, and another two chairs. The expedition was turning into an Ikea trip.

Lucas made his way to the library and pulled out as many English-language books as he could find from the shelves. Thumbing through the titles, he found a few he recognized, *The Brothers Karamazov*, *The Iliad*, *The Picture of Dorian Gray*. He had to chuckle when he found the full set of Harry Potter books on one of the lower shelves. His son had always sworn by them, and Lucas remembered seeing pictures of him from Halloween wearing thick round glasses with a jagged scar drawn on his forehead. His grin turned sour however, once he began reflecting on his lost family again. He hastily threw a few books in his pack and the rest he scattered loosely on the cart outside.

After finishing with the library, he had to hunt through the house to find Asha and finally located her back in the master bedroom. She'd torn all the sheets off the bed and dumped them on the dead cannibal on the ground so that only his feet were poking out. On the mattress she'd thrown a huge number of different outfits, pulled from a walk-in closet at the rear of the room. Clothes. He'd forgotten what it was like to even have new ones. Over time, he'd gone through a few different sets, but always came back to his military gear.

"Absolutely atrocious taste," Asha said as she noticed Lucas standing in the doorway. Lucas knew little of fashion, but the dresses she lay on the bed did seem rather loud, with severe lines and vibrant colors. And though she may have had a modeling career once, Lucas couldn't imagine Asha reverting back to couture gowns and cocktail dresses in their current conditions. Rather, she was pulling the plainest items she could find, which included jeans, slacks, shorts, T-shirts, and tank tops. A few pairs of boots and running shoes were strewn nearby. Anything with heels had been tossed haphazardly in the corner.

"The 'his' closet is over there," she said as she motioned to a mirrored door on the other side of the bed. Lucas stepped around the pile of bloody sheets and looked inside. Row after row of suits, ties, and dress shirts were items he would never again need. A few tuxedos and even a kilt were at the very end of the closet, which was larger than his first office. Like Asha, Lucas began to hunt for ordinary items and found a large drawer of boxers, socks, and undershirts, all in shades ranging from white to gray to black, that would be a welcome addition to his nonexistent wardrobe. He grabbed a few pairs of pants, and though he couldn't decipher the Norwegian sizes, the waist and length appeared comparable to his own dimensions. A black thermal jacket was his last acquisition. It seemed silly, but it wouldn't hurt to be prepared for anything.

As he exited the closet, he rounded the corner and was caught off guard. No cannibal greeted him this time, but Asha was standing with her back toward him, wearing nothing on top and revealing a canvas of tan skin. A few white scars distracted from what was otherwise an appealing sight. She flung a dark blue T-shirt over herself and turned toward him without a hint of embarrassment on her face.

"A little baggy, but they'll do."

She held up a rather large red laced bra.

"I don't know how this woman walked without falling over. Lucky guy, I guess."

She dropped the bra and pointed to Lucas.

"Anything good?"

"Good enough," Lucas replied quickly as he stuffed the clothes into his pack with the extras draped over his shoulders. What he'd just seen was probably the most pleasant scene he'd come across in years, though Asha would likely cut his head off if she knew he was thinking that. He put it out of his mind and continued with the task at hand.

The final room they discovered was one they'd hoped to find. Covered in layers of dust, a brightly painted child's room sat unused in the far right corner of the second floor, almost touching the mothership. The collapsed ceiling had made the door stick shut, and it took both of them to smash it open. Perhaps it was why the area seemed like it hadn't been touched in years. The pristine room was somewhat off-putting, a remnant of a far happier time. It was unclear what had happened to the family that lived there, but the reality that there were no happy endings in the current climate made Lucas a bit sad for them.

Inside the room they were able to find an intact crib, and the shelves were lined with children's books and stuffed toys. A relief, since Lucas had worried Noah would be forced to play with shell casings or alien power tools with nothing onboard remotely appropriate for a child. They threw everything in the crib and together carried it down the stairs where they perched it on top of the cart.

The way back was the hardest trip they had to make all day. The furniture, books, clothes, and assorted other trinkets vastly outweighed the initial weapon haul, and they had long ways still to go, having come all the way from the mansion. The path back was on a slight slope downhill, which made it easier, but they had to remain vigilant so the cart didn't gather too much steam and roll away from them. They periodically stopped to rest and drink water. Lucas opened up another can of tuna and split it with Asha, who downed her half in seconds. It wasn't much longer now until they'd have to test the merits of Alpha's "nutrients."

During one of the rest periods on the way back to the ship, Lucas and Asha wandered down a side street to stretch their tense muscles. With Natalie out of commission on his back, Lucas had turned to his recently acquired sawed-off shotgun as his primary weapon. Granted, if anything attacked him from more than ten yards away, he'd be in trouble, but Asha would be able to handle anything at range. He hoped.

They approached the remains of a burned down building, completely in ash and ruin. It must have been made entirely out of wood, a rarity in the mostly stone town, and there was too little of it left to deduce what it might have been.

But something caught Lucas's eye. A skull. Not an unusual sight here. But this one, it was small. Too small.

"Oh god," Lucas involuntarily exclaimed.

Asha stepped into the ashes and began loosely kicking around rubble. Another skull, and another, attached to tiny skeletons. Lucas put it together.

"*Barna, barna*," he said.

The old woman. She was trying to free the slaves in the church to help her save the children from the burning nursery across town. She pleaded with Lucas to help her do the same, but he didn't understand. But Alpha understood, which is why he remained silent. He must have known Lucas would want to go off on a hero's quest to save the children.

Lucas looked around. They were so small. Not one of them could have been over three. In their own twisted way, the cannibals really were trying to start some kind of reborn society. A nightmarish one to be sure, but one that involved procreation.

The woman was likely kept alive as a caretaker, and after receiving no help from the three of them at the church, she went to the nursery to rescue whoever she could. And she saved Noah, bringing him to the only place that seemed like salvation. The ship.

Asha agreed with Lucas's analysis of what had happened, though was additionally disgusted by the rape that had assuredly produced all of these children in the past few years. Lucas felt a rising anger toward Alpha, as he'd purposely left them in the dark about what the woman was telling them. They could have saved all the children had they known, not just one. Lucas felt sick as he surveyed the ashen graveyard.

They returned to the cart and spent the next two hours in silence pushing it through the loose sands of the bay. When they reached the Ark at last, Lucas didn't stop to unload; he marched straight into the engine bay.

"There were others, Alpha," he said sternly.

Alpha was tinkering with the white core and his mechanical fingers continued to work even as he turned to face Lucas.

"What do you speak of?" he said flatly.

"Other children, besides Noah."

"Oh, you have given it a name. How pleasant."

"That woman, you knew what she was saying, and I didn't realize what she meant until now. There wasn't just one child she was trying to save; there were many."

Alpha's mech hand stopped its work on the core.

"I concede. I kept this information from you purposefully."

Lucas was livid, but before he could speak, Alpha continued.

"But an attempted rescue of children would have doomed our entire mission. Our capture almost caused us not to reach the core before irreparable decay. Further delay and the window of opportunity would have been closed completely, and we would be stuck in your lifeless solar system until we died as well."

It made sense, though the fury was still boiling inside Lucas. Alpha pressed on.

"It was pleasing that an infant did manage to survive, and I welcomed him onboard. But you were struggling with the concept of caring for one child. What would you have done with five? Ten?"

Lucas was now speechless, and couldn't formulate an answer, internally or externally. Instead he stormed off, and Alpha returned to work on the core. He spoke loudly as Lucas walked through the doors.

"Watch the skies. We will be leaving soon."

On the bridge, the sky showed nothing, and Lucas didn't expect Omicron to break through the cloud cover any time soon. *It took a while to get here, didn't it?*

He was still simmering about Alpha and the children, though logically, he had to concede the point. They had reached the core with minutes to spare after all, and he couldn't even imagine ten children running around the Ark's corridors. He'd thought himself hard after all these years in the wild, but the tiny blackened skeletons were stuck in his mind, as were the pleas of the woman. There was still hope however, and he would be remiss to let Noah suffer just because his brethren had perished. Lucas had brought him a stuffed T. Rex from the cart outside. Placing it in his hands, he waited for some flicker of emotion to register across his face, but none did. He eventually pawed at it with his burned arm, but when it toppled over, he lost interest. Lucas began to wonder if the child's emotional state might be beyond repair. His thoughts were interrupted when Asha broke through on the comm.

"Are you going to help me with this shit or not?"

He headed back to ground level and helped Asha move the items out of the cart and into the storage bay. They debated where they should set up quarters. Alpha couldn't be bothered with such trivialities, so they decided to explore the ship to choose locations.

The armory was now full of weaponry, but there was enough room to set up a mattress and a few choice pieces of furniture. Asha immediately claimed the area for herself, and added that she'd be able to sort through all the weapons in her free time, cleaning them of blood and dirt and matching up the scattered ammo. Lucas found the idea agreeable and helped her move in. A queen-size mattress, some thousand-thread-count sheets, a table, and two chairs made the space cozy enough. It was definitely preferable to a claustrophobic, nightmare inducing sleeping pod.

Lucas wandered around the rest of the ship by himself, going up and down levels in the lift. He returned to the pod area and found that though the room was quite large in total, the more than one hundred pods crammed in there made for limited floor space. Also on this level was the water storage area, and the blue tanks glowed to show they were as full as ever. Their water consumption had barely made a dent.

Lucas then took the lift to the LABORATORY level, where he hadn't been before. The hallway dead ended quickly and the door on the right said "Research." Lucas tried the controls but they were locked. Alpha's quarters, he imagined. The lab from the video earlier. Turning to the other door across the hall, the label was an array of alien symbols that for some reason hadn't been translated. Also locked. Lucas tried to pry the cracks of the door open, but quickly gave up as it became obvious it wouldn't budge. Returning to the lift, he rode further down to the brig and engine level.

Before the large and secure doors of the engine bay were the four jail cells where at one point Alpha and Asha had both been kept. Three of them were caked with a decent amount of dried black blood and two had consoles that were sparking loudly and brightly. One room, however, had no blood at all and its console was burnt out, but quiet. It was too small for him, but perhaps Noah? He doubted he would mind the confined space. A short trip down the hall to the storage bay and he had the crib along with the selection of toys and books placed methodically in the room. He slapped the cushions in the crib against the wall and rid them of clouds of dust. It occurred to him to do the same with the animals, and he coughed as he accidentally inhaled a few particles. Surveying his work, he was satisfied. It wasn't much, but it would have to do.

Finally Lucas decided on the water room for his own quarters. The ambient glow of the tanks was somehow comforting, and he set up his mattress at the far end of the corridor between the last two units. He put a desk and chair a few feet in front of it and stacked his books in piles on either side of the table. Shelving hadn't exactly been a top priority when selecting furniture in the mansion, nor had storage, and he piled his recently acquired clothes a few feet away on the ground. Finally, he unslung Natalie from his back and mounted her above his mattress on a part of the wall that jutted out. She deserved something resembling a place of honor, and he wasn't about to toss her out with the other scrap metal.

His muscles ached from hauling the cart through shifting sands and rough cobblestone all day. His leg and ribs were feeling markedly better however, and he couldn't deny the effectiveness of Alpha's healing apparatuses. Lucas kicked off his boots, lay his shotgun and buck knife down on the metal floor, and was fast asleep before he could strip any further.

11

It was time to leave. Not Norway, but Earth.

The prospect had been looming since he'd met Alpha and his working ship, but it appeared the moment was finally at hand. Lucas had been awakened by Alpha's booming voice in the water chamber, and he and Asha had hastily assembled themselves and reached the engine bay where they'd been summoned.

Alpha had worked through the night, and Lucas didn't know if he'd taken a single break the last two days. After learning of the slaughter of his entire family, was this how he dealt with grief? Or were they really just in that much of a hurry? He looked fatigued but resolute as he pointed out his finished work on the white core. It stood in place of the old blue one, but Alpha had built up a large amount of machinery around it, and every console in the cavernous room seemed to shine more brightly than ever. Whatever he'd set out to do, it seemed he had done it, and he informed them they were ready to leave immediately.

"The new core should allow us to travel at range, and once we are far out enough in space, we can use it to reach our final destination."

"Which is where again?" Asha asked.

"A place that requires an explanation longer than we have time for. Once we are en route, you will have the answers you seek."

He played around with a few holocontrols and the room made some odd noises.

"You're sure this is going to work?" Lucas asked, motioning to the core. "You said this ship wasn't supposed to be able to use this thing to travel."

"The fact that the core has been installed without detonation is a positive sign. The calculations indicate the ship will hold while traveling in [garbled]. We have no other option but to attempt escape."

"Wait," Asha interjected. "You're saying that when you were hooking this thing up, the entire ship could have exploded at any time?"

"That is . . . correct."

"And you didn't think you should tell us this?"

"I did not."

Asha fell silent. Lucas supposed it was hard to fault him. It certainly would have robbed them of a few nights' rest.

"Before we begin the longest stage of our journey, we must survive the shortest. The Sentinels wait outside your planet's atmosphere and have almost assuredly been issued capture or kill orders by High Commander Omicron. They will be waiting for us."

"What exactly are these things?" Lucas asked.

Alpha brought up a display of an object on his wrist. It was a long column with spindles poking out around the center. It almost looked like a satellite or space station.

"Sentinels are unmanned robotic drones that monitor a planet's life and resources. But in our case, they will transform into their secondary function: defense."

He tapped the display and smaller machines began to shoot out of the central station. Pulling his claws apart, he zoomed in on one of them. It had three fin-like protrusions with a central chamber in the middle. Guns were mounted on all three wing tips.

"These drones are the Sentinel's defense system, and they will be pursuing us. They're smaller than traditional fighters, and don't have the instincts of a living pilot, but they can be quite deadly in swarms. Their [garbled] cannons can damage us beyond repair if we take enough fire. We may be destroyed, or merely disabled, depending on Omicron's orders."

The holograms began firing tiny projectiles that disappeared into the air in front of them. They spun around and flew in tiny loops, demonstrating combat maneuvers.

"How am I supposed to avoid these things?" Lucas asked.

"And how am I supposed to kill them?" added Asha.

Alpha closed the hologram.

"It will not be easy. We are a transport ship and not nearly as maneuverable as a fighter, nor with as much firepower. Our sole advantage is that the new core allows us to move more quickly than the craft could previously."

"So just dodge and weave," Lucas said.

"I am not a combat pilot, but yes, that would likely be advisable."

"And I'm still using the same gun as I did there?" Asha said, motioning toward town.

"Only at extremely close range. Though the main gun is offline; it would not have mattered as the drones are too small and fast. But your arsenal has expanded, as you now have access to [garbled]. To a stockpile of missiles."

Asha was taken aback.

"We had missiles this entire time, and you weren't letting me use them?"

"There was no reason to unleash them on the village, when the light gun served its purpose. Furthermore they are designed for extra-orbital combat, and I knew we would need to employ them in our escape attempt."

Alpha was once again logical, but it didn't make Asha any less annoyed.

"Additionally, I will join you in the secondary turret. The engine is now more stable than it has ever been, and we will need all the firepower we can gather to avoid destruction by the Sentries."

"I thought you weren't a soldier," Lucas asked.

"I knew this day would come, and I have trained myself accordingly. Do not concern yourself with my abilities. Additionally, there is no longer a chance of our weapons overheating."

"Thank god for that," Asha said.

"So what's the plan? Kill all these robots and turn on hyperdrive?" asked Lucas.

"What is this 'hyperdrive'?" Alpha said, confused.

"The new core, it makes us go faster than light, right?"

Alpha looked amused.

"Your notions of science are derived from your fiction, not fact. The core does not make us 'go faster' to travel at range. You have heard of what you call 'wormholes' in space and time?"

"Yes."

"The core generates a pathway that we will travel through that will cut through the galaxy to our destination. 'Going faster' would have all of us dead of old age before we even reached [garbled], much less [garbled]. This way will still take some time, but substantially less than a million years."

Was that sarcasm? Couldn't be.

"So how does that work?" asked Asha.

Alpha was the one starting to look annoyed.

"From interacting with the pair of you, it is obvious neither of you are well versed in the sciences. But even if you were, attempting to convey the elaborate and exact concepts behind intergalactic travel to even a genius of your civilization would be as if you were to try to explain how one of your 'airplanes' functioned to an ancient ancestor more intimately familiar with the workings of sticks and stones."

Lucas didn't appreciate the condescension, but he knew he probably couldn't understand the depth of Alpha's knowledge even if he was Einstein or Hawking.

"Alright, no need to be a dick about it," Asha said. "When are we getting off this rock?"

"Presently," said Alpha. "Report to stations."

When Lucas fired the ship up this time, things were different. Taking off in open air rather than underground was certainly a relief, but it was more than that. The controls were responding much more quickly, and green 100 percent indicators lit up across the board, which revealed that every primary system on the ship was now surging at full power. The thrust of the engines was more powerful than ever, and as he left the ground with ease, he found that the ship felt a great deal lighter than it had previously. The weight had obviously not changed, but the integration of the new core had given the Ark a complete overhaul, and it felt like an entirely new ship.

Lucas watched the ravaged town at Kvaløya disappear below him. The place had almost been his tomb on more than one occasion over the past few days, and he was glad to be rid of it. But it occurred to him that the horrible little village was the last place on Earth where he would ever set foot, and he regretted not savoring the moment a little more, even if the place was a hellhole.

Turning his attention to the cloud cover, Lucas found it to be quite a bit higher in the atmosphere than he had anticipated. They were rising rapidly, and had been for some time, but had not yet broken through it. Alpha and Asha were visible in two floating monitors to his right and left. His hands swirled around through ship status reports and diagnostics so quickly he was barely conscious of what he was doing. It was the virtual training at work again, and his brain was firing even faster than his hands. Hopefully the ship would allow him to process information that rapidly when avoiding Sentinels in a short while.

Finally, the Ark broke through the clouds. Lucas was speechless.

The sun shone as brightly as it ever had, and the bluish black sky was a stark contrast to the red swirling clouds below it. To the east, Lucas could even see half of the moon in the distance. Earth's old friends were still there as they'd always been, watching as the planet slowly decayed. It was miraculous to see them once again; he never thought he would.

They kept rising and the blue turned darker and darker and stars began to appear in the distance. The ship rumbled and Lucas could see the hull turn a fiery red as they broke through what was left of the corroding atmosphere.

Amidst all the carnage and heartbreak and despair he'd experienced in the last few years, this moment was simply glorious. He remembered watching the space shuttle launch from Cape Canaveral with his father as a boy. Soon after, he went through a prolonged phase of wanting to do nothing but be an astronaut. To go and see the stars and come back and tell everyone about them. Now he was actually going there, at the helm of an alien starship. His childhood self could not have imagined anything more spectacular.

His perfect moment was cut short by Alpha on the monitor.

"Do you see them?"

Lucas checked his readouts and saw that two of the rotating satellite stations Alpha had showed them earlier had been detected nearby. Zooming in on the viewscreen, he scanned the star-filled horizon until the computer located and outlined both of them.

"Increase speed," Alpha said.

Lucas dialed up the engines and was temporarily pinned back in his seat. He glanced over at Noah, who was still in his cylinder on the floor a short distance away, with no time to move him to his new quarters in the brig. Alpha assured them that the ship's artificial gravity system would keep in them in place and minimize G-force, no matter how elaborate their maneuvers in space.

The curved edge of Earth was now visible in the viewscreen and, as Lucas suspected, the cloud cover stretched far and wide over the horizon. Earth probably looked more vibrant from this angle back when it was a mass of green and blue, but it was still an undeniably impressive sight.

Lucas couldn't savor it for long. As the Ark moved further out into space, he could see the two stations drifting to either side of the viewscreen. He was going to pass right through them. Was it possible Alpha was wrong? Maybe they had been left offline with the planet in ruin, as there was nothing of substance to report. No one breathed as they moved silently through the pair of Sentinels. The speed readout said the Ark was travelling at close to 200,000 miles an hour, but it felt like he was riding a raft down a lazy river. Noah had apparently even fallen back asleep.

Alarms. Everywhere. The game was up.

Half-translated danger readouts flashed in front of Lucas's eyes. He scrambled to see what exactly was going on, but could only make out the words ENEMY and APPROACH. The Sentinels were behind him now, but one of his monitors with a rear view of the ship showed what was happening. He flung it up on the main viewscreen.

Robotic drone fighters streamed out of the stations like hornets from a disturbed nest. It was impossible to tell just how many of them were pouring forth from each station, but what was clear was that they were approaching fast, even as Lucas increased their speed to 500,000.

"Here we go!" he yelled into the monitor, and he tried to silence some of the proximity alarms that were blaring in his ears. He was flying away from Earth, but the viewscreen continued to show the view to the rear. The planet was almost entirely encircled by cloud cover, with a few rare areas showing brown or dark red blotches. More pressing, however, were the objects in the foreground, as the drone fighters were gaining on them.

Alpha fired the first missile, knowing their range and capability more intimately than Asha. The canister burned a bright blue and spiraled toward a cluster of Sentinel drones. They attempted to scatter, but the detonation consumed two of them while three others spun crazily out of control, heavily damaged. Asha didn't waste any time after seeing Alpha unload, and launched a missile of her own. The drones reacted more quickly this time, but one was incinerated and another injured so that it fell back, unable to pursue.

It was their turn. The foremost drones fired a stream of shots that Lucas had to dodge entirely through reflex. Without the added neural stimulation of the captain's chair, he doubted he would have reacted in time, but using the holocontrols wrapped around his arms, he wrenched the ship to the right, avoiding the stream of fire.

The battle escalated quickly as more and more drones caught up. Asha and Alpha were now firing missiles in sequence, and through a pair of small monitors to his left, Lucas could see their targeting systems cycling through possible bogeys and then deploying the missiles once there was a lock. Drones were going down, but they were incredibly nimble, and on occasion would be able to dodge the missiles entirely, which would shoot past them toward Earth, growing ever smaller. Their speed was now well over a million, but all systems appeared to be holding. Lucas spun right to avoid another series of blasts from the drones. Even when the ship was upside down, the internal gravity didn't change at all, and Lucas imagined he was feeling far less nauseous than he would be at the helm of a human fighter jet.

The battle was fraying his nerves, however, and he could feel his heart beating in his throat. Every split second he was dodging more fire. As increasing numbers swarmed the ship, he couldn't avoid them all, and the Ark started taking hits. Blasts peppered the hull and readouts flashed at him angrily. He scrambled to try and fix the affected systems on the fly. Mercifully, there had been no breaches, yet.

Missiles continued to rip the drones apart, but some had managed to get along the sides of the ship, despite its ever-increasing speeds. Asha caught on, switched to the manual turret, and unloaded into three on the port side. When they were in pieces, she did a complete 180 and tore apart four more starboard. Alpha too switched to the turret's cannon and blasted a few spindly drones that were moving dangerously close to the engines.

The Ark was traveling at five million miles an hour, and Lucas wondered what the upward limit was with the new core. Earth was barely visible, and he hadn't even had time to notice they were approaching a dull reddish-orange orb in the distance. *Mars*, Lucas realized, but was jolted by another series of blasts connecting with the hull. He spun the ship around for three full rotations to avoid further impact.

"Will you hold the damn thing steady for two seconds?" Asha yelled through the monitor. "I'm trying to kill these things!"

"I'm trying to keep *them* from killing *us*!" Lucas shot back. Two more drones blew apart and it appeared Asha was making do.

Lucas switched the main viewscreen to a frontal view once more and his blood instantly chilled as he saw a formation of four drones heading toward him, each unloading all three cannons at once. Their initial volley hit, but Lucas quickly jerked the ship straight up to arc over the rest of their fire. Only stars were in view now, but the Ark was immediately rocked by a huge impact. The readout in front of his face read COLLISION, followed by an even more terrifying notification: HULL BREACH—CARGO BAY. Lucas immediately checked if the seal was still intact on the bay door, and breathed a sigh of relief when he saw that the rest of the ship wasn't compromised. Had one of the drones actually hit them? What else could collision mean? Checking readouts, it became clear one of the advancing drones had connected with the underside of the ship, where both turrets were. The monitors revealed both Asha and Alpha were still present and accounted for, but Alpha's turret had a multitude of warning lights surrounding it.

"Alpha, what happened? Are you alright?"

Alpha launched another missile into a drone cluster.

"This station was weakened by that impact. I must abandon the post before it gives way completely."

He shot a barrage that tore the wing off a passing fighter.

"I will move to the engine bay and prepare us for our final departure."

"And when exactly is that?" Lucas asked, dodging another volley from the rear.

"We must be further away from your sun," Alpha replied coolly, even as the ship took fire all around him. "That will require holding off the Sentries for a short while longer."

"Fantastic," Asha said, as one of her shots failed to connect.

Alpha left his turret as the danger indicators attached to it continued to look more and more dire. Now the Ark had half the firepower, but it seemed as if the drones were finally thinning out. They still buzzed around the ship, but there were no more large clusters, and their automated formations seemed to be growing sloppy. Lucas wondered if they were too far away from their central stations. Were they even meant to travel this far? Was their own ship?

The Ark was now moving through space at twenty million miles an hour and was starting to shake a bit. Whether it was the speed or recent damage they'd taken, Lucas couldn't be sure. He kept swerving to avoid fire, and another Collision indicator told him he'd clipped a drone on the right, though it was a heavily armored part of the ship and he'd done no actual damage to their craft.

Asha kept picking off straggling drones, and a readout indicated that she was almost out of missiles. They'd launched almost their entire supply in their escape attempt, and as the Ark was meant to be a transport above all else, there wasn't anything else in the arsenal to turn to. Lining up a shaky formation of three drones, Asha launched a precious missile, and as all three machines erupted, she could see it was well spent.

A new monitor showed that Alpha had reached the engine bay and was swirling controls around near the core. Lucas looked at his turret, and found the danger readouts had reached critical mass.

"Shit."

The weakened viewscreen of the turret bay shattered and the entire gun was ripped from the bottom of the ship and flung into space. It stunned Lucas, but he quickly saw that there had been no depressurization of the nearby passageways with the area sealing itself off automatically. He breathed a sigh of relief, but halfway through exhaling had to jerk the ship away from another barrage of incoming fire.

Trying to keep track of every angle of the ship via a string of monitors was extremely difficult, and it was compounded by all the floating readouts of the ship's various systems in differing levels of distress. He was constantly racing back and forth between them, all the while steering the ship away from fire, and he was certain he wouldn't be able to keep up without his enhanced cognitive functioning. Despite all their weaving, the cables remained embedded to his temples, and were likely the only thing preventing his brain from shutting down due to an overabundance of information. He took a split second to glance back toward Noah's cylinder bed, but couldn't see him over the lip. He turned to the other side of the chair, and tried to see if he was crawling around somewhere, but there was no sign of him. Could a child that age even crawl yet?

Lucas was snapped back into reality by another drone speeding at him from the front. He dodged the tri-gun assault and watched it explode as he and Asha were apparently on the same page for once.

Thirty million and rising. Mars lay suspended before him, its red coloring unmistakable. They were a long way from home now, and the planet grew larger as they sped toward it. It was a breathtaking sight, but as it grew bigger, Alpha chimed in on the comm.

"Please refrain from striking that planet."

Lucas took offense to Alpha's estimation of his piloting abilities. He veered the ship to the right and watched Mars slowly pass them by in silence.

It was too silent, actually.

Lucas scanned his various monitors and saw that the Sentinel drones had stopped firing, and had all fallen to the rear of the ship, keeping their distance.

"What the hell are they doing?" Asha said, and she stopped firing as the drones were now too far out for turret fire and too spread out for missiles.

Lucas switched the main viewscreen to look forward once again and saw a strange sight. Of the hundreds of thousands of stars that populated his forward view, there was a distinct section that was completely black. It was like the space had swallowed up everything around it, and all that was left was complete and utter darkness. A black hole? No. Even with Lucas's limited scientific knowledge, he was certain there were no black holes within the solar system itself. He called down to Alpha, who was still near the core.

"Are you seeing this, Alpha?"

Alpha pulled up a monitor and saw the darkness for himself. He immediately sprinted over to another console and furiously whirred the fingers of both his claws. When he spoke his voice had an urgency Lucas couldn't remember ever hearing before.

"Asha, fire all remaining missiles in succession at these coordinates!"

He flung some data to a screen and it popped up in front of Asha.

"The computer says there's nothing at that point," she said.

"Override! Immediately!" Alpha said, his metallic voice as close as it could get to yelling.

Asha unleashed a stream of five missiles, their last five, and they shot out into space ahead of them. They trailed each other in a helix pattern until the lights of their propulsion systems were too dim to see and then disappeared into the black void.

"So what did—"

Asha was cut off by an explosion that lit up the viewscreen. The missiles had collided with their target, and the dark void flickered ahead of them until a distinct shape came into a view. A ship.

It was sleek and black, and though the missiles had disabled its cloaking field so it was now visible, it reflected the surrounding starlight so well that it was still camouflaged. It was longer and thinner than their craft, but Lucas couldn't estimate its true size. He turned to his holoscreen, but there was no data for the ship the way there had been for the mothership and Sentinels. Just a jumble of incomprehensible symbols. As they drew closer, Lucas could see where they'd damaged it with their blind missile barrage. But even injured, blue lights were beginning to spool up in the front of the ship. Suddenly, the viewscreen changed.

Omicron.

The menacing black creature growled something, and Lucas's readout gave him an extremely rough translation. Only two English words appeared out of the mess of symbols.

"RETURN . . . HOME."

On the monitor, Alpha flicked his claw through a virtual switch. The white core glowed brightly and every light in the ship went out, the main screen along with them. In an instant, everything came back online and the viewscreen exploded with blinding white, purple, and blue light that seared Lucas's retinas. Omicron's ship was nowhere to be found. The neural enhancers detached themselves from Lucas's temples, and he immediately lost consciousness in the chair.

12

He was jostled awake on a bench by a blurry shape in front of him. A face soon came into focus. Adam.

Around him was a grassy park and, in the distance, a recently risen sun. Another reality, one already past. Adam spoke.

"Hey Lucas, you alright?"

Adam flashed a brilliant smile as he put his hand on Lucas's shoulder and sat down next to him. He was in his dress blues that echoed his eyes and had a slew of decorations on his chest Lucas couldn't identify, though he'd heard tales around the dinner table of what he'd done to get them. The fact that he was here at all was a miracle in itself.

"Yeah, I'm fine," Lucas replied. "It's just been a long week."

Lucas adjusted his bow tie; his shirt was too tight around the neck and felt like it was choking him. He undid the top button in surrender. Adam was still tan from his trip overseas, though his blond hair had grown back and was not the close-cropped buzz cut it had been when he left. It was perfectly trimmed and swept in an arc to the side, his white hat in his other hand. His ceremonial sword was perfectly polished. Not a fiber of his entire ensemble was out of place.

"That's understandable. It's been a whirlwind, I imagine," he said.

"You have no idea."

The Portland breeze grazed his face. July was one of the few months it truly felt like summer here. It really was a perfect day, and they couldn't have been luckier.

"How are you feeling after last night?" Adam asked.

Lucas rubbed his head instinctively.

"I'm good."

"Things got pretty out of control there for a while. Even for a bachelor party." Adam's smile dimmed a bit.

"I know, I'm sorry."

Adam looked out toward the city.

"She's my sister. I need to know you're going to take care of her when I'm away."

"I will, I promise."

"I know you will," he said earnestly, without a hint of a threat.

Behind them, men and women scrambled around setting up white folding chairs in an outdoor park. A gazebo was coated in more flowers than Lucas could count. A tiny, barefoot girl in a yellow dress went running down the empty aisle. Lucas turned back toward Adam.

"I'm afraid," Lucas whispered. He was ashamed to admit that to someone so brave, but he had no one else to turn to. Adam had been a good friend during the past few months, and Lucas couldn't help but admire him. He was a greater man than Lucas could ever hope to be.

"He who sees all beings in his own self, and his own self in all beings, loses all fear."

Lucas looked at Adam incredulously.

"Where'd you get that from?"

Adam laughed, his broad smile returning.

"It's Hindu. Don't tell my mother."

Lucas chuckled.

"What I mean is that once you marry her, you're one with her. If you can see yourself in her, and realize that she's now a part of you, the fear will fade, as you can conquer it as one."

He adjusted his decorative sword, which was poking through the slats of the bench.

"It may sound like crap, but it's helped me a lot with Grace when I've been away. She's what helps me get past the fear over there. It's not only about survival; you need something to be fighting for."

He took a breath, and ran a white gloved hand over his hair.

"I know you have your own struggles, but now you're fighting for her. You're fighting to be the man she needs."

Adam was such a stand-up guy it almost made Lucas sick. Or perhaps that was the handle of Jack from the previous night. But he was right.

"Anyway, we've got to go. Sonya's almost ready."

"Thanks, Adam."

"Any time."

"No really, I mean it."

Lucas extended his hand. Adam shook it firmly, then stood up and hoisted Lucas to his feet. He stood a few inches shorter than Lucas, but he never felt like the smaller man.

Ahead of them, people were starting to trickle in and take their seats. In the distance, a large white tent stood rooted to the ground by a few dozen stakes. A bridesmaid opened the flap to walk in and Lucas caught a glimpse of her. Sonya was standing there in her radiant white dress as women swirled around her touching up her makeup and making sure her blond hair remained in place. Even at this distance, the sight was breathtaking. The flap closed and Lucas turned back to Adam.

But he was gone. In front of him, the guests had all disappeared as well, and the entire park was empty. The blue sky turned red, a nearby fountain evaporated in a hiss of steam.

Lucas awoke in a pod, a halo rising up from his head. Another memory, which he'd realized as he'd been living it. But again, the sound of Adam's voice and the breeze lingered for a moment before all traces of them faded. At least this thing wasn't necessarily a nightmare machine. That had hardly been a traumatic moment, though it was one that stayed with him. It was the last time he would see Adam before he shipped off to Afghanistan again the next day. At least the pod hadn't thrust him into the terrible day six months later when Sonya got a phone call and collapsed to the floor in a crying heap. Lucas's stomach knotted even thinking about it. Adam deserved better than to die in a desert during a conflict no one understood. Had he lived until the creatures showed up, no doubt he would have been leading the first retaliation strike force as soon as they opened fire. It would have been a slightly more noble death. As strong as he was, he wouldn't have survived in the world after the war. He had too much honor, and the wretched souls who remained would have killed him for it.

And Sonya. The memories were so vivid it was like he'd actually gotten to see her again, if only at a distance. Before the fights, before the tears. The day in the park had been fantastic, one of the best of his life. But reliving it? It pained him to see Sonya and Adam again, especially when they'd seemed so real. Even if it didn't constantly plague him with the horrors of his past, this machine was still dangerous.

The translucent door slid up and he found himself facing Asha in the pod across from him. She was visibly upset, and as she stepped down from the platform her legs buckled and she had to steady herself.

"How the hell did I get in that thing again?" she asked, her voice shaking.

Lucas's legs were a bit wobbly as well, and he reached out and grabbed a nearby pod for support.

"I've no idea. What's the last thing you remember?"

"That ship, the message, that light."

"Same here, then I woke up in a memory."

Lucas turned to notice one of the pods had been ripped out of the wall and placed horizontally on the ground. It was still connected to the wall with cables, but the door was shut, and the inside appeared to be filled with some sort of gas. A dark shape moved within.

"Holy shit!" Lucas exclaimed as he dropped to his knees, understanding what was in the pod. As he drew closer, he could see the door was trying to open, but the mechanism was stuck. He gripped it and pulled upward with as much force as he could muster, which wasn't a lot given that his arms felt as weak as his legs. Finally, the door popped open on his third try and the gas dissipated in an instant. In the gelatinous backing lay Noah, looking groggy but unharmed. He thrashed his hands and feet around and let out a large yawn. It was as active as they'd seen him. His burned arm and shoulder looked noticeably better.

Asha bent down to pick him up, and he threw his arms around her neck. But she was still scowling as she turned to Lucas.

"Where's Alpha?"

They found him on the bridge, sifting through a giant grid of symbols projecting from the central holotable. Asha marched up to him and set Noah squarely in the middle of the display.

"What happened?" she asked sternly. "Why did we all wake up in those nightmare boxes?"

Clearly her vision was far more jarring Lucas's his had been.

"I am pleased to see you are refreshed after your slumber," Alpha said, a baby now obstructing his view of the symbols.

"Our slumber?" Lucas asked. "How long were we in there?"

"A mere three days."

Three days? It had seemed like only a matter of minutes.

"I placed you in the [garbled] after our escape attempt. The intensity of the actions you performed caused your bodies to shut down when they were disconnected from the ship. The controls were not designed with your neurological systems in mind, and you lost consciousness immediately afterward following the prolonged combat experience."

"And what about him?" Asha said, motioning to Noah who was gazing up at the moving symbols all around him with a smile. It was the first one they'd seen him wear.

"The child insisted on constantly crying once you both were away. I do not know how to raise your young. Rest, medicine, and nutrients should have satiated him. The same is true for the both of you."

Nutrients, that's what the gas was in Noah's pod. And they'd been absorbing them as well. Lucas's stomach felt empty, but he wasn't hungry and despite some lightheadedness, he felt more energetic. He also noticed his leg and ribs barely hurt anymore. And Noah had been crying? That was a first.

"Why didn't we have to rest after the aerial village raid?" Lucas asked.

"That was a far simpler task. Escaping Earth and engaging the Sentinels required complexities far beyond that of the first assault, and your brains had to be stimulated to the point of collapse in order to be able to maintain focus."

Lucas remembered how his mind had raced to keep track of the controls, readouts, and array of monitors during the engagement. Asha likely had as much on her plate as she tried to shoot down dozens of fighters while traveling at a few million miles per hour.

"You regained consciousness in the [garbled] a day ago, but I kept you suspended for a while longer to ensure your full recovery. I would have thought you would be grateful."

"Those things . . ." Asha said. "They're not meant for us."

"More hallucinations?" Alpha asked, bemused.

"That's not what they are," Asha said coldly.

Lucas changed the subject.

"What happened to Omicron? What was that light?"

"The coordinates I gave you were the precise location of his ship's central power node. The missile barrage caught his defenses unaware, and hopefully disabled it for a period that will allow us to reach our destination without capture."

"How did you know exactly where their power source was? I couldn't even see a ship there at all."

"My father designed that vessel, and its cloaking system. It was built as a unique craft for the High Commander and presented to him as a reward for winning the siege of [garbled]. It is one of the most advanced units in the entire fleet, and we were fortunate to catch it off guard in the manner we did."

Noah was now swatting at the holographic symbols on the table excitedly. It was the most engaged he'd ever been with anything. It appeared the pod agreed with him, if not with them.

"He came all the way here to get you himself? And why didn't they just blow us up instead of hiding?"

"I have perhaps underestimated the significance of whatever my father did that brought about the destruction of my clan. The fact that we are alive implies they need to capture, not kill me. At least temporarily. Why, I do not know."

"I bet he'd tell you," Asha said. "If he wants to speak with you so badly."

"Perhaps, but I fear after I was informed and forced to aid them in some way, I would be executed or enslaved. And it is obvious you three would be expendable even if I was needed alive."

"We're an endangered species. Doesn't that count for anything?" Lucas said, half joking.

"It does not."

Alpha seemed to only have a sense of humor when it suited him.

"And where exactly are we?" Asha asked. The viewscreen was full of data and readouts, not stars or the celestial fabric of space.

Alpha swirled a switch next to the squirming Noah who reached out and tried to grab at his claw. The viewscreen's display was wiped, and a soft glow of blue, purple, white, and green light shone in front of them.

"You activated the core," Lucas said, though he'd already guessed it.

"I did, and yet we live."

There were no shapes to be found in the ether, just hazy patches of light. It reminded Lucas of the one time he'd caught a glimpse of the aurora borealis on a flight across Canada. Alpha swiped the controls again. The data reappeared and the hypnotizing display of colors vanished.

"And what about Omicron?" Lucas asked.

"It will take him some time to repair his ship. He will likely have to call for maintenance assistance and a new core which will set him back even further behind us. Though that does not mean he cannot catch us once we are out of [garbled]."

"Out of what?"

"You do not have a word for this state. How to describe it? The in-between. Space between space. We are on a path that transcends space-time, allowing us to travel great distances in a short span."

"And how much time is that exactly?" Asha asked.

Alpha paused for a minute to think. He brought up some data on the monitor, much to Noah's delight.

"In relative Earth-time, five months."

"Five months? We're stuck in this coffee can for five months?"

"Would you prefer five hundred thousand years?" Alpha replied with an audible snort. "Dilation shrinks the perceived time of the journey, but it will feel like a hundred and fifty-eight days to you."

Lucas realized now was the time to ask the question that had been dodged for a week now.

"Alpha, for the love of god, where are we going?"

13

After a long pause, Alpha spoke.

"We are defecting."

Noah was crawling dangerously close to the edge of the holotable. Lucas scooped him up before he got any further.

"Defecting? To where? To who?" Asha asked.

Alpha hesitated again.

"You may not be able to process this information. It is something we still do not fully understand."

"What are you talking about?" asked Lucas. Noah squirmed in his arms trying to get back to the table.

"I suppose it would be best to show you. To explain I must integrate the [garbled] language into my translator."

Alpha adjusted a few symbols on the tiny hologram protruding from his collar and then sifted through a few readouts on the table. Suddenly, a three-dimensional picture of a woman's head appeared. She was silver haired with fair skin and blue eyes and looked to be about sixty.

Lucas and Asha were confused.

"Who is this?" Lucas asked.

"Talis Vale, ruler of Sora."

"Sora?"

"Sora."

Alpha brought up a hologram of a large green and blue planet with unrecognizable continents surrounded by vast oceans.

Lucas understood.

"No . . ."

It was impossible.

"They're . . . human?"

Asha looked astonished as the stern-faced woman rotated slowly in front of them.

"'Soran' is what they call themselves, but yes. Your genetic makeup and biology is almost identical to theirs."

Alpha brought up a hologram of a cross section of two human males, though one was presumably Soran. Lucas scanned both but could see almost no difference between them. He only counted one kidney on the Soran, and two fewer ribs, but no other marked dissimilarities jumped out at him. Incredible.

"How is this possible?"

The hologram of the woman reappeared.

"A common ancestor presumably, though we have not been able to trace the exact location or nature of their origin."

Next to the woman, a smaller depiction of her planet spun in a slow rotation.

"This is who you're fighting your war against? More humans?" Lucas asked.

"Sorans, but yes. And it is a war that has plagued us for a long time. Too long."

He brought up another holographic sphere, this one was a dark red planet with only hints of blue and green. Lucas recognized it from the bridge of mothership.

"This is the planet the Sorans call 'Xala.' To us, it is [garbled]. It is my home."

Lucas couldn't tell if it was disgust or reverence that was in Alpha's black-and-gold eyes.

"The two planets are a mere ten trillion miles away, using your own system of measures. The proximity has allowed the war to be fierce and constant, but never truly winnable by either side. The conflict has raged for many millennia now, and is only growing more intense with the passage of time."

Asha finally spoke for the first time, having absorbed all the recent incredible information.

"Why are you at war?"

"At first it was to survive, but now, it seems the greatest motivator is purely revenge."

"Revenge? For what?"

"It is a story that's been passed down for generations. Many ages ago, the Sorans found our civilization soon after intergalactic travel across space-time was discovered. We welcomed their arrival and embraced their wondrous technology, which was ages ahead of our own. They called the planet 'Xala' and us 'Xalans.' In their tongue, the words mean 'strange' and 'stranger,' while 'Sora' means 'home.'"

Images were playing on the larger viewscreen now. It was a video of Sorans landing in a large spacecraft. They were dressed in bulky metal suits that covered every inch of their body, including their faces. They were greeted by Xalans, or creatures, as Lucas knew them.

"But as the decades went by, it became clear that our planet was more valuable than we were. Posing as friends, they siphoned off all our resources, including our most precious one: water."

A rich, lush planet onscreen slowly decayed into the red rock that was Xala.

"After a hundred years of being trampled, we decided to fight back. Our revolution was bloody and swift, and though we suffered huge losses, we eventually drove them from our planet. But the damage was done. Xala barely had enough resources to carry on, and the dwindling population had to make do."

The screen showed a wretched bunch of Xalans in a dilapidated city full of strange-looking buildings. The screen then jumped to scientists working in haphazardly constructed labs.

"It should have driven us to ruin, but it drove us to ingenuity instead."

"Wait," Asha interrupted. "Why did they need to take your resources and all your water? They've got oceans full."

"Yes, that is true, and more than you could know. Here is the actual scale of these planetary bodies."

He flipped a holoswitch back at the table and three planets appeared. Xala was small, a tightly packed ball of red. Next to it was Earth, a little larger, implying the dark planet was a touch smaller than Mars. But Sora? It was massive, a half dozen times the size of Earth at least, and looked to be comparable to a body like Neptune.

"Sora is resource rich, and they did not take our water. They destroyed it, along with negating the formation of the nearly all the clouds that would produce more."

"Why?"

"To prevent us from reaching their level of scientific progress. To avoid us becoming a threat by unlocking the mystery of cross-system and intergalactic travel."

"What do you mean? What mystery?"

"Water. There is a reason finding the resource in large quantities across the universe is so exceedingly rare. Combined with a certain synthetic element, which your race had not yet discovered, it is a power source far more incredible than any you could ever imagine and has the ability to open a rift in space-time when utilized properly."

"Water? This ship, and all your ships, are powered by water?" Asha scoffed. Lucas thought of the tanks below in his makeshift quarters.

"I know of your planet's scientific history. You were likely a long ways off from discovering the process for yourselves, if you did not destroy each other first."

"No, you did that for us," said Asha coldly.

Alpha ignored her.

"I do not expect you to believe what I am saying, or understand how the process works, but I assure you, it does."

Water. The idea was preposterous, but suddenly something became clear.

"Our oceans. That's why you came here. That's why you invaded us. You needed our water to help fight your war."

Alpha nodded.

"Eventually, despite a lack of resources, our scientists discovered the process to create the cores needed for long-range travel. When the Sorans learned we had invented the technology, they returned to attempt to wipe us out entirely. But we were ready."

The screen showed an enormous space battle with types of ships Lucas had never seen before firing at each other.

"We held against the onslaught, but knew we could never best them completely with our homeworld's now limited resources."

Alpha paused, and then brought up the bust of a Xalan on the holotable.

"My clan was gifted with intellect, and generations ago, my ancestors were responsible for the research that eventually allowed us to travel further and further out into space. Technology that the Sorans did not even possess. We were able to find other habitable planets with resources near our region of the galaxy. Not many, but enough to help fuel us in our ongoing struggle."

A litany of worlds were flung up next to Sora, Xala, and Earth on the holotable. A few had large areas of blue, but were quite a bit smaller than any of the others. The ones that were close to Earth's size had far less water, and were almost entirely brown with only select patches of blue.

"When we arrived, we were amazed."

He brought up another video feed on the main viewscreen.

"More Sorans."

The archival footage showed a group of dark-skinned tribal humans clutching elaborately carved spears and wearing armor made of bark.

"It was not until we annihilated them that we knew they were not tied to Sora at all. The same species simply existed on planets across the sector. We lay siege to all of them, and not one put up a fight. How could they?"

The viewscreen showed an astonishing sight. Playing were five separate videos of battles that showed Xalan ships and soldiers raining fire on human civilizations. A planet spun in the corner of each feed, named by unidentifiable symbols. One showed the tribesman throwing spears at drone fighters, another was a medieval-looking castle under attack by spaceships. To the right, a large stone palace was crumbling as foot soldiers brandished swords and shields against hordes of creatures approaching in power armor. Next to that was an army of infantrymen wearing ornate metal armor, marching in formation while firing odd-looking mechanical guns and hoisting flags full of bizarre designs. The last viewscreen simply showed nude humans with matted, stringy hair waving wood clubs and flinging rocks at Xalan ships flying far overhead. The entire display was surreal.

"Their civilizations were infantile. Despite their biological similarity to Sorans, they possessed not a fraction of their technology. It was not a war, but a slaughter. Each new planet we discovered managed to fuel our conflict for another era. And then, there was 'Earth.'"

A familiar-looking globe appeared on the viewscreen as the battle scenes faded.

"Earth looked the way Xala once did, according to record. It had far more water than any habitable planet we had discovered and raided previously. It could have been the key to our ultimate victory, rather than the disaster it was."

The viewscreen showed a shot of the original creature ship hovering above New York.

"We underestimated your civilization's technological progress. Though your space travel capabilities were pitiful, we did not anticipate your ability to destroy. Imagine, a civilization that would willingly keep weapons that could annihilate itself a thousand times over. Incredible."

The screen flickered with battle scenes from the assault on Earth. Mushroom clouds erupted across the landscape as Xalan ships disintegrated.

"We sent reinforcements, but not enough, and not as quickly as we should have. Once we understood the full capability of your 'nuclear' weapons, and how they interacted with our own antimatter bombs, your planet was poisoned by the ensuing fallout."

"The clouds," Lucas said. "The water."

"All rendered useless in the aftermath of the war. Not only did we sustain heavy military losses, but we only managed to extract limited resources before they were corrupted completely. I do not know how the botched campaign was received back home, but I would imagine it has been a significant setback for the war effort."

"Just a minute," Asha said, her arms folded in front of her. "If you were discovering all these habitable planets, why didn't you just relocate there after mopping up the local wildlife? Why continue the war?"

Alpha brought up the five other planets beside Earth once more.

"This has been the subject of debate for many years now. We do in fact have colonies on many of these worlds, as they've helped to alleviate the issue of our rapid population growth. But the ruling council decrees that the war must continue until Sora is ours. The Sorans must not be forgiven for what they did to us, and their rich planet is the crown jewel of the galaxy, which they do not deserve."

"You don't sound like you believe that."

"My clan has always been wary of such claims. For generations we have worked for the betterment of the Xalan race, and war improves the lives of no one. While there is a sect that wishes for all our people to leave Xala and migrate to these new worlds, the ruling party, which has been in power for thousands of years, demands Xala hold firm as a military force to be supplied by the other planets. The vast majority of Xalans believe wholeheartedly this arrangement must continue. Our species has been battle-born for thousands of years and war is all we know. Pride has killed more Xalans than Sora ever did."

Intergalactic war that lasted millennia. A mammoth planet full of humans. Even with all Lucas had experienced over the past few years, it was a lot to take in. He understood why Alpha had needed a quiet moment to explain it all to them.

"Where do we fit into all this?" Lucas asked.

Alpha brought up the original hologram of the woman once more.

"We will go to Sora. I will offer Talis Vale all my knowledge of the Xalans and our military operations both on- and off-world. I also possess the knowledge that would allow them to travel further than they have ever been into deep space. I would be infinitely valuable to them."

"They'd raid your colonies," Asha said.

Alpha sighed.

"It is a risk I must take. The war must end, one way or another. Omicron and the council must not be allowed to continue plotting this course toward mutual destruction. The war may be ended without the annihilation of either side. I believe uncovering my father's research will be key to understanding the solution I seek. I believe it is why he was killed."

"And what about us?" Lucas asked.

"You will astonish them the way they have astonished you. They have not seen these other worlds, full of creatures like them. They know nothing of Earth. To learn they are not the only Sorans in the universe will undoubtedly be a shattering revelation, and they will want to hear everything you have to say about your world."

"And showing up in this Xalan hunk of junk, they're not just going to blow us out of the sky?" Asha asked.

"I hope they would be more curious than vengeful when they encounter as strange a phenomenon as two of their own piloting the craft in tandem with their enemy," Alpha said.

"You hope?" Lucas asked.

"Hope is the basis for this entire endeavor."

Lucas lay on his mattress in the water chamber, clad in new khaki cargo pants and a black T-shirt from the mansion. His head was still reeling from all Alpha had told them about Sora, Xala, and the eternal conflict they were now squarely in the middle of. Nearby, Noah was playing with the only toy that interested him. It was the disc Alpha had given Lucas when they'd gone into the mothership, and the child was waving his arms excitedly through the various maps and interfaces, giggling as they changed shape before him. Having broken out of his sullen state, Noah would certainly help to improve morale if he began to develop as a normal child would.

Lucas's quarters had needed some reorganizing, as even with the artificial gravity of the ship his stacks of books had been thrown across the floor during the Sentinel firefight, and Natalie had fallen off of her perch above his bed. He remounted the rifle and ran his finger through the gaping metal wound once more. It still pained him to see his old friend mangled so.

Lucas browsed through a data disc Alpha had given him after their chat on the bridge. It contained a large amount of Xalan-gathered information on their destination, Sora, and Alpha had advised the pair of them to study it closely. Thumbing through the basic information, he found the planet's vital statistics. Sora was about 40,000 miles in diameter, which dwarfed Earth's 8,000. It took the equivalent of 486 Earth days to orbit around the central star of its system, and the days were thirty-seven hours long.

There were thirty-five major continents and almost a hundred smaller ones, though the entire planet was governed by a singular ruling body. The total population was estimated by Xalan military officials to be around one hundred billion, with another five billion or so scattered across nearby planets and moons. They had forward military bases in other star systems on the way to Xala, but none of the planets were particularly hospitable, and as such they were merely used as stopovers.

The data packet was surprisingly light on Soran history. The tactical information was highly detailed, but in terms of the actual history of Sora as a society, not much was to be found. There was a sparse timeline that started with a brief note about the invention of interstellar travel with attached scientific notes Lucas didn't understand. A note said something about a machine uprising that didn't go into detail. After that was a huge chunk of time with absolutely nothing listed, and then suddenly the discovery and invasion of Xala appeared out of nowhere, with a litany of battles marking the many years after. The data file contained much to look through, but Lucas would have thought that the Xalans would know their enemies in and out and would have an infinite amount of information about them. Instead, there seemed to be pretty large knowledge gaps that didn't make sense for a race with such advanced technological capabilities.

Lucas tossed the data display over to Noah, who was delighted to have a second colorful plaything. Lucas thought of their own upcoming timeline. Five months aboard the Ark? It was barely a week ago that he reached Portland, and though he was growing more accustomed to his new extraterrestrial surroundings, it was still a long stretch of time, and the vessel was not that big. Stuck with a baby that had now figured out how to cry, a woman who had almost killed him on a few occasions, and an alien with an assumed death wish, it was going to be an interesting ride.

14

In their own personal tunnel through space-time, there was little to disturb them. Far from the whirlwind of the first week, the Ark and its inhabitants were now in a place of relative calm. No cannibals, no drones, no stealth cruisers or alien warlords. Their journey was no longer a race but merely a drift, outside the bounds of physical space. On the other side of the passageway they could find anything, but for now they were allowed some sort of reprieve.

It had been a few weeks since they'd activated the core and started the final leg of their journey toward Sora. Lucas had a routine down that kept him sane and healthy. He was slowly adjusting to the thirty-seven-hour clock of Sora, as Alpha told him that his twenty-four-hour cycle would hinder his ability to function there, and though it exhausted him at first, he found sleeping fifteen of the hours gave him enough energy to stay awake the other twenty-two. He kept to his appropriated mattress and sheets and hadn't dared go back to the pods for fear of what visions might plague him.

After he woke up and dressed in the water chamber, he ingested his first nutrient vial. As he and Asha refused to sleep in the pods, Alpha gave them portable inhalant devices that shot the nutrients straight into their lungs where they were then filtered into their bloodstream. It was almost entirely tasteless, but there was a musty iron smell that took some getting used to. Water was still plentiful, but a few of the tanks were starting to drain noticeably as the core drew on them for power. From the looks of it, they should have enough to last the months required, but the exact calculation of that fact Lucas left to Alpha.

When "breakfast" was over, Lucas began the first of a few workout regimens he'd crafted to help him pass the long, sunless days. Though there was no more solid food to be found on the ship since they'd gone through the last of the canned goods, the constant supply of nutrient packs allowed him to return to a healthy weight. By the end of his journey to Portland, he had wasted away to almost nothing, and he was lucky to be able to walk a few miles a day in the heat. But now, with proteins, vitamins, and whatever the hell else was flowing through his system, he did dozens of wind sprints down the metal grated hallway of the water chamber, aided by a pair of athletic shoes he'd looted from the mansion. When he was winded, he dropped and did as many military push-ups as he could manage, and the number was increasing daily. There was an overhanging section of the wall he managed to use for pull-ups, and it had taken him a week of recovery to even manage a pair of them. He cycled in various other isometric exercises he remembered from high school football camp decades earlier and would repeat variants of the routine two more times before the day was over.

After downing two full cylinders of water after his workout, Lucas headed upstairs to the barracks to check on Noah. The prison cell nursery had been abandoned when it became clear that Noah loved sleeping in the pod Alpha had laid out for him. He slept soundly through the night, every night, which was stunning for a child his age. Lucas assumed he took to the pod because he had no real memories that could haunt him. The system was a godsend as it allowed him to wake up rested, fed, and happy each morning, and the gaseous nutrients meant few messy diapers. On this particular day, Lucas brought him a new holographic toy Alpha had thrown together in minutes. It was that the size of a tennis ball and had colorful symbols that shot out of all sides when it was touched. Lucas threw it up in the air and the symbols disappeared, and when he caught it, they immediately sprang out again, which pleased Noah greatly and he reached for it with outstretched arms. His burns had continued to heal, but Alpha warned that without more advanced medical supplies, they would likely never fully disappear, and the child would be permanently marked by his former planet. After handing him the ball, Lucas stepped over the welded storage cubes that made up a makeshift playpen, and the child remained enraptured by his new plaything.

Alpha had been spending a large amount of time in the lab, which was now unlocked as he didn't mind visitors while he was working. Lucas supposed Xalans craved interaction like any other creature, and Alpha was doing his best not to fall back into isolation the way he had been before the pair of them came along. Lucas was glad for the company as well.

"What's the project today, Alpha?" Lucas asked as he came in through the main door. Though the lab was always open, the door across from it remained permanently locked.

"Something that should prove useful when we reach our destination," he replied. He didn't have his power tools out today, but rather was programming something onto a small chip like the one Lucas had used for holotraining.

"What is it?"

Alpha held up his hand, the chip levitating a couple of inches above it. Lucas still didn't understand how it did that. Some sort of magnetic trick? He grabbed it from Alpha's outstretched claw.

"It is the entirety of the Soran language, translated into English. This program will help you master it, and you should be fluent in a short period of time. As should Asha."

He presented a second, identical chip.

"When we do finally make contact, I imagine the Sorans would be far more receptive to you if you know the language 87.3 percent of their people speak."

Lucas left Alpha to his tinkering and headed up a level to the armory, where Asha was sure to be found. He entered the large room and found a familiar sight: her reassembling yet another one of their confiscated cannibal weapons.

"Don't you ever get tired of that?" Lucas asked.

"Keeps me sane," she said, not lifting her head to acknowledge his presence. She was wearing a dark green tank top and a pair of white cropped pants streaked with grease. And she was barefoot, as usual. She too had been regaining some of her lost strength, and was not as rail thin as she once was. Her arms looked noticeably more muscular, and he'd seen her bench pressing storage cubes on occasion when he came by to visit. She never asked for a spotter.

The room was far more organized than when Lucas first came across it. The guns they'd taken from the village had all been carefully cleaned and organized by caliber, matched with appropriate ammunition that filled cubes on the ground. The three sets of Xalan power armor they'd taken hung on racks with the energy weapons propped up next to them. Though they'd all been meticulously polished by Asha, none of them were working as they hadn't yet gotten Alpha's attention.

Lucas tossed the chip at Asha, who caught it instinctively.

"What's this?"

"Time to learn how to speak Soran."

Asha rolled her eyes.

"We have to learn their damn language? I already speak Hindi and French. Can't Alpha just make us a pair of those translator necklaces?"

Three languages? Lucas had almost failed out of AP Spanish in twelfth grade.

"You really want to sound like a robot like him? Besides, what else do you have to do?"

Asha looked down at the gun she was rebuilding for the fourth time.

"Alright," she said.

She stood up and walked past Lucas toward the far side of the room.

"While you're here, come take a look at this."

She picked up a heavy cube full of ammo and set it on the ground. It had been sitting on another, larger storage device. One with a holographic lock on it.

"I found this hiding in the corner here once I finally got this place sorted out. I've tried everything under the sun with those controls and I cannot get it open."

A few bullet indentations near the display indicated she'd tried more than just sifting through the lock's display. A machete lay on the ground next to the cube, snapped cleanly in half. Lucas had become more accustomed to the design of Xalan displays, but as he attempted to unlock the container, he was met with multiple flashes of angry red. He couldn't translate the symbols that appeared when he failed, but he understood their general meaning, warning him to back off.

"I've no idea. You should ask Alpha."

She sat down on the cube and put her feet up on another container nearby filled with belt-fed light machine gun ammo.

"I'm wondering if he's the one who put it there. If his friends cleared the place out before they abandoned ship, why wouldn't they have taken it with them?"

Lucas didn't have an answer to that.

"Anyway," Asha said. "I'm going to go check on the kid."

Over near her bed was a floating monitor that showed a view of Noah rolling around in the barracks. Lucas had a similar display in his own quarters that he could bring up to keep an eye on him.

Asha marched out of the room before Lucas could say another word, and there was more grease on the back of her pants than the front. Their relationship wasn't what Lucas would call "friends," but they were getting dangerously close to "colleagues" as their recent battles had forced them to pull together and, at the very least, allowed them to trust each other to a certain degree. In the weeks after their brief moment of personal revelation about her harrowing childhood and his lost son, they hadn't talked much about themselves, sticking to the safe topics of the Ark, Alpha, Noah, Xala, Sora, and intergalactic war.

Lucas arrived in the CIC and stared at his primary source of entertainment these past few weeks: the captain's chair. With over twenty hours a day to kill, he'd finished his combat flight school holotraining, completing all thirty-three levels of the program for the Ark's ship class. Even when unplugged, his brain whirred with flight formations and intercept tactics. Growing tired of attempting to best his highest scores in the simulator, he thought about trying to learn how to fly a virtual fighter instead of a transport, but at the moment he had a new program to investigate.

The chip flew immediately into the console when he released it and familiar cables sprung out and attached themselves to his temples. The rush of information was something he was slowly getting used to, but this was his first experience with an entirely new type of program. There were no virtual spacecraft or foreign moons to fly around, rather his field of vision exploded with a countless array of geometric symbols. It took him a moment, but he began to understand what he was looking at. The Soran language.

A voice began speaking in English, and he was stunned to find that it was actually his own.

"Welcome to basic Soran," it said calmly, sounding exactly as he did.

Lucas was puzzled, but then something clicked and he understood. With no other English speakers around, Alpha must have taken a speech sample from one of their many conversations and used some sort of editing technology to allow him to say anything he wanted. He programmed it as a virtual guide for Lucas, as surely the lesson would be easier when he could already hear himself speaking the unfamiliar words. All he had to do was copy.

An hour or so with the audio tutorial and Lucas thought he was getting the basics down quite well. The language didn't sound like any he'd heard on Earth. It wasn't as slow as an American drawl, nor as intense as Japanese or Chinese. It lacked the flow of any Romance language, nor did it have the unpronounceable sounds of Arabic or African tongues. It was entirely unique, but Lucas, aided by his own voice, was learning to assemble simple phrases with ease. It was that good old neural stimulation at work again, allowing him to process information at lightspeed, but he wondered how much he could retain when the program was shut down.

The tutorial broke from its audio lesson and turned to a visual representation of the language, the geometric symbols from earlier, which looked far different than the Xalan words scattered through the ship. These icons were clean and organized while Xalan was more primal and almost hieroglyphic. As virtual Lucas talked actual Lucas through the layout of letters and words, he began to understand. Each sound corresponded with a shape. An "o" sound was a square, a "u" a circle, an "a" a triangle, and so on. Non-vowel sounds had more complex shapes. When they were combined into a word, the different sound shapes assembled themselves into one complicated glyph. If you knew what each shape meant, you could read the word. It took Lucas far longer to catch on to this system than when he'd heard the language audibly, but after a few hours, he was creating his own symbols by drawing them in the air, his finger turned into a virtual pen by the program.

Eventually he grew tired of the sound of his own voice droning on about the intricacies of Soran grammar, and spent another hour trying to top his best score in the particularly difficult level twenty-eight transport training exercise that required him to dodge enemy ships while weaving through a canyon only a few meters wider than his craft. He had to decrease his speed to not crash, but too often he would slow down so much that his overall marks would suffer because of it. Having just shot down two fighters on his tail, he was on pace for his best score yet, but a surprise blast into the side of the canyon wall caused him to lose focus and clip a nearby rock pillar. The damn program changed each time he ran it, and there was never any predicting what would happen next. He spiraled out of control and felt a familiar jolt of pain when his ship was dashed into a million pieces on the red rocky surface.

"Goddamnit!" he said audibly, and shut down the program in frustration. He got up from the chair and paced around, but soon his anger subsided. Even after using the chair for hours, he wasn't nearly as fatigued as he used to be, and he assumed his body was forming some sort of bridge with the device. His neurological system was growing accustomed to the virtual stimulation.

Thinking back to the language program, he tried to remember what he'd learned. Surprisingly, he discovered much of the information had stuck, and he started spouting Soran phrases out loud in the CIC.

«My name is Lucas.»

«Where are you from?»

«Do you have any water?»

«How do you get to the spaceport?»

«Death to Xala!»

The words coming out of his own mouth sounded bizarre, but he could at least process what he was saying. He wondered if the Sorans would be thrown off by his assuredly American adaptation of their language.

«Impressive,» Lucas heard from behind him.

Alpha was standing there, his spindly metal claw tapping on some controls.

«Thank you.»

Lucas reverted back to English, as after a few hours he imagined he couldn't carry on an actual conversation in Soran yet.

"Yeah, it's not too bad."

"The program is satisfactory?" Alpha asked.

"So far, though it's a little off-putting that I'm my own teacher."

"I figured the voice most familiar to you would be the best option."

Lucas thought briefly that he might prefer having Asha's voice relay the lessons to him, but he kept the idea to himself.

"Oh," Lucas remembered an earlier question. "We found a sealed box in the armory. All the other crates have been stripped, but this one is locked up tight. Do you know what it is?"

Alpha shifted, then responded after a pause.

"No. I know the object of which you speak, but it is above my clearance to open. I have tried myself, but the mechanism is too secure."

"And the room across from your lab?"

Alpha didn't look at Lucas when he answered.

"Yes, the same security measure is in place there as well. It would be best to not tamper with it, as it could prove dangerous."

Something was odd about Alpha's tone, but Lucas didn't press the issue further.

"Noah says thanks for his new toy by the way."

Alpha looked surprised.

"The child speaks now?"

"No, no, it's a figure of speech."

"I see," said Alpha. "It took a mere minute to build. It is pleasing to see him take to foreign technology rather than childish artificial animals and the like."

"Every kid should have a stuffed animal or two."

Alpha kept tapping on the console.

"The norms of your world are no longer relevant. If the child is to survive, he will have to be strong from an exceptionally young age."

Lucas thought of Noah's likely permanent burns.

"Well, he's not off to a bad start."

After another pair of workouts, a few more hours of Soran, and a game of "fetch the holoball" with the now fast-crawling Noah, Lucas was off to bed in the water chamber. He liked to read actual, physical books before he attempted over a dozen hours of sleep. It was a nice reprieve from the constant flood of technology everywhere else onboard. He'd polished off the Harry Potter series in a week and finally understood what all the fuss was about, though he was a bit miffed that Potter didn't end up with Hermione Granger in the end. Now he had started on *The Picture of Dorian Gray*, and was wishing that he'd managed to find some CliffsNotes in the mansion library as well, as it was quite a bit more dense than a tale about wizard school.

Thumbing through the pages to see how long until the current laborious chapter ended, he glanced up at the monitor, which showed a closed glowing pod on the ground where he'd placed Noah a while earlier. He was about to look back down to his book, but did a double take as he saw Asha enter the room. She bent over Noah's pod briefly, but then stood up and began examining the others on the walls. *What is she doing?*

Much to Lucas's surprise, she stepped inside one of the pods and a halo descended onto her head as the door closed in front of her. Lucas was perplexed. She'd hated the machines and had looked even more chilled than him each time she'd emerged from it. Why would she willingly go back to them now?

The question bothered Lucas until he finally drifted off to sleep where he had dreams he would barely remember. In one of the stranger moments, he found himself floating in empty space, a brilliant supernova erupting in front of him. A black, shimmering ship shot out of it and raced toward him. A voice could be heard from within, but it wasn't growling. Rather, it was speaking in broken Soran.

«You . . . do not . . . belong.»

Omicron's ship hung there in space with the supernova's light refracting off its hull.

«Return . . . to your . . .»

The voice was growing fainter. A whisper.

«Your dead . . . world.»

Lucas turned behind him and saw Earth. The all-encompassing cloud cover had dissipated, and only a husk remained. A scorched red and brown planet without a hint of blue, white, or green. Against his will, Lucas began speeding toward it. He blasted through space at speeds he couldn't comprehend and surged toward the outline of North America. He fell to Oregon. To Portland. To the crater.

Lucas woke up in a sweat, but the dream didn't stay with him for long the way pod memories did. After a fresh tube of nutrients and a vigorous workout he'd forgotten all about it.

What he did not forget was what he'd seen last night, and when he woke up, the monitor showed only Noah crawling around. The pod Asha had been in was empty. He confronted her about it in the armory, where she sat reading her old copy of *Paradise Lost*.

"Yeah, so what?" she said dismissively, not looking up from her book.

"So I thought you hated those things."

She casually turned a page.

"I haven't been sleeping well, and those nutrient packs taste like ass. Despite its . . . flaws, the pod gives you way more energy and the nutrients you need for practically the entire day."

Her messy hair and eyes laden with dark circles didn't make it look like the pod had helped her recharge all that much.

"Why do you care anyway?" she asked, finally glaring at him.

"It just seemed odd, given what those things can do to us."

«Mind your business,» she shot back in Soran. Lucas was momentarily caught off guard.

"You spent some time with the program?"

She put down her book and turned toward him, happy to be rid of the pods as a subject of conversation.

"Yeah, in the turret yesterday."

Her turret had all the same capabilities as Lucas's chair in terms of running simulations. He had seen a similar-looking one in Alpha's lab as well.

"Did yours have you teaching yourself?" he asked.

"Yeah, it's a little creepy."

Lucas got up to leave, but stopped.

"Oh yeah, I asked Alpha about the box. Claims it's above his security clearance. Same with that room outside his lab."

"And you buy that?"

"Nope."

"Yeah, like the genius son of a super-scientist doesn't have that clearance, or can't hack through it. He's hiding something."

"He's always hiding something," Lucas mused. "But we're still alive, so I'll let him have a secret or two."

As Asha left for her turret, Lucas headed upstairs for another day of Soran lessons. This time he stayed in for almost eight hours, and by the time he came out, even his thoughts were in Soran for a solid twenty minutes after disconnect. He gave the alien fighter variant of the flight program a try and found it to be far more intense than his transport training. The smaller ship was capable of much higher speeds in close combat, and was infinitely more maneuverable than his present craft. At first he died so often than he almost passed out from the amount of pain he was receiving as punishment, but slowly he began to correct his errors and managed to pass the first four stages by the skin of his teeth.

His nerves needed a rest, and he closed down the simulation and brought up the various monitors linked to different parts of the ship. Alpha was in the water chamber, noting the various levels in the tanks on an electronic pad. The next view of was of the armory, though only the front half of it as Asha had smashed the second camera that showed the rear of the room where her quarters were. A fair attempt at some privacy, but Lucas hadn't bothered to do the same in the water chamber. Lucas was surprised to see Noah crawling around the storage cubes. Despite Asha's concession that the child should be saved, she didn't usually spend all that much time with him. Lucas saw him shaking an assault rifle magazine like a rattle, so perhaps that wasn't necessarily a bad thing. But at least she was taking an interest.

That night, he watched her crawl into the pod again as Noah slept, and when he woke, she was gone. This pattern repeated itself for several nights until one morning he awoke and found her pod door still shut. After his morning workout, he returned to the monitor and found the same scene, despite the fact that Noah had crawled out of his own pod an hour earlier and was busying himself with his colorful techno-toys.

Lucas went up to the barracks to investigate, but when he got there, found Asha stepping out of the pod looking exceptionally disoriented, breathing rapidly. She jumped when she saw him in the room.

"What the hell are you doing here?" she asked angrily.

"I was about to ask you the same question," he replied. "This doesn't look like it agrees with you."

"Some nights are better than others," she said as she rubbed her bloodshot eyes. Noah rolled his metal ball toward her foot, but she didn't even notice it. Instead, she turned and walked out of the room without another word. Lucas looked cautiously at the open pod next to him. He picked up Noah and headed to Alpha's lab.

"I have an idea," Lucas said as he reached the laboratory a floor down.

Alpha was working on some sort of device that Lucas couldn't decipher. It looked like a cross between a lamp and a dehumidifier.

"And what is that?" Alpha asked.

Lucas put Noah down on the table, and he immediately began crawling toward Alpha's project. In a few seconds, he pulled a piece of fragile machinery off. Alpha sighed and calmly used his good claw to slide the child a few feet away across the metal surface of the table. In the past few weeks, Noah had grown increasingly curious about Alpha and treated him the way a child on Earth might a Great Dane. Alpha had initially snapped and demanded the child be kept confined so as not to interfere with his work, but over time he seemed to warm up to Noah and was becoming more tolerant of him by the day.

Lucas continued.

"If the chair speeds up neural functioning in Asha and me, would it do the same for him?"

Noah was crawling back toward Alpha, but reacting swiftly, he shoved a blinking metal disc at the child. Noah was quickly enraptured by the glowing lights and progressed across the table no further.

"The thought had not occurred to me, though I suppose it would be possible. The programs would have to be far less intensive, and he should only stay connected for a brief period of time."

"Do you think it would make him speak and walk more quickly?"

"Speech, perhaps. Mobility is more a factor of muscle development however, and it would likely have little effect."

Alpha was perhaps wondering if more mobility would be a good thing for the already fast-moving child. Lucas imagined it might compound the trouble he could get himself into.

"It is indeed how we train our young, and as such, they develop cognitive reasoning and logic skills quite quickly. Human biology is not used to such technology, but perhaps if the child was trained in its use at a young age . . ."

Alpha escorted Lucas to the bridge, happy to be out of his cramped lab. Lucas set Noah in the chair as Alpha tinkered with the Soran language chip, which he'd plugged into his mechanical wrist. Noah squirmed in the chair, but calmed down when Lucas produced his holoball.

"I've crafted a basic speech program that is below even the basic levels that you utilized. I have programmed in Asha's voice. Your scientific texts have shown children respond better to their mothers."

Lucas was a bit miffed, as the absent Asha wasn't even around to witness this, nor had she come up with the idea. In fact, over the past week, she'd barely paid any mind to Noah at all. *She's no mother.* The state she was in that morning indicated she could barely even take care of herself.

Alpha finished his tweaks and the chip flew into the console. Cables attached themselves to Noah's head and he looked momentarily shocked. He began to show a little fear, and was almost about to cry when suddenly the program lit up the space in front of him. He calmed down immediately and let out a large chuckle that made Lucas grin. The kid did love his holograms.

Alpha monitored Noah's brain activity as Asha's voice guided him through basic Soran words like colors and numbers, which were universally recognized entities it seemed. A discussion had taken place about whether or not to have him taught English, but Alpha maintained he could pick that up from them, and Soran was the priority if he ever hoped to have a future, should they survive this journey.

After about a half hour of an Asha-voiced lesson full of bright colors and soothing sounds that seemed to hypnotize Noah, Alpha signaled Lucas to shut the chair down. As the display disappeared and the cable retracted from Noah's tiny head, he looked around confused, wondering where all the fun had gone. His mouth started moving, and Lucas and Alpha watched in anticipation.

But no words came. That would have been too much of a miracle. Alpha checked some readouts.

"His cognitive functioning is above average. Despite no external result, the session seems to have agreed with him. Repeat daily, and perhaps you will achieve what you seek."

Alpha sounded like a pediatrician prescribing ear infection medication.

"Alright little man, playtime's over," Lucas said as he scooped Noah up off the chair. Alpha returned to his lab, and Lucas took Noah back to the barracks, but not before he brushed past an irritated-looking Asha in the corridor. She didn't acknowledge their presence, and looked equally as unkempt as she had when she stumbled out of the pod earlier.

After dropping Noah off in his cobbled-together playpen, waiting briefly for him to say anything other than babbling nonsense, Lucas headed back up to the bridge. The promise of hours of virtual training stood before him, but he forced himself to do a hundred pushups before he plugged himself in. It was a constant struggle to stay in shape confined in a relatively small vessel, and the chair required hours of motionlessness. As stimulating as it may be for the brain, it was in no way a physical workout. Lucas's chest burned during numbers ninety through a hundred, but he was impressed with how far he'd been able to come in a relatively short amount of time. He was able to run more windsprints than ever, and do double the amount of strength exercises he could a week ago.

He collapsed onto the metal floor, then pulled himself up into the chair where the cables found his head. He was determined to figure out how to fly this damn virtual alien jet fighter, and he'd stay in all day until he could master it.

And that he did, peeling himself off the chair fifteen hours later. The vast majority of it had been spent in flight sim, and only a few were devoted to any further Soran instruction. He still had another four months, and figured there was plenty of time as he was picking up a large amount of the strange tongue already. His body told him that he'd overdone it in the simulator, and couldn't even muster up the strength for his nightly workout. He told himself he'd make it up by doing an extra one tomorrow.

As he crawled into bed, the monitor showed Asha's now frequently used pod closed already with Noah's unit also shut on the ground alongside it. He thumbed through about five pages of *Dorian Gray* before he passed out with the book on his chest. He was too exhausted to dream.

What seemed like minutes later, he awoke and tiredly pulled his wrist over his head as he lay on his mattress. Alpha had built him a makeshift watch based on the thirty-seven-hour clock, which had proved to be essential since it was almost impossible to tell time any other way. The tunnel of space-time had no rising or setting sun, and his body's internal clock couldn't be trusted any longer. He glanced at the barracks monitor and saw that while Noah was crawling out of his pod, Asha once again remained in hers. He didn't feel the need to go extract her, as despite him being a few years her senior, it wasn't his responsibility to regulate what she did on the ship. She was always quick to remind him of that fact.

Lucas surprised himself by being able to complete a number of handstand pushups, leaning up against the wall. Despite a lack of solid food, the so-called nutrients really were boosting his physical prowess. After only a month he reckoned he was in the best shape of his life. It was a strange feeling. He had been on the verge of death such a short while earlier, and he almost felt foreign in his own newly powerful body. Noah too was looking healthier than ever, and even Alpha seemed to have a new sort of shine to his usually dull gray skin. The only crew member who had looked worse for wear was Asha, as after a stint of regaining muscle, she had now wasted away. The pod seemed to be atrophying both her body and mind.

Lucas found Alpha doing some work at the holotable on the bridge. He was zooming through planets and star systems too quickly for Lucas to process. The speed of his gestures looked a touch panicked.

"Everything alright?"

Alpha looked up, startled. He quickly waved the images away and a host of Xalan symbols appeared.

"Yes, yes, just working on some . . . calculations. What are you doing up here?"

Lucas cocked his arm to hold up his watch.

"Chair time."

He strolled over to his usual seat, but turned to Alpha.

"Do you think you could put any other languages on here?" he asked, holding the Soran chip out.

Alpha was bemused.

"Other . . . languages? For what purpose?"

"Yeah, Xalan for one. I know that I'm never going to speak it, but it might be nice to know what the hell everything says in this ship. The English translations are pretty rudimentary."

Alpha considered the request.

"Alright. I will work on something."

"Oh also," Lucas added, "a virtual Norwegian dictionary would be nice too."

"It is bizarre you would request to learn an extinct language," Alpha said, confused.

"Can you do it?"

Alpha threw up his claw in surrender.

"Very well."

He shut down the holotable completely.

"I must retire, there is much work to do. Do not over-exert yourself with simulation."

Alpha started walking out the door. He spoke with his back still turned.

"You will not be needing to fly a fighter any time soon."

Lucas swore he heard a mechanical chuckle as the scientist left the room.

Alpha's parting words got to him, and he spent most of the day diving headfirst into his Soran chip, determined to master the language faster than Asha. He wasn't sure if she was continuing her sessions in her present state. The tutorial was growing more and more grammatically complex, as were the attached geometric words, but his fast-firing brain appeared to be keeping up. The program began glitching a bit when he ran into words that had no direct English translation. Many had to do with technology, and with no clear picture of the objects or concepts in question, it was a bit hard to process. The use of water as a power source was discussed, as was the element that was employed to make the kinds of cores they'd been accumulating on Earth, but it didn't have a pronounceable name. The computer simply subbed in the term "null" for the synthetic element.

From his readings about the Sorans, which Lucas brought up onscreen beside his lesson, null cores of all shapes and sizes powered every bit of their technology from household lighting to starships. The more powerful the core, the more transmuted water it needed and the more refined the null element had to be, an expensive process. A null core's color indicated its power, and practically the entire rainbow spectrum was classified. Blue, which was what the Ark had used to get to Norway, was on the higher end, while white, their new power source taken from the mothership, wasn't listed at all. The null core was the technological breakthrough that the Sorans were determined to keep from Xala initially, but now both sides employed the technology that was driving the war into an eternal stalemate. But the Xalans had eventually developed cores more powerful than the Sorans, which had allowed them to travel further out in the galaxy and discover other inhabited planets like Earth. The Sorans didn't have a word for these types of super cores, and Lucas understood the significance of the glowing white object in their engine bay. It was a higher power variant, above anything the Sorans ever manufactured.

Lucas's head began to swim attempting to process all the technology that was millennia past anything he should be able to comprehend. The program was a language tutorial, not a science class, and even with neural stimulation he doubted he could even begin to process the concepts behind it all.

Still, Lucas was learning a great deal, and his brain seemed to be less fatigued by the influx of information he was exposed to every day. It appeared the journey had allowed him to not only recuperate physically, but mentally as well. Out in the wild, he was lucky if he managed two hours of sleep without waking up in a panic after all the horrors he'd witnessed. Here however, he was sleeping fifteen uninterrupted hours at a time.

After years of nothing but misery and despair, the ship felt like the closest thing Lucas had to a home since the war began. As his lesson ended, he wandered back to his quarters, saying complex phrases he was now able to put together.

«This ship was our salvation.»

«We were outnumbered a hundred to one in the battle.»

«My planet is dead, and my people are all but extinct.»

When he reached the water chamber, he collapsed onto his bed, his mind too full of Soran to effectively process any English books. He glanced at the monitor to find Asha already locked in her pod for the night, an hour earlier than usual. Thoughts of her fled from him as he drifted out of consciousness.

No talking ships or celestial events appeared to him during his long slumber, and when he awoke, it was as if he had just deactivated the lights moments ago. He swiped through his watch to kill the alarm that sounded vaguely like an ethereal air raid siren. 1500 meant it was time to start the day, but apparently everyone didn't agree with that. On the monitor, Noah was sleepily crawling out of his pod on cue, but Asha's remained shut. Lucas was half annoyed at her sloth, half concerned with her well-being. Though he'd likely hear an earful from her, he went upstairs to catch her when she came out and attempt to talk her out of her new sleeping quarters.

But when he reached the barracks, the pod remained shut. Even Noah was a bit unnerved, as he pressed up against the glass with his hands and tried to peer inside from the ground. Lucas didn't know how to open the pod from the outside, but as he was flipping through the half-translated menus, he found something disturbing. A timer.

53:08:16

53:08:17

53:08:18

These were hours. She hadn't left the pod in well over a Soran day.

"Shit!" he cried out, startling Noah. Lucas hurdled over the storage cubes boxing the child in and raced down to the lab where Alpha was soldering a chip.

"We have a problem," Lucas said frantically.

Alpha accompanied him back upstairs where he sifted through the readouts at the front of the pod. The timer reappeared, and Alpha quickly waved it aside as he found the control he was looking for. The manual override caused the door to raise, and a hiss of vaporized nutrients dissipated when the panel came up. Asha was slouched against the back wall as the halo lifted off her head. She was scrawny and pale, and her eyes remained shut. Lucas reached out to touch her arm. When she didn't react, he shook her, calling her name.

"Asha! Asha!" he shouted as he jostled her. "Is she alive?"

"Yes," Alpha said, checking the readouts. Her breathing was shallow but her chest was rising and falling ever so slightly.

Lucas put his hand on her shoulder and shook once more.

"Ash—"

Suddenly her eyes snapped open with a look he'd seen too many times before. She lunged at him and he was propelled all the way to a pod on the opposite wall. His head cracked the translucent door and his vision exploded into a brilliant array of stars. Her fingers raced for his eyes and he barely had time to grab her wrist and wrench her arm away. Lucas's other hand caught her throat instinctively, but he threw her backwards before he crushed her windpipe out of habit. Alpha caught her with his good claw and restrained her against the pod, his eight-foot frame towering over her. The fierceness in her eyes subsided, and she collapsed, sliding down the gelatinous surface behind her. Next to her was Noah, who was bawling at the turn of events. Lucas rubbed the back of his head and pulled his hand away to find it coated in blood.

"What the hell, Asha?"

She looked disoriented.

"But you were . . . I thought . . ."

The thought was left unfinished.

Alpha spoke next.

"It is clear that prolonged [garbled] use has adverse affects on human biology. I am deactivating the system for both of your biological signatures."

Asha's wild-eyed look returned.

"No! You can't!"

Lucas threw his arms out in front of him.

"What are you doing sleeping in these things anyway? You and I both know what they do. Why would you want to subject yourself to that?"

Asha sat with her knees folded and her arms crossed and covered in goosebumps.

"Because I want to see him," she said coldly.

"See who?"

"Christian."

The photo. The young man with the bright eyes and wide smile. Her ring.

"Impossible," Alpha said sternly. "I need to run some tests. Accompany me to the lab."

"No!" she yelled, her raised voice causing both Noah and Alpha to jump. Her eyes weren't wet, but her voice was cracking a bit.

"I haven't seen him yet. It's been mostly . . . bad things. But I know I will. Next time. Just one more time. There are so many memories . . ." Her voice trailed off.

"You can't do this, Asha," Lucas said sternly.

"These . . . memories you experience only serve to degrade your mental condition," Alpha added.

Lucas pressed her.

"I thought you were stronger than this."

That got her to her feet, and up in his face. Lucas's head was still throbbing as he braced himself for possible impact. Her green eyes burned with rage.

But she turned and stormed out of the room, kicking a formerly welded storage cube out of the way as she went.

15

After debating what to do with Asha, Lucas and Alpha agreed that keeping her confined was the best solution until she would allow Alpha to run tests on her, or they could effectively force her into compliance. The full extent of the damage to her psyche was unknown, but after the encounter that day, it was clear she was highly unstable. When she fled back into the armory, Alpha locked the door behind her. An hour later when she tried to leave and found she couldn't, she started yelling all sorts of vile threats and violently threw herself against the door. The problem was that the room they trapped her in happened to be filled with assorted amounts of weaponry, and extracting her was a risk neither of them wanted to take. Alpha set to work synthesizing a nonlethal toxin he would release into the room to knock her out, and afterward she could be analyzed at the lab. The hastily improvised compound would be ready by morning.

Lucas had trouble sleeping that night, disheartened by what he'd seen that day. He had felt he was growing closer to Asha, but now that seemed impossible as her mind had been corrupted by her search of a lost loved one. To Lucas, it didn't make her weak to search for Christian, even though that's how she had appeared. It actually made her seem strong. Surely she had to endure night after night of unimaginable horror just for a chance of seeing him again. Lucas however had been terrified from the beginning to relive any moments from his former life, good or bad. The disturbing things he'd witnessed in the last few years were scarring to be sure, but seeing Sonya or Nathan again? Feeling like they were still alive the way he'd seen Adam? The thought was too much to bear and was a journey he had been too scared to attempt, even before the psychological effects were made evident.

After a few hours of dreamlessness, Lucas awoke. The lights were still off in the water chamber and there was only the blue glow of the tanks. His eyes were out of focus, but as they adjusted, he felt a presence. Then he saw her.

A silhouette stood at the foot of his mattress, and this was no dream. He heard a click and Asha raised her Magnum. He froze.

"At last, you bastard."

Her voice was calm and cold.

"You thought you could hide in Alaska? You didn't think I'd find you here?"

The blue light illuminated the metal of the gun. Lucas raised his hand.

"What are you talking about? What are you doing?" he said slowly.

"Don't act like you don't remember me. How could you forget what you did? Are you really that much of a monster? You betrayed him, killed him in cold blood when he trusted you."

Lucas's heart was thundering in his chest.

"Asha, I know you, but this isn't Alaska, I didn't kill Christian. I'm Lucas."

Her tone remained icy.

"So you do remember me. And call yourself whatever you like; it makes no difference. Changing your name and denying your crime doesn't erase what you did."

Lucas's eyes darted around the dark room, trying to find a way out. Reason didn't seem to be on the table, as Asha was clearly in an entirely different place. She stepped closer and raised the gun.

"Asha, I'm—"

With his right arm, he whipped up the floating monitor that showed the view of the barracks. The hologram illuminated her face and showed her vacant eyes in the darkness. She glanced at the sudden apparition and it was enough to give Lucas the split second diversion he needed. He propelled himself up off his mattress and tackled her. The Magnum went off, sending a deafening echo throughout the chamber, and the pair of them smashed into the wooden desk, knocking it and all its contents loudly to the floor.

Lucas went for the gun in her left hand, but her knee found his mended ribs and the breath was knocked out of him. She whipped her right fist around, catching him in the throat, and breathing went from difficult to impossible. He rolled to his back, gasping for air, and she leapt onto his chest. Bringing the Magnum around to his face, he barely had the presence of mind to swat it sideways with his forearm before it fired again. The noise made his ears ring and he couldn't hear the sounds of the ensuing scuffle.

He launched his torso upward and managed to headbutt her cheekbone, which was all he could reach. It stunned her momentarily and he was able to shove her backward off of him as he scrambled to his feet. With her still on the ground, he swung a kick at her gut and heard the gun clatter to the floor. Wheezing, she searched the darkness for the weapon, but when Lucas came after her with another kick, she was ready. Asha grabbed his leg and twisted, and Lucas felt a surge of pain as something popped near his knee. She released her grip and then sprang to her feet, immediately whirling around to connect a roundhouse kick to Lucas's jaw.

Blackness was encroaching on his vision from the pain as he staggered away, and he focused his eyes in time to see her locate the Magnum on the ground. He stumbled forward, grabbing her wrist just as she pointed it toward him, and the gun fired again, this time blasting a hole in the water tank behind him, which began to bleed its precious contents out onto the floor.

"Asha, please. I don't want to . . ."

She raked her nails across his neck with her free hand, and Lucas was forced to counter with a pair of body blows. He summoned one final burst of strength as he lifted her from her feet, spun her around and threw her into a nearby water tank, which shattered from the impact. Water exploded out into the metal corridor as untold gallons coated both of them before pouring through the grating below. Something underneath them was apparently generating a large amount of heat and the water vaporized instantly and steam shot up through the grating, blanketing the room. Asha lay unconscious and soaking wet on the floor of the tank. Lucas fell to his knees in exhaustion, innumerable parts of his body in agony as fresh blood sprang out of injuries the water had just washed.

Suddenly the lights came on, and through the steam, a familiar-looking shape appeared at the end of the corridor. As Alpha saw what had transpired, Lucas watched him lose his usually calm and collected demeanor.

"No, no, no! What have you done?" he exclaimed as loudly as his translator would let him. Lucas struggled to catch his breath.

"She escaped . . . attacked . . . I had to . . ."

But Alpha wasn't listening. He sprinted over to the wrecked tanks, one shattered and one losing water rapidly out of a large hole the Magnum had blown through it. It was already about two-thirds empty. Alpha raced behind it and came back with a long, wide hose. He sealed it around the hole, and dragged the other end around to one of the tanks that was empty, but intact. Water began to pour into it, but the vast majority of the second tank's water had seeped into the grating. The other tank had lost the entirety of its contents mere seconds after Asha went through it. She remained motionless inside.

With the second tank secure, Alpha walked over to the ailing Lucas, sitting among his drenched books that littered the floor.

"How did . . . she get out?" Lucas asked as he shook from a sudden chill that ran through him.

"I am uncertain," Alpha said, still scanning the carnage around him.

"She's lost it. She thought she was in Alaska and that I was someone she was trying to kill back on Earth."

"We must go to the lab and attempt to make sense of this destruction," Alpha said, exasperated.

He walked over to Asha and pulled her out of the broken tank, avoiding any shards that might catch her. He slung her over his back the way he had when Lucas had knocked her out the first time in the desert, though considerably more of her blood was now streaming down his back.

"Follow me."

Lucas dragged himself upstairs and filled his wounds with the gelatinous fluid Alpha had used to heal them before. The scientist tended to Asha on a nearby table. Her arms and legs were restrained with metal devices, and a hologram of her brain appeared floating above her physical skull. Alpha examined it carefully.

"Prolonged exposure to the [garbled] has indeed induced deep psychosis," he said matter-of-factly, like he was looking at an unconscious lab rat.

"Can you bring her back?" Lucas asked. He winced while the gel hissed closed the claw wounds across his throat. His ears were still ringing from the close proximity gunshots.

"She will require an extended period of treatment and observation. I will keep her here until progress is made."

He attached two nodes to the side of her head. A large bruise was beginning to form on her cheek where it had met Lucas's fore-head. Alpha flipped a switch and the hologram of the brain showed certain sections lighting up colorfully.

"Good response," Alpha said.

"I didn't mess her up too badly, did I?" Lucas asked. She had lost so much weight and he'd gained so much muscle, when he'd thrown her through the tank she felt like she barely had any substance to her at all. But still, she'd put up quite a fight in her primal state, and he'd be seeing some bruises of his own soon enough, which would join his bloody scratches and possibly dislocated kneecap.

"She is injured and unconscious, but stable, and I will keep her sedated until I can repair the brain damage from the [garbled]."

"And you're sure you can do that?"

"Better equipment would help, as this is not a medical vessel. Hopefully I can build a few of the tools I am missing. Even our most rudimentary medicine is leagues beyond your homeworld's capabilities."

Lucas didn't think Alpha was being purposefully condescending, but if it meant Asha could be saved, it didn't matter. He was . . . frightened to lose her. A level of attachment to her existed that he wasn't even aware of until she lay mentally and physically broken before him.

Lucas didn't sleep much at all the next few nights, and his days were full of distraction. He routinely checked in on Asha in the lab, each time greeted by Alpha who maintained treatment was in progress as he attempted to try and rewire her brain with an unfamiliar electronic device. She was still sedated, and would be until the procedure was complete. Soon after she was deemed stable, the pair of them searched the armory footage to find that she'd stacked storage cubes up to the ceiling, pried open a loose panel with a blade, and dropped down into the hallway, Magnum in hand. Even impenetrable alien locks couldn't contain a crafty, determined, psychotic human.

Lucas kept his mind off of Asha by spending more time than ever in the chair. In between Asha's treatments, Alpha had programmed the chips Lucas had asked for. Learning Xalan symbols was straightforward enough, and the intricacies of the controls all around the ship began to reveal themselves to him. Their written language was much easier to comprehend than Soran, and their fifty-one-character alphabet was ingrained into his mind in only a few days. Words and phrases began to follow soon after, though his learning was limited to written word, as audible speech was beyond his biological grasp.

He also spent a bit of time with Norwegian, and found it much easier to learn than Xalan or Soran. The letters were ones he was familiar with already, and neural stimulation made retention a breeze. Unfortunately, the reason he was learning the now-deceased tongue had taken a bit of a beating during his and Asha's brawl. The cannibal chief's journal that he had taken from the mansion surely contained all sorts of intriguing insights into the mind of the man he'd killed, but water had soaked it to a degree where the vast majority of the ink had bled into illegibility. That night, Lucas tried to read a section that had been preserved.

It's been a week since we cut up the last creature in town. There is no more food, and scouting parties have turned up nothing but water in a month. The creatures were all the sustenance we had left, and now they too are gone. Another large raiding brigade flung themselves at the wall today, thinking we had supplies they could pillage. The men gunned them down quickly. There was talk of hanging their carcasses outside to ward off other invaders. Such ideas repulse me. We are not barbarians like them; why should we behave as such? With the world torn asunder, we still have a functioning village, a town of friends and allies. Though now that the food is gone, I wonder how long we will remain that way.

The ship looms ever present, cleaving the town, and the mansion, in two. I've been petitioning Aleksander that our best hope of survival is opening that ship. Who knows what untold supplies and edible creatures linger within? But after forced entry failed, they now just laugh at my attempts to unlock the vessel with reason. They believe, because of my size, that I am a brute, but they are mistaken. It seems only yesterday I was at university, extolling the virtues of space travel to a sea of eager young faces. How quickly things change.

Conscription forced me to fight, for whatever good it did. I remember watching the ship fall in our final stand, but what did it matter? The entire region was decimated. I declared my forced tour of duty over and decided to stay.

But now I hunger. Deeply. It's all I think about. It consumes my every waking moment. A week ago we caught Harvald chewing on meat. Red meat. A dead raider. We expelled him from camp immediately, but I fear that such behavior will only increase in frequency. What happens then? What do we become?

The rest of the entry became illegible, as did many pages after that. Lucas had to flip far forward to find a section where the Norwegian words were still visible.

I killed Aleksander today. He gave me no choice. I watched him sacrifice one of the older women, one without "purpose," so we may eat. Murdering our own for food? I couldn't allow it. Raiders and wanderers are one thing, a reality I was forced to accept despite it seeming to spring from my darkest nightmares, but our own citizens? Those we've been protecting all this time? Where does it end?

The only thing anyone in this town respects now is pure force. I shoved a spear through his eye in the middle of the town square, and no one said a word. Whether they are now with me out of belief in my cause, or out of fear, I do

> *not know, but I suppose either purpose will suffice. My first order was to send a larger party to head back to the mainland. They found a creature a month ago. Perhaps there is still hope further savagery can be avoided.*
>
> *The taste. It is mentally sickening, but physically . . . pleasant. This is what causes me the most anxiety. This was a line I swore I would not cross. What will we do next, in the name of survival? Is this life even worth living?*
>
> *The heat is growing unbearable. The endless clouds look angrier by the day. The ship's door stands there mocking me. I suppose with Aleksander gone, the mansion is mine. More time to spend with the door. It is our salvation, I am sure of it!*

More ruined pages, and Lucas flipped to near the end of the tome where he could read once more. The handwriting was harder to decipher, and it looked like it was written in a panic with shaking hands.

> *There's a conspiracy to kill me, I know it. I see it in Veigar's eyes. Well, his eye. He's the most educated, the most devious. He pretends to be my advisor, but I know the truth. The armor is almost complete. Once it's assembled and active, I will be invincible, and immune to treachery. I tested the gun on one of the women yesterday. It cooked her almost instantly, a useful tool. But now the weak are starting to thin out. Their sacrifice serves to keep the rest of us alive.*
>
> *The remaining women grow nervous. After the runaways this week, Olaf suggests we keep them in the church under lock and key. They deserve it. They don't understand the world now. The weak must make way for the strong. If this world is to survive, they must do their part to repopulate, though it seems few will do so willingly. How can they be so blind? So selfish?*

My son was born today. The ship speaks to me. It tells me he will be a legend. He is strong, healthy. I killed his mother, the pretty one from Oslo. Now she may not produce a rival with another. This angered Henrik, and so I killed him as well. We ate like kings that night.

As I look into my child's eyes, I know the world will return to its former glory on the backs of men like him. He is the first of a new generation, a new Earth. We will rule the world as gods.

The entry was marked eight months ago; Lucas's mouth hung open as he understood the implication. Noah. Though he did not know how many other children perished in the fire, the probability certainly seemed likely, and the child was big for his age. The mad chief's heir, playing with alien toys in the barracks upstairs. He would never know these things. His life needn't be burdened with a wretched history such as this.

The rest of the pages were a jumble of stained words and nonsense phrases as the chief lost his mind at an increasingly rapid pace. Lucas had seen prolonged flesh eating lead to similar conditions many times. He was shocked at how dramatic the transformation was in this case, however. A reasonable man, even a good one, turned into a monster in such a short stretch of time. Perhaps it was good Earth was dead, if men like that were all that remained.

Lucas closed the book and rubbed his jaw. One of his back molars was loose after Asha's kick, and Alpha had nothing for that onboard. He was the smartest being Lucas had ever encountered, but human dentistry was not in his skill set.

Dimming the lights with a specific wave of his hand, he fell into bed. Days later, he was still jumping at shadows after Asha's nocturnal assault. With Natalie cold and still, he was now sleeping with his sawed-off shotgun under his pillow. He had scoured the armory and found a few stray shells of rubber pellets. Should he have to forcefully deal with another Asha escape and murder attempt, he didn't want to have to blow an actual hole through her chest to stop her, even if she did have it coming at this point.

He dreamed in Norwegian.

When he saw Noah the next morning, he searched him for signs that might tie him to the chief. Resemblance was hard to gauge. The man had been so hairy he resembled a grizzly bear more than a human. And there was no telling what the mother looked like, and she might explain the fact that he wasn't a full-blown giant, content with being perhaps slightly larger than your average infant. But his eyes, they were the same rich blue as the chief's, which Lucas had seen in the man's final moments. It was true then. A truth that would stay buried forever.

Noah had been taking to his chair sessions with great enthusiasm, and the way his face lit up, it was clear the colorful symbols paired with Asha's narration were the highlight of his day. Lucas had taken him to see her the day before. Pawing at her face, he looked forlorn when she didn't respond. Today he was in a much better mood however, though no magic breakthroughs came when the lesson ended. The invented words he babbled still weren't any from Earth, nor any other planet they knew of.

After Lucas put him back in his storage cube–lined playpen, he headed down to the lab for one of his many daily visits. This time, he was stunned to enter and see her eyes open, staring straight up at the ceiling.

"She's . . . she's awake?" Lucas asked cautiously.

"No," Alpha replied. "She remains unconscious for the moment."

"But her eyes . . ."

"A necessary condition of this phase of the procedure."

The effect was unnerving, and Lucas waved his hand over her face. She blinked, but her gaze remained unbroken, looking past him to the lights of the ceiling. She was still wearing the bloodied clothes from the night of their fight and was starting to smell.

"She's filthy."

"It is not of importance."

"Maybe not to you, but she shouldn't wake up like this."

"Do what you will," Alpha said as he adjusted some controls near the device fixed to her head.

Lucas returned with a fresh pair of clothes he found in the armory and was relieved to find her eyes closed. He wasn't entirely sure the navy shirt matched the black pants, but they'd recently been steamed (the closest they could get to washing), and were leagues more sanitary than what she had on now. He swung by his own quarters to grab a worn shirt and a container of water.

Back at the lab, he soaked the shirt and started wiping away the crusted blood that coated parts of her body. Alpha had healed her wounds, which included many small cuts from the shattered water reservoir, but the blood remained behind. Lucas undid her restraints and peeled away her odorous clothes, leaving her sports bra and underwear in place as he already felt strange enough changing her in this state. He quickly wiped down the rest of her body, and could now see how much it had truly atrophied. Muscle gave way to skin and bone, and he could count every rib she had. He quickly dressed her in the new shirt and pants he had acquired. Tossing the clothes away, the stench was already dissipating. She looked gaunt, but less like a car accident victim after having been cleaned up. Alpha hadn't even noticed the process and shooed Lucas away to reattach the device to her head. The hologram of her brain reappeared, and began pulsating with light. Lucas could decipher a few of the Xalan symbols for a change. He could make out "cortex," "synapse," and "improvement." It sounded promising.

16

A day later, as he was sitting in the captain's chair, Lucas tore the neural cords from his head when he received a simple message from Alpha over the monitor.

"She is awake."

When Lucas arrived out of breath at the lab, he saw Asha still strapped to the table, cursing loudly. As she saw him, she broke her stream of profanities to release a more coherent thought.

"Can someone please tell me what the hell is going on?"

Alpha looked to Lucas.

"Attempt to speak with her. She will not listen to me."

Lucas went to her side.

"Calm down, Asha," he said forcefully.

"Why am I strapped to this thing and why do I feel like I've been beaten with a sledgehammer?"

She paused as she saw Lucas.

"And what happened to your face?"

Lucas touched his still-bruised jaw.

"This is your handiwork, and the reason you're strapped to the chair. Have you seen yourself lately?"

Asha looked down at her chest, which was peppered with small white scars that were still healing. No mirrors were present, so she couldn't see the giant bruise covering half her face. Lucas turned to Alpha.

"Memory loss?"

"None other than the escape and assault."

"What are you two idiots talking about? Let me out of this thing."

Lucas went over to Alpha's workstation and began typing on the virtual Xalan keyboard. Alpha seemed taken aback that Lucas knew what he was doing with the complex interface. A holographic monitor appeared and Lucas dragged it with his hand and placed it over Asha's head. A video began to play.

"You thought you could hide in Alaska? You thought I wouldn't find you here?"

Asha looked stunned.

"When did . . ."

"You killed him in cold blood . . ."

"I don't remember . . ."

"He trusted you."

The fight began, and Asha looked horrified as she watched herself attempt to blow Lucas's brains out with her Magnum onscreen. After she was thrown through the tank, Lucas stopped playback.

"What's the last thing you can remember?"

Asha was no longer heated, and responded quietly.

"The last few days have been . . . blurry."

"The last eight days you've been on this table. Alpha's been repairing the damage the pod did to your brain."

"God, I had no idea. It all just blended together. And I don't remember any of that," she said, motioning to the monitor by raising her chin, her only free body part.

"But everything else, your past, the ship, me, Alpha, Noah. You can recall all of it?"

"Yeah, where is the little guy anyway?"

"Probably chewing on a very important piece of machinery," Alpha said in a huff.

"He's been by to visit. He should be happy to see you."

Asha looked down at her body.

"What the hell am I wearing?"

It took about six more hours of tests before Alpha finally agreed to let Asha out of the restraints. It would be even longer until she was allowed back in the armory, and Lucas was relocating her personal effects to a detention cell on the lower level. She wouldn't be imprisoned there, but the door to the armory would no longer respond to her biological signature (the ceiling panels had been sealed as well), nor would the pods in the barracks. All had been deactivated completely, save Noah's, as the boy had been thriving in the device. Asha put up a fight about not having access to her beloved, well-polished arsenal, but when shown the assault video once more, she reluctantly conceded the point.

Lucas hunted through the armory for any scraps of her belongings he had missed. He discovered a few books lodged in the cracks of some ammo boxes, and then found himself staring at the locked container once more. He thumbed through the display and found that he could now read some of the words. "Danger" and "contaminant" were two that stood out. As he attempted to open it, the word for "NO" appeared in bright flashing red. *Well, that's straight to the point.* But now he thought better of opening it at all, with all those descriptors attached.

When Alpha finally cleared Asha to move freely about the cabin, she came down to see her new quarters where Lucas was still attempting to arrange her belongings throughout the small room. To avoid further anger, he'd even brought down her treasured Magnum, which rested on the center of the round table where she usually sat to read. Bullets, of course, were nowhere to be found.

"So this is what I've bought myself, huh?" she said as she glanced quickly around her new tiny living space, once originally meant to house Noah before he took to the barracks instead.

"Hey, this is generous. If our roles were reversed I'm pretty sure you'd have me living on the outside of the ship."

Asha paused. "That's probably true." She sunk down against the wall and came to a rest on her mattress.

"How do you feel?" Lucas asked.

"Fine. Really. Not insane, though I suppose that's what an insane person would say."

"To be fair, I thought you were crazy before this entire thing."

She scoffed, shrugging her shoulders.

"Look around, don't you think you'd have to be a little bit crazy to be where we are right now?"

Lucas sat on the floor as well, leaning up against the console that was meant to activate the light barrier that barricaded the cell. The scene reminded him a bit of their first conversation on the ship months ago, back when she was still just the nameless siren who left him to die in Georgia.

"You know, you don't look anything like him," Asha said suddenly, looking Lucas over as he sat across from her.

"Like who?"

"He called himself Roy, but who knows if that was really his name."

"Who was he? And . . . who was Christian?" Lucas pressed.

She tilted her head back against the wall and let out a long sigh.

"Christian and I were engaged. He was my favorite photographer. He could make me look better in his shoots than anyone else in the industry. Once we were together, I found he could make me not only a better model, but a better person as well."

She paused.

"Our wedding was set for a week after the first ship showed up. As you might imagine, that really threw a wrench in things, and we were desperately trying to get back to our families in California after being on set in North Carolina."

Asha hadn't started out her journey all that far from him, Lucas realized.

"When the war began, we were lucky to escape Charlotte alive. The city was wiped out almost immediately. Soon after, we joined a group, as most everyone did. Ours was about thirty deep, and led by Roy. He was short, stocky, and balding, someone you would never take for an authority figure. I still to this day don't know what he did in his old life. He wasn't military or police, but he spoke loudly and with confidence, and that's all it took to be a leader in those days."

Lucas disagreed with that statement, as he had been rather soft-spoken as his own group's leader, but he supposed at the time he did exude a sense of purpose. He remained silent and let Asha continue.

"Things got bad. People died. Roy wasn't so confident anymore. The West Coast was supposed to be annihilated, and he swore Alaska would be our salvation as the temperature rose each day under the red sky. But he was starting to lose it."

Asha walked over to the table and picked up the Magnum, checking to make sure it was indeed as empty as it felt. No snide remark followed.

"One night, when I was in the woods attempting to find usable firewood, he came after me. Told me he deserved me for all he'd gotten us through, for keeping us alive. He clawed at me and was stronger than he looked because he'd been hoarding much of the food for himself. I was weak and couldn't fight, so I screamed. Part of me wonders what might of have happened if I hadn't."

She stared down at the pistol.

"It happened so fast. Christian came running, and drew his gun immediately. His father's revolver that had saved our lives many times the past few weeks from humans and creatures alike. But Roy was quick, and without even re-buckling his pants, drew his own pistol. Both fired. Roy's shoulder blew apart. Christian took a round in the chest."

She stopped for a long time, and neither of them said anything. The Magnum's significance was clear now.

"I picked up Roy's gun from the forest floor. There was terror in his eyes as he looked down the barrel, but I couldn't pull the trigger. It was frozen. Or I was frozen. He ran away, clutching his wound. I heard him yelling to the rest of camp that he'd been attacked by bandits, and Christian and I were already dead."

She set the gun back down.

"But we weren't. Christian lived for a full day afterward. I couldn't move him, and the medical supplies were gone when the rest of the camp fled from the imaginary invaders. Toward Alaska. Christian didn't have any last words, because he couldn't speak. His eyes pleaded with me as he kept motioning to his gun with the only arm he could move. I told him I couldn't. No way. His killer got away, and he suffered until the end because I was weak. After that day, I was never weak again."

Lucas sat in silence.

"I'm sorry," he finally said. It was the best he could come up with.

"For what?"

"For how you lost him. When my own group was slaughtered, it was horrific, but I didn't know them, not really. I lost my family in an instant, thousands of miles away, and I didn't even know it. What you went through, I can see how it would change you. I can see why you'd follow a man like that to Alaska."

She sighed.

"I never saw him again, except in the pod. I had to relive that night, that entire next day. No first date memories, no New Year's Eve proposal. The pod wouldn't give me what I wanted, but I realize now, even if I did get to go back to one of those moments, it wouldn't last. I'd wake up and Christian would still be dead, and I'd still be on a spaceship a billion miles from home. The future is all we have now."

"He'd be happy you survived."

"I suppose he would."

"So what do you live for now, if not revenge?"

"I don't know. I guess I have to figure that out. What about you?"

Lucas thought of a response, but was interrupted by a large eight-foot frame at the door. Alpha was standing there with Noah seated in his good claw. It was the first time Lucas could remember seeing Alpha hold him, even if he was handling him like a piece of fruit.

"The child would have words," he said.

As Noah saw Asha, his eyes lit up and he waved his arms in her direction. Then suddenly . . .

"Ah-sha!"

Lucas's mouth hung open.

"Ah-sha!

She broke at last, and tears streamed down her face as she took Noah into her arms.

Lucas looked at the strange band before him. The woman, the child, the alien. He thought of what Adam had said to him in his final pod experience.

"It's not only about survival; you need something to be fighting for."

He would fight for them.

17

Lucas slept soundly for the first night in a week, plagued by no further visions of shadowy figures near his bed. Asha truly seemed healed, and it was miraculous what Alpha had done over the past week with her mind. Had she undergone such a breakdown on Earth, surely she would have ended up institutionalized and doped up indefinitely, but here, a week later, she appeared to be entirely cured. It really was a shame the Xalans hadn't come in peace. Who knew how Earth might have changed as a result of such scientific breakthroughs? But it was a pointless thought now, as it was clear the planet would never recover from its mortal injuries, and no amount of technology would change that.

As he prepared for his morning workout, a voice rang out through the corridor.

"Crew to command."

Alpha rarely summoned them together anymore, and it had to be something rather important to issue such an order this early in the morning.

Lucas hastily dressed and got to the CIC where Asha and Alpha were already waiting. Asha looked leagues better than she had even yesterday. Color had returned to her face and it seemed she'd gained back five pounds overnight. Lucas wondered if Alpha had prescribed her additional nutrients that would return her to a healthy weight. She glanced at Lucas and gave a half-smile that caught him off guard. Perhaps recent events had brought them closer than he realized.

Alpha derailed his train of thought.

"We have an issue that I have avoided discussing while Asha's recovery was taking place. But now it is a subject we can avoid no longer."

The holotable showed the Milky Way with several points of interest marked.

"What kind of issue?" Lucas asked.

Alpha moved his claw and the galaxy map turned into a video of their brawl in the water chamber.

"You may have been too incapacitated to notice, but your altercation destroyed a large amount of our water supply."

The video showed Asha being thrown through the container and the water turning into steam instantaneously once it poured through the grating. The tank across from it was leaking a large amount of water itself, pierced by a shot from the Magnum.

"I noticed. Sorry, but I didn't really have a choice."

Alpha scoffed.

"I believe you could have handled the situation in a way that didn't involve the destruction of 7 percent of our fuel, but apologies are not required. We must simply deal with the task at hand."

Asha spoke, not bothering to apologize for her role in the fight.

"What task at hand? Is 7 percent really that much?"

"Simply put, yes. I was already a bit concerned we may fall short of our final destination as we burn through our fuel supply at an increased pace with the [garbled] core. But even with those consumption rates, there was an 87 percent probability we would reach our final destination."

"And now?" Lucas asked.

"There is a zero percent chance. Seven percent of our water supply tipped the balance of the calculations, and even if we make it 96.738 percent of the way to our destination, as I predict, in a best-case scenario we will still be several trillion miles out with no means of reaching Sora."

The room fell silent. Was their journey over? Had they really come all this way just to die floating in space, running on empty? Alpha read his mind.

"There is a plan to avoid this fate, one I have been developing over the past week, which now needs to be shared with you."

Lucas breathed a sigh of relief. Alpha always had a plan.

"There is a fuel depot in the upcoming system of [garbled]. It is the midway point between Xala and the colony [garbled], and is one of many such depots that have been dispersed as stopovers all around this quadrant of the galaxy."

The map returned, and a section of one of the spiral's arms was highlighted.

"So we can just fuel up and be on our way?" Lucas asked.

"It is unfortunately not that simple. Fuel stations are not automated; they are manned by a small crew."

Asha was already thinking ahead.

"And right now you're Xala's most wanted."

"I am likely a high priority target, based on Commander Omicron's personal interest in securing me."

Lucas continued the thought.

"And you said any ship that you fly is tagged with your signature."

Alpha expanded.

"And their sensors will also pick up Soran life-forms onboard the vessel."

"Meaning us. So how the hell is this going to work then?" Asha asked, arms crossed.

Alpha entered some commands and a stream of Xalan symbols appeared in place of the galaxy. Lucas could pull out a few, but they were moving much too fast for him to process what exactly he was seeing.

"I have been developing an algorithm that will mimic the effects of a solar storm. It will disrupt their sensors without appearing as if they are being purposefully disabled. They will be unable to scan the ship, and will not recognize that you are on it, or that it has been flagged as being piloted by a traitor."

Lucas shifted and leaned up against the table.

"Sounds easy enough."

"Perhaps, but I do not know how long the system will take to detect the malfeasance. Hopefully long enough to allow us to refuel and depart before they are the wiser. If not, we will have larger issues to deal with than a lack of water."

Asha had a suggestion of her own.

"Why bother with all this? Why can't we just attack the station, take the water, blow it to hell, and leave?"

"A direct assault would immediately alert the entire fleet to our whereabouts, including Commander Omicron. We will already be losing time on him by making this detour, but if he's alerted quickly enough, he could divert his course and arrive before we are able to escape."

Asha looked annoyed at the suggested absence of violence.

"Additionally, though the crew is relatively small for a space station, they are still trained soldiers, and fifty of them in a relatively confined area would not be a fight we would be capable of winning in a head-on assault."

"You want us to just sit on the ship with our thumbs up our asses while you smooth talk your way into some fuel?" Asha said.

"I do not understand much of your phrasing, but yes, you will remain onboard while I relay a cover story to the crew as to why we are here. A lone transport this far out into dead space will raise some questions of its own. Even without their equipment, the presence of our ship will be . . . curious."

"And what happens if your hack fails or they don't buy your bullshit?" Asha asked.

"Then more drastic action may be required. For this reason, you will be hiding in the armory."

Lucas thought briefly about being trapped in a room full of guns with the woman who just tried to kill him for the third (fourth?) time, but he supposed in this case, it was unavoidable.

"This sounds incredibly dangerous," he said, thinking more of the entire plan than Asha's recent instability.

"Yes, but of all the fuel stations I researched, this is the most isolated and very much understaffed. Mathematically, it is our best chance for survival. It is our only option."

The room fell silent after that.

The unpronounceable star system they were approaching was still five days out. There were no more fun fighter pilot diversions, nor learning reflexive Soran verbs. Lucas and Asha spent their time training in real life, with her especially attempting to regain much of the strength she'd lost. Should her services be required, she had to be in top form, and she was pushing herself to a degree that surprised Lucas.

Asha returned to her storage cube–based lifting routine, but cycled in many of Lucas's own isometric exercises, and the two of them sprinted against each other down the longest hallway they could find. Lucas won every time, but by the final day, she was within a half-second of catching him.

Panting, Lucas attempted to catch his breath, as the ten back and forths they'd just completed had him winded. Asha walked around with her arms above her head, her tank top completely soaked in sweat.

"See what you can do with a good night's sleep?" Lucas said in between breaths.

"Please, I've had personal trainers since I was sixteen. Do you really think this is a tough workout you've crafted?"

Her breathing was already returning to normal. She started boxing the air furiously, and spun around with a barefoot kick that Lucas remembered connecting to his jaw the last time he'd seen it.

"Are you really going to kickbox eight-foot-tall aliens to death?"

"Well, you won't let me in the armory yet, so I have to make do. Besides, it's about speed and flexibility."

She flung out three sharp jabs and an uppercut before Lucas could even blink.

"And yeah, I think if push came to shove, I could knock one of those things out cold."

Lucas doubted this was the case, but she had come a long way in under a week.

He decided to relay to her the information he'd learned about Noah. He was in the hall with them, busying himself with a bit of foam tubing he'd managed to pry off somewhere, but even if he had spoken, he didn't have the cognitive abilities to process what was being said. Afterward, Asha merely shrugged.

"No thoughts?" Lucas said, a bit caught off guard.

"I mean, we knew he was the kid of one of those monsters. What does it matter which one? I guess he'll be bigger than us in a few months, but other than that, it doesn't really matter."

Lucas supposed she was right. Yes, he could see the chief's mental state deteriorate in the pages of the book, but given the circumstances he was in, it hardly seemed like a genetic trait. And other than his initial bout of silence and his burns, Noah was a happy, healthy kid. At least until the next cosmic disaster turned their little group on its head once again. And one was looming.

"Do you think this is going to work?" asked Asha as she leaned up against the wall.

"I've no idea. Alpha's smart, but it seems a bit far-fetched, even with everything we've been through so far. Won't they . . . recognize him if he's some top-priority criminal?"

"*Puh*, would you recognize him? They all look alike to me."

It was xenophobic, but undeniably true. Other than being various shades of gray, only minor variances like eye color and slightly differently sized and shaped facial features were noticeable.

The only one that had ever really stood out to Lucas was the dark black Omicron. Suddenly they heard a voice from behind them.

"The crew is a long way from Xala, and there is likely no reason they would have been dispatched my image given their remote location."

Alpha stood with some sort of electronic pad in hand.

"And yes, of course we can tell each other apart. It is a trait of any living species."

"I was joking, Alpha," Asha said drolly.

Lucas interjected.

"So why is Omicron black when the rest of you are light or dark gray?"

Alpha pondered the question.

"He is a [garbled]. Naturally, you do not have a word for it. The closest equivalent term might be 'shadow.'"

"Is he just a different race, like the same way we have different skin tones on Earth?"

"No, it is not the same, though Sorans do share that trait. Rather, a Shadow is a specific creation. All Xalans are altered genetically from birth to increase strength and intelligence, but Shadows are different."

He paused for a moment as Noah had crawled over to him and was grabbing his toe claw.

"My father has . . . had argued against the procedure for years as inhumane, but with the escalation of the war, its use has only increased."

"What exactly is a Shadow?"

"They are Xalan, but genetically enhanced to . . . unsafe levels. Only one out of every 1,145 survive the procedure, making it both highly dangerous and tremendously expensive. But those who emerge on the other side have tremendous speed, strength, and reflex capabilities, with the darkening of the skin an inescapable side effect. They also process information at a much faster rate. Imagine the way it feels when you are plugged into the [garbled] cables. A Shadow thinks at such a speed at all times with no cerebral fatigue. As such, Shadows are often found in positions of great power, like Commander Omicron. Some say he was the first to ever live through the procedure."

Alpha walked past Lucas and Asha and twirled his metal claw, then stretched out the fingers.

"Additionally, in extremely rare cases, Shadows have exhibited psionic abilities. This development is recent, and we barely understand it."

"Psionic abilities?" Lucas asked.

"What do you call them in your language? Telekinesis, telepathy. In small amounts, but it's only been recorded in a handful of Shadows, all of which were quickly scurried off to covert operations before anyone could study the mutation."

"Does Omicron have these powers?"

Alpha shook his head.

"Not that I have heard. If he truly was one of the first, or *the* first Shadow as he claims, that mutation was still two generations away."

"How old is he exactly?" Asha asked.

"I would say he's approaching 450 cycles. Or the equivalent of six hundred of your years. But do not let his age fool you; he is still exceptionally dangerous."

Asha and Lucas looked at each other.

"Alpha, how old are you?"

It was an obvious question neither of them ever thought to ask until now.

"Two hundred and fifteen Earth years. No, two hundred and sixteen. Time has been difficult to keep track of as of late."

The pair was stone-faced.

"Ah yes, I forgot you endure short lifespans on Earth. What is it, a hundred?"

"More like eighty," said Asha.

"Simple advances in medicine can double that. Complex procedures can extend life even further. These days, most Xalans live to be around five hundred. Shadows, quite a bit longer."

Asha and Lucas contemplated what they'd heard. Alpha continued.

"If you will excuse me, I must finish work on this corruption algorithm. Perfection takes time."

The conversation shook Lucas up a bit as it reminded him exactly how over his head he was in this whole situation. As if space travel hadn't been enough, now he had genetically altered psionic monsters to deal with, too. He felt like a medieval knight being tossed into battle with a Navy SEAL squadron centuries in the future. But in this case, the gap was untold millennia. How the hell would he survive this?

But here he was, one of the only three humans left from Earth. He chalked it up to luck and blind chance, but maybe Asha was right. Maybe he'd earned his spot here. He'd survived bloody battle after bloody battle and had only a few scars to show for it. What others who may have been considered Earth's greatest warriors were now left stranded on the slow-cooking rock. But if they'd come across Alpha and his ship, wouldn't they have just killed and eaten him on the spot? Perhaps Lucas had overlooked one of his most important qualities, restraint.

Asha was something else entirely. There was a savvy about her, a will to survive that superseded all else. And yet, she still managed to hang on to her humanity unlike so many of the bloodthirsty left on Earth. She was an all-consuming inferno when she needed to be, but could bring herself down to mere embers in quieter times. Her recent brush with insanity was driven by love, not hate. She had passion in a world without hope. It was . . . strange to see.

Alpha was perhaps the biggest mystery of the three. He was like them now, a creature without a family or a world. His relatives were slaughtered by his own people, and after being branded a traitor to his planet for refusing brutality, Alpha was now being hunted across the galaxy. His only refuge was the very civilization his race had been trying to destroy for thousands of years. Through all of it however, he had kept a cool head. There was always a fix for each problem, an answer for each question. Logic was his salvation, though Lucas wondered what sadness and rage brewed beneath his gray skin with all he'd been through.

Poor little Noah had to grow up in this insanity. Lucas supposed it was better than a cannibal nursery, but the risk of death seemed to loom greater onboard the ship. They'd barely escaped the solar system in one piece, and now they were charging straight into another risky venture. Lord only knew what they might find if they ever reached Sora. With the planet's history with Xala, Lucas couldn't be sure their menacing ship wouldn't be destroyed immediately, without a question asked. And what was the alternative? Assured extermination by genetic supercreature Omicron. Quite the array of available options.

Suddenly, a voice rang out through the water chamber where Lucas had been gathering his thoughts.

"It is time."

18

When they deactivated the core, Lucas sat in the captain's chair. He was responsible for maneuvering the Ark into Alpha's designated position. They were arriving at the refueling station's star system a day early in order to start bombarding them with the fake solar storm Alpha had concocted. Should they show up at the exact moment the scrambling started, it would obviously be suspicious. Alpha deemed that a day would give them a reasonable window without letting Omicron gain too much ground.

The glowing lights of the space-time tunnel slowly faded, and the ship made a loud noise that sounded like someone powering down a colossal vacuum cleaner. Soon, stars began to reappear in the viewscreen, arranged in formations Lucas had never seen.

As he veered the ship around to the newly plotted course, Lucas saw the central body of the system, a star burning an unfamiliar bronze color. A brown dwarf, Lucas remembered from his limited time in astronomy in school. It was smaller than their own sun and governed over a system that had no natural life at all, like so many billions of others that lay just as desolate, according to Alpha.

The sun grew larger and larger as Lucas raced toward it, until finally he saw his primary target. A small ashen planet not even the Xalans had bothered naming. It hung there, motionless, and as Lucas approached he saw that its gray surface was peppered by craters. They would begin their electronic assault from orbit around the scorched rock. The station circled a more distant planet on the other side of the star, but Alpha was confident his signal would travel the necessary distance. Once the ship was locked into its rotation, Alpha started broadcasting the faux solar storm out into the ether. In Lucas's monitor, the signal was visualized as a pulsating sphere, and a few minutes later its color changed and a readout indicated the disruption had found its intended target. The fuel station's sensor systems were going haywire.

For the next few hours, Lucas stared at the sun, shaded to a safe visible spectrum by the viewscreen. He was tired of training, both virtual and physical, and the celestial body allowed him a peace he hadn't managed to find in a long while. Once again, he quietly marked a milestone for humankind, the first of his species to reach another solar system. Too bad he wouldn't get a parade if he ever returned.

In the distance, another planet loomed. The sphere was bright blue, but Alpha told him not to mistake it for water. It was purely gaseous and of no use to anyone. There were only five planets in the system and the fuel depot orbited the one furthest from the central star. Being stationed in such a desolate place was undoubtedly not the most prestigious military assignment, and Lucas could only hope the soldiers there were foolish enough to believe Alpha's tricks.

On the monitor, the scientist was tinkering with the core, making sure it had powered down correctly and would be able to reactivate once they made their escape. Asha, meanwhile, had finally been granted access to her beloved armory, and was busy scurrying away weapons into locked storage bins in case the ship was searched. Each of their respective living quarters had been stripped of the books, furniture, clothing, and mattresses, all hidden away in various parts of the craft. It looked as it had the day they'd come aboard.

The plan was for the human trio to hide inside the inner wall of the armory, should the ship warrant a walkthrough by the creatures. Noah rarely cried, but soon he would have to remain as silent as could be, and Alpha debated sedating him for the duration of the mission.

Later that day, while they were busy removing the panel where they were to hide, Alpha appeared in the armory with one final directive.

"There is an additional complication."

There always seemed to be one.

"Readings indicate that there is a [garbled] class cruiser parked at the station that is currently being repaired."

"And how big is that?" Asha asked.

"Smaller than the ship we encountered on Earth, but much larger than this vessel, and one equipped with a full squadron of functional fighters."

"That doesn't sound good," said Lucas.

"It is not. It means after refueling, we will have to destroy the station and the ship to ensure our escape. We are out of [garbled] missiles and the main gun remains offline, but even if this were not the case, Xalan fighters would shred this transport, even with the added maneuverability of the new core."

Alpha projected a hologram of a sleek-looking ship that dodged and weaved in space. A fighter. Lucas recognized it from his time spent in the simulation he had yet to master. Alpha wasn't joking when he said they were far more maneuverable. They packed a hell of a punch as well. The fighters' weapon systems easily outclassed what they had available on the transport.

"What happened to smooth talking our way into the fuel station, and leaving here in peace?"

Alpha shook his head.

"Repairs have already begun on the station's sensors to combat the alleged solar storm. The scrambling may prove effective by the time we arrive, but I am no longer certain their equipment will remain jammed for the duration of our stay in the system. We must make . . . contingencies."

Alpha began walking through the piles of weapon-filled boxes, looking for something. When he found it, Lucas recognized the container immediately.

"You son of a bitch. I knew you were lying."

Alpha dragged the locked crate into the center of the room.

"I have indeed kept something from you."

Asha rolled her eyes.

"What else is new?"

Lucas couldn't bother spending more than a second being annoyed.

"Alright, so what's in it if it's not above your 'clearance level' after all?"

Alpha typed a complex code into the lock, and the container hissed as it opened. Inside, the box was ray shielded, the way the prison cells had been, but Lucas recognized a symbol through the light barrier immediately. The yellow-and-black circle was unmistakable.

"Tell me that isn't what I think it is," Lucas said breathlessly.

"It is a nuclear device of human creation."

Asha's eyes weren't rolling anymore, and were wide open instead.

"You mean to tell me I've been sleeping in the same room as a nuclear bomb this entire time?" she said angrily.

"The container has contained all harmful radiation. Even now, we are being shielded from its effects by the [garbled] screen," Alpha said

"What the hell are you doing with a nuke?" Asha asked.

Alpha played with some controls on the box. Lucas recognized the Xalan word for "stable."

"I came across it in my travels. A human underwater military vessel had been beached a few miles inland. I salvaged the important parts from one of its warheads, as I figured it might be of use at some point in the future, perhaps even as a power source. Though I did not imagine this would be its function."

"You want to blow up the station . . . with a nuke you took from a submarine?" Lucas said slowly.

"It is the only way. We simply do not have the firepower to bring down the station or its docked ship ourselves."

"This is insane," Asha said. Coming from her, that was saying something. But she was right.

"What exactly happens when you detonate a nuke in space?" asked Lucas.

"The same thing that happens when you detonate it on land. But in silence."

Was that Alpha's version of a joke?

"And what about us?"

"At that point, we must be a safe distance away, or we will share a similar fate."

Lucas's head was swimming with this added "complication" that involved the use of the most powerful weapon mankind had ever created. Alpha continued.

"We must move this downstairs and prepare for departure. We should arrive at the station in a few hours time."

He closed the lid of the nuke container. They all breathed a little easier.

It was dark. The only light came from the cracks in the wall and the soft blue glow of the communicator Lucas clutched in his hand. Asha was cradling a sleeping Noah, who had in fact been sedated for the good of the mission and would be out for hours. There was almost no space inside the armory wall and Lucas was pressed up against the metal and Asha like a sardine. The sooner this was over, the better.

Alpha had to be the one to pilot the ship into the station, and had promised to keep them posted through the communicator. His brainwaves were now translated not through the speaker on his collar, but through the remote device, meaning he could speak to them from afar, and the other Xalans would be none the wiser. Additionally, he believed that as he processed what the others said to him, he could relay that through the communicator as well, allowing the pair of them to hear the conversations he had with the station's soldiers. The downside of all this was that they had no covert way of communicating back to him that wouldn't draw suspicion, and he had simply ordered them to obey his commands to the letter.

Lucas brought up a tiny monitor from the communicator that showed Alpha's viewscreen. They were approaching a dark planet and Lucas could barely make out what appeared to be the station a short distance ahead. It looked like a much larger version of the Sentinel orbiters from Earth, with a more robust center and spindly arms branching out from all sides of it. Alpha made his first attempt at contact.

"Come in [garbled] station. This is transport 1138-19455 requesting permission to dock and refuel."

Silence.

"Come in [garbled] station. This is transport 1138-19455 requesting permission to dock and refuel."

Silence.

"Come in . . ."

Alpha was interrupted by a burst of static. A fuzzy image of a creature appeared on the viewscreen, but the feed was distorted, as was the audio.

"Copy, 1138. This is [garbled] we read [static]. We are [static] having difficulties with a [static] storm."

Alpha replied.

"Yes, I am having similar issues. Permission to dock and come aboard to speak in person?"

"[static] granted. Why is a [static] all the way [static] here?"

"It is difficult to understand your transmission. I will speak to you onboard shortly."

"Copy."

Alpha guided the ship toward the station, which was much, much larger than it looked from a distance. It was now clear why it would take a nuke to destroy it. A few minutes later, a loud clank indicated they'd docked. Alpha spoke directly to them through the communicator.

"Scrambling appears to be intact. If readers were functional, my identity and your presence would be known. All is normal. Stay where you are."

Lucas flipped the monitor's view to show Alpha walking down to the port side of the ship. Alpha tapped a few controls and the airlock slid open. A pair of unarmored creatures stood in the doorframe. They were right next to the nuclear crate, which Alpha had placed in the entryway earlier. The taller of the creatures spoke first.

"Greetings Captain, apologies for the technical difficulties. This storm is one of the largest we have seen in years, and it was not in any of our forecasts."

"No apology necessary," Alpha said. "I know how unstable the [garbled] system can be. My cousin was stationed here two decades ago and complained often of such things."

"That was before my time," the tall one said. The short one looked around the ship curiously then spoke.

"What is a transport doing in such a remote sector? And where is your crew?"

Alpha took a deep breath.

"It is fortunate this station is still in operation, or I fear I may have been left drifting forever. I am part of the crew of a recovery vessel sent to Earth." Alpha presented some sort of chip, which the tall creature scanned. After he did so, he immediately stood at attention.

"Sorry sir, I was not aware of your rank," he said. Alpha had forged himself a convincing identity.

"Earth?" the other creature was skeptical. "We have not seen any returning ships from Earth in a few years now."

"I am aware. My mission was of the utmost secrecy. We were sent to retrieve an artifact from the planet that would aid in the war effort." Alpha motioned to the locked nuclear crate on the ground next to them.

"What is it?" the tall one asked, lightly kicking the box with his claw.

"It is above my clearance to know, and certainly above yours as well."

"Errr, yes sir. Apologies."

"I was sent here from my [garbled] class ship, which is stranded a few sectors away. We took heavy asteroid damage during our departure, and the ship leaked fuel to the point where it could travel no further and communications are down. They equipped this transport with the [garbled] core in the hopes that I might return with fuel and assistance."

The shorter one spoke.

"You are running a [garbled] core in this transport? Is such a thing even possible?"

"My commander is . . . talented with such things."

"And who is your commander exactly?"

"That is classified," Alpha said calmly.

"Of course, sir, but we will need to verify this with central."

The tall one spoke into his comm.

"Set up a link to Xala, and in the meantime, start giving our friend here some fuel."

"It is greatly appreciated," Alpha said. "I will ensure your cooperation is relayed to command."

The comm crackled.

"The storm will not let us connect to Xala, chief."

The tall one grunted.

"Unfortunate, I should have known. Care to come inside for some nourishment while we wait? It seems as if you have had quite a harrowing journey."

"Of course," Alpha said.

The short creature spoke.

"I will assemble a team to sweep the ship."

Alpha looked a bit unsettled.

"Is that really necessary?"

"Protocol," the short one said. "Anything from Earth has to be archived and searched with a report sent to command. I believe they are looking for something. Maybe your artifact."

Alpha thought quickly.

"Yes, perhaps. I am told it is of exceptional importance. Would you mind if I brought it aboard for safe keeping? I am not supposed to let it out of my sight."

"Absolutely sir, bring it inside."

The tall one motioned to the short one who grumbled. He began to push the crate, which was on gyroloader, but was still rather unwieldy. He bumped it against the wall, which made Alpha snarl.

As they turned and walked off the ship, Alpha directed his thoughts to Asha and Lucas.

"Check fuel status."

Lucas thumbed through the communicator controls and saw that water levels were going up by the second. They'd gotten what they came for.

"Stay hidden," was Alpha's next command. And soon it was clear why. Six soldiers marched through the airlock. They were only lightly armored, lacking full combat gear like the invasion troops he'd seen on Earth, but they were brandishing power weapons. He glanced at Asha who had her eyes fixed on the monitor. As the team spread out, Lucas split his view into as many screens as he could, trying to keep track of them all. Four were still visible, with the other two veering off to places unknown. The ones they could see scanned the bridge, and two made their way down to the elevator.

The comm crackled back in and Lucas realized that he could still hear Alpha's conversations, despite no longer being able to see them via monitor.

"Sir, what can you tell us about Earth? Outside of your classified mission, that is?"

Alpha paused.

"It is a wretched place, and the Sorans there are among the most savage I have seen."

"We heard the raiding fleet was defeated?"

It was hard to tell which creature was talking now.

"We . . . underestimated their resolve, and they were more advanced than the Sorans we encountered on other outlying worlds. We took what resources we could, but the planet is now desolate and useless."

"Except for the artifact."

There was a hint of disbelief in the tone.

"Correct."

"Do you believe the invasion was a mistake?"

"I am not one to speak ill of my superiors, and neither should you, crew chief."

"Of course sir, sorry sir. I did not mean to imply—"

Suddenly, Asha motioned at the monitors violently. Lucas looked and saw a pair of guards outside the entrance to the armory. He immediately flipped off the comm, and they stood deathly still in silence and darkness. Noah stirred briefly in Asha's arms.

The door opened and Lucas could hear the sound of claws tapping against the metal floor. He attempted to regulate his breathing as best he could and tried to ignore the fact that back on Earth, he'd been rather claustrophobic. Such petty fears had no place here or now. The soldiers stalked through the room, grunting at each other. Suddenly, the familiar electronic sounds of a keypad rang out. They were trying to open the locked weapons crates. After a few attempts, the harsh tone of rejection kept ringing out, and the soldier barked something at the other, and the two left the room.

Lucas breathed a little easier.

"I don't like this," Asha whispered.

He flipped the comm back on.

". . . and that's why the [garbled] is docked here. But repairs should be done within the week. They keep the crew onboard at all times however. They are not supposed to fraternize with us off-worlders."

"This is most unfortunate, because there is a petty officer onboard that is exceptionally attractive. I was stationed with her back on [garbled]."

The conversation was interrupted by another voice.

"Sorry to interrupt sir, but we have made a connection with Xala."

He sounded nervous. This made Lucas nervous.

"The storm let you through?"

"Yes, the effects appear to be lessening."

Alpha shot a mental message through the comm.

"If fuel is ready, depart."

The nervous voice returned.

"They said the item they are searching for is not any 'artifact,' but a Xalan. A traitor. They are patching through an image."

Another transmission from Alpha.

"If fuel is ready, depart."

Now another voice joined the scene.

"Sir, something must be wrong with the scanners, we are now detecting fifteen Soran life-forms onboard that ship."

"No . . ."

"If fuel is ready, depart. And detonate."

The sounds on the comm became a garbled mess, as someone let out a bloodcurdling scream. Alpha? They'd been discovered, and Lucas's heart thundered in the darkness as Asha let out an audible gasp.

"Subject has been apprehended. Crew chief [garbled] is dead. Take the traitor to level seventeen immediately as we await orders. Contact the highest ranking officer onboard the [garbled]."

"Shit, shit, shit," Lucas said as he kicked the panel out from in front of him. He stepped out into the light, shielding his eyes for a brief moment. Asha emerged behind him, holding Noah.

"We have to get to the bridge and get the hell out of here," she said.

"The bridge? We have to get Alpha!"

"Are you crazy? He's on lockdown with god knows how many of them in there with him."

"How are we supposed to fly this thing without him? How are we going to make it to Sora?"

"You heard what he said. 'If fuel is ready, depart and detonate.'"

"You'd just leave him?"

"What choice do we have? And it's what he's telling us to do! He said to obey his orders at all costs."

"We know where they're keeping him."

"What, level seventeen? And you know how to get there?"

"We can figure it out!"

Lucas paused to catch his breath. Adrenaline was surging through his system. He spoke again.

"Since when are you one to run from a fight?"

That hit the right note. Asha stood there scowling for a minute. She turned and placed Noah on the ground inside the wall, then reattached the panel.

"For the record, this is insane."

"Well then you should be onboard."

Asha set to work unlocking every storage crate around her. Dozens of weapons revealed themselves.

"Take what you need, fast. If we're lucky, the entire station won't be alerted yet," Lucas said hurriedly.

Just then, a wailing alarm sounded.

"Fantastic."

Asha had her Magnum already loaded up and her hatchet on her belt. She scooped up a few grenades and threw them in a pouch on her hip. Lucas grabbed his knife and sawed-off shotgun. He rifled through the box until he pulled out a Scandinavian assault rifle with a few matching clips strapped to it. Thank god Asha was organized. She pulled out a rather long machete from the box.

"We should go quiet when we can."

Lucas took his knife and fixed it to the front of his rifle as a bayonet. He wished Natalie was here with him now; the new weapon felt unfamiliar in his hands. But they had to work with what they could pull together in mere minutes.

Once they were equipped with as much as they could carry, Lucas shuffled through the monitors. The soldiers onboard were now running all over the place and two were currently marching down the armory hallway toward them. Lucas signaled Asha to move to the door. He put away the monitor display and readied himself for what was to come. They stood on either side of the entryway. The door opened and two soldiers entered the room. Just as their peripheral vision recognized the threat, it was already too late. Asha leapt onto her creature and drove her hatchet through his skull, which erupted with black blood. As the other creature turned in horror, Lucas shoved his bayonet through the back of his neck and he instantly fell into a heap on the ground. Wiping the dark blood from her eyes, Asha spun out into the hallway and Lucas followed. The alarm still blared, echoing down the corridor, reaching from the station itself. The airlock was still open. As they approached the hallway that would lead them to the station, they peered around the corner. Three guards stood there, clutching weapons menacingly.

"Now what?" Asha said, black blood streaming down her neck and chest.

Lucas looked around, and quickly put a plan into action. He aimed his rifle down the adjacent hallway they had just come from and opened fire. The bullets bounced around the hall, as did the echo of the blasts. The three creatures immediately took notice and two of them ran toward the sound. Lucas and Asha stood with their backs on the walls. They didn't need to communicate to know what to do next.

As the first creature arrived, Asha swung her machete upward and it got about halfway through his head before it caught on a piece of unmovable bone, snapping the blade cleanly from the handle. The second creature met a similar fate as Lucas shoved his rifle into an exposed part of gray skin and ripped the blade upward. The creature fell over with a wail as blood spilled out of its midsection and Lucas smashed the bayonet into his temple.

Suddenly a blast from an energy rifle came ripping through the corridor, and blowing a hole in the wall and knocking them to the ground. The third guard had seen the fate of his two comrades and shot off two more quick bursts in their general direction, again missing the mark as he frantically adjusted the settings on his gun. After sitting idle for months at a desolate station, these soldiers didn't know quite what to do in such a circumstance. Asha ended the creature's panicked shooting with a well-placed Magnum round that took off most of his head. The pair of them sprinted through the airlock and found themselves onboard the alien space station.

19

The interior of the station was cavernous, the hallways meant for eight-foot-tall beings with long strides. It was dimly lit, illuminated mostly by the glow of holographic consoles. The alarm coated the area in red pulsing light and echoed off the metal walls at a volume that was almost deafening. Quickly, Lucas and Asha ducked into a nearby room that was mercifully empty. Asha closed the door behind them, familiar with the controls since they were the same as those on their own ship. Lucas scanned the room and found a unit he recognized as a data terminal. As he approached it, a holographic menu system appeared before him.

"What the hell do we do now?" Asha said as she had holstered her Magnum and was trying to wring black blood out of her hair.

"I'm trying to find out how to get to Alpha." Lucas quickly scanned through the system. He could recognize words, but it was difficult to access data when he couldn't comprehend large chunks of what he was seeing. Finally, after what seemed like an eternity, he managed to pull up a three-dimensional blueprint of the station, easy to navigate with simple touch controls.

"Got it," he said. "We're on level twelve already, so seventeen isn't that far. They've locked down the lift, but there should be a maintenance tunnel five rooms over that should get us there."

Lucas shut down the terminal and he and Asha readied themselves to leave the room. They burst out into the hallway and almost collided with a Xalan who was sprinting the other direction. He spun wildly into the wall to avoid them, and when he saw they were human, his eyes widened and he turned and kept running. He wasn't wearing armor and must have been a civilian or an incredibly ill-prepared soldier. By the time they regained their footing after almost being bowled over, he was already rounding the corner. They ignored him and pressed forward, past four more doors.

When they came to a fifth, it was already open. Peering inside, they could see a team of Xalans standing around the locked storage crate that contained the nuke. It was the room Alpha had been taken to when he first boarded the ship. A tall, dead Xalan lay on the floor and blood pooled around their feet and the crate. They were scanning the storage container with small electronic devices and wearing protective suits that were apparently supposed to shield them from whatever danger lurked within.

Asha turned to Lucas with a worrying look in her eye.

"Those crates are strong, right?"

"Yeah, why?"

She gave a rare half-smile, reached into her bag, and pulled a pin on a grenade.

"Oh shit."

The group inside had just enough time to notice the bouncing metal object before it exploded and tore through the five of them. Smoke shot out of the doorway. As Lucas and Asha entered the room, three were motionless on the floor with assorted limbs missing. One writhed around on the ground, howling in agony, and another was stumbling wildly around the room, blood pouring from the eye holes of his protective suit. Asha silenced the one on the floor with her axe as Lucas emptied a three-round burst into the chest of the blinded creature who crashed into the wall and ceased moving. The crate sat in the middle of the room, scorched but undamaged. The fact that they were not incinerated along with the rest of the station indicated the risk of the grenade had been worthwhile.

They quickly shut the door and Lucas scanned the room for the entrance they sought. It took him a few minutes, but he managed to find the symbol for "repair" and pried off a panel revealing a long downward tunnel.

"This is it," Lucas said, staring into the abyss.

"After you," Asha replied.

There were loud bangs on the door behind them, prompting Lucas to disregard his misgiving and climb into the dark passageway. The opening was much too small for a Xalan, and would barely even fit them. Maintenance must have been done by some sort of robot. Asha followed him in, securing the panel behind her so as not to give away a probable path. Lucas imagined the station was in such a state of chaos, they wouldn't be able to organize anything like a coordinated search effort for at least a few minutes longer.

The pair of them grasped at pipes and wires and slowly lowered themselves down. Lucas activated his comm and hooked it to his stained shirt. The glow lit up the tunnel and he was able to see the Xalan symbol for "13" on a panel in front of him. Only four more to go.

Suddenly, the comm spat out some static and he could hear voices. He hadn't turned it on since they'd left the ship, and it hadn't occurred to him it would still be active. Two creatures spoke.

"The traitor is from the [garbled] clan? Were they not obliterated during that Soran raid?"

"I thought the same, but apparently he shipped out to Earth with the invasion fleet."

"What is he doing on a ship with all those Sorans?"

"I do not know, but I am assuming that is part of his treachery. A science team is inspecting that object he brought onboard with him. They do not want to relocate it as it might be a trap."

Suddenly Alpha's voice broke through. It was weary and hoarse, a reflection of his mental state.

"Detonate . . . Detonate."

Lucas slipped and slid down the tunnel until he caught himself on a tangle of wires. Alpha's voice continued.

"Perhaps you are dead, as the station should be vaporized by now. I am sorry, I have failed you."

The other voices broke in.

"It seems High Commander [garbled] himself has been hunting him across the galaxy."

"Personally? Has such a thing ever happened before?"

"Not that I know of. Do you believe the station will receive a reward for his capture?"

"I would hope for a placement on [garbled]. That would be reward enough."

"I would prefer my own ship."

"An amusing fantasy."

"Detonate . . . Detonate."

Lucas climbed lower still.

"At least we know he's still alive," he said

"So this suicide mission still has some sort of purpose to it," Asha replied.

Lucas's hands were coated in a mixture of grease and blood, and it was getting increasingly hard to hold onto the sides of the tunnel. Asha slipped and her boot struck him in the forehead. He gritted his teeth but said nothing. They were only one level above the detention floor.

"Quiet now; we don't know how thin these walls are," Lucas said as he switched the comm off.

The alarm was barely audible now; it seemed to be confined to the upper docking floors. Lucas heard growling in the adjacent room, and lowered himself down another few slippery rungs.

Finally the jagged glyph for "17" appeared in front of him. He grabbed Asha's calf, halting her descent. Slowly, he unhooked the panel and gently swung it outward. Light flooded into the tunnel and Lucas squinted.

The room in front of them was empty outside of some shelving units and a pair of holographic screens. Lucas stepped cautiously onto the floor and Asha followed him out. He wiped his greasy hands on his dirtied cargo pants and drew his sawed-off shotgun. Asha clenched her Magnum with both hands. Her entire upper body was caked in dried black blood. Lucas imagined he probably looked the same.

As they crept into the hallway, they could hear the familiar guttural sounds of Xalan communication, though there was no way to tell how many there were. Lucas unhooked the knife from the rifle slung on his back. He spit on it and wiped it off on a clean patch of his shirt, which was not easy to find. He held up the blade and used the mirrored surface to see the hazy shapes of creatures in the next room. He held up four fingers to Asha, who nodded. She reached into her pack for a grenade, but Lucas raised his hand to stop her. In the cloudy view from his knife, he could make out that Alpha was strapped to the far wall to the right of the guards. Cuffs held each of his upper and lower claws in place, and even his neck was encased in a brace. Lucas couldn't tell the extent of his injuries from the murky reflection, but it was clear further use of explosives was out of the question.

Wild West it was then. Lucas signaled to Asha, holding up three fingers. Then two. Then one.

They rounded the corner together, Lucas unloading both barrels of his shotgun into the two guards on the right, Asha putting two Magnum rounds in each of the others as they scrambled to raise their weapons. All four hit the ground at the same moment, and not one stirred afterward, though Lucas and Asha both stood ready just in case. When it was clear the battle was won, they turned to Alpha, who was breathing heavily and bleeding from slashes across his body. Lucas turned on his comm when he saw Alpha's communication collar on a table a short distance away. It still worked at range. They heard his voice immediately.

"This was a most unwise decision."

"Hi Alpha."

"Why are you onboard?"

"I'd never been on an alien space station before," Asha said sarcastically.

"You should be a light-year away. Did you not receive my messages?"

Lucas pried at the cuffs, but they wouldn't budge.

"If you could read our minds, you would have known that we weren't going to leave you here to be roasted by a nuke. How do we get you out of this thing?"

Alpha nodded in the direction of the crumpled pile of Xalan bodies.

"A chip."

Lucas walked over and dug through the gore until he pulled out a device that made Alpha nod. He stuck it into a slot near the base of the contraption and the cuffs all sprung open at once. Alpha dropped to the floor and collapsed backward onto his knees. Lucas offered him a hand. Alpha grabbed it with his good claw and wearily rose to his feet. He scooped up his comm collar and mechanical hand, which sat on the nearby table. His next acquisition was an energy pistol pried from the hands of a dead guard.

"We must leave before reinforcements from the cruiser arrive. This station is sparsely manned, but the ship docked here will have a full battalion of troops."

Lucas looked around the room.

"We crawled down here, but you won't be able to fit through the way we came."

Alpha waved his hand dismissively.

"It is of no importance. I will override the lift lockdown."

Alpha marched across the room and Asha and Lucas followed. At the far end, a door remained closed, and Alpha tapped away at the holocontrols next to it.

"A simple encryption," he said as the door flew open. A startled-looking pair of Xalan soldiers stood inside the elevator. Lucas raised his shotgun, but by the time his finger reached the trigger, Alpha had blown a hole through each of their heads with a pair of shots from his newly acquired pistol. He calmly entered the lift, stepping over their bodies. Lucas and Asha looked at each other and did the same.

The lift was almost as slow as the one on their ship. As they rose, Alpha plucked Lucas's communicator from his shirt. He pulled up a multiple monitor view of the Ark, and the scene they saw was troubling. On every screen, Xalan soldiers swarmed throughout the ship, tearing it apart, hunting for Sorans.

"That's a lot of them," Asha said. "What exactly is the plan here?"

Lucas was wondering the same thing. Alpha cycled through a few different screens.

"Contingencies," he said coolly.

Alpha pressed a button and the airlock door connecting the Ark to the station slid shut.

"What are you . . ." Lucas said slowly before Alpha's next action revealed his intentions. He slid his claw to the right, and the monitors showed every door in the ship springing open. Including the external airlocks.

Soldiers flew across the monitors too quickly to see the looks of horror on their faces. The airlock cameras showed Xalans being pulled through the hallways and flung out into the vacuum of space. With the docking bay sealed, only the ship was venting, not the station, and the sole door still closed within the Ark was the armory, where Noah remained inside the wall. After thirty seconds or so, no more soldiers were visible as Alpha cycled through the monitors, and only bits of debris whirled through the screens toward the exits. Satisfied, he slid the switch back. All the doors closed, and the entryway to the docking bay reopened. Just in time for the elevator to reach its final destination.

The door opened, and no one was there to greet them, other than the piercing wail of the alarm. They sprinted down the hall and into the docking port, running across the pathway into the Ark. Once they were inside, Alpha shut the door behind them. His mechanical voice rang out through the hall.

"Bridge! Turret!" he commanded and Lucas and Asha sprinted to man their respective stations. Assuredly Alpha was heading down to the engine bay to prep the core.

Lucas reached the bridge and fumbled through the controls looking for the seldom used "disengage" command. He finally located it and the ship groaned as it detached itself from the station. Lucas brought the engines to life, and the ship banked hard to the right, veering away from the fuel depot. His monitor showed Alpha and Asha in their respective stations, both scrambling to get all their systems in order. Alpha shouted into the screen.

"Accelerate, quickly, before the fighters launch!"

Lucas had forgotten about their potential pursuers. The docked ship loomed in their rearview, but both it and the station were growing smaller in the distance.

"Approaching safe distance. Detonation in seven. Six. Five."

Lucas dialed up the speed even further.

"Four. Three."

His eyes were glued to the viewscreen.

"Two. One."

He watched the station. Nothing.

"Alpha?"

He was staring intently at the station in his own monitor.

"There should be—"

Suddenly a flash of white light enveloped Lucas's entire field of vision. There was no sound, but when his sight returned, amidst the red spots, Lucas saw distant pieces of debris spreading outward from where the station once hovered, and a readout explaining that the installation had ceased to exist.

"Touchdown," Asha said through the monitor.

A faint glow was all that remained in the distance. The entire ship fell silent for a moment. Lucas looked down and saw they were already approaching twelve million miles an hour, but it felt like they were standing still. Alpha's voice cut through the quiet.

"Core activating."

On the viewscreen, there was a brief flash of an image that registered for less than a second. It was Omicron, his dark skin and bright eyes unmistakable. But in an instant, he was gone. The stars blurred and after a large moan and a worrying shudder, the view turned into the hazy tunnel of light that signified they'd arrived in their own custom-made wormhole. As Lucas waited for a minute, then two, then five, Omicron did not reappear and his readouts were blank. Eventually, Lucas felt his entire body relax for the first time in hours. He unplugged the neural cables from his temples and walked around his chair, stretching his arms out above his head. They'd done it again.

A few minutes later, Asha came walking through the CIC entryway holding a yawning Noah, recently recovered from his hiding place.

"Look who missed all the fun," Lucas said, smiling as the pair approached.

"Yeah, good thing Alpha didn't vent the armory, or he'd be floating in space along with all those creatures. And our weapons."

"I had hoped you secured the child properly," said Alpha, entering from a different hallway.

"We clearly thought of everything," Lucas said, walking forward to meet the trio.

Alpha touched his recently sealed slash wounds and winced. Though they were healing, the cuts would remain tender for some time.

"I wanted to . . . thank you, for boarding the station to retrieve me."

"Thank him," Asha said. "I was ready to blow your gray hide to bits the way you were telling us to. But he had other ideas."

Alpha turned to Lucas.

"I do not understand human honor codes, but I am in your debt."

Lucas shook his head.

"We've all been in yours for some time. Without you, we'd be dead in Portland, dead in Norway, dead next to Mars, or dead orbiting a dwarf star."

"We are not at our destination yet," Alpha said, and cast a worried look toward the viewscreen.

Asha fumbled in her pack with one hand while holding onto Noah with the other. She produced an ornately designed crystal bottle filled with brown liquid. There was Norwegian writing on it, but Asha was waving it around too much for Lucas to read it.

"It's brandy," Asha said. "I looted it from the mansion back on Earth. Something that looks this fancy can't be bad. I bet this bottle cost more than my first car."

The crystal glinted from the light of the holocontrols around the CIC.

"This seems like as much of a special occasion as we're going to get," she continued.

Lucas smiled.

"Well, sounds good to me. Have any glasses with that or are we going to have to vaporize and inhale it?"

That got a chuckle out of both Asha and Alpha.

Suddenly, Lucas heard a scratching sound from across the room. The doorway darkened for a moment, then a creature stepped into the light. A soldier. He was dragging an injured leg, his power armor was splintered, and his veins were popping out all over his body from the depressurization of the ship. He raised his energy rifle with one shaking hand, pointing it at Asha's back.

The scene was in slow motion for Lucas. He grabbed Asha by the shoulder with his left hand, throwing her and Noah behind him. She stumbled forward, crashing into Alpha as the bottle of brandy shattered on the floor. With his right hand, he raised the sawed-off shotgun. Before he could pull the trigger, there was a flash of light, and his midsection exploded.

20

He woke in a crater. The crater.

Lucas got to his feet slowly, struggling against the shifting sand, which poured off his clothing as he rose. It was night, but a brighter one than he could remember seeing in years. The menacing cloud cover was gone, revealing a full moon and a billion stars. With no artificial light sources polluting the sky, he could see straight into the heart of the Milky Way.

He looked around and found the familiar crater walls stretching out all around him. Ahead were the mangled remains of skyscraper metal, buried far deeper than the wreckage he'd previously seen. In the distance, he could see shadowy figures gliding across the crater floor but couldn't make them out. Were they human? Creature? He was too far away to tell.

Trudging through the sands, he called out.

"Hello? Anyone? Who's out there?"

No response from the shadows.

"Can you hear me?" he shouted. Only the howling wind answered him. Until . . .

"They cannot."

Lucas jumped and turned to find the source of the voice. It was a woman, clad in white, with bright green eyes and flowing platinum hair. She was iridescent, radiating light out onto the floor of the crater. She stood on the ground but did not sink into the sand. Lucas spoke to her.

"Who are you?"

She smiled.

"You know me."

Lucas searched his memory.

All my love.

"Natalie?"

The photo, brought to life. He wasn't in a pod, that was for sure. A realization dawned on him.

"Am I dead?"

"That is not for me to say," she answered calmly, staring out into the distance.

"Who are they?" Lucas asked, motioning to the shadows in the distance.

"They are the slaughtered. Your slaughtered."

The shadows grew closer.

"They come to greet you."

Lucas felt an intense pang of terror as the shadows continued to move toward him. Natalie stood calmly at his side, with a faint smile on her face.

He had no weapons, and as he turned to run, he found his feet rooted in the sand.

"What's happening?" he said, panicked.

Natalie turned to him.

"Don't be afraid."

The shadows were now so close, Lucas began to recognize them.

A mechanic. A tattooed band member. A platoon of soldiers, all marching in formation. Natalie eyed the leader as he passed. Other men, women, and creatures streamed by, all of whom Lucas recognized. He hadn't forgotten any of them. They walked past him and Natalie, empty eyes fixed straight ahead, ignoring his presence. The air was cold.

A collection of ragged cannibals trudged by him, and in the rear, a bearded giant loomed, taking one step for every two of theirs.

Behind them was a troupe of creature soldiers, taking birdlike strides across the sand. Lucas still couldn't move.

Finally the last creature shadow passed and Lucas pivoted to see the herd shuffle off into the darkness. Turning back again, he saw Natalie's arm extended.

Following her gesture, Lucas saw two more shapes walking toward him. It was far away, but it was a woman holding the hand of a child. They were too far to be seen clearly. Sonya and Nathan? Asha and Noah?

A low rumble echoed from over the horizon. The ground shook. The shadows stood still.

"What is that?" Lucas asked, his voice a whisper.

"He comes," answered Natalie.

The shadows turned to dust. Behind them, a colossal claw gripped the far crater wall. It must have been forty stories high.

A figure shot up into the sky, blacking out the moon and half the stars. A pair of blue rings shone brightly in the darkness. It was Omicron, ten thousand feet tall. He spoke in Soran, and the voice appeared to be coming from inside Lucas's own head.

«Your journey ends.»

He raised his massive claw in to the air. Natalie took two steps forward, then turned around to face Lucas. She hovered a foot above the ground and bent down to kiss him on the forehead. A second later, Omicron's claw came crashing down.

Lucas woke with a jolt on the laboratory table, gasping for air. The dream was over, but it took a few seconds for his mind to understand it. The lab was dim, but the minimal light still hurt his eyes. He looked down to find himself clad only in underwear. A long, curved scar made its way from his left hip to his collarbone with a few inflection points along the way. With bleary eyes he looked around the dark room, but neither Alpha nor Asha were anywhere to be found. But when Lucas saw what was next to him, he fell off of the table, pulling a mass of wires attached to his body with him.

It had to be another nightmare. He quickly ripped out each wire from his skin, ignoring the small bursts of pain that followed. Alarms began to sound on a nearby console, and Lucas grabbed it to help him get to his feet. As he did so, he rose up next to another makeshift table where a human body lay. It too was hooked up to machines, but was obviously dead. It was a young blond man who looked to be about twenty. He had a calm expression on his face for someone displayed so grotesquely. His entire torso was splayed open; his ribs were broken off and there was a huge gulf inside of him. Lucas saw a heart and the bottoms of lungs, but the rest was a mess of gore under what appeared to be a plastic shell.

Lucas stumbled backward, knocking over a different machine, and his stomach heaved. But no vomit came and he was met by crippling pain instead. He staggered across the room, a few wires still trailing behind him attached to his legs and back. He could barely walk, as if his brain didn't even understand the concept. Lurching forward, he dove out into the hallway and through the open door across the way. A door that had forever been locked.

Lucas pulled himself to his feet again, surprised he hadn't been jolted out of the nightmare by the surging pain through his midsection. And yet, the scene continued.

The room before him was awash in a harsh red light. On either side stood six tanks filled with fluid, and a human being was suspended in all but one of them. Lucas took one small step forward at a time as his jaw hung open.

Their bodies were wrapped ankle to neck in bandages laced with circuitry, and each had tubes coming out of multiple points on their bodies. There were five males and six females of varying skin tones and ages, though none looked older than forty. The youngest appeared to be a girl to his immediate left who couldn't have been more than fifteen. Lucas leaned up against the control panel for her tank, using it to brace himself as pain surged through him. The display showed a globe of Earth, and the unmistakable landmass of China was glowing a bright red. Below it, a heart monitor beat slowly. *She's alive.*

Lucas stumbled to the next tank. Inside it was a tall, dark-skinned man. On his globe, a country in Africa was highlighted. Zimbabwe maybe? His heart beat as well. Lucas looked to the other globes. A young woman from Brazil. A middle-aged man from Greece. The Philippines. Iran. Australia. Chile. France. Japan. Denmark. The lone empty tank showed the large shape of Russia in bright red.

Lucas fell to his knees, his head swimming and internal pain gripping him. *Wake up. Wake up.*

But the woman who entered the room wasn't an angelic visage this time. It was Asha.

"Oh shit," she said when she saw him. "Alpha!"

She raced over to Lucas and grabbed his jaw. She turned his head from side to side and saw a vacant look in his eyes. He felt like he was about to black out. He heard the familiar tapping of Alpha's claws on the floor and a metallic voice spoke.

"We must return him to the laboratory."

Asha hoisted up Lucas as best she could while Alpha took hold of his other arm and the pair dragged him into the lab where they rolled him back onto the table. All the lights came on and Lucas's eyes starting tearing up from sensitivity before they rolled back into his head.

"He's going!" Asha shouted.

Alpha grabbed a device and put it next to Lucas's temple and his vision faded to blackness.

Once again, he opened his eyes, and this time found both Asha and Alpha next to him. Looking down, he saw many of the cables reattached to his body. He started to struggle, but Asha put her hand on his shoulder.

"Stop," she said sternly. "As much as I'm glad you're awake, I'll kick your ass if you try to get up."

Alpha's head came into view.

"Did I not say he would regain consciousness?"

"Yes you did, Dr. Frankenstein."

"Was he an accomplished surgeon on your world?" Alpha asked earnestly. "I am impressed with his survival given our limited medical resources on this ship."

Lucas tried to talk, but his voice was hoarse.

"Can . . . someone . . ."

Asha fished around and came back with a container of water. She fed it to Lucas and it trickled down his throat and face. It was enough.

"Can someone explain what's happening here? Who . . . is that?"

He rolled his head in the direction of the dead body next to him.

"Oh, you mean Vlad?" said Asha.

"What?"

Alpha chimed in.

"I do not know why she refers to him as that. Specimen eleven is the reason you are alive."

Lucas was woozy from whatever pain remedy he'd been given. He fought to keep focus.

"Where did he come from?"

"This is a fun story," Asha said as she sat on the end of the table with her legs crossed.

"Specimens one through twelve were acquired on your planet before we met. Part of my mission there was to collect Sorans, humans, for further study. Perhaps your localized species would have some significant biological distinction of interest that the other worlds' populations lacked."

Lucas propped himself up on his elbows. Alpha continued.

"During the war, I collected a healthy specimen from as many diverse regions of the planet as the ship's course would allow. They were to be studied on the journey back to Xala, and housed there for further use."

Alpha checked a nearby machine that was hooked up to Lucas. He nodded, satisfied.

"But they're . . . alive."

"Technically yes, but realistically, no."

"What does that mean?"

"When the ship crashed and lost power, they went without oxygen for a prolonged period of time. By the time I was able to restore it, every specimen had ceased all neural activity."

"They're brain dead," Asha clarified.

"But how have you kept them kept alive all this time?"

"The liquid in which they are suspended is what feeds them. Their hearts beat and blood pumps through their veins, but they will never awaken."

Lucas didn't understand.

"Why have you kept them all this time? I thought you would have eaten them when you were starving, scavenging for parts."

Alpha sighed.

"It was . . . a difficult prospect to resist. But before I met the pair of you, they were to be all that was left of your species when the ship left Earth. They may not live, but their genetic material is . . . valuable. Their preservation took precedence over my hunger."

"Why did you keep this from us?"

"I was not sure how the two of you would react, as it does appear rather morbid. Though I imagine you understand the reasoning. Do you not think that your own scientists captured many Xalans for similar study?"

Lucas pondered that for a moment. The answer seemed obvious.

"I suppose so. It's still a bit bizarre to see. I was sure I was dreaming. I almost think I still am."

"You have regained consciousness, I assure you."

"And . . . Vlad? What did you do to him?"

Asha hopped off the table and took over storytelling.

"When that last bastard showed up, you got blasted pretty bad. By the time I shot him, your intestines were all over the floor. It was . . . unpleasant."

She traced her finger lightly along his scar. He was so doped up with painkillers, he couldn't even feel her touch.

"Alpha picked you up and raced you down here. He ran off and a minute later came back with poor Vlad here. By the time I could manage to ask where he'd pulled a fully grown human from, he'd already carved out his stomach to replace your ruptured one."

She looked over at the Russian on the table.

"Once you were stable, Alpha showed me the room and explained. We've kept Vlad on ice in case you ended up needing any of his other parts. So far, besides the stomach you've gotten a kidney, a liver, and about twenty feet of intestine."

Lucas turned to Alpha.

"What happened to the precedence of their lives?"

"I deemed yours more valuable than his, as you still possess cognitive function."

Alpha was always so sentimental. Lucas felt around his midsection with his hands, but again, couldn't feel anything.

"We were a transplant and blood type match? For all those organs?"

"Our medicine has no requirement of such things. The organs have been adapting to your body over the course of the past thirty-five days."

Lucas was shocked.

"I've been unconscious for over a month?"

He felt his face, where there was only light stubble. Had Asha been tending to him, the way he had with her? Though it seemed he had been out of commission for far longer.

"You should rest now," Alpha said, typing a few commands into a nearby machine.

"I've been resting for a month."

"It is a monumental achievement that you have regained consciousness, but your body is still recovering from the shock of your trauma. Rest now, and you can move back to your quarters soon."

When Lucas woke the next day, he found all the wires, save a few, detached from his body and a neatly folded pile of clothes next to him. He unclipped the remaining cords. This time, no alarms sounded. Sliding into a T-shirt, jeans, and socks, he found he had only minimal discomfort where there had been crippling pain. The table next to him was now bare, and his savior Vlad had been carted off to god knows where.

He found himself able to walk without staggering, and though his head was cloudy, he wasn't in a daze the way he'd been previously. The door across the hall was still open, and he walked inside once more, now fully aware that the existence of the bizarre room was not, in fact, a dream.

Alpha's collection floated silently while Lucas thumbed through some of the menus. There was no personal data, merely scientific notations about their height, weight, estimated age, and a few other variables Lucas couldn't translate.

«Strange place, isn't it?»

He turned to see Asha leaning up against the doorframe.

"Soran, huh?"

«You've been gone quite a while.»

«I suppose so.»

She reverted back to English.

"Can you imagine if they were awake? We'd have quite the little party on our hands."

Lucas scoffed.

"I bet we would have lost most of them between Norway, the Sentinels, and the fuel depot. They didn't have to survive in the wild the way we did. They wouldn't have been ready."

"Can't argue with that."

She walked over to a blond woman whose readout said she was Australian.

"Boob job."

Lucas chortled.

"What?"

"Absolutely."

"How can you tell with the bandages?"

"No one that skinny has a rack like that. And trust me, I was around a dozen pair of these a day in my line of work."

"Stripping?"

"Acting, smart ass."

Lucas walked over to the floating Frenchman, who looked to be about thirty.

"What was your show about anyway?" he asked.

Asha laughed.

"Ah wow, it seems like a century ago now. It was called *Cyberhawks*."

"Sounds like a 1980s Kurt Russell movie."

Lucas slid down to rest on the ground. Asha joined him.

"It was about Cassidy Clark, a sexy, ass-kicking government super spy. The big twist was that at the end of season one, you find out she's an android. We were only shooting the fourth episode when the first ship showed up."

"A spy huh? You don't seem like the government type."

"I wasn't. Cassidy was a cute blond actress they pulled off *Gossip Girl*. I played the villain, Victoria Ravenholm. She was the CEO of a bio-tech firm by day and ruler of the criminal underworld by night."

"I'd say that suits you more."

"There was far too much black leather involved."

Lucas laughed.

"Was it any good?"

"God no, it was awful. I would have been lucky if I ever worked again after that. Thankfully, aliens showed up and I never had to read the reviews."

Lucas grinned and Asha fell silent for a long while. She spoke in a different tone.

"You know you really saved our asses up there," she said, lifting her head toward the CIC above them. "Mine and Noah's. If you hadn't pulled us back, that blast that hit your stomach would have gone right through my chest, and probably into the kid."

Lucas shrugged.

"Nah, that wouldn't have been a problem. Alpha could have just given you Sydney's heart over there."

He motioned to the Australian woman.

"Oh, is that her name?"

"Yeah, and maybe he could have thrown in the silicone for good measure."

Asha punched him in the arm so hard Lucas felt it even through his meds, but she couldn't help but laugh. Her smile faded.

"But really, thank you."

It was the first time she'd ever expressed such a sentiment. And it seemed earnest. Lucas nodded.

"You should go see Noah; he's been asking for you."

"Asking?"

Noah lit up when Lucas arrived in the barracks. He crawled over to his leg and pulled himself up by the fabric. After raising his arms, Lucas picked up him up.

"Ooo-kas!" Noah said excitedly. Lucas beamed.

"You taught him that?"

"He's been to visit quite a lot. And he's really taken to those chair sessions you started with Alpha."

"Ah-fa!" Noah squealed with delight, throwing his arms in the air.

"Wow, he's acquired quite the vocabulary. What other tricks have you taught him?"

Asha folded her arms as she thought.

"Well let's see, 'noo-noo' is food. I guess he was going for 'nutrients.' He says something like 'hessip' that I'm convinced is spaceship. His most common words, yes, no, up, down, and the like, are all in Soran."

As if he understood, Noah yelled out a word.

«No!»

"I'm sure Alpha is loving this," Lucas said.

Asha took Noah from him.

"He doesn't seem to mind. He's been in the lab a lot, working around your corpse. Something strange is going on though. He's quiet. Somber almost. I thought it was just because of you, but now I'm not so sure."

Noah was back on the floor, rifling through his toys yelling «Yes!» «Yes!» in Soran.

"I feel like he's been keeping something. Maybe he'll spill it now that you're awake."

The two kept playing with Noah until he wore himself out and fell asleep clutching his favorite holoball. His blond hair had grown thicker, and Lucas guessed he'd gained about ten pounds since he'd last seen him. The past month had been good to him, and perhaps being under Asha's watchful eye wasn't quite as dangerous as Lucas initially imagined.

Over the next few days, Alpha said nothing to them that indicated something was amiss. But the truth was, he said very little to them at all. Before Lucas's injury, he was almost jovial with the promise of escape to Sora, but now? He spoke rarely of future plans, only concerned with Lucas's ongoing recovery and the continued functionality of the ship. But he walked around as if in a daze. Sometimes Lucas would pass him in the hall, and he wouldn't even acknowledge his presence. Something was wrong alright.

Eventually Lucas had enough. He retrieved Asha from her now reassembled quarters in the armory and the two of them marched into Alpha's lab, shutting the door behind them.

"Hello," Alpha said politely. "What is the purpose of this visit?"

He didn't look up from his table. It didn't seem like he was actually working on anything.

"What are you doing?" Lucas asked.

"I . . . uh, I was just calibrating the [garbled]."

"The what now?"

"It is a very . . . complex device. I cannot—"

Asha interrupted.

"Cut the bullshit Alpha!"

"Excuse me?"

"You've been moping around here for the past month. I thought it was because you felt guilty about Lucas getting shot, but it's clear it's something beyond that."

"I regret my involvement in his injury. I should have properly scanned the ship before—"

"But that's not what it is, is it? There's something else."

"How do you know such a thing? Does your species subset have latent telepathy?"

Asha rolled her eyes. Lucas answered.

"It's a bit easier than that. You're not yourself. I've only been up a few days, but I can see it. Just tell us what's going on."

Alpha sighed. He stood up from his seat at the desk and began pacing around the room.

"When we made our escape from the [garbled] station, Commander Omicron arrived in the system at nearly the precise moment we activated the core."

Lucas remembered the flash he had seen on his screen of Omicron's face.

"I thought that's what I saw, but I wasn't sure."

Alpha continued.

"As such, our voyage is now doomed."

"Wait, what?" Asha said, confused. "We've been running away from him this entire time. We haven't seen him in a month!"

"Such things do not matter. When he arrived back in the Earth system, we disabled his ship before we departed, therefore he was not able to immediately follow us. His ship would have been stranded for days before repairs were made."

Alpha increased the rate of his pacing.

"As such, I believed taking a day to broadcast the solar storm virus to the station was not putting us at a risk. It seems I miscalculated."

"I don't get it," Lucas said. "What does that have to do with our journey?"

"Omicron jumped into the system mere seconds before we jumped out of it. That means when we leave our space-time tunnel, and arrive in Soran space, he will no longer be days behind us, but minutes. The highly advanced long-range core in his craft can be reactivated after previous use in mere seconds, not hours like in most vessels. He will intercept our craft."

Lucas began to understand. Asha pressed.

"So what? We'll fight him. We took out a hundred sentinels leaving Earth. We blasted through dozens of Xalans at the fuel depot. We can take him."

"We cannot," Alpha said grimly. "Our ship has almost no reserve weaponry, and his craft is the most advanced in the fleet. We exploited a technical hole in the ship's design that only I was aware of, a trick that will not work twice."

Alpha finally stopped pacing.

"Rather, we will undoubtedly be disabled mere minutes after arriving in Soran space, and then we will be boarded. I will be apprehended and you will be executed."

Asha didn't buy it.

"We can fight. I've killed plenty of your damn soldiers. We all have. We have weapons."

"She's right," Lucas said. "We can make a stand. With what we've lived through, I like our odds."

Alpha shook his head.

"You do not comprehend. Commander Omicron travels with an escort of elite soldiers that act as his personal guard. They are highly trained, and the most deadly fighting force my civilization has to offer. Picking off starving infantrymen on Earth or ill-prepared custodians in a remote fuel depot has not readied you for this."

They were silent.

"Commander Omicron himself may be more dangerous than all the members of his squadron combined. As I explained, he is a Shadow, infused with more strength, speed, and intelligence than all of us. His feats upon the battlefield are legendary."

"Legends can be exaggerated," Asha said.

"Not in his case, I assure you."

"So what?" Lucas said. "You're just giving up?"

Alpha sat back down at his table, avoiding eye contact.

"I regret my role in causing this. We should have raided the fuel depot outright instead of waiting an additional day. This all may have been avoided."

"And we might have died in the attempt or he might have caught us anyway! There's no point in thinking like that."

Alpha said nothing. Lucas circled around him.

"The Alpha I know would have a plan. You've had one every step of the way so far. As the smartest person left alive in your civilization, it would be a disgrace for you to roll over now without even trying."

Asha broke in.

"What about your family? Your people murdered them. Omicron probably did it himself for all you know. Don't you want to know why they died? Don't you want to avenge them?"

Alpha threw his claw up dismissively.

"Of course! But such desires are not possible. We do not have the resources to survive this upcoming encounter."

"Then make them," Lucas said. "Build them. It's what you do. We have time. How far away is Sora?"

"Forty-three days."

"You're telling me you can't make us battle ready by then? That's an eternity!"

"We have no materials for such projects."

"Of course we do," Lucas said, raising his arms out wide. "Use the ship. Use whatever you have to that isn't absolutely necessary for us to fly and breathe. There's more technology in this thing than the entirety of our former planet."

"It does not matter."

Lucas was growing angry. He shoved his finger into Alpha's face, inches away from his sharp, gray teeth.

"It does matter! I haven't come halfway around the galaxy to die a light-year away from the finish line. And neither have you."

Lucas turned and stormed out of the room, shoving aside a piece of equipment hanging from the ceiling as he did so.

Asha turned to Alpha, her voice softer.

"He's right you know. You've gotten us this far. We know you can get us to the end. All you have to do is try, and we'll do the rest."

She left in silence as Alpha rubbed his head with a claw.

That night in the water chamber, Lucas couldn't sleep. Alpha's news was weighing on him, and he wrestled with the reality of the situation. After all this, everything they survived, was he right? Did they even have a chance? If Alpha in all his infinite genius thought the odds were impossible, what shot did they really have?

But when had any of their battles ever seemed like fair fights? A city of cannibals, a fleet of assault drones, a station full of soldiers. Were they really that outmatched here?

They had to be. He could see it in Alpha's eyes. There was a hopelessness Lucas hadn't seen since they met, when Alpha was lying helpless in the sands of the Portland crater.

The strangest part was, Alpha wasn't even sad for himself. He was confident he would live through the ordeal, though a life of servitude to the group that murdered your loved ones was hardly a wanted outcome. But rather he seemed sad for them. These humans he'd brought so far from home. Ones that by now with all they'd been through, he felt a kinship with. It was a mutual feeling, as Lucas hadn't thought twice about risking life and limb to save Alpha back at the depot. The scientist was now sorrowful that he would not be able to return the favor.

But he had, hadn't he? Lucas felt around for his long curved scar. He'd given him an almost entirely new set of internal organs, and brought Asha back from the brink of madness. If they were keeping score, they likely still owed him. But to Alpha it didn't matter. His mistake allowing Omicron to catch up with them had made it all pointless.

Lucas wondered if they would be executed like he said. Perhaps they'd be thrown in a tank like their new crewmembers and given to some other Xalan scientist for study and experimentation.

Surely that would be a fate even worse than death, and it wasn't an idea that made Lucas feel any better about their prospects. He tossed and turned, but was unable to make his bedding any more comfortable. Eventually, he gave up, and he drifted off to sleep despite his unease.

Lucas opened his eyes sleepily, minutes or hours later, he couldn't be sure. It was still dark, and as he regained focus he saw a familiar vision. A shadowy figure, standing at the foot of his bed. As it saw him stir, it took a step closer. Asha.

Please god, not again, he prayed silently to a long-absent deity, desperately hoping she hadn't relapsed into insanity.

But as she took another step, her body was illuminated in the blue glow of the tanks. She wore nothing.

Lucas's heart continued racing, but now for an entirely different reason. The light showed her graceful curves, but the darkness hid her litany of battle scars. She was truly a beautiful creature, more so than any he'd seen before. Reaching the mattress, she kneeled down and crawled toward him. He was speechless, breathless. He only managed to get out one word.

"Why?"

She looked into his eyes, and after lingering a moment, kissed him.

"Why not?"

She shoved him down against the mattress, and broke into a full smile that Lucas had never seen her wear before. Even in the darkness, it was captivating. As was the rest of her, bathed in the dull blue light.

He asked no further questions.

21

Lucas slept more soundly than he had in years that night, the weight of the old apocalypse and their imminent destruction lifted from his mind. When he woke, Asha was gone. He was hardly surprised, though he had to make sure the entire thing hadn't been a dream. Overturned stacks of books and a bite mark on his collarbone indicated the events of the night had indeed occurred, though Lucas still had trouble believing it.

Why not, she'd said. With all but certain death mere weeks away, was there anything to lose? Grab the closest, or only, person next to you and try to enjoy your last few moments.

Or was it more than that? Lucas remembered the look in her eyes, and her smile. That smile. There was something deeper there. Reflecting for moment, he realized he'd felt it for a while now, and there had been something between them that was downright palpable, especially since he'd woken up from his injury. A wound sustained while saving her. Perhaps that had something to do with it as well. He supposed he'd get some clue when he saw her that day.

He found her in the CIC, rapidly thumbing through the holotable display. She'd clearly been much more immersed in the technology the past few weeks.

She glanced up and caught his eye.

"Hey," he said.

"Hey."

There was a pause that lasted a few beats too long. Asha broke the silence.

"So, you're not going to get all girly about this are you?"

Lucas looked caught off guard by her frankness.

"Uh, no."

"Great. And don't go bragging to Alpha either."

Lucas laughed.

"You know, I really doubt he'd care."

"He was probably watching on the monitors."

They both laughed at that one, and the tension evaporated from the room. Whatever her motivations, Lucas was content to leave them a mystery.

They debated what should be done with the day. Should they train in the chair? Getting through the last few Soran lessons seemed a bit pointless now. Should they work out? Lucas had a long path ahead of him to get back to where he was before the injury, though clearly Asha had made good use of the last month. Her body was . . . well, perfect, as Lucas had discovered. His mind wandered as he watched Asha absentmindedly swirl through galaxy maps on the holotable. His thoughts were interrupted by Alpha on the comm.

"Crew to laboratory level."

Lucas was surprised. After their conversation yesterday, he thought Alpha would be even more sealed off. What was he summoning them for now?

When they arrived, the lab was humming with various devices. Alpha was at his desk, which was littered with all manner of mechanical parts. His metal claw was busy rifling through some circuitry while he worked on an entirely different set of electronics with his good arm. At the same time, he seemed to be looking over a technical readout floating in front of him. How his brain was able to process so many different tasks, Lucas could not imagine. All of them ceased when he saw them.

"Welcome," Alpha said warmly.

"What's going on? What are you doing?" Lucas asked coldly as he approached the desk. He was still displeased with Alpha.

"Thank you for coming. I understand that you felt our discussion yesterday was . . . unproductive."

"You could say that."

He closed the readout in front of him so there was nothing between the three of them.

"Last night I had a revelation."

You weren't the only one.

"Your words found a place in my core. You were correct in your assessment that it would be foolish to abandon hope after all that we have overcome to reach this point in our journey."

Lucas folded his arms as Alpha continued.

"Perhaps hope itself is foolish, but I would be remiss not even to attempt to craft a solution that will allow all of us to survive."

"So what does that mean?" asked Asha warily.

"Commander Omicron must be destroyed."

That produced a glint of excitement in her eye.

"But what about what you said yesterday?" Lucas asked. "You made it sound like he and his troops are practically invincible."

Alpha nodded.

"That remains true. It is the reason we will have to work exceptionally hard if we are to stand any chance at surviving a confrontation."

"What are we supposed to do?"

"There is little the pair of you can do to aid me with what needs to be done. Rather, you must train yourselves to be more quick thinking, stronger, and faster than you have ever been. You must maximize your potential as much as is 'humanly possible' you might say. Anything less than perfection is unacceptable for the task ahead."

"We can do that," Lucas said. His muscles had atrophied from his prolonged unconsciousness, but with thirty-seven-hour days to kill, he imagined he could inch back to his former level of fitness.

"And what are you doing?" Asha asked. She was already miles ahead of him, but knowing her, she would push herself to the absolute limit if it meant a chance to survive.

"I will train as well, but more importantly, I must craft weapons that can kill immortals and armor that can protect us from them. This shall be no easy feat."

"I thought you said we didn't have the materials."

Alpha lifted up a holographic menu and coasted through pages and pages of schematics. The designs were complex, and even if Lucas could recognize some of the symbols, it was unclear what was being envisioned in these three-dimensional pages.

"I did not sleep last night as I could not get visions of theoretical weaponry out of my head. I have created a number of designs that I think may suit our purposes. In part, they have been fashioned from military prototypes in production on Xala, combined with a few of my own ideas. Ideas that will make them actually work."

Lucas breathed a sigh.

"I knew you'd come through."

"I have not, yet."

Alpha waved his claw as he stopped on one of the designs. He sat back in his chair.

"Be forewarned. Even with such devices, should they function as intended, our chances of survival are almost non-existent. Whatever trials we have faced to date, they will pale in the face of this upcoming conflict."

"That doesn't matter," Asha said. "So long as we try. Besides, I can think of less dignified ways to die than at the hand of a legendary alien general."

Alpha scoffed.

"Commander Omicron can imagine a variety of ways to end your life without dignity, and he has done so across many Soran worlds. Do not delude yourselves with visions of an honorable death."

"You're sure they're not just going to blast us to bits the moment they see us?" Lucas asked.

"Their behavior has always indicated an attempt to capture, not annihilate. As such, we will be boarded. Much of the fight will take place here."

"And the rest of it?"

"If we survive, on the [garbled]. On his ship."

"So what exactly are you going to be making?"

Lucas peered into the floating schematics, but couldn't tell what it was supposed to be when it was all disassembled. Though one of the pieces did match the item in Alpha's right hand.

"I will inform you upon completion. I am still sorting through concepts to ascertain what should take priority in the limited time we have."

"Forty-odd days seems like a lot."

"These are items that would take a team months to craft back on Xala."

"Well, that's why you're better than them, right?" said Asha.

Alpha chortled.

"We shall see."

The next two weeks were a whirlwind of activity. Alpha was in his lab for practically days at a time, only venturing to the engineering bay or CIC on rare occasions. Usually it was to pull something out of the wall, and he was appropriating many pieces of the ship's technology for whatever it was he was working on.

They let him be and focused on their own training. There were no more Soran lessons, no flight simulators and unfortunately, less time lounging with Noah. They let him crawl around nearby as they worked out together, and he was content enough with his toys, but he had to be an afterthought. His survival depended on what was to come, as did their own, and as such they trained with a laser-like focus. Distractions were no longer permitted.

Well, almost. Every night for the past two weeks after a hard day's work, Lucas was visited by the same nightly specter, one he welcomed. Asha crept through the ship to the water chamber to recreate the events of that first night. Each evening was more memorable than the last, but every morning, she was gone. Lucas didn't bother asking why, or wonder out loud why they couldn't just share quarters. He let her come and go as she pleased.

Lucas felt more connected to her than ever. Their nights and days were spent almost entirely in each other's company. Their only sparring was physical, for combat preparedness purposes; they avoided verbal altercations entirely. The weight of probable death had whitewashed whatever problems they'd had. They had almost killed each other on more than one occasion, but the number of times they'd saved one other from death was starting to rival that tally. Lucas putting himself in between her and the energy rifle blast seemed to be the tipping point. Skepticism had turned to trust. Anger to lust. Hate to . . . love?

Lucas wasn't sure what he felt for her. Was it love? Or was it two people with nothing to lose, trapped on a spaceship for six months, surviving more near-death experiences together than was statistically possible? Whatever had sparked it, he couldn't put the flame out now. It was true, he felt kinship with Alpha and even Noah, but his connection to Asha ran deeper. He'd felt it sooner than that first night in the water chamber, but he'd shoved it out of his thoughts. Despite their wary alliance that had begun months ago, for a long time she had still felt like a possible threat.

He thought back to the most recent time she tried to finish the job, when she was driven out of her mind by pod memories. She wasn't even attacking him; she was trying to kill some would-be rapist in Alaska. But that whole event was a look into her soul. He saw the source of her passion, and her capacity to love. Love drove her hate, and it wasn't blind or sadistic the way he'd imagined. Since her recovery, he felt he understood her, and she him. That's why, without a moment's hesitation, he had thrown himself in front of that blast. His body knew what his mind wouldn't admit. He'd do anything for her. Even die. And he almost did.

Lucas wrestled the thoughts to the back of his mind, though every morning when he woke, he was a little disappointed she hadn't stayed. Despite the fact she was offering herself to him each night, there were still defenses in place. Barriers that needed to be broken.

Not that he was an open book. There was still so much he hadn't told her, about his life both before and after the war. He thought of Sonya and Nathan more often now. His love for them had sustained him during a trip through an ocean of devastation. Though he had lost his faith in traditional notions of God, he wondered if, should he die, he might see them again. He'd heard a theory about death once that had stayed with him. A condemned soul speculated that heaven might be going back to the time in your life in which you were happiest and living there forever. He thought if he died out here in space, perhaps he could wind up living in some past lazy summer. He and his wife young and beautiful, their son even more so. Maybe when they'd rented out that cottage in Cape Cod for a week. It was hard to imagine a more ideal time in his life.

But sometimes he wondered if he might come back here instead. On the Ark he had a stalwart extraterrestrial friend, an adoring, bright-eyed child, and a woman in his bed that had been worth a hundred-trillion-mile journey. If he could ignore the ever-present shadow of death, it might have felt pretty perfect itself.

Lucas looked down at Asha, fast asleep, as all these thoughts floated through his mind. He ignored pending death, forgot about a decade of drinking, an interstellar war, and a hundred murders he'd committed since. He was content.

The lights of the water chamber grew brighter as they were programmed to at 0600. Lucas squinted and found himself stunned when he saw Asha remained next to him. It was the first time she hadn't left in the night. Her eyes fluttered, and she too looked shocked at her surroundings. She stammered as she saw Lucas was already awake.

"I, uh . . . I was pretty wiped from yesterday," she explained.

"It's alright."

"Let me just . . ." She scrambled for her clothes, which were strewn all around them. Both of them looked up when there was a familiar clank in the metal hallway ahead. Of all the days . . .

Alpha was walking toward them down the corridor. These creatures couldn't quite smile in the traditional sense, but Lucas imagined that must be what he was doing. His translator wasn't verbally relaying his current thoughts on what he saw in front of him. Asha wrapped herself in the covers, her usual lack of modesty not extending to aliens, it seemed. Lucas just sat on the mattress with his arms folded around his knees.

"Hi Alpha."

"Greetings."

"To what do we owe the pleasure?" Asha said, now as covered as she could manage.

"I have something to show you. Please accompany me to the laboratory."

"And you couldn't have just told us that on the comm?" Asha asked menacingly.

"I was overcome with excitement. Apologies, I did not mean to . . . intrude."

Asha just shook her head. Lucas had already thrown on a pair of pants and shirt and walked toward Alpha.

"Alright, let's go then," he turned back to Asha, still wrapped in the sheet. "Asha?"

"I'll meet you up there," she said as she fumbled around with her hastily assembled pile of clothes.

The elevator ride was a tad uncomfortable as the pair stood in silence. Lucas felt obligated to break it.

"You know, that's not going to interfere with our training or anything."

Alpha waved him off.

"I am not concerned. It was expected."

Lucas raised his eyebrows.

"Expected?"

Alpha nodded.

"Imagine my delight when the last two sane humans on Earth turned out to be a male and female. I knew biology would assuredly run its course on the journey. Though I did not expect it to take this long, mind you."

Lucas was confused.

"You planned this?"

"I planned nothing, but it was good fortune the pair of you have become . . . compatible after much initial hostility. There may be hope for your species yet."

"What? There are whole worlds of Sorans out there."

"Yes, but you are an alternatively evolved strain. You are physiologically unique. The differences are subtle, but present. I've studied your species intensely for years now, and there are many aspects of your genetics that are remarkable."

"We're not doing this to repopulate the universe with humans. It's . . . something else."

Alpha looked surprised.

"An emotional connection? A pleasant side-effect. How fortunate for you. Though it is likely the result of proximity compounded by intense duress."

"I see you're a romantic then."

"Sarcasm. Humorous."

"So let me get this straight, you wanted Asha and I on the ship so we could be the last surviving members of our species?"

"You were preferable to my current crew, which was in stasis, devoid of brainwaves, so yes."

The elevator continued its slow crawl. Alpha quickly continued.

"Though you have proven yourselves more than capable on this journey. I am certain without the pair of you I would have never escaped the clutches of your dead planet."

He paused.

"Additionally, I . . . enjoy the presence of others onboard. Years of solitude can warp and degrade the mind."

Alpha had convinced Lucas the pair of them was more than another science project, though it was still a strange concept. Lucas thought of Earth. In the past few months, it had likely cooked even further. Soon the poles would be the only proper place to reside, and then they too would go up in flames. Outside of their brain-dead companions, he and Asha really were the last man and woman on Earth. Well, from Earth. Could love actually be found in that? Or was it just "proximity and duress" the way Alpha said?

As the elevator doors opened, Asha was already waiting for them at the end of the hall. She was dressed in baggy black pants and a white tank top and leaning in the doorframe of the stasis room. She answered their next question.

"I took the ladder. I hate those elevators."

Lucas was glad she'd missed their conversation. Alpha approached the lab door and opened it, ushering them inside.

The room was an utter disaster, with pieces of metal and wire everywhere. Lucas wondered how on earth Alpha was getting anything done. There were materials he'd pilfered from all over the ship, and Lucas and Asha had to tread carefully around it all in order not to trip. Finally, they arrived at the desk, where two long cases lay.

"This item has been crafted specifically for Asha."

The first case opened on its own accord. A long, flat, black blade was inside. The handle was laced with electronic circuitry, some of which fed into the dark metal above it.

"Take it," Alpha said. "It is not meant for my grip."

Asha picked it up, looking at it with wonder. It was quite a bit longer than her arm, and the blade was so thin that, when turned sideways, it was barely visible at all.

"It's light," she remarked with awe. "Really light. What is this made of?"

Alpha looked proud.

"An alloy that I will not attempt to pronounce in your language, but one more durable than anything you have crafted on Earth. It is what constitutes the armored parts of this ship."

"You forged this out of the hull?" Lucas asked.

"I secured a piece from the inside. Normally the alloy is not able to be rendered thin enough to forge a blade, but I devised a process to do so using [garbled] and [garbled]."

"It's . . . lovely," Asha said, enraptured by her new weapon. She held it aloft in the overhead light.

"Much of the coming combat will be close-quarters, and I thought you could put it to proper use."

"Absolutely."

"That will cut through any class of armor when wielded with proper force. Additionally, it is laced with electricity to be used as a paralyzing agent."

Alpha motioned to the handle. Asha slid her finger across a small protrusion at the hilt and the black blade crackled with blue electricity. Asha's eyes lit up in a similar fashion.

"May it serve you well."

Asha was too floored to say any more. Alpha turned to Lucas and motioned to the second case.

As the lid rose, Lucas couldn't believe what lay in front of him.

It was Natalie. Transformed.

His beloved gun had been salvaged from the brink of death, and from the looks of it, given a hell of a makeover. Alpha spoke as Lucas took it into his hands.

"Our weapons are too large for you to wield effectively. I took the liberty of infusing your damaged rifle with Xalan technology, and I must say I have created a weapon more effective than either planet offered originally."

The grip and stock and even the trigger were the same, and the faded NATALIE could still be seen etched into the rear. The sight was retrofitted with a holographic scope, and the magazine had been replaced by a cylindrical power pack. The entire frame was streaked with circuitry and a few lights on the side glowed a dim blue. Whatever personified vision Lucas had seen of Natalie in his dream, this was more beautiful.

"What does she shoot?" Lucas said, overlooking the use of the pronoun.

"Superheated plasma rounds. But ones far more volatile than anything in the typical Xalan arsenal. The technology is normally reserved for artillery, but I've managed to condense it into a much smaller package. As such, it will melt through all manner of materials with ease and produce a great deal of concussive force."

Lucas hadn't even noticed Natalie had been taken down off the mantle in his room. He supposed he'd been occupied with . . . other activities. But it felt incredible to have his treasured weapon back. Despite its new killing power, it felt like the same old gun in his hands. There was no trace of the wound that had crippled it, and the gun seemed to hum with power.

"I ask that you not test fire your weapon inside the ship. It may cause . . . complications with the hull. I have programmed a simulation that will mimic the effects of firing for training purposes."

Alpha presented them with two more gifts. Lucas received a short knife made out of the same material as Asha's sword (though not electrified) and Asha a case of ammo for her Magnum. The bullets were explosive, and Alpha said something about them containing microscopic fission reactions before his translator became a jumbled mess of sounds when he couldn't explain the technology any further. He then motioned to the rear of the room, where two unfinished sets of power armor lay stretched out, one larger, one smaller.

"I have not yet been able to complete your armor at this time. Converting from a Xalan body type to a human one is a rather prolonged process, and the weapons took precedence. But I hope to be finished shortly so that you may grow accustomed to them."

A rough metal skeleton of some other device sat a few feet away. It was large. Quite large.

"And what's that?"

"Another project. One that requires much more work. Though it may prove to be the most necessary of all. You will understand when I am finished."

Alpha turned away from the machine.

"I imagine you would like to test out your weapons. Feel free to do so, but please do not destroy the ship before we have a chance to face Omicron."

The armory seemed like the most logical place to try out their new gear. The boxes upon boxes of weapons they'd taken from Earth were largely useless now. Bullets alone, Alpha had told them, would prove futile against the advanced armor of Omicron's elite squadron, while the explosives would have to be extremely well placed to have an effect.

Asha had already chopped up a handful of storage crates with her sword and was practically giddy as she tore through a nearby light machine gun like it was foam. Her form wasn't exactly that of a seasoned samurai, but it wasn't bad either.

Lucas, meanwhile, couldn't fire the newly refurbished Natalie without carving giant holes in the wall, so he set about employing Alpha's "test fire" mode instead. The program caused the gun to simulate recoil in its three main firing modes. It could shoot a stream of small plasma rounds like a typical machine gun, it could be focused to line up a distant shot like a sniper rifle, and finally a switch with the Xalan symbol for "carnage" turned it into an area of effect shotgun, blasting a million tiny plasma particles at close range. The barrel narrowed and widened, lengthened and shortened, based on which option was selected. The kickback when he test fired its final setting was enormous, and the sound deafened them both for a few seconds. If the gun was live, Lucas imagined the metal wall in front of him would be a large, smoking hole. But he would have to wait to be sure.

Asha had no safety mode on her blade, so when she shoved it into the wall and activated the electricity, they both jumped as the surge blew out the power to the door. The controls smoked and sparked, and they could no longer close the entryway. Asha merely shrugged as Lucas glared at her.

He busied himself thumbing through the different scope options, which were a significant upgrade from Natalie's old crosshairs. Zoom went up to 20x magnification, and as he scaled back and aimed at Asha, he could see that his lenses included thermal, infrared, and ultraviolet, all of which set his target apart from the background, turning her some bright color of white, orange, or purple. He was surprised to find one last option, simply marked "X." Upon activation, Asha turned skeletal, and he found he could see through each crate, even over into the next room if he focused correctly. He could only imagine the tactical implications of being able to see through walls.

"Could you not point that thing at me?" Asha said as she ceased sword swinging. "I'd rather not be vaporized before we even start fighting."

"It's not hot," Lucas said as he tapped an indicator on the gun. It was only programmed to fire when the scope read Lucas's eye, to help prevent having his own gun used against him. Alpha said that he had entered Asha's retinal pattern as well in the instance that Lucas had been killed and she needed the weapon to defend herself. It was a morbid thought, but a logical one. As such, he let Asha familiarize herself with it for a bit, while he handled her sword.

It was light. Impossibly light, if it was as durable as Alpha claimed. Lucas picked up a submachine gun he now deemed useless, tossed it in the air and cleaved it into two with ease. He may as well have been cutting through a throw pillow. To test the mettle of his new knife, he struck it against the blade. The two were indeed forged from the same material; they sparked brightly, but left not even a scratch on one another. After only a minute, Asha wanted it back.

At the end of the day, Lucas mounted Neo-Natalie back on the perch above his bed. Sure, half the weapon was now Xalan, but it was more beautiful than ever. He thought back to his dream where the gun had come to life before him in an ethereal form of her namesake. She really was his guardian angel, watching over him during these long, hard years. He'd certainly test that title during the upcoming battle.

But she wasn't the only one in his corner. Asha walked down the corridor as she did nightly, this time with her sword strapped to her back. It was clear she was never going to let it out of her sight, and it joined Christian's Magnum as a permanent fixture on her person. Lucas sat at his desk as she approached, unwinding with a worn, water-stained copy of *Brave New World.* It hadn't occurred to him until recently that all that remained of Earth's treasured literature was sitting right here in his quarters. He had some classics sure, but authors like James Joyce, Ayn Rand, George Orwell, and the ancients like Homer and Dante were all lost to history. He'd searched around his collection and found no trace of the works of Shakespeare or a single copy of the Bible. Well, at least Harry Potter lived on.

Asha unslung her sword and flung it at the opposite wall behind Lucas. He was so used to such commotion around her that he only directed his eyes upward toward her while his nose remained buried in the book.

"Watch this," she said.

She was wearing a small metal cuff Lucas had never seen before. Bending her wrist upward, a small light activated in the center. Immediately, the sword flew out of the wall and back into her hand, fifteen feet away. That made Lucas put his book down.

"Whoa."

"Alpha just finished up the bracelet a few hours ago."

"How does it work?"

"Some sort of directed electromagnetism, but I had him spare me the boring details. It's just nice to know I've got some range on this thing if I need it."

"Even still, I wouldn't let that out of your hand too often."

She looked at the handle and swung the blade around in a circle across her palm.

"Yeah, I'm worried one of these times it's going to come back and take a few fingers off."

She walked past the desk and jammed the blade into the top.

"Hey!" Lucas cried sharply.

Asha rolled her eyes.

"You really care about this stuff?" she said, motioning to his furniture. "In a few weeks we're going to either be dead or on some alien planet. Either way, I doubt you'll be taking it with you."

Glaring at her, Lucas dislodged the blade from the wood and handed it back to her.

"Fine," she said flatly, and threw it into the opposite wall once more. Mercifully, it stuck a full foot away from where Natalie was perched. Lucas continued his glare. Asha ignored him and sat down on the edge of his desk.

"You think this new ordinance is going to get us through?"

Lucas leaned back in his chair, his scowl fading.

"Honestly, I've no idea. Truth is I've expected to die nearly every day for the last few years. Why should this be any different?"

Asha was silent, her feet dangling loosely.

"The Ark has been a sanctuary, sure. But it was always only temporary," Lucas continued.

"Yeah," Asha said. "But it's the closest thing to something like home in a long while now."

Lucas couldn't dispute that.

"I never got to defend my home back on Earth. It was gone when I showed up. At least this time I'll have a chance."

Asha lay down on the mattress and looked toward the ceiling. Lucas set his book down and joined her. Only the faint whir of machinery was audible as the lights dimmed.

"I don't want to die yet," Asha said quietly. "I want to make it there. I want to see what all this was for."

"We will."

"Will we?"

"We will."

22

The day had come.

Lucas shifted uncomfortably in his hand-crafted power armor. Even after training in it every day for the last few weeks, and despite Alpha's constant adjustments, parts still pinched him at times. The suit wasn't pretty, that was for sure. It was a patchwork of unpainted dark metal, some from the original armor they'd taken from the mothership, the rest scavenged from the Ark itself. Given an unlimited amount of time, Alpha said he could make armor almost entirely out of the hull alloy that composed Asha's sword. But in a crunch, he had to make do with a few select pieces of plating in key areas. The electronic implants in the suit allowed Lucas to move more quickly and exhibit strength beyond the capabilities of his natural body, though he had to be in perfect shape to be able to utilize it correctly. It had taken him three days and a dozen bruises just to learn to walk in the thing, and only recently had he fully mastered running and jumping.

Lucas stood with Natalie on his back and his helmet in his hand. His black-bladed knife was fixed to his chest, and he surveyed the CIC about three inches taller than he stood normally. Beside him was Asha, her own armor a similar design to his. She too had her helmet off, and her dark hair was pulled back into a high ponytail. Together the pair of them stared into the viewscreen, the hazy blue-green light of the space-time tunnel greeting them. It wasn't much longer now. Soon they'd arrive in a new solar system. Fifteen planets, eighty moons, and a yellow sun only slightly larger than their own. Somewhere out there, Sora, their haven, awaited.

Lucas was jolted out of his thoughts by a thud and a vibration that shook the floor. He looked at Asha, and the calamity repeated itself. Then again, even louder. It was getting closer. They turned around.

The central door of the CIC opened, and a giant armored mechanical monster came lumbering through, the top of it almost grazing the doorframe. Lucas marveled at the behemoth. It wasn't a threat—he knew who was responsible for it.

It continued its march toward them, each step shaking the room even more. It had two legs and two arms, all four of which were wider than Lucas's entire body. One appendage ended with a large, metallic recreation of a Xalan claw. The other arm had no digits, only a massive cylinder that had to be some sort of weapon. The torso was heavily plated, and Lucas recognized the familiar black alloy. The suit had no neck, causing the head to be engulfed into the body. Two brightly lit slits vaguely resembled eyes. The suit spoke.

"Greetings."

The familiar mechanical voice now had actual machinery to go with it.

"Holy shit," Asha said breathlessly.

The center of the mech split open, and as it did, the arms and backward-bending leg plating followed suit. Alpha stepped out and walked toward them.

"Behold, our final weapon," he said, motioning behind him. "I feared I would not complete production in time."

Lucas walked over to the mech.

"Jesus, this thing is huge."

And it was. It had to be eleven feet tall, and nearly that wide.

"I designed it making sure that it could provide maximum protection while still moving about the ship. It should be able to access all the main areas, though a few smaller corridors will remain out of its jurisdiction."

Asha ran her hand over the right arm that ended in a giant cannon.

"How did you make this thing?"

Alpha motioned for them to follow him around to the rear. As they reached the backside, a familiar blue glow was visible, coming out of the cracks of the plating. Alpha opened a panel and their suspicion was confirmed. The blue null core that had initially powered their ship resided in the base of the suit's spine.

"You're using the old core to run this thing?"

Alpha nodded.

"It was the only power source that was capable of supporting its tremendous energy needs."

Lucas was amazed.

"But that was powering this entire *ship*, and you have all that crammed into one suit?"

"Correct. As such, it should be a powerful weapon in the coming fight."

Alpha reached up to a section on the back that was almost entirely encased in the durable black alloy that made up much of their own plating.

"There is another item to show you," Alpha said as he pressed a button and the panel swung open. Lucas and Asha's eyes widened in surprise.

There sat Noah, clutching his holoball. He smiled when he saw them.

"You . . . you're putting Noah in here? You've got to be joking," Asha said.

"I know it may appear to be unsafe, but I specifically designed this compartment with his protection in mind. Believe me when I say that it is the most secure location on the ship."

Lucas was unconvinced.

"He'll be in the heat of battle! Can't we just hide him somewhere?"

Alpha shook his head.

"They will be able to find him, and there is always a chance that his location may become depressurized during conflict."

Noah kicked his feet wildly.

"Ah-fa! Ah-fa!"

"This compartment is reinforced with a layer of protection as thick as our ship's hull. It could withstand an antimatter bomb. He will be safe, I assure you. For at least as long as we are alive."

Lucas looked up at the colossus in front of him. Maybe he was right. What use was there in hiding Noah if they all were killed anyway? They might as well tie his fate directly to their own, and being fixed inside an impenetrable cocoon was probably the most ideal place to be.

Alpha left the mech standing where it was and walked over to the captain's chair. There would be no need for a turret gunner. No reason to spool the white null core up for another jump. As such, the three of them remained in the CIC as Alpha took the controls. The blue-green glow waved hazily in front of them.

"Are you both prepared for what is to come?" Alpha said as the neural connections took hold of his temples.

"As ready as we'll ever be," Lucas replied.

A million stars greeted them as the ship decelerated out of the tunnel. Unfamiliar constellations appeared before Lucas's eyes, and in the middle, one star shone more brightly than the rest. The central sun of the Soran system was a distant beacon at this range.

Alpha was not stopping to admire the scenery. He immediately dialed up the speed as high as he could muster. The ship took a fair amount of time to reach its top velocity, which Lucas had learned from the Sentinel chase back in Earth's system.

It seemed Alpha was hoping he was wrong. Perhaps his calculations had been off. Perhaps if they just flew fast enough, they'd reach Soran-controlled space before Omicron showed up.

The crew waited in silence. A minute passed. Then two. Lucas felt hope beginning to creep into his mind. Could they really outrun Omicron? Had all their worry and training been for nothing?

His gaze was captured by the large pale-green planet they were approaching. It had two rings and its surface swirled with gaseous storms. It was unlike any body Lucas had seen before. He wondered what the Sorans had named it.

The planet became enormous. Lucas kept his eyes fixed on it as Alpha barreled straight ahead. Briefly, he caught a glimmer of something that didn't look like gas movement. A miniscule shimmer that shouldn't have been there. And then, from the same spot, three bright blue lights began to glow.

"Alpha!" he cried, but as he did so, the lights fired. A pulse blast rocketed toward the ship. When it struck, every light went out, and Lucas and Asha were pitched off their feet from the impact while Alpha remained in the chair.

As they picked themselves up, the lights came back on one by one. Lucas looked out of the viewscreen and saw that they were now floating through space, their engines having been knocked out and their desperate race interrupted by the blast. The stars drifted lazily around, and the green glow of the nearby planet blanketed the room. Straight ahead, there was a void in the stars. A void growing ever larger.

"He has arrived," Alpha said solemnly. The hope of escape was gone. Alpha's prediction had been proven true and Omicron's invisible ship loomed ahead of them.

Alpha flew out of the chair as the neural connectors snapped off from his temples with an audible crack. He raced over to the holotable and whirled through screen after screen, muttering to himself.

"Engines disabled, airlocks disabled, hull intact, life support online."

He turned to them with a conclusion.

"We will be boarded."

As he spoke the words, a loud clang reverberated through the ship. There was no confirmation from Alpha, but Lucas was sure that Omicron's vessel had now attached itself to their own in some way.

The viewscreen flickered and changed from hazy stars to a familiar, imposing sight. Omicron's dark face and blue eyes appeared before them. Alpha stepped away from the holotable and approached the front of the room. Omicron snarled something in Xalan.

"What's he saying?" Asha asked.

Alpha continued to listen to his grunts. He flipped a switch on his translator, and it began broadcasting what Omicron was saying through the holotable behind them. It wasn't reading his brainwaves from this distance, but the language was indeed being translated into understandable English.

"Greetings, lost child. It seems I have found you at last."

Alpha growled back.

"I am no child of yours."

"And yet you have no father."

"Only because of your actions."

Omicron sneered.

"Your clan was killed in a raid, as you have been informed."

"A raid orchestrated by whom? And all surviving members were eliminated? An unlikely scenario, considering many are spread across the planet."

"No matter the cause, your services are required on Xala. Your past transgressions have been forgiven. From your cowardice during Earth campaign to your destruction of the [garbled] station, where you slaughtered thousands of your brethren with the aid of . . . Sorans."

His voice carried a tone of very obvious disgust as he motioned with his claw to Lucas and Asha, standing beside Alpha staring up at the screen. He let out a loud roar that shook the walls.

"And you dare lecture me about the death of your traitorous clan?"

"So you admit your misdeed?"

Omicron threw up his claw dismissively.

"What of it? Your father disobeyed an explicit directive and compromised the security of the entire war effort. He made the foolish mistake of trusting your brothers with his findings, and as such your entire clan was deemed a threat, no matter their scientific value."

"Then why spare me? Why not obliterate this ship when you had the opportunity?"

"Study of your genes has shown that you will develop into a formidable mind. It would be unfortunate if we were not able to come to an arrangement for you to continue your work on Xala, as your clan has for generations, producing some of our finest technology."

"Until you wiped them out."

"It was necessary for the preservation of our species."

"What did my father find?"

"If you learned that information, we would be forced to execute you as well, no matter your inherent worth to the cause. We trust that you will see the error of your clan's ways, and give up this foolish pursuit of refuge on Sora."

Omicron leaned forward and continued.

"For someone with such a high intelligence quotient, you appear to be a fool. Do you really think the Sorans will welcome you?"

Alpha stood defiantly, his claws clutched into fists.

"I offer knowledge, far beyond what they possess. I bring with me humans, Sorans from another world. They think themselves alone in the universe. They will embrace us."

Omicron shook his head.

"You know nothing of the cruelty of the Sorans. You think you understand this conflict. You think our regime corrupt and barbaric. You are too similar to your father. And if you do not submit, you will meet the same fate."

"You merely prove yourself the barbarian," Alpha replied.

Omicron leaned away.

"Further debate would appear to be useless, as it is apparent you have made your choice. You will return to Xala. Your ill-chosen companions will be destroyed. My men are already onboard."

The screen cut to black, and Alpha raced over to the holotable.

"They're here already?"

Alpha scrambled through monitor after monitor, but they were all deactivated.

"They disabled all of our sensors. I thought we would have more warning."

He shut down the console.

"We must depart, immediately."

Alpha walked over to his suit and crawled inside. The metal plates shifted and engulfed him.

"To Point A?" Lucas asked, remembering their plan.

"Yes," Alpha said from inside the mech. "Let us hope we are not too late."

In making preparations for the coming battle, Alpha predicted Omicron's troops would be drawn to the stasis room first, where eleven humans were suspended in tanks. The Xalans' equipment would merely detect the life-forms, not the fact they were brain-dead, and as such, they might deem the chamber a haven for a secret collection of stowaways that needed to be exterminated.

The elevator had been rendered offline, but was likely too slow for their purposes anyway. Instead, in preparation for the battle, they'd already cut large holes in the hallway floors, allowing for easy, fast access between levels. The three of them reached the first opening outside the CIC and Alpha's thundering metal suit dove straight into it. A loud, jarring clank from below indicated he'd landed. Lucas and Asha affixed their helmets while they ran toward the opening. They leapt into it without a moment's hesitation, an action they'd practiced repeatedly these past few weeks. The fifteen-foot drop was a breeze since their armored suits absorbed the impact. One more drop and they were in the laboratory hallway.

This time, all three of them landed at the same time, their collective weight making a crater in the metal floor. As they looked up, they saw Omicron's troops for the first time. There were five of them at the end of the hall, two busy cutting through the door to the stasis room while the rest stood guard.

There was no look of surprise on their faces, as each wore menacing helmets that engulfed their entire heads. Their dark armor covered every inch of them. Far from the chunkiness of their own suits, the troops' plating was sleek and streamlined. Lucas recognized the Xalan symbol for "paragon" emblazoned on their breastplate. These soldiers were not the clumsy misfits that guarded the fuel station. Alpha had warned them, but to see them now sent unwanted chills up Lucas's spine.

In an instant, the hallway erupted with gunfire. The enclosed space was a nightmare for engagement, but Alpha's giant mech suit was able to act as a shield for them. It lumbered toward the soldiers, taking shots from their energy rifles as Lucas and Asha fired their own weapons from underneath each of its arms.

They were fast. Very fast. They dodged plasma rounds and fisson bullets alike, and in seconds the back wall had been blasted through to the hull, which was the only thing keeping them from blowing a hole in the ship with their fire.

A blast from Alpha's arm cannon finally caused one of them to stagger. Lucas managed to catch him with a spray of plasma from Natalie's full-auto mode, and the rounds ate through his suit like acid.

Just as soon as he started mentally celebrating, a round caught him square in the chest. He flew backward onto the ground, and looked down to see a smoking dent in his black alloy breastplate. He winced in pain, but staggered to his feet to rejoin the fight. Asha took a grazing round to her left arm, and it cut through the armor all the way to the skin.

But the soldiers were ultimately cornered. As the trio moved closer, there began to be less time and space to dodge blasts. Alpha caught one of them directly in the chest, the explosive round disintegrating him on the spot. Asha managed to hit the leg of a soldier attempting to dive out of the way, and the fission bullet caused his leg to detach at the knee. Even over the sounds of constant fire, Lucas could hear him screaming on the ground.

Asha ducked as a stream of rounds went over her head. Lucas flipped a switch and Natalie's barrel extended. Thermal vision cut through the smoke and he targeted the white shapes ahead. A single piercing round went through the right soldier's helmet, and black blood sprayed out the back of his head.

The last soldier pulled his rifle's trigger only to find it broken—Asha had grazed it with a round—and he dropped it to whip out an energy pistol instead. They were less than twenty feet away now, and Lucas was amazed at the soldier that stood before him. Even in the face of certain death, he fired away at them, praying he'd connect with a shot. Such courage.

Lucas spun out from behind the armored Alpha and blew him apart with a shotgun blast. The noise was even more defeating than in test fire mode.

Alpha examined the door that stood next to the pile of corpses reeking of cooked flesh. A few seconds longer and they might have cut through the door entirely, but it remained intact with no piercing damage. Lucas thought he heard Noah giggle from inside Alpha's rear compartment.

"Back to command," Alpha ordered, and they began sprinting down the hallway where they'd just come from.

Lucas held up his hand to stop them. He checked a readout on his suit, a motion sensor. He slowly pointed upward toward the hole they'd come through, a few yards ahead. The quiet shifting of metal could be heard above.

Aiming Natalie upward, Lucas activated his "X" scope. Above them, he could see through the ceiling where another squad of six or seven skeletal soldiers hovered around the hole, waiting for them to climb back up.

Lucas flipped a switch. His barrel shortened and widened. He signaled to Asha and Alpha who nodded. Three. Two. One.

He blasted the ceiling just to the right of the hole. Four Xalans tumbled down to the hallway floor. Alpha immediately crushed one's head with his massive metal foot while Asha celebrated a chance to use her dearly beloved blade. As promised, it tore through the soldiers who were struggling to reach their feet. In an instant, the three of them were in pieces, black blood spatter coating the walls and their own suits.

Asha suddenly looked up and raised her sword. It blocked the first shot from the soldiers that remained above, but the second and third caught her in the chest and she rocketed backward into Alpha's mech. Lucas sprayed a stream of rounds at their knees. They dodged the barrage, except for one of them who staggered and fell through the hole. Lucas leapt on him immediately and jammed his knife through the metal mask. Blood pooled out around him and joined that of his comrades on the floor.

Alpha discharged his cannon arm and the final soldier was obliterated as more of the ceiling came down around them. Lucas ran over to check on Asha, who was writhing on the ground. He pulled off his helmet and removed hers as well.

"Where are you hit?" he asked frantically.

She gasped for breath.

"First one . . . hit plate. Second . . . shoulder. Ow."

Lucas now saw the smoking hole near her right collarbone. He searched for the release on her chestplate, and once he found it, peeled the entire apparatus off. Underneath, she was wearing a pressurized black bodysuit, as they all were. It was an organic material meant to seal itself after damage, stopping blood from exiting wounds, among other uses. Quickly, Lucas reached into his own suit and pulled out Alpha's medical cauterizing tool. He cut open the resealed suit with his knife and sprayed the gel into her wound. She winced as it hissed and steamed. Soon however, the bleeding stopped, a fresh layer of faux skin began to form over the wound, and the organic material mended itself from the knife slit. She breathed a sigh of relief.

"That'll do," she said as she picked up her chestplate and reattached it over her torso. Lucas helped her to her feet and both put their helmets back on.

Alpha's mech doubled as a ladder to the next level. He extended his metal clawed arm above his head, and Asha and Lucas were able to scramble up the suit to the barracks level. Alpha gripped the edge of the destroyed floor with his claw and hoisted himself up with boost from his mechanized legs.

They executed the same maneuver to reach the command level, but as Alpha landed, they saw another contingent of soldiers rounding the corner from an airlock tunnel. This time they were a dozen deep and sprinted toward them in formation. Those in front had some sort of large metal shields in place that deflected incoming shots.

"Retreat to command!" Alpha yelled from inside the mech. Lucas and Asha sprinted toward the door as Alpha provided cover. Then he too turned and bounded toward the entryway.

They slid inside and Lucas closed and sealed the door behind them. Soon after, he began to hear the sounds of metal being cut. They'd come prepared.

"What happened to the traps, Alpha?" Lucas asked, still regaining his composure from the recent engagement. "Those airlock entrances were supposed to blow."

They'd rigged a series of explosives on each of the external entrances using a combination of the human grenades and mines they had left over from Norway and a few of Alpha's own creation.

"It appears they either disabled the devices, or were simply unaffected by them."

Lucas suspected that soldiers this well-trained knew how to spot a booby trap, but he was disappointed they hadn't worked. But not everything could go according to plan, could it? The real plan was to not die, and that was working so far. Now, they were the ones who were trapped. The second doorway leading into the room began to emit similar sounds of metal being shorn. Behind them, the viewscreen had been covered by a large solid shield to prevent it from being shattered in a possible firefight.

All around the room there were storage crates that had been fused to the floor. They wouldn't provide much protection, but between them and the consoles, it would at least allow them some cover. Alpha imagined that they might need to make a stand in this room, and he was right.

Lucas could feel sweat pouring down his face inside his helmet. His hands started to tremble, but the stability sensors of the suit didn't allow that to translate to his aim. Alpha was behind the holotable in the mech, and Lucas and Asha were behind storage crates on either side of him. A bright cutting torch burst through the center of the first door. It was quickly removed, and a device was inserted into the opening. After a few seconds of silence, the item erupted and a huge hole was blown through the door. The Xalan forces began streaming in, shield troops in front. There were almost no gaps in the phalanx and it was nearly impossible to get a shot.

Alpha let loose a blast from his cannon which jarred the front line. Lucas seized on the moment of instability and unloaded a stream of rounds into two soldiers whose shields were now ajar. Others behind them scrambled to pick up the fallen shields and fill the void, but Asha caught two of them in the head as they attempted to do so.

Finally, the group broke formation and all of them began opening fire, abandoning the shields altogether. The storage crates and holotable were taking heavy damage and the air was filled with the smell of melting metal. Lucas watched as the central console sparked and eventually erupted in a cloud of smoke after it was decimated by round after round. His own crate was starting to be eaten away and plasma flew by, mere inches from his head. The second doorway exploded the way the first had, and another phalanx of shield-bearing troops marched inside in formation.

"Screw this!" Lucas heard Asha yell. She banged on Alpha's metal leg next to her.

"Cover fire!" she said. Alpha responded by shooting a concussive blast at the scattered troops, which drew their fire to him. Lucas popped out of his own hiding spot and lined up a sniper shot which tore through two separate soldiers who were caught unaware.

Asha, meanwhile, had leapt over her barricade and was full-on sprinting toward the shielded unit at the other side of the room.

No way.

As the Xalans turned their attention toward her, Lucas and Alpha hammered them for not recognizing the more immediate threat, and four more of them went down. Lucas looked back just in time to see Asha throw her sword at the middle shield bearer. It ripped through the metal and hit him square in the face as the shield slumped down to an angle. Continuing her sprint, she ran up the downed shield like a ramp and launched herself twelve feet in the air, aided by the mechanisms of her armor. She curled her wrist slightly and her sword shot up out of the dead Xalan below and into her hands, just in time for her to come crashing down and split another soldier in two. The phalanx shattered, and Asha was now whirling around in their midst. Black blood and limbs flew into the air.

She's insane, Lucas thought as he sprinted over behind Alpha on his way to aid her. When he reached the pile, the group was so focused on her they didn't even hear Natalie fire as the rifle ripped through the backs of four of them. Lucas kicked one soldier away and slashed his knife across the throat of another. Finally he reached Asha, still swinging wildly with pieces of Xalan troops everywhere. She almost took his head clean off before she recognized him. Her armor was cracked, and bits of blackened skin shone through where she'd been hit. But whatever pain she was feeling, she kept fighting. Lucas wrestled with a soldier trying to take his rifle away, while she split another Xalan's midsection open and then shot him in the head at point-blank range with her Magnum. Lucas flipped the switch on his gun to "carnage," and fired a blast while the creature was still clutching it. The round hit a soldier to the left of them, and the recoil allowed Lucas to wrench it away from the creature. He spun it around and fired a second blast, which immediately caused the surrounding area to rain black blood. Asha stuck her blade in the center of one final soldier, and Lucas watched as, with a flick of her thumb, blue electricity surged through the creature and smoke poured out of the cracks of his armor.

The second phalanx was now completely decimated, and Alpha had whittled the first wave down to almost nothing, despite taking heavy fire himself. His mech had blast marks all up and down it, and bits of machinery were spilling out in places. It was still moving and firing, though a bit slower than before.

Natalie's barrel elongated and Lucas took down a soldier from across the room with a single shot. Asha ran toward the last Xalan standing and threw her blade at his heart. It stuck straight through his chestplate, and as he slowly fell down to the ground, Asha recalled the sword back to her hand. When she reached him, she used it to cleave his helmeted head off in one quick slash.

Lucas lowered his gun and winced in pain. He removed his helmet, and tried to look around at his back. He could see smoke rising from behind him, and the distinct smell of burning flesh indicated a shot or two in the frenetic firefight had made its way past the plating, though his organic suit had since sealed the wounds. Asha looked even worse for wear, her armor was missing huge chunks and her bodysuit was visibly mending itself around her bloody wounds and burns, closing them up until they could be further treated. She pulled off her dented helmet, which had fortunately kept her head free of serious injury.

Lucas walked over to Alpha's mech, and went around behind him. He opened the rear compartment, and found a very frightened-looking Noah with tears in his eyes. He dropped his holoball, which rolled down the charred floor away from them.

"Hey buddy, it's okay. We're just playing a little game out here. We'll be done soon."

Noah sniffled.

"Can you be brave for just a little while longer?"

Noah merely waved his hands around. Lucas walked a few steps away and picked up the ball. Noah blinked away his tears as he took it into his hands and it lit up with a rainbow spectrum of colors once again.

Lucas walked around to the front of the mech. Alpha had opened the metal head so that his own face was visible.

"How'd we do, Alpha?"

Alpha shifted the mech slightly. It groaned.

"Both the pair of you and the mech have sustained damage, but we are victorious."

Asha slowly approached, dripping blood in her wake.

"Let's get you patched up again," Lucas said, and he needed her to return the favor. He reached for the medical tool once more, but as he did so, heard a familiar sound.

Behind Asha, another phalanx approached, and similar noises could be heard coming from the other hallway.

"Impossible," Alpha stammered. "He should not have this many . . . It's unheard of that he would travel with . . ." His thoughts kept breaking down midway through. He looked down at the pair of them. Lucas was in bad shape, Asha in worse.

This is it, Lucas thought. *This is the moment.*

Death had been both everywhere and nowhere these past few years of his life. He'd seen so much of it, yet it always escaped him. Until now. There was no way they'd survive another battle like the one they'd just fought. Natalie's scope display flickered. The gun was as damaged as he was.

Asha pivoted toward the phalanx, marching in unison down the hall. She turned her blade outward, and her Magnum was pointed at the ground in her other outstretched hand.

Lucas walked up beside her, Natalie crackling in his hands, but still willing to fire. He looked at Asha. Her eyes were full of determination and tears as she stared straight ahead at the alien army ahead of them.

"Are you ready?" he asked, as smoke billowed around them. He wasn't sure if he was asking about fighting or dying.

"Yes," she said, an answer to both.

He gripped her by the arm, turned her toward him, and stared into her brilliant, green eyes, burning with rage or passion, he couldn't be sure.

"Asha, I—"

"Do you trust me?"

The voice was not hers, but Alpha's, coming from behind them.

"What?" Lucas asked.

"Do you trust me?"

"Alpha, there's no plan left. This is it."

"There is always a plan. That is the reason for the question."

What new insanity had been hatched inside that mind?

"Yes, Alpha. I trust you."

"Why not?" Asha echoed.

Alpha nodded, satisfied.

"Then put your helmets on, and prepare yourselves."

Lucas and Asha obeyed, and the helmets hooked into their chestplates with a hiss.

"Prepare for what?"

The phalanxes were now both visible, and had almost reached the CIC.

Alpha turned toward the viewscreen and pressed a button inside the mech. The metal barrier slid down as the armor closed around his head. A view of the stars and nearby ringed planet reappeared. It took Lucas a moment to process what was happening.

No.

Alpha charged up his cannon and let loose a blast at the viewscreen. It made a loud thud, but it remained intact.

No.

He shot another blast, and cracks began to form on the surface.

No.

Alpha started sprinting toward it as fast as his damaged mech would muster, and fired one more shot. The cracks expanded to the entire screen. He plowed headfirst into the damaged pane and the whole thing shattered as he flew out into space.

The air was sucked out of the room instantaneously, and Lucas and Asha along with it. He could barely keep a grip on Natalie as he was flung out into the vacuum, and he saw Asha doing cartwheels next to him. In a second they were outside of the ship. He saw streams of Xalan soldiers flying out of the opening, each flailing wildly about. A metal shield shot past Lucas, almost colliding with him. The damaged holotable had ripped out of the floor and was spinning around next to Asha.

A soldier drifted toward Lucas, unable to control his movements. Lucas tried to fire Natalie, but apparently the rifle wasn't meant to shoot in a vacuum and remained dormant. Instead, the soldier merely drifted by him, struggling with his own weapon, which wouldn't work either.

Lucas wondered why he wasn't dead. He remembered the holes that peppered his suit, but another thought occurred to him as he floated weightless through space. The bodysuit! The constant sealing also acted as pressurization, and between that and his still functional helmet, he was alive in the airless environment.

And what an environment it was. Outside of the pirouetting soldiers and debris, he was suspended in deep space in complete silence. All around him shone the light of a billion stars, and the distant center of the Milky Way was more visible than ever. This system must have been quite a bit closer to it than Earth. To his right, which was a constantly changing identifier as he couldn't stop spinning, was the great green gaseous planet he'd seen earlier, a fresh storm brewing on its surface in the form of a large spot visible between the two rings. Below him was the Ark, battered from their time together, and dwarfed by the ship attached to it. Omicron's vessel was no longer cloaked, and Lucas could finally see it's elongated form and true size, which was at least twice that of their own ship. It reflected the starlight and was far more elegant than the usual bulky, mechanical ships he'd seen throughout the course of the war.

Lucas caught a glimpse of Asha, a hundred feet away. She was grappling with a large Xalan soldier that had been flung her way. His first instinct was to attempt to swim over to her, but the effort proved futile, as it was an ineffective way to move about in space. He lacked propulsion of any kind to come to her aid, but was relieved when she saw her plunge her sword into the creature's thigh. His suit depressurized, and he clutched his neck as he shook violently. Soon he was still, and Asha removed her blade and let him float past her while she batted away crystals of frozen black blood.

Lucas searched for Alpha, but couldn't find the mech anywhere. How was this a plan? It seemed like a peaceful form of suicide if anything. Lucas was unsure of the air reserves his suit contained, but he knew there weren't any large tanks attached to his back, so it couldn't be long. Already his breath was starting to feel shallow, and he forced himself to remain calm before he hyperventilated and used all his remaining oxygen. At least the stars and nearby planet were a tranquil sight.

23

After admiring the enormity of deep space for several minutes while his breathing became increasingly shallow, Lucas jumped inside his armor when he felt three metal claws wrap around his waist. He looked around in surprise and saw that Alpha's mech had snuck up on him in the silence. And they were . . . moving? There were jets shooting out wisps of white underneath each giant metal foot, and it was clear Alpha had designed his suit with an emergency propulsion mechanism for such an occasion.

They soared through space toward Asha, and Lucas had to deflect an armored Xalan body part away from his head as they flew through lanes of debris still streaming out of their ship. Soon she was within range and Lucas reached out and grasped her hand while Alpha came to a halt as best he could. Lucas pulled her into his arms to ensure she wouldn't float away when Alpha changed course. They were supposed to have comms inside their helmets, but Lucas's was no longer working and he could only guess at Alpha's intentions.

They flew further away from the Ark and drifted closer to Omicron's ship. Alpha wheeled around and Lucas had to tighten his grip on Asha to keep her from floating away. She was moving slightly, meaning she was still conscious, but it was getting harder to breathe for Lucas, and he imagined the same was true for her.

Alpha jetted toward the black enemy craft, which was still sitting dormant, silhouetted against the nearby green planet. They moved closer and closer to the front, and Lucas realized their intended destination. The larger ship had a rather wide forward viewscreen of its own.

Alpha began a barrage of cannon strikes as he rocketed toward the front of the ship. The artillery was silent, but the vibrations from the shots reverberated all the way through Lucas to his core. Alpha was focusing all his fire on one particular point in the viewscreen, and Lucas couldn't tell if it was achieving its desired result. As they zoomed closer, he could see there did appear to be an area that was cracked, but it was far from destroyed. Alpha kept firing, and Lucas was starting to get dizzy as the air inside his suit was desperately thin. The cracks were starting to spread. Alpha fired one more round and turned himself so that he was diving head first at the weak point. Lucas braced himself as best he could.

What happened next was complete chaos. Lucas felt an impact shake his whole body and he flew from Alpha's grasp. They slammed through the screen and onto the bridge of Omicron's ship. A metal curtain rocketed down to seal the shattered viewscreen. Pressurization returned, as did sound and gravity, and Lucas found himself rolling on the floor, Natalie tumbling out of his grasp.

But that wasn't a priority. Lucas's first action before even standing was to rip off his helmet. Fresh air rushed into his lungs, and he could finally catch his breath, his chest heaving inside his breastplate. A second later, he managed to look around the vast command center and saw that a number of Xalans were getting to their feet as well. Lucas scrambled forward to grab Natalie and put two of them down before he even realized they were unarmed and unarmored. Two more shots from across the room and he saw that Asha had dealt with those on her side as well. Presumably they were navigators, comms officers, or maybe even pilots, but whatever role they had on the ship, they weren't expecting combat.

The room they were in was enormous. Holographic consoles lit up every wall, and there were three central chairs instead of the one they had onboard the Ark where Lucas had spent so much of his time. Their holotable was a bit further back, but it was colossal. There was no galaxy or planet floating above it, but rather a three-dimensional rendering of the Ark. Lucas scanned through the flurry of symbols surrounding it, and found that he was reading through KIA reports of the Xalan boarding party. It appeared none remained.

Lucas's attention was snapped away from the display when he heard a loud metal groan. Alpha was struggling to right the mech, which was planted face first on the ground amidst the wreckage of a console it had plowed into. The suit was badly damaged, and Lucas saw that its metal claw was severed and lay a few yards away. Alpha was struggling to push himself up with his cannon arm, but the mech wouldn't budge. Something was sizzling inside one of the leg mechanisms, and it contracted and expanded rapidly as if it was out of Alpha's control. Asha came over to help Lucas push the mech's head and torso upward, but the thing weighed as much as a semi truck, and even their enhanced armor couldn't help them right it. Alpha wasn't talking. Presumably his external communicator had been destroyed in the crash.

The top of the suit opened, and Alpha had to crawl his way out of it onto the floor.

"You alright?" Lucas asked cautiously, scanning his body for blood.

"I am intact," Alpha replied hoarsely, readjusting his translator collar.

Lucas climbed up the shoulder and onto the back of the mech. The blue core's light was flickering and seemed to be unstable after the trauma the suit had just endured. Lucas opened the black metal hatch and found Noah safely swaddled in the lining of the gelatinous pod, having endured the recent cataclysm without incident.

"Leave him in there," Alpha said as he reattached his mechanical claw. "It is not yet safe aboard this vessel."

He was at the holotable, rifling through menus and readouts. A display of Omicron's ship floated up above him. He scanned through a number of pages of symbols and came to a conclusion.

"Only one life-form remains onboard this vessel."

"Indeed."

Lucas jumped, as did Asha, who ripped off her helmet and looked around the empty room. The last voice was not any of their own, and sounded as if it had been spoken right beside his ear. His eyes darted around as the voice continued.

"It appears I have misjudged your taste in allies, traitor."

The voice was deep and dark, speaking in perfect English. It was coming from inside Lucas's own head.

"They will have to be studied and dissected instead of destroyed. This species subset is the most violent we have encountered to date. And these two, to fight on your behalf with such devotion and ferocity? Fascinating."

Lucas couldn't help but look around, even though the voice was within him. Asha looked similarly unnerved, while Alpha stood coolly at the base of the holotable. It was clear he was hearing the voice as well, as he spoke back to it.

"Telepathy, Commander? I did not know you were one of the Chosen."

There was a laugh that made Lucas's skin crawl inside his armor.

"A recent mutation. Though I fear one that pales in comparison to the abilities of the newer Shadows. I am an old man, after all."

Alpha slowly circled around the table to the front of the room.

"Too old it seems. You have miscalculated this fight. Your troops lie in pieces or now orbit this planet."

There was a snort.

"My mistake was trusting others to do a task I should have completed myself. In fact, I was just preparing to come aboard. I am grateful you have saved me the trouble with your misguided escape attempt."

"This was no escape," Alpha growled.

"No, I suppose it was not."

The large door at the end of the room slid open. Standing in the middle was Omicron, clad in armor to the neck. He was taller than most Xalans, and thinner too. His dark skin and blue eyes were visible, which indicated he felt he had no need for a helmet. His plating was even slimmer than that of the soldiers they had seen, and was contoured exceptionally close to his body. Organic claws poked out of the tips of his gloves and the bottoms of his boots. He had no visible weapons either in hand or on his hip. He didn't move from the doorframe, and his electric blue eyes glanced across the room to each of them. Lucas and Asha had their guns raised, Alpha had apparently scavenged an energy pistol from inside his downed mech and it was also pointed at the unarmed Omicron.

The only sound in the room was the faint whirring of machinery. Pools of black blood were starting to dry around the Xalan bodies that littered the CIC. Omicron stood motionless, his gaze now directed toward the ground. As he slowly raised his chin, the voice returned.

"Well Earth-warriors, what are you waiting for?"

Asha didn't need to be asked twice. She fired off a pair of shots from her Magnum, and Lucas and Alpha followed her lead a split second later, emptying their own weapons at him. But it was already too late. As soon as the first crack of a gunshot could be heard, Omicron was already four feet to the right. Lucas fired a stream of rounds toward him, but the creature kept dashing sideways and ran up a nearby console. In the split-second it took Lucas to understand his next move, Omicron was already ten feet in the air above him.

His feet hit Lucas's chest before he could re-aim Natalie. He was pinned to the ground in an instant, and heard a loud crack come from his torso where his armor splintered. Before the pain even registered in his mind, Omicron had leapt off him and landed next to Alpha. In one claw swipe, he disarmed the scientist and kicked him in the chest so he flew backward into the downed mech.

In the mere seconds this took, Asha had enough time to draw her sword. As Omicron leapt toward her, she slashed through the air and he had to twist himself to avoid being cut. When he landed, she swung with a flurry of strikes, hitting nothing but air as he dodged and weaved around the blade. It seemed impossible for a creature so large and so old to be this agile. "Inhumanly fast" was not the correct term, but Lucas had never seen another creature move like that.

Finally Asha swung the blade around in one giant arc and, when she froze, Lucas thought he had caught it in his hand. His claw was raised in the air above his head, the sword suspended motionless with it. But as he struggled to his feet, Lucas saw that there were six inches of air in between the blade and his armored claw.

Impossible.

A look of terror crept across Asha's face as she realized the true power of the creature before her. She didn't have the sense to react when he plowed a clawed fist into her midsection, sending her rocketing back into the far wall. Lucas finally got his finger to Natalie's trigger and sent another stream of plasma his way. Sensing it before it even arrived, Omicron did an arching backflip that put him once again adjacent to Alpha, who was attempting to recover from the earlier blow. Omicron didn't give him a chance, and ravaged him with a series of claw strikes before flinging him toward the doorway where he slid to a stop, a trail of black blood smeared on the ground behind him.

Omicron turned his attention toward Lucas, who fumbled with the "carnage" setting until it finally snapped into place. As the creature sprinted toward him, Lucas unleashed a blast. But Omicron twisted out of the way in a split second and the burst ripped apart a nearby console instead. And then he was upon him.

Lucas couldn't shield himself from the barrage of blows and slashes he was enduring at a lightning pace. Pieces of his armor flew off in chunks to the ground, and his alloy knife bounced away behind him. After raining down the barrage of strikes, Omicron kicked Lucas's legs out from under him, then landed a forward shoulder thrust that sent him flying into a control cluster. Lucas's back arched from the impact, and his vision was mostly white from the searing pain that surged through his entire body. Blood was spilling out of his armor out onto the floor; his organic undersuit couldn't mend fast enough to seal all his fresh wounds. The console he'd crashed into was sparking and smoking while he tried to pry himself out of it. Once he did, he immediately collapsed to the floor.

Omicron walked toward him, but had to dodge reflexively as a fission bullet whizzed past his head and took a chunk out of the back wall. Asha was back on her feet. Omicron ripped a nearby piece of machinery that was as tall as he was out of the floor. The lights and displays flickered then went dark when the cables attaching it to the ground were snapped off one by one. He took it in his arms, spun it around once, and flung it at Asha. She tried to leap out of the way, but Lucas saw the edge of it hit her hip, which sent her flying. She tumbled to the ground and didn't stir once she stopped. Alpha remained motionless as blood filled the cracks of the metal floor beneath him. Blood in his own eyes, Lucas felt around on the ground for Natalie, but the gun was nowhere to be found.

Omicron surveyed the destruction he'd caused, and turned his attention to the mech. He slowly climbed on top of it and checked a readout on the forearm of his armor, which didn't have a scratch on it after the recent battle.

Lucas watched in horror as he realized what the readout said.

"There is another," spoke Omicron's cold voice in his head.

He pried open the rear armored hatch with his claws and stood up when he saw its contents. He turned toward them.

"You would bring a child here? Perhaps you are more savage than us."

Lucas finally found a familiar stock with a familiar etching in the back. He pulled Natalie into his arms and used the battered rifle for support so he could bring himself to his knees. Omicron turned back to the open hatch. Lucas could hear Noah crying from across the room.

"This one is so early in its development cycle. The scientists will love it. They might even keep it alive."

Omicron shifted his cold gaze back to them. He paused before speaking again.

"But alas, I am not one to cater to the sciences. Perhaps this mission was impossible to complete. Perhaps the subjects were all too weak, and were slaughtered before they could be captured for study."

His voice was dripping with venom inside Lucas's head.

"Yes, I believe that is what my report will say."

Suddenly, a black blade flew across the room, launched by an injured Asha, hobbling on one leg at the far side of the chamber. Lucas felt a microsecond of elation, one that quickly evaporated as the blade fell short of its target, embedding itself in the mech a foot below Omicron. He hadn't even flinched, as he must have predicted its path.

"Your accuracy is unfortunate," he scoffed.

Asha was breathing heavily, and spoke through clenched teeth.

"Is it?"

She pressed a button on her cuff, and the blade erupted with blue electricity. It coursed through the mech and up into Omicron's suit. He was caught unaware by the weapon's secondary function and seized up in agony as the voltage surged through him, rooting him to the mech.

Lucas didn't hesitate as he brought Natalie around, the barrel already extending. It took him a quarter second to line up the shot, and he exhaled as he pulled the trigger.

The round flew through the room at hypersonic speeds and ripped through Omicron's throat as he remained fixed to the top of the mech, unable to leap out of the way. The electricity left him, and he crumbled to the ground in a heap, his body smoking and black blood splashed all around him.

Still on his knees, Lucas struggled to his feet. He limped toward the body and saw that Alpha had pulled himself off the floor as well. He was covered in his own blood, but was able to walk. Asha followed, heavily favoring one leg, her armor in tatters.

They reached Omicron's body at the base of the mech, and they could see his chest still rising and falling. His throat was open, and making unpleasant noises as blood poured out of it, but he was alive. Furthermore, his injury didn't impede his ability to communicate without words.

"You are as much a fool as your father," he spat out, his voice noticeably weaker inside Lucas's head. *"He would have us destroyed. As would you."*

Alpha reached down to the ground where his energy pistol lay. Standing back up, he aimed it at Omicron's head, which continued to project his thoughts.

"You may kill me, but I will join my true Xalan brothers. Those who have fallen for millennia fighting this war for the good of our people. I will be in a place you will never go."

"Nor would I want to, should I find you and your brethren there."

Omicron coughed as more blood poured out of him. His voice became quieter.

"You will understand why we did it. We needed to be a proud people if we were to thrive. We could not allow the masses to know the truth."

"What truth?" Alpha asked, his pistol shaking.

"With my dying breath, I will not betray the oath I swore."

His piercing blue eyes stared directly into Alpha's.

"May you suffer as your father did. As your brothers did. As your—"

A smoldering hole in his forehead prevented further elaboration. Alpha dropped the pistol as their minds went silent and Omicron was still at last.

24

"Goddamnit."

Lucas doubled over, fully aware of his injuries now that the fighting had subsided. His armor was decimated, shredded to ribbons from Omicron's razor claws. His organic suit was attempting to seal the many slashes across his body, but blood was spilling out onto the floor regardless. He stumbled over to the rear of the mech and looked down to find a teary-eyed Noah. The gelatinous insulation had kept him safe from the electrical surge generated by the sword. Asha pulled her blade out of the mech, and slowly fixed it to her back once more. Her face was badly bruised, her lip cut and bleeding, and she limped a few feet away to pick up her fallen Magnum.

Alpha had gotten the worst of it. Outside the mech, he had no armor. He was painted in his own blood, but was trying to seal his wounds with cauterizing gel. He winced as it hissed, and some of the gashes were too large to close immediately. His only saving grace was the fair amount of natural armored plating Xalans had across their chest, abdomen, and back. But even those areas were obviously injured.

He tossed away the empty gel gun and shambled over to the large central holotable.

"It must be here," Alpha said, his mechanical voice strained and his breathing labored.

"What must?" Lucas asked, but was ignored as Alpha ripped through the display at a lightning pace.

Asha sat down against the mech next to the still-warm body of Omicron, which was oozing black blood onto the ground. His blue eyes were still open, staring straight above him in a haunting manner.

"Not so tough now, are you?" she spat at him, as she leaned her head back to rest it against the mech.

Lucas was still trying to process what had just taken place. Omicron fought unlike anything he'd ever seen, a frenzied demon, a whirlwind of pure carnage. Alpha had warned them of his prowess, but it was now abundantly clear the Shadows were exceptionally dangerous weapons. Omicron was unarmed, and nearly killed them when a legion of elite soldiers could not. He stopped Asha's blade in midair using . . . what, his mind? Even with all they'd seen, such power was beyond anything Lucas could comprehend.

Lucas undid Noah's restraints and took him into his arms. The child whined as he carried him away from the scorched mech, and he didn't dare set him down on the floor, where black and red blood mingled. He walked over to Alpha who was still racing through the readouts of the holotable, typing furiously into a circular virtual keyboard.

"What are you doing?" Lucas asked once more. Alpha's eyes raced at lightspeed across the stream of symbols.

"I am inside the ship's mainframe and am attempting to form a bridge into the Commander's personal files. They are heavily encrypted, but I believe I have developed the correct override algorithm."

Symbols poured down vertically in the floating display, constantly shifting and swirling. One stopped moving, then two and eventually a string of thirty of them became locked into place, and Alpha breathed a sigh of relief. The screen changed to show a list of data packets, which Alpha quickly scrolled through. Almost immediately, a certain cluster caught his eye.

"Messages for me, from my father," he said breathlessly. "Sent over the course of Earth campaign."

"You never got them?" Asha said, lifting herself off the ground and hobbling toward the table.

"I never received any correspondence from my clan for the duration of the assignment. They must have been intercepted." He peered curiously at one particular file.

"One message is further secured at a level beyond the others."

Lucas recognized the Xalan symbol for "treason." Alpha began working on the virtual encryption using gestures that Lucas probably couldn't emulate with his own five-fingered hands. Noah squirmed in his arms and flung them out toward Asha. Lucas passed him over and saw he was now quite dirty, having been propped up against the bloody, ashen armor. But he had survived without so much as a paper cut; Alpha's mech had done its promised duty of protection. Noah set to work attempting to grab Asha's ponytail as she wiped away fresh blood from her chin with her free hand.

The symbols in the display turned green; Alpha's hacking was a success. The room lit up as a giant hologram was projected out of the table above them. It was a Xalan, one with many lines on his face, but familiar gold rings in his eyes.

Alpha pulled the chip from his translator collar, and placed it onto the holotable. The floating figure began growling, but his words were broadcast in English.

"Greetings, my son."

Alpha stood in reverence of his deceased father, towering larger than life above him.

"I do not wish to endanger your life with this message, more so than I already have by causing your exile to the Earth campaign. But this information must be disseminated to as many members of our clan as possible to ensure that the public may someday learn of it. I fear I have already given myself away, and my own destruction is imminent because of what I have discovered. My only hope is that, if I am killed, one of you may find a way to make the truth known to our people. The truth about the intertwined histories of Sora and Xala."

Lucas was enraptured by the broadcast, as were Alpha and Asha. The pain of his wounds was melting away as he focused solely on the giant hologram.

"As you know, our clan's field of research has exclusively focused on technology, mechanical, electrical, physical, and otherwise. We have been forbidden from doing genetic research for millennia, those duties assigned to the covert operations scientific enclave responsible for the horrific Shadows, along with other nefarious biological modifications to our people. I have never had an interest in such deplorable practices, but when a prototype armor set required access to the subject's genetic makeup to compensate for inborn faults, I was forced to break protocol and delve into the DNA of our species. These operations were done in secret, and for weeks, I found nothing unusual, and the project progressed smoothly."

Alpha slowly walked around the table, still craning his neck to see his father who seemed to follow him as he moved.

"But in the final stages of the process, I uncovered something deep within the genetic code. Something that was impossible, some sort of contaminant within the sample. I found Soran DNA."

Lucas's eyes widened and Alpha let out something resembling a snarling cough.

"I tested sample after sample, but always the same indicators were there. Soran genes. Mere traces, but they were consistently present. I told no one of the discovery, and set aside my work to further understand what I had found. I spent a month attempting to infiltrate the genetics core, the most secure server on the planet, accessed only by the Shadowmakers themselves. The encryption was a masterwork that took ages to decipher, but once cracked, I was able to access the entire alcove of data undetected."

The hologram flickered briefly, but continued.

"What I discovered was more astonishing than any explanation I could have imagined. A common celestial ancestor would have been fascinating enough, but what I found was a secret that had been kept for thousands of years."

The video changed from the portrait of Alpha's father and showed a great shining city in front of a crystal blue bay. A voiceover continued.

"This recorded archive was on the server, stolen Soran intelligence that no one has been allowed access to for millennia. 14,645 years ago, far before first contact, Sorans had invented machines to do nearly all laborious physical tasks for them. From construction to mining to harvesting, the machines were the core of the planet's economy. But centuries passed and the technology evolved at a rapid pace to produce artificial beings that were more intelligent than their creators. War broke out as the machines tried to seize control of the planet."

The beautiful city was ravaged by explosions. The feed cut to a battle scene that showed robots of all shapes and sizes rampaging through the street, butchering Sorans left and right with weapons Lucas had never seen before as other flying machines soared overhead dropping ordinance that consumed everything nearby in a blazing inferno.

"Eventually, the machines were defeated and technology regressed, forcing Sorans to work for themselves the way their ancestors had. This peace lasted some time until they became slothful once again. They were tired of backbreaking labor, and they began to experiment in a new field of progress, organics."

Lucas was beginning to understand.

"Synthetics could evolve at a rapid rate, their intelligence dooming their creators as it expanded exponentially. But organics? Such quick evolution was impossible, and living things could be engineered to be docile. They tried countless combinations of DNA, using nearly every animal variety on the planet, even inventing entirely new species. But the final products all disappointed. There was something missing, and one day they finally realized what it was."

The picture changed once more, and showed a small gray creature standing next to a male Soran. It had three clawless fingers, and short backward-bending legs resting on stubby feet. It stood a foot shorter than the Soran, and had an elongated snout with large white and green eyes. It almost looked . . . friendly.

"Using just a tiny fraction of Soran DNA, they created the first Xalan."

Alpha was standing transfixed. He let out a loud growl that wasn't able to be translated by his disassembled collar. Lucas himself could hardly believe what he was hearing.

"The new creature had the labor capabilities of a thousand different beasts, but the creative spark of a Soran, which allowed it to perform more complex tasks that the other prototypes could not. After initial success with the docile, intelligent creatures, they were slated for mass production. They assumed all the laborious tasks the Sorans were so desperate to avoid. After decades of free Xalan labor, the population grew fat and lazy once more. The Xalans were subject to abominable working conditions. Many died doing dangerous jobs, many starved when food was deemed an unnecessary expense. But they never complained, never seemed to lament their plight. They were bred not to care, and not to speak."

The video showed legions of small Xalans marching into a mine, covered in black dust.

"Others kept them as pets. A family's personal Xalan would do housework, supervise children, whatever was required of it. They were slaves, but cheerful ones. They became an indispensible part of Soran life."

A Xalan was shown playing with a pair of Soran children. One sandy haired boy tugged on one of its fingers, and it appeared to smile, revealing teeth that weren't sharp at all, far more square than the needles Lucas had seen a thousand times in snarling present-day creatures.

"The trouble started when the Xalans were put in charge of their own creation. The scientists no longer wanted to be bothered with the endless churning out of new organics, and so they tasked the Xalans with the responsibility. The process was uneventful for a century, but eventually one particular Xalan working in the genetic lab . . . altered things."

The video showed a specific Xalan, but he was indistinguishable from the others. His eyes were gold, not green however.

"The Sorans now refer to him as 'Zero' in their history scrolls. He was a mutant, one that managed to slip by inspection after the Xalans were put in charge. He came to work in the lab himself, knowing he was different from the others. Zero had a sense of self-awareness, which his brethren all lacked. He felt complex emotions, he could . . . imagine. After years of secretive research, Zero located his mutation, and introduced it into the system, crafting it as the new template for Xalan production. The change went undetected.

"He was merely the first. After him, with each subsequent generation, the Xalans were increasingly intelligent. New mutations were added into the template. Each new lifecycle made them perhaps a centimeter taller, with skin a millimeter thicker. The Sorans did not detect these subtle changes, and did not realize that the Xalans had grown as clever as them a mere three hundred years after Zero's first alterations."

The scene changed to show an uprising. Xalans took up arms, no longer docile and gentle looking, but snarling and furious. They were still far from the creatures that had invaded Earth, but were definitely first generation warriors, that much was clear.

"Another rebellion, one by creatures who had seen their strength and intellect increase drastically over the past few hundred years in secret as they continued to be treated with disdain. The Soran people were caught unaware and suffered heavy losses after so much time living in peace. Xalans almost conquered the planet, but after decades of fighting were finally driven back and their ranks decimated.

"There was much debate among the Sorans about what to do with the few remaining survivors. Many wanted genocide. Complete extermination of the species. Others wanted mercy for this new race of self-aware beings. After years of argument, the last Xalans were put on a ship that was set on a course for a nearby planet in a neighboring solar system, which could sustain life."

The circular sphere of Xala floated before them. It was the ravaged rock they'd seen before, red with the occasional patch of green and blue.

"The planet was almost barren, but there was enough oxygen and water to survive."

The feed showed the surface of Xala, with a few hundred creatures living in a makeshift village.

"The ones who remained made an oath. Their children must never know how they came to be. They swore revenge against the Sorans, but they would invent a tale about invasion and decimation of their world. They did not want future generations to learn they were once subject to the Sorans and were a mere genetic accident. They were to be their own people, fierce warriors who would terrorize the Sorans until they had wiped them out completely.

"They had little technology, but had the knowledge to create it. In less than a millennium, great cities had been erected, genetic laboratories had been crafted, and the population had grown dramatically. Genetic modification facilitated drastic changes in the population, and eventually, Xalans were molded into a lethal species. Once Xala had built up a comparable military force, they attacked Sora and the Great War began."

The screen showed a progression of various Xalan mutations over the years. Teeth and claws grew longer, plating appeared across the body. Their limbs and claws elongated and they shot up in height until the final frame depicted how the Xalans appeared today.

"These new generations were brought up believing all Sorans were pure evil, as they'd transformed Xala from a lush paradise into a nearly lifeless rock when they invaded years ago. The lie became truth, and only a select few carried on knowing the true origin of our species. The Council, military elite, and the Genetic Science Enclave all carry the secret, but no more than a few dozen out of billions know. The myth remains in place for the masses.

"There are records of a few that have discovered the truth over the years. The Sorans have been trying to enlighten us for millennia with propaganda promising a reunification of our people, but it is almost always intercepted and destroyed. It is why diplomatic relations do not exist with the Sorans and why self-destruction of soldiers and ships is mandated upon capture. Those who did manage to catch a glimpse of the truth have all been executed. As such, I now fear for my life. I could have kept this information to myself, rather than endangering the clan, but I have a responsibility to the truth, even if it means risking those I care about in the hope all Xalans might someday know these things. That they may know they have been deceived for thousands of years and that this eternal war is based on a lie.

"If you receive this, it is likely I am already dead. I hope your brothers may avoid extermination, but the reach of the Council is vast. If you survive the Earth campaign, and this message reaches you securely, you must find a way to broadcast this information and these documents to our people. That is your mission. I believe we can end this war if the truth is revealed. I understand this knowledge is a heavy burden, but despite your age, you were always the strongest of us, and I know it is something you can bear."

He paused, and raised his clawed arm to his chest.

"Be well, my son."

The hologram flickered and disappeared. Alpha stood with his claws resting on the table, his head down. He was silent, but soon growled something under his breath in Xalan. Eventually he reached for the chip and affixed it to his translator. The muttering was now understandable.

"It cannot be."

He started rapidly sifting through scenes from the message, the Soran uprising records, the genetic reports.

"Authenticated footage, officially sealed documents. It is true. All of it is true."

He turned to Lucas, his eyes full of fear and despair.

"An entire civilization, built on a lie. Thousands of years of history fabricated, used to stir the masses into a frenzy for war. Astonishing. Terrifying. We are Soran. The most important piece of us, Soran."

Lucas had nothing to say. He understood the enormity of the revelation and the crushing burden Alpha now had on his shoulders. His father had tasked him with spreading the truth, something no one in his civilization had been able to do for thousands of years. No wonder his family had been targeted. Omicron's last words made sense now.

"You will understand why we did it. We needed to be a proud people if we were to thrive."

A race of former slaves would surely be far less proud than a race of warriors fed the tale of a destroyed homeland. According to Alpha, Xalans had been bred from birth to fight. But would they continue to do so if they knew that deep down it was ultimately Soran DNA that made them creative, intelligent, and adaptable? Alpha addressed the unspoken question.

"If word of this gets out, the public will lose all faith in the ruling class. Rebellion, a civil war to end this galactic war."

Lucas finally spoke.

"Would that be worth it?"

Alpha paused and pondered the implications.

"They must know the truth. The Sorans didn't decimate Xala, nor did they ravage our civilization. They created us; they spared us."

"But you were slaves," Asha added. "They were playing god and created an entirely new species."

Alpha nodded.

"They are not blameless, but their crime is sloth, not wrath. This war for vengeance is unjust. The records show Xalans could have, and likely should have been exterminated after the uprising. Instead, we were granted a chance to survive across space, a chance we threw away for more bloodshed. There are many other Xalans like me who wish the war to end. Information of this nature would drive them from words to action."

The holotable sprang to life, untouched by any of them. A warning symbol flashed as a dull alarm sounded. Alpha immediately took to the controls and discovered the source of the interruption. Lucas recognized the phrase "Proximity Alert" in the flurry of Xalan symbols.

"The Sorans have arrived."

The view switched to an external monitor that showed eight warships heading toward them. The craft looked significantly different from the curved Xalan ships; they were far more angular, with seven appearing to be cut from the same model and one looming larger than the others. It came to a rest in front of them as the other smaller ships fanned out to surround them. A light began flashing on the table.

"We are being hailed," Alpha said. "This is the moment you have studied for. First contact."

He paused.

"Answer, and bridge human and Soran for the first time."

Lucas looked nervously at the light, but eventually brought his hand up to press it. An enormous portrait rose above them. It was an older man, with fair skin, close-cropped silver hair, and a granite jawline. His dark-green uniform was clearly military, though Lucas recognized none of the symbols that adorned it. After seeing Lucas appear in front of him, the Soran couldn't contain a look of surprise, but he spoke with a calm cadence.

«This is Admiral Tannon Vale of the Fifth Soran Interstellar Fleet. You are in restricted space operating an enemy combatant's vessel and in violation of more edicts than I can count. What are you doing out here?»

Lucas's brain raced to pull his many Soran lessons to the forefront of his mind.

«My name is Lucas, I come from the planet Earth,» he stammered, staring into the hologram's eyes. Strangely, one was green, the other blue. «We have come a long way to seek refuge on Sora.»

The admiral looked down at a readout offscreen.

«We're picking up thirteen Soran signatures onboard your vessels, with one live Xalan. Whether you are refugees or mercenaries, I don't know, but that doesn't give you license to be in this quadrant, nor pilot these ships, no matter how you came to acquire them. Prepare to be boarded.»

The feed went dead. The monitor showed ships closing in on the pair of locked Xalan craft.

"Well, that went well," Asha said, placing Noah down on the table.

"It does not matter," said Alpha, who was sifting through the holotable controls. "We will be able to explain further once we face them in person."

"What are you doing?" Lucas asked.

"Deactivating the self-destruct sequence on this vessel. All Xalan ships are programmed to explode if subject to capture to prevent acquisition of sacred technology."

Lucas looked around the room warily. The table readout showed airlocks opening in various parts of the ship. The Sorans were onboard.

"The time for fighting has ceased," said Alpha calmly. "Do not resist capture, lest this journey be for nothing."

Lucas couldn't fight any more even if he wanted to. His body was racked with excruciating pain, only pushed away by the adrenaline surging through him having just spoken with humans from an entirely different part of the galaxy.

Alpha put his energy pistol on the holotable. "Deposit your weapons."

"No way," Asha said, her hand instinctively reaching for her Magnum.

"We do not need to give them a reason to destroy us."

Reluctantly, Lucas unslung Natalie from his back and set the weapon gently on the table, taking Noah into his arms as he did so. Eventually Asha came around and did the same, placing her Magnum and blade next to one another on the glowing surface.

The three of them walked around to the front of the room and could hear metal footsteps approaching. The door opened, and a score of Soran troops marched in, head to toe in gunmetal armor, fully helmeted with identical rifles raised and pointed at them. They spread out around the room as one more helmeted figure emerged. He strode toward them with a pistol in one hand and he removed his headgear with the other. It was the admiral. He stood a few inches taller than Lucas and looked to be about sixty in Earth years, but who knew what his true age was. He eyed Lucas up and down and directed a suspicious gaze toward Alpha.

«Analyze.»

He directed the command toward a soldier next to him, who shouldered his rifle and brought out a device Lucas didn't recognize. It emitted a green light and was swept across himself and Noah, then over to Asha and Alpha.

«No explosives on any of them,» the soldier reported. «Moderate to severe injuries. They require medical attention.»

The admiral looked around the room and saw the dead Xalan crewmembers. Taking a few steps forward, he saw Omicron's black body on the ground.

«A Shadow!» he exclaimed, unable to hide his surprise. «And you killed it? Where were you trained, soldier?»

Lucas cleared his throat and spoke, his head throbbing. Noah squirmed in his arms.

«We are from Earth, sir. It's a—»

The admiral cut him off.

«Why is your prisoner not restrained?» he asked, motioning to Alpha, who wasn't going anywhere with a dozen rifles aimed at his head.

«He is not a soldier,» Lucas said. «He is our ally.»

The admiral scoffed, until Alpha spoke.

«He speaks the truth.»

Every soldier took one step back as they heard their native tongue spoken from his translator collar.

The admiral shook his head, a look of astonishment on his face.

«In all my years, I've never come across a scene like this. You have some serious questions to answer. Take them, and find the others.»

The soldiers began to close in around them.

«Sir,» the soldier with the scanner spoke again. «This one is with child.»

Lucas looked down at Noah in his arms, but then saw that the soldier was motioning to Asha.

«Take her to medical and get it out of her,» the admiral said gruffly.

"What?" Asha said in English. She began to struggle against the soldiers who were already upon her. As one came around in front of her, she cracked his helmet's visor with a headbutt, which drew blood from her own forehead. A violent kick sent another one sprawling.

The admiral raised his pistol and fired a single silent shot. Asha's head snapped back and Lucas's heart leapt out of his chest as the air escaped from his lungs. But as her face came back into view, there was no wound, just a light green splash on her forehead, and she crumbled to the ground, unconscious. A tranquilizer. The soldiers started to drag her away.

"No! Asha!" Lucas cried, unable to fully process what he'd just heard. She was with child? *Get it out of her?* He began to struggle against the metal arms that were trying to pry Noah from his grasp. They wouldn't take her.

"You can't!" Lucas yelled, ignoring the fact that he was no longer speaking their language. To his right, Alpha was calmly offering his outstretched hands to the troops who were encircling him. Lucas elbowed a soldier with his free arm, but Noah was ripped from his grasp. The admiral raised his pistol once more. Lucas felt the stinging impact, but all his pain faded away in a few seconds when the world went dark.

25

Only a few moments to dream this time. He was lying in bed, one bright summer morning. Sonya was beside him, her blond hair spilling onto the pillow next to her. In between them, Nathan, only a few months old. Lucas didn't know if this time had ever actually existed, but he felt a sense of euphoria as he looked around the sun-soaked room and into Sonya's oceanic blue eyes. She smiled at him in a way he hadn't seen since . . .

And then she was gone. Nathan was gone. Lucas sat up straight, and rifled through the sheets, but there was no trace of them. He called out their names to no avail. The room was now baked in red light, the clouds outside menacing as lightning crackled between them.

He got out of bed and raced through his house. He should have been familiar with it, but it had become a labyrinth, with each door opening to somewhere he'd already been. Finally, he came to the front door and tore it open. He walked out into his yard, the grass scorched to a brown crisp. Ahead of him was not the road, but a vast chasm where the earth simply ceased to exist. He turned back to his house, which was now aflame and crumbling, and when he pivoted once more, Asha was standing on the precipice of the cliff in front of him. She held a child in her arms. One with dark hair and without burns. She looked intently at him, then smiled. That same smile.

Then, in an instant, she threw herself backward off the cliff. She hung suspended in midair, falling slowly as Lucas tried to sprint toward her, but he was moving at the same glacial pace. Clutching the child, she dipped from beneath his view. When he finally reached the edge, there was nothing but blackness. Blackness that was slowly fading as light crept into his eyes.

He blinked twice, three times. The darkness was lifted and white light was reintroduced to his vision. When his focus adjusted, he saw he was in a circular room with curved walls. He was sitting in a chair with both of his arms and legs secured by unmovable metal. To his right was a large viewscreen showing a dazzling array of stars. In front of him was the admiral seated on the other side of a long metal table. He was no longer armored but back to his green cloth uniform.

«Finally, you've stopped yelling.»

"Where am I?" Lucas said hazily, his mind still jumbled.

«What kind of daft language is that?»

«Where am I?» Lucas corrected.

«Onboard the SDI *Starlight*, en route back home, where you'll be formally charged.»

Lucas shook his head. He wasn't in any pain, which was a surprise.

«Charged with what? Where's Asha? Where's Noah?»

«The child is secure. The girl?» the admiral raised his eyebrows. «She's still in medical; her injuries were more serious than yours. I'm surprised you allowed her to fight in her condition.»

«She's . . . she's pregnant?» Lucas stammered, recalling what had happened just before he blacked out.

«You didn't know? In any case, she'll be relieved of that burden soon enough.»

«You're monsters,» Lucas spat out. The admiral looked at him, confused, as if he didn't understand the accusation.

«Where are you from, son?» he said. «I won't ask again.»

«I told you, Earth.»

«Earth? What province is that in? I can't place your accent.»

«It's not a province,» Lucas said. «It's a planet. My homeworld was destroyed by the Xalans, and we escaped to seek out refuge on Sora once we learned of its existence.»

The admiral was not amused.

«I don't have time for this, and insanity will not excuse you for your crimes. And I don't care if you did kill a Shadow.»

«What crimes? Listen, you have to—»

«Let's see, operating a vessel in restricted space. Piloting an unlicensed spacecraft. Consorting with an enemy combatant. Failure to register weapons. Engaging enemy troops without credentials or orders.»

Lucas was frustrated.

«You don't understand. Talk to Alpha, he'll—»

«That thing? He's claiming to be some sort of scientist. He's the first one I can remember who hasn't self-destructed or slit his own throat after capture. They're not usually a talkative bunch, but this one won't shut up. Though he's making about as much sense as you.»

The admiral slammed his fist on the table, and the sound echoed throughout the circular room.

«I have thirty-odd dead Xalans in pieces, a Shadow among them, a ship running technology my men can't even fathom, eleven vegetative Sorans in stasis tanks, a pregnant girl, an infant, an enemy defector, and you. Running interrogations is way below my rank, but this is unlike anything I've ever seen and *I want some damn answers!*»

The man's metal wrist cuff began to glow. He pressed it and a voice spoke.

«Admiral Vale, you're needed on the bridge immediately.»

He pressed the same button on the cuff and got up to leave.

«Don't go anywhere.»

A curved sliding door shut behind the admiral. Lucas's thoughts immediately turned to Asha, and he struggled with his chair in futility. He swore he'd protect her, and this is what had happened? Now it wasn't only her life in danger, but that of an unborn child. Had there been signs that he missed? Had she known? But according to what the admiral suggested, it was all for naught. Whatever was happening to her, Lucas swore he'd find her. He loved her, he knew that now without question or hesitation, and he hadn't gotten a chance to tell her in the lulls of the firefight. As he struggled even more violently in the chair, the metal dug into his skin, and tore through his organic suit. A light went on in the armrest, and Lucas felt a wave of fatigue sweep over him. It appeared misbehavior wasn't tolerated by the chair. A faint gas swirled around him, and in a few moments he was unconscious once more.

When he awoke, Lucas found the circular room packed with people. Six additional chairs had been added to the table in front of him, with the admiral in the middle. Behind him was a large assortment of other officers and a few men wearing ornate suits who didn't look military. Armed guards stood a few feet apart along the wall. Next to him was a soldier injecting something into his arm. It surged through his system and he was fully awake almost immediately.

«There we go,» the admiral said, standing up from his chair and resting his palms on the table.

«What's . . . what's going on?» Lucas asked, finding twenty pairs of eyes looking directly into his own.

The admiral was no longer irritated, but spoke calmly.

«Preliminary results have come back from medical. Treatment of your injuries has revealed that your genetic makeup is not of . . . Soran origin.»

The room was silent. Someone coughed in the back. Lucas saw what appeared to be a tiny camera lens floating next to the admiral's shoulder.

«We searched the flight logs of both Xalan ships, which are the first we've captured that haven't subsequently exploded. In them we've found a great many things. We found Earth. Your Earth.»

The admiral presented a flat disc, which projected a floating hologram of Lucas's home planet from it. It hung suspended on the table in its formerly lush green-and-blue state. Every face in the room wore an expression of unbridled awe.

«Tell me Lucas, who are you?»

They understood. They believed him. Everyone had assembled in this room because they knew a new chapter of history was being written with each word spoken.

«How did you get here?»

On the viewscreen to Lucas's right, an enormous green-and-blue planet came into view. A gorgeous collection of unfamiliar continents and oceans appeared before him. His journey was over. A new one had begun.

«Why have you come?»